Legacy of the Defender

Jacob Spadt

Legacy of the Defender

Cover art by Abner Hernandez

Edited by Chad Donohue

First Printing August 2015

Library of Congress Catalogue Card Number:

ISBN-13: 978-1514693261

Visit www.legacyofthedefender.com

I dedicate this book to the idealists in the world.

To those who dare to dream

Make your dreams reality

Acknowledgements

I would like to thank:

Kenneth MacGuffin, you started me down the road of gaming. You have opened my eyes to so many possibilities. Your guidance has been critical in my spiritual development.

Thank you, Chris Anderson, for believing in me and supporting me when things got rough. Your creative ideas inspire me.

Sean Duval, I could not imagine my life without you my friend. You supported me from the start. It has been an honor to have you in my games.

My cousin Tami Myers for proofing the content of my story and asking questions that made me explain things better.

Jesse Patton. You inspired me to stand up for myself in all of our adventures as kids.

Adam Raetz. You shared your stories with me and kindled the fire inside me to put my own ideas finally to paper. You are missed my friend.

Trevor Carrol, Todd Forsland. The two of you influenced my ability to come up with great stories in so many ways. You both shined a light on my life with your creativity.

Shannon Cheek for providing valuable feedback that allowed me to make the story even better. You asked the right questions to make me think.

Thank you to my gaming groups through the years that gave me the opportunities to be creative and dove into my story lines.

My editor and sound board Chad Donohue. You are not last on this list by far but joined my creative team last. Your concepts and ideas changed the way I approached writing. Like any good coach or mentor, you made me so frustrated and appreciate you even more when I got over myself. Because you questioned everything, you made me a better writer.

Abner Hernandez, you made my visual images such a reality.

Lastly, but in no way the least...
Deanna Fallon, you inspired me to finish my journey. My life will never be the same. Thank you for being my muse, for without you, I would never have finished.

Prologue

"How did you become a Defender?"

I panned the clearing. Many sets of eyes sat transfixed and hanging on my every word. It was an honest question, which no one ever asked before. The world knew the existence of someone, or something, like me had turned the tide when it mattered most.

Where to begin? My mind drifted back. To answer this question, I had to go back to what defined me as a child.

My fourth grade teacher, Mrs. Styles, one day asked the class what we wanted to be when we grew up. I lived in a small town called Snohomish where nothing very exciting ever happened. Some of the boys said they wanted to be police officers, others said doctors or firemen. A few of the girls said they wanted to be ballerinas, which made the boys laugh. I said nothing. The teacher responded to all the students as they gleefully spoke of a positive future they openly hoped was in store for them.

The teacher noticed my silence.

"Dieter, how about you?"

She pressed me for an answer, but I did not respond. There was a feeling inside me that I could not explain. Words escaped me. The class was starting to whisper and point fingers at me for being weird. I did not mind. My mind probed my depths for the answer that eluded me. Outside, the proverbial dark cloud had settled over the school. Leaves blew across the playground grass. We could see the wind in the trees outside the window.

A storm was coming. A storm was always coming.

"Dieter Gutermuth you will answer my question," she repeated as the other kids began to laugh at the mention of my last name. They played on the words saying gutter mouth for several moments. "Dieter, what do you want to be when you grow up? There must be something that sounds interesting to you."

The answer finally found my tongue. Silence hung like smoke in the room.

"Alive," I said.

Part I

I

Sasquatch

Why me? That is a good question.

I had no way of knowing that my life would lead me down a dark path beyond my wildest dreams. My fate was to become a Defender. No one knew what a Defender was, or of their existence. There were no myths or rumors surrounding it. No fairy tales told to small children or recorded accounts passed down by word of mouth by the Bards of old.

Certain people know certain things in life. Sometimes in a church or a government there are secrets guarded with the pain of death if they ever come to light. There was no secret military program. No school or training camp that you could sign up for to see if you had the mettle to be all you could be.

Sometimes people go through life convinced that aliens abducted them. They tell the story in a way that makes you certain they cannot be lying. You know they are. They have to be because it is too outrageous to believe; but they are not.

So much has changed. For the person that stands face to face with a creature of myth, a Sasquatch, knowing what they saw...reality is a hard pill to swallow. Often it is a slap in the face. Back then, people would laugh at someone and say, "Yah right!" All those people are crazy, completely nuts. Nevertheless, some of them are telling the truth.

4

Legacy of the Defender

Now, to answer the question of how they chose me to become a Defender, I was compassionate to a Sasquatch.

Jason Patterson, my close friend, would not admit what we saw until much later. He claimed it was hallucinations for many years to come, but he knew the truth. I was on one of my time outs from the "dungeon" – my *room* as my mother referred to it – and found myself at his house. After a brief negotiation, the lake came to mind, and we were off. Neither of us imagined the events of that day or where they would take us. Several hours away from home always did my existence, however meager, some good.

The day had been a blast. We met two girls at the lake. One girl named Sandra and I looked at each other nonstop, and somehow my confidence allowed me to kiss her. Not knowing what had come over me, I went with it. In my younger years, I used to think girls fixated on kissing. As a fascinated boy, I remember hearing them discuss it. Experiencing it was mind blowing. I was floating.

That afternoon we all went swimming, and the fun continued. Nothing went past playful kisses, and a few that lingered. Our comfort with each other grew steadily. I was really into Sandra and Jason was into the other girl, although her name slips my mind due to what I had been doing most of that day. A good portion of the day passed. Plans to meet formed as the light faded. The grin I wore must have compared to what was plastered all over Jason's face. A silly grin.

The trip home was cloud nine. It was the first time a girl had shown real interest in me. I was not a jock or a great looking guy, and to say average looking was amongst the least of my qualities. She saw something in me she liked, and I saw many things in her that I liked, and everything felt good. The kids at school the following year would be surprised if the mystery of a girl I met over the summer clouded my return. A smile tattooed itself on my face permanently. The dark cloud ceased its downpour on my life. I felt the warmth of the sun at that moment, even in the dark.

As we rode home, a somber silence hung gently about both of us. Inner conversations and sweet remembrances gave way to the recognition that the light had faded to the ambient glow of the moon growing in its luminance by the moment. We took the long way home because we escorted the ladies most of the way to their houses.

Usually, there was a bit more of a twilight effect, because one's vision had to re-adjust as the setting sun's rays became more powerful due to the mountains shearing them off like jagged teeth. There was a pause; an inhale, before the moon would appear as a beacon. That night, not only was it brighter than usual, but it continued to get even lighter. Had it been any less, we might have missed an event that changed us forever. My thoughts turned as we progressed towards Jason's house. Growing up, I heard stories and rumors about Sasquatch, more commonly known as Bigfoot. The tales had been that they attacked people way out in the logging camps clearing the forest. Sometimes there were stories, almost like old wives tales, that would circulate through town. My step father had told me once that they were responsible for taking large tires from worksites; tires that weighed over a ton. That very concept scared the hell out of me, but their existence fascinated me.

Occasionally, television shows talked about strange things that go bump in the night. With luck, I would find one about the Sasquatch. The accounts ranged from what people saw to how they smelled; often the odor of rotten eggs. On one show, a guy spoke to some reporters on the back deck of his home. He was explaining a noise he had heard coming from the woods on more than one occasion. Suddenly, off in the woods, came a strange jabbering sound. The man stated that this was the Sasquatch communicating. This reverberation sent chills down my spine because it sounded guttural…if you knew what *guttural* sounded like, that is. Nothing in my life compared to those sounds.

The memory of sitting in front of the television, and the fear rolling over me, gave me goose bumps. That night the fear followed the sensation of eyes peaking in at me. I remembered turning the lights out and becoming the hunter as I looked outside and watched. The eerie feeling soon passed, but never forgotten and, on occasion, it revisited.

Another story a friend of mine heard involved a local sheriff who hunted. He saw what appeared to be a large rotten stump dark brown or blackish blend of colors. Upon bending down and touching it, the peculiar shape and size became apparent. It crumbled in his fingers and broke apart, not like a rotting stump. It was no stump! It was dung. He could see rivulets where the urine ran down away from the pile. Animals did not return to one place to defecate or urinate. Fear hit him, and he looked up and froze. Thirty feet from him, crouching beneath a branch was a Sasquatch. It stared at him with darkened eyes. The bough hunched beneath stood seven or eight feet high, and the creature crouched under it; its head touched the bough above it. Their eyes locked.

Legacy of the Defender

The sheriff sat there frozen, unable to move. Even with a rifle and camera on hand, he was unable to act. Fear took hold of him. I imagine it was much like a deer in headlights, he was surprised and flatfooted. The Sasquatch left after about five minutes leaving the sheriff paralyzed with fear for a half an hour. Upon returning to camp, he asked a few of the loggers about it. They denied nothing.

The loggers said it was no big deal to see a Bigfoot. The company they worked for told them to hold their silence. Speaking of it was bad for any and all's health that were involved as they usually turned up dead. Cut break lines coming down a mountain bought a lot of silence. In short, they lived with the fact that their workplace was hostile on both sides from the environment and the company.

As we rode, my thoughts turned again to the sound of the Sasquatch speaking. To this day, I remember that sound as if it was yesterday. A lolling sound repeatedly vocalized with different pitches like words on an untrained tongue. It was both beautiful and scary. Anyone hearing that would be both mystified and probably scared, as was I the day of the show. This thought was actually on my mind when I saw one standing downhill from us as we approached on our bikes. It stepped onto the road at least one hundred yards away, illuminated by the moon is such a way there was no question what it was.

The creature stood at *least* eight feet tall. No exaggerating because it stood next to a sign posted on the side of the road. Jason referred to it jokingly as a real life Wookie, but the broadness of its shoulders dwarfed even that image. I was transfixed on it, almost paralyzed, that the reference did not even catch at first. My mind simply could not believe what I saw. Wrapped with long, dark fur covering a powerful frame walked this creature of legend. The head was conical shaped with human but dark features. Fur ran along its face but did not fully cover all of its features. Lines of the face were still distinguishable, much like a human would be. It was amazing.

I paused in my thoughts for a fraction of a second as this vision unfolded. Its long stride took it halfway into the lane as we were rolling towards as it. As we neared the creature, we noticed the detail was magnificent. In those few moments, I found it strange that the Sasquatch did not hear the approaching car or notice us until it was almost too late.

It all happened so fast...

"Look out!" I yelled towards the beast, not considering its linguistic skills.

It was weird; there I was, seeing a being that had eluded capture for God knows how long, and all I could think about was its safety. Stopping on the road, it turned its head. Maybe I should not have yelled because the creature paused to look. The oncoming car swerved. Without my warning, the beast might have cleared the road. The car missed the creature; Jason and I were thirty or so feet from it in the other lane going with traffic. That was the last thing I had remembered before the pain hit.

The car struck both of us. The impact threw me about forty feet backwards and knocked me out cold. When I talked to the doctors, they let me read the police report that described the missing pieces of the puzzle. It did fill in some holes, yet part of me felt as if I had already seen it from afar. I somehow recalled poor Jason's plight. He was not so fortunate. His bike folded around the front of the car, and there he stayed while the driver lost control of the vehicle. Flying off the road the car rolled over, taking Jason, the new hood ornament, with it. How he managed to end up under it is still a mystery.

When my eyes opened, what I saw was even more amazing, our new friend was helping Jason. It gently lifted the car with ease as if made out of paper. The stories of humans being able to lift cars off someone did not compare to what I saw. I had always imagined the great effort involved. There was no noise, not even a grunt or groan besides the creaking of metal, falling glass and the ringing in my head.

Jason does not remember anything. The accident knocked him out. The driver died instantly when the vehicle rolled because part of a tree came through the windshield and impaled his face. I was the only witness to this heroic event by a fabled creature. Bigfoot carried Jason over to me, who was unconscious, setting him down next to me. My body was propped against a tree with my bike folded around me. With ease, he removed the bike folded around me and straightened out my broken femur. Things began to go blurry from my cracked melon.

I looked at it rather curiously. It felt like a gift. Moisture ran down my cheeks onto my shirt. The large furry beast seemed to melt away before my eyes. There were many lights flashing. I could hear cars stopping and then there were people. Those first arrivals probably never thought twice about the story that I was rambling about, other than the fact that a car hit two boys. I did not know this until much later.

Trauma does funny things to your body, especially head. Medical personnel could not stop the internal bleeding or the severe swelling that led to my coma. Miraculously it stopped on its own. They said Jason was the lucky one even though he had a car sitting on him for only a few seconds, crushing the life out of him. No one knew this fact, and I sure did not move it with a compound fracture. I always wondered what one of those was. Your curiosity wavers when you are looking at your bone poking through your skin, and it is looking back at you for the first time. That image stapled itself to that moment in time.

My rambling was brief.

The Tullenbrooks seemed like nice people if memory serves. Silence should have been golden. I really hated that I told them what happened in retrospect. With the pressure forming behind my eyes and the redness appearing, my lips moved on their own. That is all I could see for a blood vessel had burst in my head and came out my eyes, nose and ears. I tried to get all the words out because it was obvious something was wrong and time was short. My slurred speech sounded like English to me. To others, it might have sounded like gibberish and incoherent words. Much of the story was most likely lost in translation.

In hindsight, they probably did not understand a word I said.

The young couple was busy trying to calm me down. My words made no sense I am sure. The sight of me covered in blood must have been a bit much. I do not know when my eyelids went heavy for the last time, and the blackness came. Apparently the paramedics pronounced me dead when they arrived on the scene much later, then suddenly detected a faint heartbeat. I hovered near death for a long time but remained technically alive.

Legacy of the Defender

In sleep, I traveled.

*　　*　　*

I spiraled into a dark fog.

The sense of falling was present but felt more like floating on a tube in a river. My mind turned in all directions, and a gentle breeze caressed my face. Faint images greeted me at first, but little by little became clear. It made no sense why I could see everything all around me, but none of it was in focus. I heard once or twice when you pass out…you are out. If you were lucky, you would dream about something cryptic and wonder for the rest of your days what it meant. I probably would have taken the opportunity, had the chance been available. Moments turned in to minutes; minutes turned into longer still. Ghostly images formed all around me, and yet I could not tell if I was asleep or awake.

I felt the ground. My body gently elongated on its own in an almost animated fashion. It felt like a puppeteer was having their way with me and playing with my limp corpse. My eyes were now open, and awareness told me that my body was lying there in the fog on some soggy surface. The moisture soaked into my clothes slowly, kind of like a creeping doom. Fear rose up in me. This could not be real, but it could not be a dream either. I bit my lip for a reality check. There was no pain. So I bit hard and yelped. The taste of blood made me feel a bit stupid. I began to take in other senses.

It was very cold, yet I was not shivering. The smell of new aromas assaulted my nose making it itch. Very pungent and earthy at the same time, these scents brought different emotions to the surface of my mind one at a time before they dissipated. Blood in my mouth began to accumulate in the recesses under my tongue. I was trying to find a way to process the information my senses provided. The excitement overwhelmed and scared me at the same time if that is possible from not knowing where *this* even was.

Where was Jason? Where did that couple go? That creature, was it real? A car hit me! Wait...I remember leaning against a tree and getting very sleepy. The last thing I remembered was everything was red.

"Jason?" The name gurgled off my tongue, and I swallowed some blood and gagged. There was quite a lot of it, and I had not realized how much. The crimson taste laced with the hint of iron uniquely clung to the insides of my mouth and with every breath I could re-taste it. As my breath exhaled, the moisture danced in the air for a bit then hung in front of me. Within moments, more light came from the distance illuminating. Shadows and shapes around me shimmered slightly, and aspects of this place began to form. The eerie light did not move but shimmered all around.

Sudden realization hit me in the stomach, and I felt sick. Did I die? I felt my throat get wet as it does before you vomit, but nothing forced its way out.

"Holy shit!" I gurgled forward again, this time mixed with saliva and blood.

"I can assure there is nothing holy about that no matter what culture you are in." A reply came.

I freaked out. The voice was all around me; feeling like it was in my head as well as every part of me heard it speak. It sounded both feminine and masculine at the same time. Two sounds moved in unison and harmony. I began to look around and now felt panic rise in me like my insides were going to empty. My pulse was racing so fast it seemed like my heart was not beating against my ribs but in my throat. Dry mouth followed by nausea made my stomach knot again.

A figure approached out of the swirling mist. He looked like some tribal chief or holy man to some ancient tribe. He had big feathers in his hair and some crazy looking staff. He walked right up to me as if he had been expecting me. I could smell something not identifiable, but sweet and pungent. The gag reflex hit me again, and my mouth filled with fluid this time and instinctively swallowed it back to where it came from leaving a burning in my throat. My head was hurting now. A sudden fatigue rolled through me, but I managed to sit myself up by the time he reached me. Out came a hand and lifted me effortlessly off the ground by my clothes. He was remarkably strong. He towered over me. My feet dangled.

"There is a storm coming; you shouldn't be here," he said as he started to move me off some direction. "It is not your time to be here yet; you are not ready." As we moved, I noticed there was some sort of cave ahead. It seemed to appear, and he headed right towards it. A whiff of some God-awful smell, like swamp gas or something just as nasty assailed my nose.

"Where am I? Is this a dream?" I asked aloud, not sure if I wanted him to answer. We entered the cave, and he boldly strode in as if it was his or that he at least belonged there.

"It's no dream. Your spirit is here. I assure the strange sensations you feel are real. Your physical body is in the hospital. For now, you are here.

"Am I dead?" I blurted out, suddenly afraid, thinking of all the things I had not finished. I might be sixteen, but I was not a complete waste of a being.

"No, you are not, not yet. Time will tell. If you survive the tests, then you will be worthy of the greatest gift ever unknown to man. If you do not survive then death will come swiftly, I assure you. But it will be pain-less."

He set me down in a lit cave, warmed by a large fire in the middle. The smoke rose gently up. *No pressure there,* I thought as his words rang in my mind. *Weird! How was it that I could forget what my mother told me ten seconds after she said it? His words played forward and back words, faster and faster, as they sunk in.*

Something drew me to the smoke as it began its lazy ascent. Images and symbols danced forwards and backwards upon it as it went. The symbols not recognized from any book or text. They seemed almost surreal at first glance but very old and tired. As I watched, I began to see images more clearly of some tribe. A very old and ancient tribe by the look; they lived life right under the stars. Sitting around a campfire, I could see that they were telling stories of great battles and victories with tales of faraway lands full of adventure. Strange I understood, for they spoke some language that did not sound like anything found in the world today. *This must be several thousand years ago.* I saw many scenes of the life of these people. Their life...their death. Death? *Wait* I thought, *back up,* something was missing. It was as though I had blinked, and they were all gone. Nothing but a large bear remained. It made noises as if a great grief or misery had aflicted it. I could feel pain. They were its people and friends that I saw and then everything changed. The image zoomed in on its eyes. It seemed like a male. Something tragedy unfolded.

Then images started again. There were different people, different clothing, from a different time apparently. I could tell it was hundreds if not thousands of years later just by looking at the shift in the stars. The travel patterns that the universe goes through over time as it expands was obvious to me. Astronomy had never been a strong suit for me but see the changes in the stars the astral drift with the naked eye through an image had me reeling. *How could I know this without studying? It was perplexing!* Something was different, but this time the faces of the people were clear. They seemed to be more of an Indian heritage then a Stone Age tribe.

The bear was gone, but there was a familiar figure in the midst of them. Bigfoot. He seemed to be teaching them. Again, I understood what he was saying although the exact concept was complex. With amazement, my attention held while he instructed them; from hand-to-hand combat to a math that was very basic. Drawing on the ground as the villagers responded with answers like it was an actual class. I was able to see the words and hear them more clearly this time. The language was still very strange to me yet I could understand as if it was English. This was not possible. My history was not that bad, and this was not the thirteenth century or later when English was finally developing.

Ages passed as I pondered.

The image went fast-forward just like a movie. The village changed and grew, and children got older. Life seemed to repeat itself with new faces emerging from the shadows. They learned; they mated and died. Always there was Bigfoot; always teaching them.

Then it happened. The image changed to one of chaos and darkness. There was a rift or tear in the very air itself and there where creatures, thousands of creatures, pouring out. I did not recognize what they were from any pictures or books. It was an apocalypse. The village was being destroyed and almost its entire population slain. Fires blazed everywhere, and the villagers consumed like dry leaves in a fire. Amidst the smoke, there was a large shadow, fighting hand-to-hand with these creatures. It tore the very life out of them. The villagers fought hard, but they could not stand against the tides that poured from this opening. Bigfoot howled with righteous anger as he felled his foes.

He had scores of wounds.

The blood flowed freely in his matted fur and reddened the ground with his very essence. I could hear and feel the earth itself crying out in pain. It was as though that portal was tearing into its very core and releasing cancer that wanted to spread. Bigfoot fought on. However, in the end, he fell. There were just too many. The horde of beings filled the very air in which I watched. They seemed to be no end to their numbers.

There was a flash. Rolling thunder followed by howling winds that were so loud my ears hurt. These winds pushed the beasts back into the opening. They did not go quietly or peacefully as the wind tore at them. Lightning struck several times. The smell was awful. It hung thickly on the air. I could feel it getting into my pores, and the taste of burnt flesh was in my mouth. The reflex to wretch hit me hard. Images blurred for a moment.

Then I saw the bear return swatting and clawing at the remaining monsters. Slaughter is too nice of a word for the carnage witnessed. It was gruesome to the core. I liked it. The thick blood was everywhere. I could taste it now as it covered everything, saturating the soil. The blood was ichor-like and tasted horrible, but I began to feel the rush of power as it fueled this bloodlust drawing me in. The bear gained speed as it waded through the army falling backwards before it. Walking bipedal his mighty claws swatted and crushed the remaining tide, pressing the advantage. It felt like an eternity before the energies holding open the gate wavered, and it slammed shut. A bellowing, rage-filled roar came forth from its mighty maw and collapsed, where he lay for many days.

Thinking it to be dead, the emotions welled up inside of me. Without realizing it I spoke, urging the bear to rise that this was not its time. The blood flow lessened and it healing itself caught me off guard. My lack of faith was apparent, as I had given it up for dead. Time passed. The bear arose, to my everlasting joy, many moons later. Then something happened I did not see coming. It changed its shape into that of a man, the very man that had carried me into the cave earlier.

I found my eyes practically glued shut from keeping them closed for a very long time. The process of locking onto one of the runes visually must have transferred the image directly into my mind. My eyes naturally closed. It was a muscle cramp or a twinge that brought me out of this trance. Upon my opening them, he had taken up position across the fire from me; behind him stood a familiar figure. The Man looked very wise and very tired as though he had seen several millennia and fought many battles. We sat there, for what felt like a small eternity, before he spoke. Bigfoot remained quiet. I do not think I could have handled him speaking.

"Those people..." I began.

"They are long gone from your world. They lived and died long ago, an entire age."

"Why? I do not understand!"

"You will, but now you know what they were. In time, you shall too be able to see."

"What am I supposed to be able to see?"

"Should you pass the rest of the test, you will see your destiny." He grinned. I was looking at the smoke again and could not see any symbols anymore. Puzzled, I looked at him.

"Was that part of the test to be able to see the past?"

"If you have to ask that after what you have seen, try looking forward. It works both ways. It will provide you with answers you seek. However, the answer is yes. That was the first test."

I began to focus on another flame lazily floating above the fire and tried moving past the images on my own. At first, nothing moved, my will was unsuccessful at getting anything to change from the last image seen. Sweat beaded on my forehead as the intensity within me began to build. I felt the ground shake in my image. It was slow at first. Like when a train starts to lumber forward as it picks up speed. The images started to crawl. Moving as molasses, but defiantly moving. I saw the village disappear over time. The seasons began to change. There was nothing left of the village or its people. Soon animals began to wander in and reclaim the area back to nature.

I stopped. "Can I look at different locations?" I asked him. I felt quite exhausted. His answer was not a surprise. I am glad he said it.

"In time."

I closed my eyes for a moment as I sat, thinking about what had just taken place. All that had just happened. The car, Jason, the fire, the visions, and my head swirled again. I just wanted to sleep. I do not even remember waking up there, or if I ever did.

II

Beginnings

Such a strange dream.

My hands worked to rub the sand from my eyes. The events of the dream stayed with me. Normally, I did not remember my dreams so clearly, but this one had been particularly vivid. With my eyes clear, my surroundings came into view. My hands touched down to raise me up. A woven mat with an intricate weave had been my bed. The patterns were amazing. A quick pan of my surroundings made me shudder.

It had not been a dream.

Perhaps it was a dream within a dream. This notion fled when something hit my groin. I fell backwards with a deep groan, hands cupping my crotch.

The item that had hit me remained in place while I lay there, breathing and clutching, trying to will the pain away. Moments passed, allowing enough air to stem the pain. My strength returned as I sat up, and my hand found what struck me. To my surprise, it was a loaf of bread. It was a large and rather hard loaf at that. Mindlessly, it found my lips and the realization of hunger hit. Nearly breaking my teeth on the first attempt, I tore it open and started to eat. My eyes examined the cave.

The man, if he was a man, sat on the other side of the clearing with his staff resting across his knees. He gazed at me with a blank look. I stared at him for a few minutes still clutching myself and deciding on whether or not I should say something about the assault on my groin. I decided not to challenge someone with his aim. I tried, instead, to gather information.

"So last night was not some crazy dream?" I asked the man. Words found gaps in my consumption. The taste of dirt or mold hit me about the third swallow. *At least if I got an infection the bacteria might fight it off,* I thought and chuckled, waiting for an answer. Until then, I had never questioned if my meal was a health risk.

"No, it was and is not. You are here. Today I give you another test and if you succeed you will get your first mark and begin your training."

"Are you sure you have the right person? Just because I could watch that stuff in the fire, you could have given me something to make me feel funny. I may have never taken any drugs, but I know they can make you hallucinate."

"I assure you, there are no substances in your food, the fire, or the surrounding area that would affect you in that manner. If I wished it, you simply would see what I wanted you to see. You have your free will to perceive what you will."

"That's comforting. So who are you a magician or something? Like a Druid? I do not believe in magic, or I should say I did not until I woke up here. If I am supposed to be a chosen then why did you say I should not be here?"

"You would not have survived the storm out in the open. You say you do not believe in magic, well magic is just energy bended to someone's will. Look outside the cave, you will see tremendous holes in the forest floor." He pointed towards the entrance around the corner to the right. Rising, my body felt very sore. The pain triggered nervous laughter. My hand held my ribs as I balanced myself and walked toward the entrance. Around the corner my feet froze.

The view of the outside was devastating. The man was not kidding. I could see smoldering holes as far as the eyes could see as if sprinkled over the countryside by a giant hand. It looked like small craters had sprouted overnight out of nowhere. The earthen color of the scattered dirt and huge rocks bore the scorch marks in the aftermath of the storm. The land was devoid of vegetation for dozens of feet around each of these craters; that extended down several feet. Beyond the charred area, vegetation wilted from burns. Smoke rose lazily as if from a small fire or embers left over from a cooking pit. The complete awe of the scene stayed my feet from moving farther.

I heard and felt movement behind me. The man was suddenly there. He did not say a word as we both over looked at the devastation. No words could describe this accurately but it resembled the carpet-bombing from the Vietnam War from the linebacker campaigns my seventh grade class studied but with smaller craters and much wider devastation. Sickness gripped my stomach, and the little bits of bread previously consumed came back up. A hand on my back lent comfort while my stomach my purged for a few more seconds. His touch was very strong and warm, like a parent's touch to their child. It caught me off guard. A reactive flinch pulled me away abruptly. To my surprise, he was smiling.

"Sorry," I said, full of embarrassment. Even my manners knew it was bad to lose your lunch in front of the host. My hand cleared any remaining bits while spitting a few times to clear my throat. Out of nowhere, he handed me a cup.

"Rinse and drink."

I did as instructed. My insides felt much better from the fluid in the cup. It seemed shamefull to waste it, but spitting a few more times ensured my mouth was clean. The liquid had a very sweet flavor to it. As it went down my throat, it was warm and cold at the same time. My stomach felt instantly soothed. The feeling spread to all of my limbs slowly, and within a few moments I realized the soreness faded. I looked at him wide eyed. His smile widened.

"Why the smile, I just puked on the door step of your house?" The smile was still there.

"You passed the test. Seeing nature destroyed invokes such emotions in you and only someone that truly loves life in all its forms would have that response. Your other actions have brought you to this point. Seeing the Defender and the runes were the other two tests. Your training begins tomorrow. You should rest."

"What should I call you? Master? Teacher? Sensei?" I asked him as he walked back in the cave leaving me alone with the smell of my rejected breakfast. He did not answer. He walked away.

I stood there contemplating what had occurred. Confusion set in and I paced the mouth of the cave. My nerves felt jumbled. A creeping sensation made me feel out of place and out of time. I had no clue where I was. Who the strange, cryptic man was that had made me feel amazingly comfortable with him despite the oddness. My unease was in truth over the witnessed devastation. It went for miles, as far as the eye could see.

Growing up in the forest, I had an appreciation for nature. Sure, we cut down trees for wood to burn but we never took too much, and we always used what we took. We owned the land, or technically my parents did. So much death and destruction put a hole in the middle of my chest that I could not just ignore. I could not bear it anymore and went back inside the cave to the fire pit. The man appeared to be meditating on the ground.

Sitting down on my sleeping mat, I let my gaze fall on the flames. Runes danced within. My focus fell to all of them...not just one. The chaotic dance lured me in. There was no way to tell what the full spectrum of each image was until my gaze locked on one, and it expanded. The man had told me, that with proper focus, all of history was open to me. I picked a rune and thought about yesterday and the creature. An image came up of the two of us riding down that road after leaving the lake.

A feeling of control popped into my mind, so I imagined moving the image forward to the spot to where the Sasquatch stepped out. Sure enough, there it was in all its mystery, moving like a giant upright ape but with Neanderthal features that were drastic and pronounced.

I watched it walk out of the woods and step onto the road. Focus was difficult. The image shifted to the Sasquatch, and the view changed to what it was seeing. Excitement mounted when I heard my voice call out to warn the creature. Then the squeal of tires came from its left as the car rounded the corner. The car passed in front of Sasquatch. I could see it clearly. It swerved into our lane. I heard bike metal break and the sound of bodies hitting the hood.

The impact was sickening

It is a strange feeling to see oneself flung at incredible speed into a tree. I could not believe the contact with the car did not kill me. The look on my face was horrific; as my body hit the tree, there was an even more bone breaking thud. I lay there like a limp rag doll. Blood came from every orifice on my face and ran down my clothes. My blood covered the ground around me like a balloon with red paint exploding from it. It had even shot out of my eyes. The tree was covered.

It was horrific to gaze upon my face. The expression was that of death. Tears welled up in my transfixed eyes and started to roll down my cheeks when a hand on my shoulder squeezed. I could not look away from this image. My body was broken. Both arms and legs twisted the wrong directions, and it appeared as though my torso caved in a little. There was no breath. This viewpoint was not the Sasquatch's, but mine, and it hung in the air in front of my body.

I could not break my stare. A figure appeared and laid a hand on my body in the image. It had many bracelets and other ornate pieces of jewelry made of carved wood inlaid with precious metals. It looked familiar, and I glanced over to the hand on my shoulder. They matched. My gaze returned to the rune and watched the hand touch my forehead. A white glow flowed from it and traced the outline of my body in the image.

Moments passed the flesh and bone began to mend. Everywhere glowed white for several moments then faded. My head and one leg remained damaged. Femur bone protruded from the leg and blood trickled from my eyes and ears. Ribs popped back in place, and my chest began to rise and fall in short breaths. I glanced at the man next to me, tears still falling from my eyes. I died yesterday and had just witnessed myself brought back to life.

He looked back at me with smiling eyes with a partial grim look upon his face and nodded. He knew I understood what had happened. The image faded when I stopped focusing on it, but I no longer cared. We stared at each other, and before I knew what I was doing, I rolled to my side onto my knees before him. I bowed before him and felt his hand upon my head. It was warm and comforting. The weird aspect of his presence and mannerisms became an intrigue to me now. I sat with my hands at my side and my head bowed. Emotions ran strong. A few tears fell.

"Dieter. You have seen something that most people cannot handle in your position."

I looked up.

"What do you mean?"

"Others have tried and could not cope with their death. You have passed the final test far sooner than even imagined."

"I thought you said there were only three tests?" I asked, puzzled.

"You are correct; those were to get you ready to train. Students then spend years in training and eventually they want to see how they got here. As you know, you had a very horrible accident. Right before that happened you showed compassion on something that invoked fear in the heart of men – men who are ignorant of their own roots. Your compassion for all life is the basis for your skills and will be the source of your powers. You discovered your origin within the first few moments of your new life, and you did not lose yourself in pity or grief. You recognized what you saw and accepted it."

"Wait, Master, do you mean I am ready?"

He laughed quite heartily at that for several moments.

"No, my son, you have not even begun yet. Get some rest."

"What should I call you then?"

"I am not your master, but your teacher. One you will learn to rue before tomorrow is through." The words hung in the air for a second before hitting me. I was about to start something, and I had no idea what to expect. But in truth, I was already committed to it, for this man had brought me back to life. I was lost in my thoughts for a second. The tears stopped. My life had a purpose for the first time. I bowed before him.

"Oh get up; we will have none of that."

"I thought that I shou…"

"Do not think anymore. Do as you are told and you will be better than any man on your entire planet or in the heavens" The words hit me hard. How was I supposed to do that? I could not even beat Jason in sparring.

"You will be able to soon."

Did he just read my mind? I thought.

"Yes."

I shuddered. This was not going to be fun. Reflections in the light danced off the flames as we sat there staring at the fire. I was rather unnerved by my teacher whose I name I did not know. He had the ability to read my mind, even as I sat wondering what his name was. Not only could he read my mind, but he could also speak directly to me. It was comforting to know I would not be alone in my thoughts – which someone would always be with me. At the same time, I would not be alone in my thoughts! He would know everything, I thought, before I realized it. This scared me. My privacy was a thing of the past.

He sat across from me. His open eyes reflected the dancing fire like it was alive. He mediated. The Flames moved at their own rhythm. He appeared to command the fire. Thoughts drifted to what else he could do. Could he shape water to his will? Perhaps the wind itself held no sway over him. Such wonders I was beginning to see as they unfolded before me in this land. Where ever "this land" was.

Sleep started to take me when a whisper in my mind came...ever so subtle. "I am Malnuras."

I did not even jump. A smile crossed my lips.

III

Test

The bright morning rays peeked over the realm and found their way into my eyes. I tried to fight off this intruder by swinging at it with an open hand, not realizing it was only the sun. My efforts seemed in vain when suddenly it went dark. My hand lowered instinctively, only to feel something strike me right on the sweet spot, still sore from yesterday. I winced and coughed as the rib moved. My muscles started to spasm. Both eyes shot open, and I struggled to focus on the shadow.

"Get up. It is time to train," said a voice.

I started to mumble under my breath about unfair treatment and got another jab to the rib. It amazed me how fast he was. For someone who gave the appearance he was not martial in any way, he regularly beat the daylights. Fortunately, he used lessons to do it. He saw me wince and lose my balance only to catch it again before falling towards the fire. A very warm stone saved me. A few choice words escaped my lips while I regained my feet. Holding my side, I managed to catch my breath.

"It is not healing yet?" he asked.

"No, it is not. I think that staff strike broke a rib."

"That is unfortunate. However, you cannot allow it to slow you down. When you are surrounded by your foes, they will not relent just because you are wounded." He poked me in rib on the most painful spot and I nearly blacked out.

30

"I get the point of the lesson, Master," I said, grimacing.

"Stop calling me that. I am not your master. I am your teacher. Soon you will meet the one that you will call master," he said.

"When will he come?" I asked.

He ignored my question. It seemed to me that whenever I asked an obvious question, there was never an easy answer. He spoke in riddles. A forthright answer would be nice. Watching martial arts movies taught me that masters were always full of riddles. Once, after he punched me in the face, I asked him why.

"Because I can," was his response.

My nose remained broken for weeks because he kept smacking it when my attention wandered.

It took weeks for me to get used to his constant strikes. Then one day they stopped. When asked why he stopped the response was always silence. His ways seemed odd on so many levels. My training was never dull.

My studies progressed from basic hand-to-hand fighting, which I loved, to an introduction to weapons. Jason tried to teach me staff, but that did not prepare me in any way for the first day of weapons' training with Malnuras. Without a word, he attacked me with his staff and managed to break mine in two. I attacked with a flurry of blows using the two halves, but it did not matter, for none of them landed. My surprise was apparent, yet he did not break a smile or show any emotion during the brutal onslaught.

As we trained, Malnuras finally told me about the hand-to-hand

31

style he had taught me. He said it was the art taught to many warriors of the ancient world. The Spartans had mastered it and even changed it to become the root system for all the martial arts back on earth. They called it *pure form*. It was fast, deadly, and beautiful all in one motion. The Spartans took the grace out of it and made it straight killing. I had never thought of myself as graceful, but now, after many days of learning, he handed me a staff.

"Defend yourself."

We sparred for quite a while. Then he hit me so hard I flew back and landed flat on my back against a jagged rock. My rib was obviously broken again. The beating he delivered was brutal, but my state of conditioning could usually take it without breaking too many bones. Exactly how many times my muscles had been sprained or torn during training was beyond counting. This time it was severe enough that he stopped and addressed the damage. To both our surprise, the rib was protruding. His ability to heal me was still very weird for me. It took a while to accept that magic existed and that there was more to the world than even the world knew. Seeing it, as he mended my flesh, was unreal.

It soon became commonplace to me. Injuries occurred less and less due to my learning how to fall, roll with a punch or kick, and take a hit properly. In turn, he healed me less frequently, teaching me to rely on my body to fix itself. My life had turned into daily damage control because even though my skill was good, his was masterful. I had to get faster and act, not react. My strength was building up to be able to hold my own weight in any position, and my reflexes were coming along to the point that falling and losing my balance was rare. Although they were superior, my teacher's skills had wisdom and experience behind them. He always found an opening, and it always hurt.

Our campfire was still burning hot, providing much needed warmth. The sun's rays began to warm the ground, and the mist rose gently, blocking the view of the mountains. The mist showed no signs of dissipation. Sometimes it hung thick like a veil cloaking everything in a shroud of moisture.

Our camp was located in a small valley that had a box end canyon a few hundred yards deep. It would be difficult for something to traverse the surrounding terrain to get at us. Without knowing what to look for, there was no real path to the untrained eye. In the event a random intelligent life form happened to see the carefully concealed pathway, it would not know there was a camp nearby without the aid of other senses. The fire was not only smokeless but also created by unnatural means unknown to me.

There was always food ready to go in the morning. Some meat that tasted like bacon, though a mystery, cooked to perfection every time. Hard-boiled eggs sat nestled in a bowl covered with a towel made of some strange looking fiber. It was delicious food and stayed with me for most of the day. An assortment of different fruits and vegetables always grew near the camp even when we moved it. With so much plentiful food, the need to snack or eat very much was not there.

After breakfast, my first task of the day was to head to a river that was about a mile or two away and wash my clothes from the day before while bathing. Malnuras told me that staying clean was just as important as eating good meals. A healthy life style was something I learned at home but had never truly put it to the test before, as my mother provided all of these things for me. It fell to me to handle this task myself after my teacher threw me in the water fully clothed to bathe and wash the smell. I smiled. That day seemed so long ago already. My teacher had a sensitive nose, but it was more about establishing dominance over me or maybe even just teaching me a lesson about taking care of me every day.

As I left, Malnuras had his nose in his tome. I was barely outside of the camp when I heard his voice. "Do not forget your sword."

"Pardon me teacher, no offense but that is not for real fighting. I am just doing my laundry. I am sure you can smell me." He did not speak another word as I departed with my task.

This morning was an exceptional day being that I could barely move but strangely felt good. The trail to the river was not a rough one but did require good balance and land navigation skills to avoid many cuts and bruises. It took me about thirty or so minutes I guessed, since I had no clock or watch, to traverse the terrain that day. Walking did hurt from yesterday's lesson, but each step and knowing how good the water would feel gave me new vigor, and I stepped up my pace. It was hard not to hasten my steps, but I learned that lesson already. We chose our camp with this in mind.

Standing over the river, I gazed at my reflection and then looked at a low hung tree behind me near water. It showed me to be a little taller with a pronounced jawline. Mirrors did not exist here, and the last time I used one was the morning my life changed in fact. Days ran into weeks or months. How much time had passed escaped me now? It was a different feeling knowing that your body was lying in some bed in a hospital asleep. Malnuras did not tell me what the condition was other than being in a coma, only that I was recovering from the accident. Having seen the actual event, it had not been a pretty sight. Sadly, my memory of it was sparse so seeing it first hand by using the campfire was the only real way I could see it. It all seemed so long ago.

My thoughts went to Jason for a few moments, wondering how he was and if he recovered okay. *Maybe he was out in the woods. Did he even think of our time as friends or our adventures?* I could not imagine what he must have been going through regarding that day's events. I hoped he was okay. He had to be. Aside from my stepfather, he was the toughest person I knew in my life. Nothing could keep him down.

My thoughts shifted to the girls at the lake. Had Jason gone back there later in the summer? Was he dating one of them by now? He always had better luck with the ladies. The crazy things we were doing to try to impress them by jumping our bikes off the dock made a smile for a moment. The other girls name still escaped me.

A bubbling sound in the river caught my attention and jarred me back to the present. Things were different, of course, and my priorities had changed drastically. Malnuras told me my new life was beginning the morning after arriving, the day he quite literally threw me in the river after commenting on my smell.

It was so many days ago, I lost track.

Malnuras had really yet to tell me where we were. He simply referred to it as a realm that was not on earth. The only time he ever really talked about it was the first few days after we arrived. I asked if we were somewhere on earth; he cuffed me on the back of the head, telling me to focus on the task. Never striking me out of anger, he always had a purpose to it, even if it felt abusive. I always felt he had a reason for it other than to cause me pain. Strangely, he seemed to be doing what my father failed to do: make a man out of me the right way.

I fell back into my task of cleaning my clothes. The substance used was like soap, but would not hurt the river. I did not know its composition, but it did the job even in the cold water of the river. Even when rinsed, the residue from it vanished as if it was never there. In the end, the clothes were clean and smelled good. Many moments passed trying to figure out what it was which delayed the task of cleaning my clothes. My previous tardiness earned me undesirable tasks usually involving a shovel and the latrine we had made near the camp.

The river moved with its gentle current. I could wade across it without the water reaching my chin, fish swimming around my feet the whole time. Sometimes they brushed up against me, which used to freak me out. It was sort of funny that I did not have to fish for dinner. I simply walked into the water and grabbed one or two. They tried to get away once that happened, but it was almost as if they knew they were to become dinner and did not swim away at my approach. Sometimes, they even came up to the shore and swam around me while I washed my clothes or myself. The shoreline allowed me to step down into a slight rocky bottom, which made it ideal and was why I came to the location. The depth was about two feet right at the bank.

That day was different. There were no fish, and the water was muddy as if something had been disturbing it. *Something swam in the water!* I rose

36

from a squat position and slowly stepped back, watching the surface in anticipation of something about to reveal itself. There were minor ripples as the gentle current flowed by me. I found it odd that even with a current that the water remained cloudy in this area. Something had to be in the water because no fish were by the shore and the visibility was gone. A noise came from my left. I realized my mistake when there was an explosion of water to my right and something flew out of the river, knocking me over in an attempt to pin me down.

All I saw was a blur until it was on top of me. Dark gray skin covered a sleek muscled frame standing on two legs. It moved so fast it was not possible to get a look at it until its jaw latched onto my leg. There were spikes on the top of its head for causing puncture wounds, more than likely deep, bleeding wounds. The bleeding would wear down its opponent. Thankfully, the spikes missed and I did not go down. Its teeth were, however, very sharp but smaller, like a lizard. I could feel dozens of punctures on my leg. I knew these wounds could easily turn into large gashed if the monster or I started thrashing too violently. The creature did not take me down.

The creature had no arms, but very large tendrils protruded from its cheeks that enabled it to hold onto its prey. A fluid oozed onto my skin, followed by a numbing sensation likely to cause paralysis. Seconds passed before it started to grind its teeth. The flesh began to rip and a small part of me was almost thankful that it dulled the pain slightly as the debilitation started. A cold sensation worked its way up my thigh, slowly at first. Within seconds, it hit my hip and my balance failed. I toppled over and started punching the thing repeatedly in the head as hard as I could.

Legacy of the Defender

The creature squealed each time I struck. Sounds echoed from my right, bringing me hope it was Malnuras. Sadly, I was mistaken; a second set of tendrils hit my arm, yanked me off balance even more, and held my torso slightly off the ground. The teeth sunk in and the fluid flowed, numbing me further. I tried to pull my right arm free and continue to hit the one on my leg intermittently. Its skull was not cracking and it showed no signs of letting go. Changing my tactics, I aimed for its eye. Using my thumb, I pressed into the soft tissue and hard as possible. Fluid burst forth and a roar came out of its mouth. It did not let up but increased the pressure, finding bone.

With my vision swimming, my head felt lighter and lighter. Darkness rushed in on my thoughts faster than I could react. My grip on the creature relaxed. My thumb slid from its eye socket, but I continued to try to strike. Each attempt grew weaker. Regaining my footing was difficult due to the rocks on the shore. They were slippery with blood. Gravity put me flat on my back. I tried to call out but could not as the numbness came into my neck and shoulders. The creatures were starting to eat my flesh as my strength left me. I lay there panting and almost paralyzed. The numb sensation turned slightly euphoric as it allowed the creatures to ease me gently toward death. My arm dropped to my side, struck a rock, and started to bleed.

My other hand found its grip somehow and closed around the sharp stone. I mustered everything from deep within and sat up. Swinging the stone, I smashed the creature's skull with devastating force. It let out a short cry and fell limp, releasing its grip on my leg. Teeth slid down my flesh, tearing me open even more. The creature gently bobbed and floated away once it let go of my destroyed leg.

The second of the two beasts saw these events unfold and renewed its claim on my right arm. Very little strength remained as the damage worsened. My right leg was no longer recognizable, and my arm was practically down the creature's throat. It did some sort of frenzied move, as if to swallow my entire arm. I was thankful for the numbness now, since such pain would certainly have caused my body to shut down and go into shock. Getting up on my left elbow was more than a chore and I tried to find another sharp rock, but to no avail. Blood flowed freely from my right forearm and made it hard for me to grip anything.

Seconds rolled by and panic was setting in. The adrenaline finally hit me while the anger and the sheer force of will were fighting to stay conscious long enough to kill the thing. If that succeeded, I did not know. Self-doubt hit. I worried that walking was not going to be an option and camp was not even close. For a moment, I wondered where my damn teacher was and how this could have happened after everything I had learned. Finally consumed and digested by something unidentifiable was irony within irony.

Refocusing yielded a stone and the strength to swing it mustered in my core. The blow glanced off the creature's thick hide, making it squeal again. Yet it kept chomping away on my arm. Swinging repeatedly, I saw a few chunks of its scaly, thick hide break off. Blackish, rotten-smelling blood oozed from the creature. Nearly spent and out of strength, I started to believe I was about to fail and lose this fight to something that was even lower on the food chain than I was.

Blood covered the shoreline, theirs, and mine. A vile stench overcame my senses and the need to vomit struck. Breakfast came back up and it hit the creature right in the eyes and splattered all over its face. Howls of pain ensued as the acid and food particles got into the sockets and began to burn. It thrashed around for a few seconds before I lost sight of it and passed out. Blackness must have taken me suddenly, for I had no memory of hitting my head on the ground.

*   *   *

The wind blew gently across my face causing goose bumps to rise up, which, in turn, caused pain in the damaged areas of my body. I felt cold all over. My eyes barely saw the sun setting in the sky, and the brightness that shone on the hills intensified right at dusk. Everything hurt. Lying there, my other senses began to register the feelings of more pain and cold and wet. It took a moment to orientate myself to my surroundings. My brain even hurt with sickness and I felt dizzy with weakness. The lingering taste of my breakfast reminded me that I had released it into the face of a creature. My throat burned from not getting a chance to rinse it out.

Hard to do that when you are out cold.

I tried to raise my head, but more pain followed, then nausea. I fought to hold down what food remained in my stomach: food that would provide me with the energy to keep warm. Rolling my head to my right, I scanned the scene to see what I was up against, but my eyes failed to locate any attackers. The one that had been chewing on my arm had departed after I vomited in its face. The thought of it stumbling around and becoming something else's dinner made me smile – a fitting end to the food chain, in my eyes. I did not feel so superior at that moment.

My right hand throbbed. Upon raising it, the memory of losing its digits replayed. The blood still oozed, but at least clotted. It was all that I could do not to pass out again when I realized my leg was still in the stream. At least the cold kept the muscle tight, so bleeding was minimal now. My attempt to move caused shooting pain. My tongue got in the way of crying out and I bit down hard, adding insult to injury. My right forearm was missing a fair amount of flesh, further complicating my trauma. I was a mess.

As I struggled to move, funny sounds came from my mouth, grunts and half cries of pain. The noises were irregular and sounded like a drunken ape giving birth to a rhinoceros. I had to laugh a little, and forced myself to sit up and take stock of my leg. The bone was visible in several places where the quadriceps was missing. The wound still bled, but barely. The ice cold water in the stream had kept me from bleeding out. For this, I was grateful.

My senses were coming back faster than I wanted, and a slight panic hit me for a few seconds while I assessed my situation. My shirt was still lying there. I grabbed it and tried to tear it in half with my damaged left hand. A growl escaped my lips. Clouded thoughts hampered my work as the blood started to flow again. I only had a few minutes to find a sharp rock before I would bleed out.

Holding the shirt in my teeth and under my good arm, I worked hard to tear the material. The task was still rough. It took a few seconds to start, but once it did, the fabric, along with the skin on my chest in a few places, sliced easily. I finally used my teeth and tore it the rest of the way.

Now for the fun part!

Trying to wrap my leg up one handed was a comedy act. It took me a few tries to secure my leg so the strips stay tied by themselves. Thinking back to my days in CPR class, I wished I had paid closer attention. I knew this was going to hurt like hell and my mind prepared for what was about to be done. I pulled as hard as I could. My head swam, and all went dark.

*   *   *

Light again.

My eyes popped open. The cold flow of the river stirred me awake. My body was shaking uncontrollably and felt incredibly numb. My muscles were stiff beyond fluid motion. Death should have taken me then in its icy embrace. How I survived was beyond me. Forcing myself to sit up, I found that movement came a little easier. My morale lifted slightly. It took me a few tries and lots of rolling back and forth to get my good leg under me, and an explosion of pain was my reward; that, however, did not deter my motivation to live. Fire was needed and fast.

Several seconds passed with attempts to regain my balance resulting in falls each time. Once up, limping made me wince with every step as I made my way back to camp. All my items remained there at the river's edge, including my other clothes and the cleaning supplies. Everything became irrelevant at that point. The pain was returning in full force with every movement, and the intensity increased with every footfall. My body kept shivering. With movement, I warmed up slightly but the temperature continued to drop. The battle was slowly being lost.

The sun gave me a small measure of warmth and was the saving grace in the journey back to camp, located over at least one hill as the crow flies. Time was running out. I could not slow down. Climbing over even a small hill would prove troublesome with a broken body. I could not risk the delay or loss of strength. The decision to stay on the "known" path and not risk the hill seemed to be the wiser choice. I was able to keep a regular pace for a few minutes at a time, but had to slow down and let the muscles recover every so often. The most difficult terrain was last, thankfully, as it gave me some time to work up to it.

I had been hobbling for several hours, and camp seemed so far away. My morale sank with each step. The feeling of hopelessness hung on each moment. However, giving up was not an option. If nothing else, my training had taught me that. A Defender does not quit, no matter what.

Exhaustion and hypothermia were not far off. I was naked, had no shoes, and was losing blood with each step. A large drink of water should have been on my list, but my wits had not been about me before I left the river, and all I could think about was getting back to my teacher. His comments about responsibility rang in my ears. I tried to be more careful with my surroundings. His logic was to know the environment and avoid letting the enemy have any advantage. Even though the river was familiar to me, they had the advantage, for I had never run into them before. Perhaps they had just arrived in the area.

Pondering the attack gave me something to do, so pain was not the only thing on my mind. My steps labored with each footfall, becoming more tiresome. I lost track of my thoughts and found myself not even thinking about the turn towards camp. I was just three steps past the trail when I realized my mistake. After turning around, I walked down the final stretch down into the vale and heard the crackle of a warm fire. The last few hundred feet seemed to be the easiest as help was now close, as long my teacher did not choose to torture me for my incompetence. Death felt as if it was behind me tapping me on the shoulder when the light of the fire came into view. Light was fading and dusk settled in over the camp as my hobbled form arrived.

"Teacher?" I croaked with a broken voice on approach. He sat by the fire, nose still in his tome. My footfalls suddenly became heavy to the point it was now shuffling that brought me to his side. He did not show any signs of coming out of his trance. On my approach, the fire already began to warm me up. I stopped next to him and touched him on the shoulder with my good hand.

"Did you come back for your sword?"

I wanted to cry. I walked over and obediently tried to don the cross baldric. The blades never felt so heavy. I grimaced and tried not cry out as the worn leather brushed my fresh wounds. I turned and looked at my teacher expecting to pass out at any moment.

"You have passed the test. You will continue to be trained." He did not even look up at me, and I moved and sat down next to him. It was more of a fall, actually, and I came down hard wincing and trying not to cry out.

"You are really hurt, yes?"

I looked at him and did not say a word. He reached out his hand

and took my left in his. He looked at my missing fingers and then back to my face. To my surprise, he smiled and it felt slightly uncomfortable at that moment, but I forced a half smile back that was more of a grimace. Suddenly, healing energy coursed through my hand and down my arm. It was so soothing. My mind felt sleepy.

He muttered under his breath in a kind of chant. Energy grew more intense as it flowed throughout my broken body. Muscles began to relax as they started to weave themselves back together. It is a strange feeling when flesh knits itself and grows at the same time. A blue glow came from his hand and flowed over my arm. He continued to chant.

Many things swirled in my mind, but I lost all of them before a thought could form. I sat there staring at him while he chanted and muttered. The glow of the fire caught my eye with its dancing flame. The plumes of flame seemed to dance in rhythmic harmony to Malnuras's voice. With each phrase he spoke, the energy of the fire would vibrate back and forth. It moved in such synchronicity that I found myself hypnotized by its heat and light as well as its sound. His voice fell farther and farther away, like I was falling into a well and the sound of him speaking echoed off the walls and grew quieter and quieter. Yet I could still hear him.

The light began to form into runes coming right off the fire, and the flames pushed them higher and higher. Smoke swirled and kept the rhythm going and the runes floated away and up. I tried to focus on them as they formed in the fire. Then I realized they were the words that he was speaking. The sound of his voice was creating a pattern in the flames. The very air around us was heavy and still, as if we were in a room with no circulation.

The intensity in his voice built even though he was still getting quieter. Then silence came. Dancing flames continued to form runes, and the smoke continued to push them up and away. A sense of protection fell over the vale.

I relaxed. Mentally, I felt like I could take on anything. A renewed strength filled my mind. My body felt strong and ready. The wounds had healed and my missing fingers had reappeared, allowing me to flex my hand into a tight fist without pain. I was not used to magical healing. It fascinated me truly. The fact that he could do it so easily always made me wonder at the source of his power. I could not logically process nor fathom the answer. Malnuras finished his incantation, and his meditation state seemed to fade as he opened his eyes and stared at me intently.

"You seem to be receiving more wounds even with victories achieved. Why do you think this is? Have I not trained you well?"

The answer eluded me. No reason came to mind beyond it being a natural part of war to take casualties. Then a simple answer came forth.

"Training builds character in oneself. Lessons will bring wisdom. With each wound I suffer, a lesson is learned; thus, more wisdom is gained in failure than in victory." I was surprised to hear such words flow forth from my own lips. I smiled at him for a moment before he spoke in return.

"You are correct. Failures become lessons if you learn from them. Therefore, there are no negative experiences, only those we create ourselves. It is time for you to gain your first mark of achievement. Step over here." I rose and walked over, very unsure what he was going to do but trusting that he had my best interest in mind. He motioned for me to kneel so I did.

"Life is a balance of pain and suffering. Lessons gained through pain are the same as lessons gained through pleasure. They balance each other out, for without one there is not the other. Remember this lesson, for it is going to hurt, but the joy you will feel from the accomplishment will balance out the pain you will experience."

I swallowed hard and held my chin up. He placed his hand on my stomach and the other hand on my forehead and began to chant.

A burning coursed through me and its intensity grew. My blood felt as if it was on fire. Patterns traced themselves on my abdominal muscles. I could not see what they were, for they ran deep, like my insides were having something forcibly added to them. It hurt as if nothing ever felt before and worse than any wound, for the pain did not knock me out. My mind was fully aware of what was happening, but I did not know how to process it. My body trembled. His hands glowed brightly, as if they seared my flesh.

Will power failed and the question "How long can I endure?" formed in my mind, when he stopped and the glow faded and went out. The pain started to bleed off, but it took a few minutes for it to dissipate entirely. My skin was still on fire, and I had no idea what he had done, other than mark me somehow. It felt like a burn mark. Branding was something that *gang member pledges* did for initiation, and it felt similar to that. I was certain it had to mean something. There had been no metal in the fire or in his hand. He used pure magic to achieve his purpose.

Feeling my stomach, I noticed my abdomen was still sensitive, but the there was no more pain. A raised portion of the skin was all that remained. It was slightly elevated, but not pronounced, and it tingled when I touched it. My parents forbade tattoos in their household. Therefore, to have something worse on me would make my mother's blood boil. A smile formed at the thought of finally being my own man. I looked down and noticed dark red ink as well. Then it started to move. I pulled my hand away suddenly. Malnuras laughed.

"It is a symbol that will heal you when you invoke its power. Each side of the mark will balance out the healing energy needed to repair you. You will learn how to use it in time. For now, you need to focus on letting yourself heal," he said.

I looked at him puzzled for a split second and did not even see him draw the knife and slash me deeply across the chest. I fell back with a gasp. I rolled and came to my feet shocked at what had transpired. He did not press the attack but simply sat there and watched me bleed.

"Well now, heal yourself," he said.

Panic hit me hard. I was going to die!

Dropping to my knees came easy, for my head swam at the blood loss. After the fight at the river, I did not think I had much blood left to lose. The rest of it was spilling out now, all over the campsite. Bewilderment followed the dizziness, but realization finally sunk in. A demonstration of my healing powers. Embarrassment would not be the result today. An image of energy flowing through me and knitting the flesh back together came to my mind. My endorphins kicked in because the wound was deep.

Nothing happened. My vision started to blur. He finally spoke.

"Imagine a path from your mind to your mark and channel the energy to the wound," he said, calmly.

I attempted what he said to do. At first, there was nothing. Consciousness was fading when, suddenly, something ran from the mark to my head then down to the gouge in my chest. The energy coursed like a pulse from one area to the other. A euphoric feeling flowed forth and I noticed the free flowing blood starting to diminish. My frown turned to a smile. Sweat poured from my brow due to the intense concentration. It fell to my chest and mixed in with the wound causing a slight discomfort as it rolled right in.

After the wound finished closing, leaving a phantom pain in its wake, I took a deep breath. My chest was tender to the touch. My focus stayed on breathing for quite some time. Not having a concept of time bugged me a little, but not having to worry about it also had it benefits. Moments passed. Further examination revealed the tissue was closing nicely. Still sensitive to the touch, but nothing like it had been moments before, it tingled as the healing turned off. As I sat there in amazement, it dawned on me. This was what my teacher had been doing for me for however long my soul had been there.

I had just worked magic, even though the origin of it had not been mine. From that moment forward, I was a true believer. A new sense of awareness came over me. Feeling connected to my teacher for the first time as if we had shared something special made me fall inside myself for a moment. I sat replaying all of the events that had just taken place.

"How do you feel?" my teacher asked as if he did not already know the answer.

"I feel really good," I said.

Next thing I knew the dagger flashed three times before I could even blink. The sudden trauma hit me before my mind could even register what he did. I must have given him a pitiful look for the expression on his face actually surprised me. The ground rushed up at me.

"You didn't think I was going to let up on you, did you, Dieter?" His voice was calm and slightly mocking.

"No, Teacher," I responded, staggering.

It was going to be a long day. I glanced at my arm and saw a scar shaped like the hideous pattern of a jagged-toothed mouth. At least I was going to have an impressive scar. The glint of steel flashed again.

This time, however, I blocked it.

IV

Meet Your Master

Warrior's Prayer

Shadows dance from candle flame
Spelling out my future bane
With each rise and fall of light
Gives to me the strength to fight

The tears of mother earth have spoken
Her word to man will not be broken
I am to stand alone this day
To stave the hoards that come my way

I question not my task at hand
To give my life to save the land
What future holds in store for me
I must succeed mankind lives free

To God above my prayers do go
give me strength; more then I know
For If I fall and fail this day
Forgive me now of this I pray

What would it mean to be a Defender?

I asked myself this question often. The result lately was poetic words about my life. Sometimes only bits and pieces formed while others formed in moments. I could write twenty lines and it would all rhyme, but at the end of the day, I would forget them due to exhaustion. With no paper or writing device, charcoal was my best friend. There was a suitable depression in a cave now covered with my writing. To my surprise, the words

51

stayed with me all night long and were on my mind when my eyes opened.

I was still irritated at Malnuras for letting me almost die, but the lessons learned had shown me that tests are not always fair. Getting over it was something each person had to deal with. What mattered most was learning to adapt and stay alive. By graduation day, I had more than learned this lesson. Though I was still on my feet and had managed to arrive back at camp on my own strength, I felt in some way the day was a small failure. The satisfaction of achieving graduation did sink in, not that I had much to be proud of. However, surviving a fight with two monsters was certainly a victory.

My teacher thought my vomit tactic was probably what saved the day. Had the second creature continued its chewing run on my arm, it might have caused me to bleed out or it could have taken away my ability to tie a tourniquet, or worse. I did not argue with his assessment. His different point of view was true. We watched my first solo battle in the runes several times in silence before he began to analyze my technique. Choosing not to argue, but simply nod instead, seemed to be the best response. Every point he brought up made me think. Luck is always a factor to a point, but skill saved me.

It is hard to debate, however, when you are watching a recording of yourself. Every flaw magnified itself; every advantage diminished. To go for the rock was my best but in truth it was a reflex. My teacher shrugged when it ended.

"Okay teacher, what did I do wrong?"

"There are always other options. You will have to study this and figure them out."

"I will do as you suggest." The next day I dissected my performance. I found nothing wrong with my performance and still felt it to be effective, if not improvisational. When I brought this to Malnuras's attention, he cuffed me and pointed to my sword. I bowed and went back to the fire pit, feeling stupid for not returning with the obvious answer of preparation.

I really wanted to please him, but at the same time, the urge to be the best and to achieve something that no human had been granted drove me to work harder. The chance to defend the planet against the darkness was like a dream. In the mission, I found purpose. Yet even the heavens were not safe. The daemons that we did find had to come here the exact same way they had to get to earth. It just took less energy. My teacher did not explain this to me, but left me guessing and asking more questions.

He said simply, "It is time."

The next morning started, like all mornings, with my studies. The test was the subject and trying to find one of these mysterious options was the goal. I was concentrating when Malnuras strolled into camp looking rather occupied in his thoughts. I started to speak when his hand raised and motioned for silence. My voice trailed off as he went to his pack and pulled out a stone. A rune decorated the surface. My curiosity piqued. What was its purpose? He threw it into the fire, and within seconds, an image appeared in a flame and formed its own plume. This plume seemed different from the others as the shape of it truly looked as if it was too perfect to be of natural origin. The image was crystal clear, yet it did not flux to the heat of the fire like the other runes.

Legacy of the Defender

The image formed. A man in armor fought atop of a wall adorned with ladders with men on them. His enemy climbed ladders. It was a siege. He bore a cloak with gold embroidery that was in constant motion behind him as he moved. The man was not very large but had a frame built for dealing damage. His helmet made it hard to make out any features on his face, had they been important. Blades flashed in the light so fast that it was hard to see his movements. Instinctively the thought of slowing the image down came to mind and the picture responded accordingly.

I began to study his style of fighting. He had two swords and wielded them with deadly precision. Men fell from the ladders left and right from his nimble, yet effective, strikes. It appeared as though he was barely contacting them with the weapons as they went either rigid or limp, and then plummeted to the ground dozens of feet below. The fighter ran back and forth between twenty feet of wall section at an impressive rate, and seemed to be holding the section of wall single-handedly. The entire time bolts from crossbows or arrows were raining death on his section of the wall. As the warrior ran, his swords remained in motion the entire time and were so blurry at times that not all the contacts he made with the men on the ladders were visible. At the same time, he deflected arrows with ease. This got my attention. I had seen men fight before, but this was amazing.

I took the time to absorb every maneuver, every act, of this warrior. Not one arrow or bolt touched him, and he held his section for hours until the tide slowed and the enemy withdrew. It took several minutes of watching him pace, catching his breath before other men showed up and gave him water. The newcomers pulled the ladders up instead of pushing them down for obvious reasons. This warrior must have finally lost his adrenaline rush for after about five minutes of no activity, he fell down and lay still until the end of the image. A look of wonder must have openly showed on my face. I had just seen a combat god do the impossible. I could not even describe the feeling of elation having watched it, but sadness did rise because I wanted to be as good as him, but I felt that it would never happen. My gaze drifted to my teacher. He sat in silence while my search for words ended.

"Teacher, I want to learn this way."

He looked at me with the kind of look a teacher gives a student that declares desire, but the will power or skill could be a hindrance. Unease at his glance caught me slightly off balance. I knew the issue lay with me, not his ability to teach. It did make me nervous that he did not speak for moments and he stared as if he looked right through me. His intense face made me think of Jason when he tried to teach me something and had to watch me fail repeatedly. This look continued. He did not move and I sat there waiting. My attention finally turned back to the rune that still hung in the fire and started the sequence over again. Within seconds, a thought came to mind.

No movement was wasted; every strike, even if it was a block, did something to his opponent.

With Malnuras not saying anything, I submerged myself in my studies. It still fascinated me beyond words to be able to watch these battles from any vantage point and that the vantage point could be changed, backed up, and even forwarded if needed. Simply by watching and recreating, I learned lessons that the greatest warriors would only hope to gain. I did not have two weapons yet, only the one, and my staff, but stepping through the movements repeatedly became my preferred learning. The lessons helped me advance faster without having a live opponent trying to kill me.

Days passed into weeks without a word from my teacher. He moved around the camp at times, but he filled his days with meditation. When I did glance at him from time to time, he barely moved. My attention was engrossed in combat training. If he left camp, he was not sneaky about it.

I started developing combinations. Many of the moves were impossible for me to do or just straight up beyond my skill level at this time. It was hard to flip over a target that was not there, cut its head off, and run another imaginary target through. So I stuck to what I could do, incredible combinations with my hands. My speed had almost doubled. My coordination was unreal at times. I executed some moves flawlessly. I was trying to pay attention to footwork and balance on one particular day. The hand-to-hand training that I had just finished weeks before was really coming into play here. Balance became the key to every move and stance; now it seemed my every routine. I developed new stances and forms that required exceptional balance. Simple maneuvers transformed into deadly combinations. My survival hinged on the perfection of these skills.

My mind focused on an aerial move that allowed me to block an incoming attack and counter in the same motion. I was working on the move when Malnuras finally spoke. It had been several hours since he came into camp on this occasion and he had a staring contest with the stones. His voice jarred my focus with its ability to command and penetrate the mind. My first reaction was to try to make some witty comment, but as I looked at him, the seriousness struck me like a gust of wind on the ocean. Something was not right. A calm chill came over me.

His gaze did not leave mine. I sensed a mile marker approaching. I braced for bad news.

"A decision has been made that I do not know is right for you," he began as he stared into the fire. "The Archangel Michael was to be your master, but he has been gravely wounded by Lucifer in an epic struggle to save one of the other realms much like this one. You are going to be given a master that knows weapons better than Michael but is not so strict in his discipline, which you need."

I started to comment but the words did not leave my throat. It suddenly became dry the moment I tried to speak. His words were rather odd here. Trying to debate something when one truly does not know the subject matter may be fun, but it can also bring unwanted trouble. If this wizened man had taught me anything, it was that asking too many questions was bad, especially if asked in the wrong place or the wrong time. Therefore, I listened intently, and we continued to look into the fire at the chosen lesson.

Silence hung over the area like a wet blanket. It conforms to everything and the cold wetness crept into every corner. It was a little uncomfortable at first, but I knew better already. Malnuras said just as much with his silence as he did with his carefully chosen words. At times, what he did not say was just as emphasized as what he did say. Even just a glance from him was a thousand words. The night passed uneventfully as lessons repeated until I had memorized the subject matter. I learned each tactic until it was so basic that I did not even have to practice. Malnuras asked me to demonstrate what I had learned, then grunted as though he did not approve of my learning so quickly. His disapproval did not sit well with me, as my desire to make him proud had been my focus, more than the actual learning itself.

Silence found my tongue again, and I chose to let it stay there, feeling it best leave him be, especially if he had thoughts that were beyond me. He was fair. It took a while to separate the teacher and master aspects of our relationship, but with enough strikes from his staff, I began to get the lesson very quickly, especially if I slipped and called him Master.

*   *   *

Dawn's rays of yellow light began to peak over the hills to the realms again. The morning was slightly cold and dew clung to the plant life and everything else quite heavily. I always liked to watch it burn off. The steam lifted skyward to the blue oblivion beyond. My cares followed the dissipating steam as it separated into smaller and smaller clusters of water and vanished in the atmosphere.

Around the campsite, wild grasses grew in a variety of colors. Deep greens and light yellows were common colors. The grass was similar to grass on Earth, but the texture was soft and the blades very thin. It was a dense, thick carpet, more concentrated than the grass back home. The main difference was this grass seemed alive and you could almost hear it whisper in your ear as you lay on it.

Legacy of the Defender

Sometimes the whispering grass made me wonder if I was hearing things. At other times I knew that it spoke to me. The messages always had something to do with my lesson from the night before, something that I needed to learn or perfect. I wondered if the grass was in cahoots with Malnuras. Malnuras was nature-driven in his teachings, so it made sense that he would use the plants to transfer ideas into me. Anytime I asked him about the grass, he did not give me an answer. A nod here or a grunt there was his only response. I gave up asking.

One particular morning, I awoke to whisperings. They were loud, more so than normal. Hearing them so prevalent caught me off guard. As I lay there with my eyes closed tight, I let the orchestra of melodic voices soothe me and tried to relax again. My mind could not explain it. There were so many different sounds that trying to understand it became taxing, as if it was purposely testing me. I was about to give up after several minutes when I finally heard a phrase ring out of nowhere.

"He is here. He approaches," the voices spoke in unison from all around the campsite. I took seconds to process the message, and, upon hearing them, I jumped up and grabbed a staff sitting next to the fire. Whoever or whatever he or it was, there was going to be a fight. In my mind, not just an ordinary fight, but the fight of all fights. I stood ready. Whatever bothered us would get more than it bargained for.

The energy flowing about the campsite put me on edge. I knew better than to allow this to affect me but hearing the warning, made me wonder if there was cause for alarm. Hastily glancing around the campsite, I noticed neither Malnuras nor the mystery creature or person was in sight. My mind

59

quieted for a second. Knowing that someone soon would come, and it would be my master, was comforting. If my master was approaching, would the ground be in a panic?

The light coming from the sun dimmed slightly for a second, and I soon realized a shadow was near. At first, it did not look like a man at all, but an apparition. It coalesced right in front of my eyes, as if out of thin air. I stared for many moments as the image unfolded itself and took form. Seconds to contemplate my actions were not enough. I had lost focus on my problem and concentrated more on whom or what was appearing. Was it a foe or something worse? I gave up on logic and chose to swing my staff to connect with this shadowy stranger when a gauntleted hand caught my staff with ease. It felt heavy in my hands or my mind succumbed to my fears, and then something tore the staff away from me. I found it upside my head knocking me over from a well-placed strike that, surprisingly, did not hurt.

I rolled and came to my feet in a defensive stance ready to face whatever kind of test this was. It was unlike my teacher to downplay a master showing up in this fashion, but my discounting it would be a big mistake. The outline of a very large humanoid, back lit by the sun, stood before me, holding my staff. I squared off and took my strongest stance, waiting to size up my foe. A small stalemate seemed to be unfolding in my head as I began running through scenarios in my mind. The first one involved me grabbing rocks from the fire pit to hurl at my opponent. I was about to take action when a deep, penetrating voice sounded.

"Grabbing the rock will improve your chances of survival by about a fraction. Discovering if your visitor is indeed friend or foe increases your chance to half. Choose," he said and the staff started to spin in a most impressive display. It then struck downward, reverberating against the nearest rock and showering the area with sparks. I wanted to urinate but maintained control of my bladder and my composure. The figure strode forward out of the sun's blinding rays and stood in the twilight. I still could not see who it was.

"Are you friend or foe?" I asked.

"Lucky for you, child, I am neither. I am your master." With blinding speed, he crossed the fifteen or so feet and swept my front leg with ease before my muscles even twitched in response. My body found out how soft the grass was and it still knocked the wind out of me. "Yes, Master."

"Lesson number one, take all your opponent's advantages away. I caught you with the oldest of tricks and took away your most important senses: your sight and your ability to rationalize," he said, watching to make sure I was listening.

"How is rationalizing one of the senses?" I asked. His hand was suddenly locked on my throat and lifting me high in the air.

"You were unable to make a proper decision so you could not think. If you cannot think then you cannot perceive. If you cannot perceive then your actions will most likely be foolhardy." He dropped me, and I landed hard, buckling my knees. I half expected him to continue dangling me by my throat for my accidental insolence. Instead, I found myself standing on my own accord looking up and into the eyes of the largest man I had ever seen in my life.

"I am Mathias. You can call me Master until I tell you otherwise."

"Yes Master."

"Have you learned your first lesson?" he asked.

"Yes, Master."

"Good, now prove it," he said. "Catch me some game without using a weapon."

I caught myself looking at him as if he was crazy because hunting was not one of my skills. I managed to nod then turned the nod into a bow rather quickly. Far too many kung fu movies ended badly when a student was not proper to his teacher. The items near my sleeping mat seemed of little use suddenly, so grabbing my water skin and leaving camp was my only recourse.

"Before you leave, your old life is dead to you. Dieter is dead...You need to discover your real name. It will come to you when you least expect it."

I left confused. My old life was over, that was a given but my name too. His audacity only outweighed that he could probably kill me with a thought...But telling me to change my name? I had no response to that. I felt camp post haste.

As I hunted, my new teacher and his intensity became as much of my focus as my task. I was relieved he had given me a free pass without knocking me senseless. Perhaps my initial score would have been better in his eyes had my reaction been to attack without hesitation. Something told me that would have been worse.

My path took me away from camp. I tried to figure out how to accomplish catching game without a weapon. Soon, a small deer drinking from a pond was in my path. While considering the deer, a growl sounded behind me.

I froze.

Not knowing what to do, I slowly turned to see what was there. A large saber toothed mountain lion stood on a rock. I was too preoccupied to notice he was in a striking stance. It had given me a warning that was barely audible but loud enough for me to hear. I quickly looked down and started backing away slowly. The deer continued to eat and drink, unaware of its surrounding. Several slow steps carried me fifteen feet when the energy in the air changed and the saber sprung. There followed a squeal when its lethal jaws locked on the unsuspecting deer. My second lesson of the day had just unfolded before me.

This was going to be a difficult task. Today granted me two chances. Wasting either one of them was not my intent. I backed up even farther giving the large cat due privacy while it ate. I would have to find my own prey and that meant tracking it. With a sigh, I sat down on a rock and cleared my mind.

Today was going to be a long day.

V

Training

My lessons were brutal.

Each one connected logically to the next, giving me lethal skills. The cost was great but the reward was greater. I had mastered movement and weapon skill like a natural. Master showed me techniques that mortal men did not do, for they did not possess the physical prowess. With one swing of the blade, I could cleave a small daemon easily. Medium sized daemons took a bit more power, but I used their mass against them.

I was dangerous.

The medium sized, flying daemon approached. It was the biggest I had faced in combat so far. It was as tall as a man was. The smell of sulfur emanated from it, and its hot breath washed over me on its first pass. Its breath would melt the flesh of a mortal man. There was a chemical reaction with human flesh. In my first encounter with these types, I had not known about the effects of the breath. Master never told me. In my ignorance, I allowed its saliva to saturate my face. The skin hardened and burst as the muscles underneath seized up and expanded. My face had frozen in a grimace of death with my eyelids wide open. Bits of my flesh flapped in the wind as I danced around slashing. Talk about freezer burn. I could not imagine a more terrible way to die.

Its first pass had been a clash of steel on claw. Now it came around for a second pass. I hated fighting the fliers. There were too many angles to defend, and I had not mastered defending all the quarters. It is one thing to fight fast ground creatures, but another thing to take on speedy fliers. With runners, there were fewer attack lines. Fliers could come from anywhere. I had to look at the tactical advantage that fliers had on me. My speed was fast on the ground, but in the air, they were superior. Gravity intensified most diving attacks. Objects speeding toward the ground already had momentum. Add the benefit of streamlined beating wings and you have one fast bastard.

Smaller fliers were the worst. Their agility forced me to learn to predict movements. When close enough to perceive the smallest course adjustment in their bodies or the slightest rotation in the tip of their wings, I could predict movement. This gave me a near-telepathic skill at times.

My heart pounded. It was the size of an average human male, with huge wings, teeth, nasty breath, and a whole lot of attitude and hatred in it. They came in hordes, like aerial piranha, only much faster and with no limit to their movements. I admired their innate ability to fly in such large number with close proximity to each other. When the flying horde approached, they blocked out the sun.

For my training, I had only faced a handful at a time. The one circling me now was a tougher test.

Hundreds of days before, I had learned to focus my inner strength and release it in a burst that propelled me several meters into the air. A dual set of runes painfully appeared on either hip. Although I could not see them, unless looking at my reflection, I could feel the welts. The daemons had a hard time escaping my blades when they got too close, even though I could not fly. The key was to time my strikes to avoid their teeth and claws as they passed. My favorite tactic was to cleave their wings and watch them furrow into the ground.

It was a standard tactic for them, seen many times before. The daemons would dive straight at me in a lance-like formation. If I moved one way or the other, one of them would make contact. The last thing they would expect was for me to stand my ground and strike from the middle. While it gave them more hitting power, it also offered them less maneuverability.

It circled again, diving at me…faster this time.

My inferior training blades flashed out wide. It cried out as my metal passed through its leathery hide, sinewy flesh, and ribs…then clean out the other side. Just like the pressure you feel when pushing your finger into an orange that still has its peel, tough and hard at first, but then the tension releases as the skin breaks, allowing access to the softer inside. The ribs were never an issue. That sensation always gave me satisfaction. I pulled my weapons clear of the carcass before it hit the ground, and with a small flick of my wrists flung any clinging fluids to my sides. Last one for that group. You would think they would learn that flying faster meant dying faster. That would have been difficult with only one blade. I was thankful for finally receiving a second blade some time ago. I loved dual wielding.

With a satisfied grin, I looked to my master, Mathias.

Mathias trained me in every weapon known to man…even a few never seen before in movies or books. Everything from bludgeoning weapons to large two-handed swords; we covered everything. The training was

66

brutal. My master had taught me so much in such a small measure of time. As I looked at him each day, my desire to be just like him increased. I quickly became a weapons master because I learned faster than his previous students had. It was hard to avoid being prideful, but my view was very humble and I was excited for what was to come.

Mathias was a towering figure for what I thought to be a man. He had chiseled features like a Grecian statue, only even more defined. His body bulged with muscles for which they did not have names. A firm, square, unbreakable jaw. Flaming red hair adorned his shoulders. It was straight but seemed to get brighter towards the tips. When not pulled back, his hair looked alive, as if it could move on its own. I could have sworn it deflected my blows a few times when luck was with me. His eyes freaked me out at first; they had no pupils so you could never tell where he was looking. It was a bit unnerving for a while. He had no facial hair either. When I started to ask, he just smiled and hit me.

I had never seen legs as powerful as his, even in what little bodybuilder magazines I had read or pro wrestling seen on television. His ability to leap vertically was superior. On his descent, he drifted slowly as if he commanded the elements to carry him. His power of control was amazing for I had seen him land so hard that he cracked the ground on other occasions.

"Will I ever be built like you?"

He smiled and hit me.

He reminded me of my teacher...only Mathias spoke even less.

My training was more than just weapons. I learned that inner peace and calm was the key to surviving the most horrific events. Mastering my fear would have to come later. He taught me to control pain and to focus my inner strengths when battling fatigue. Fighting when you have reached total exhaustion is a monumental feat. Overcoming such exhaustion with the right frame of mind, that was the key. Although my skills had begun to blossom, they were nowhere near what they needed to be.

Seeing this man in action was a thing of grace and beauty. I had always heard that most muscle bound fighters had no finesse. His movements were like the flow of water, breaking upon his enemies with thundering force. There was no wasted movement, as each strike set up the next one. He gaited back and forth so fluidly. I aspired to move as he did and took inspiration every time we sparred. Each lesson filled my heart as well as my mind. Multiple aspects flooded my mind daily. It was up to me to apply the knowledge.

We relocated to a different part of the land, with light all the time. The sun never set. I lost track of the hours and had to be told at times when to sleep and, sometimes, when to eat. I focused so much that there were days I did not sleep. The conditioning was fierce, but I could not get enough. Each passing day was more grueling than before and more challenging, but my spirit cried out for more. When sleep finally found me, my hands rested on my blades. They became part of me. In this realm, with swords in hand, I felt more at home than I ever had on Earth. Through all of this, it never occurred to me to ask him about armor, and he never brought it up.

More time passed. Eventually, my body developed its own clock. Master began to drill me verbally. His words inspired me to forget about tomorrow, especially when strength training started.

"There is here and now and nothing else matters," Mathias drilled into me.

"Yes Master," I said while holding a large bolder over my head.

"Focus all your thoughts, energies, and skills on the task at hand," said Mathias.

"Yes Master." The words bubbled forth with my head barely above water. How I managed to tread water and hold that damn bolder over my head was beyond me. "How does this have this have anything to do with fighting daemons?"

The words had barley left my mouth when he smiled and hit me.

I sank.

*   *   *

Every time my swords were in my hands, excitement filled me. Swinging those blades brought a smile on my face. Joy knew no boundaries, for my path was set before me. My mission was clear. My purpose established. Put daemons in front of me and they will die. That was all that mattered.

By this time, my physical stature had grown. I was still about and inch shorter than Mathias, who stood at seven foot six. He could still overpower me, but my speed surpassed his. The lessons still hurt, but with each day my skills improved. I learned more from live instruction than from watching the runes in the fire. My mind was a sponge. Lessons at the fire pit were painless compared to live instruction, unless I fell in. The real advantage of the runes was rewinding and re-watching from different angles. Also, *they* did not hit back.

With constant light, it was hard to track how long we stayed in this night less location. It felt as if years were passing. Even though I was present mentally every day of training, the relevance of how long we were gone did not become apparent. So I asked.

"Master, how long have we been here? I feel like I am significantly older. How many years have we been here? I think I was with Teacher for over a year or more before you arrived."

He made a playful motion of looking at the sun that never moved. He looked at me and how tall I was next to him, as if that mattered. There was a long pause before he spoke. "Time passes differently here than on earth. If an educated guess could be accurate, it would be around ten years."

"Oh. How many years have passed on earth?"

"You ask too many questions, Dieter. Return to your studies."

Later that day, I found something. My interest in swords drifted to the Eastern empires of ancient Earth. Because I was adept at manipulating the runes, I began to study something I always loved. It felt like sacrilege to watch and analyze the greatest Samurai of all time, Miyamoto Musashi. He was so skilled that he used wooden swords to best his opponents. I loved to watch how he beat his foe into submission with one or two strikes.

Could I beat him?

My attention was so engrossed I failed to notice my master standing there. He was not barking orders. I jumped up and bowed.

"Dieter, I have something for you before you return to Malnuras to continue your training." He held up something very long wrapped in cloth.

"Master?" I said, hesitating.

"Has your true name come to you yet?"

"My true name? How will I know?"

"Yes, your true name. It will be obvious."

"What will be obvious?"

"Just open the package and stop asking questions," he smiled.

I stepped up and took the item from him. A purple material covered the item that was both soft and firm. A silver cord ran along the lines of a square cloth bag. The end had a drawstring fastened with a shield-shaped brooch of bluish silver with two swords crossed behind it. Carefully unfastening the drawstring, I slid it back, revealing a sturdy box that had metal bindings at the corners. Symbols like those in the fire decorated a wooden box. Its weight was less than expected.

The covering slid gently off the ornate box. Its length was easily five feet. Metal clasps fastened it at six locations. Each one released as soon as my hand touched it. The lid opened silently and light shone out across me, its luminance growing brighter and brighter. As the opening increased, the familiar shape of two blades greeted me. Two magnificent blades sat nestled in the box. They were Celestial swords, for the angels used them exclusively. The design was a cross between a scimitar and an oriental blade, only deadlier and faster. I saw them in use every day when fighting my master.

My hands slightly shook as each blade emerged from its encasement. When I held them in my hands, they felt as though they belonged there.

Their weight was astonishingly light. They felt like more than an extension of my body; they were my body. My eyes must have been wide with wonder as my gaze fell to Mathias. He simply nodded and smiled subtly for the first time. A hint of pride came from him though he tried to hide it. I guess a master is not supposed to show emotion to his student.

The enchantments tingled in my hands as my own energy began to reach out to the blades. My life force started to enter each blade while the weapons own power extended into me like a key in a lock. A sense of completion washed over me, as warm as the sun's rays caressing my skin, but on the inside. I was smiling uncontrollably.

They were so light. I swung them around and could feel the very air cut before the blades, creating tones which sang to me in harmony with each other. There were almost words coming from each of them, as each movement was different from the last. The sound was incredible. This musical sensation continued to swirl inside of me and touched the root of my emotions.

"Can you hear that, Master?" I asked.

"No, only the wielder hears his songs. In time, you will not even notice it audibly, for it will be only in your mind. That is how they will talk to you," he said.

"That is a shame. I rather like it," I said.

"Each blade will create sounds as you learn to wield them. As you perfect your moves, the sounds will diminish, telling you have achieved the synchronous and you are at one with the blades. You will have to learn their properties and make them your own; the swords ability enhances its wielder.

No two swords are the same, and they will manifest in their own time. Some abilities are set from creation. You will have to discover these as well. It will take many hours of meditation and concentration, aside from practicing each day, to master your new weapons."

"Thank you, Master," my bewildered response came in wonder of these finely crafted blades. His words faded for a few moments, for I was lost in a sea of thoughts. These new instruments of death had a feel all to themselves. I probably missed something important for he was still speaking when my focus returned.

"Tonight I suggest you meditate with each blade separately, then together. It will seal the blending process and allow growth and discovery to begin." Mathias sat down on his mat. I stood swinging the swords calmly. The moving blades created a beautiful duet of unintelligible words. A trance like state came over me.

The night passed.

Mathias left before I awoke the next morning, leaving me a note. Reading over it, my emotions elevated gently in the fond memories of his teaching. He told me I would see him soon as his duties had taken him back to where he came from to resolve some things. It was time for me to prepare for the next leg of my journey. I never had an opportunity to thank him for his instruction. He was, after all, Heavens weapons master and had been teaching people to fight since the beginning. I could only imagine how long that must have been.

I spent the day meditating with each blade before returning to the camp to find my teacher was waiting for me. Malnuras greeted me in his usual way, with a nod, almost never locking gazes with me. We used a portal that Malnuras opened with a ring he wore, taking us back to the original campsite where I met my Master for the first time. I let my pack drop on my bedding, but the box for the blades, I gently lay down and opened to reveal the pride of my existence. From behind me came a voice.

"You have earned some rest my young swordsman. I see you have your blades now, so your focus needs to be on finishing the melding process," he said.

"Yes, Teacher. The next leg of my training is about to begin I was told."

"You are correct," he replied as he pulled a book from his pack and began to read.

A few weeks passed, by my guess, each day filled with conditioning and fighting. On one particular day, Malnuras sat to my left up on a small bluff. He was eating some sort of root that he had found earlier that day. Even though his attention was elsewhere, he always knew when mistakes of mine happened, for he would call them out to me during each encounter. Mistakes did happen, but due to the limited number of assailants, there was little danger yet. I felt he was going to challenge me very soon with something big.

For several days, my teacher directed the fights to gage my skills again. This last group consisted of about three-dozen large leapers and a several medium flyers. I wiped my blades clean on the grass. The gore these creatures left behind was visually disgusting, but the smell after battle was intoxicating. Blood and ichor had a curious scent. It fueled the bloodlust within me to continue the righteous vengeance. I controlled it to this point, but did take a moment or two to realize my enemies were all dead. Sheathing my swords, I strode up the hill to where he sat. My backside found a rock to sit upon to await my battle evaluation. It took longer and longer with each one since fewer mistakes happened, and the number of foes increased. I felt confident by this time. My work had been flawless in my eyes.

Some time passed before Malnuras spoke. I had enough time to walk through the battle in my head three times before he broke the silence. My anticipation was always great. I hated my own failures and shortcomings with a passion. Each encounter I tried to incorporate his finding to avoid making the same mistake. It was easy for the most part. Occasionally in the past, his assistance was required to avoid serious injury. Fear had not been part of me for some time now. Even though he kept a pretty sharp eye on me during the battle, it was hard to tell he was watching, as his attention seemed to be elsewhere. Yet he always knew what happened and could criticize where needed.

"Your choice of technique has me curious," he began. I was just finishing replaying it in my mind as he spoke. Sometimes his cryptic way drove me crazy. He might have a point, but there had not been any bad choices this fight.

"Teacher, at what point did you feel that I was not one with the fight?" I asked. He always seemed to pause before sharing his assessment. It made me feel better if I could catch the error so I started to go over the engagement aloud in the manner he usually preferred.

"You let them get too close before you deliver the killing stroke.

Your energy is vulnerable to attack. Always remember there are many ways the enemy can attack you. Strike each opponent down before he reaches you. This will ensure that both physically and spiritually you are safe. Fighting two battles at once is never a favored strategy. Next time defeat them before they get too close, or you might find yourself under siege mentally. They must get close for you to feel those effects. Very few of them can assault you at range in this manner," he said. "Their close proximity to your life force is a threat. Remember that. They will drain you."

Taking his words to heart, I came to a realization. It was true. I did wait until they got close. Something about seeing the life fade from their eyes made it more satisfying. I could not help it. In my lessons, Malnuras had never been very clear about what made the daemons so deadly until now. Even though he closely monitored the training, I still felt some of the actual danger involved even in such small numbers. My reaction to this was to try to make the battle a challenge and not go for the kill too soon. Part of me wanted them to suffer also. My strategy was working so far. I had not lost any battles yet, but the odds told me it would happen eventually.

He knows I want to take my time, but knowing they can drain energy...

"Now get down there and do it again. Do not wait so long to strike, for if too many get in close, I will not be able to get to you before they eat your intestines." He gave me a sideways look then returned to the root he was peeling with is teeth. Lord knows what it was. It was rare that he had me fight two battles back to back. I always wondered how it was that he could sense when there was going to be more daemons, or if he had a way of conjuring them up. Part of me wondered if they were just a clever illusion.

Maybe, for training purposes, they were not even real.

I leaped off the rock and noticed that the descent took a few seconds longer than normal. *Did I just float?* During the past weeks, there had been a change in how the lessons started. While dropping, I saw the next set of daemons flying in a formless pack and heading my direction. Why they always found me down below instead of harassing Malnuras was a bit of a puzzle. Dumb question! My feet touched down and I readied myself. My teacher's words still in my mind, I panned the skies.

There were over fifty of them, large enough for me to see several thousand feet away. As I completed my count, I felt my stomach sink. This was the largest group of this size I had ever faced, by more than half, the last group being only several dozen. I looked back to the bluff. Malnuras was actually watching me at the time. I did not know if that was good or bad, but part of me found comfort in feeling his eyes at my back. I knew he grossly understated how fast he could move. Yet I did not want to test the theory.

In swooped my enemies.

"For the Defenders!" I bellowed, calling both swords to action.

Why this cry escaped my pursed lips puzzled me. I am not sure where it came from, but energy coursed through me. My soul was on fire. Heat poured from my hands, engulfing my blades. Down the edges it ran, enveloping them in some sort of Eldridge fire. I was rather hypnotized for a brief moment, watching the flames dance from the metal. This was new.

I crouched down, taking one last look at the mystical flames dancing on the swords and leapt. Out snapped my arms as I rotated to the right. My left arm rolled over, so both blades were leading the spin. The move was predictable because the daemons acted as if they anticipated it. All but the last three pulled out of my path. I sliced the first two in twain. The third took a mortal wound, leaving trails of blood as it plunged downward.

My ascent came to a crescendo. I started to drop. I stopped my rotation to get a bearing on my enemies. Although they did not travel in formations, they did attack in them. A most common tactic was a wedge or spearhead. While its original use was to penetrate enemy lines, they used it in an attempt to surround me.

They circled behind me, where I anticipated they would be. What surprised me was they split into two groups: one of about thirty and one of twenty. I touched back down, trying to posture for my next move. My mind began to race through the scenarios that Master had taught me. They were obviously trying to flank me. How could I use this to my advantage? Watching for clues, I studied each of them.

Maybe I could use one group as a shield while attacking the other.

The smaller group dove in and I charged at them before leaping. At the last moment before engaging, they broke off and swooped away. While turning to track them, it hit me; or I should say they hit me, on my flank. The larger of the two groups swung around. Upon impact, claws, teeth, and horns took their toll. My feet met the soil then legs collapsed. Down I went; one of my swords slipped from my grasp. All I could do was strike side to side with the other.

My desperate flailing was working. Two of them to my left took deep wounds and disengaged from me. I continued my fury of blows, striking at all quarters of my surrounding area. One to my right fell, missing its head, but not before it had opened up my right leg. The blood flowed freely down my thigh.

A quick glance of the battlefield revealed that some surrounded me, and others dove at me from the sky. I needed my other blade and fast. Amidst my strikes, a glint twenty feet away caught my eyes. The blade's fire had gone out, as had the flame on the on in my hand. With frustration, a roar bellowed forth, and from a crouched position, my legs exploded into action. The wind felt good on my face. A trail of my blood fell to the soil below. The daemons responded in kind, and four took to the sky to join the others. Six of them were down, and I was bleeding badly.

Landing with a roll, my hand found my other hilt as my feet took a firm stance. Dizziness overtook me for a moment, and I refocused my eyes. The one group had joined the others and had formed a spearhead. They dove right at me. *This was going to take perfect timing.* Just as they neared, right outside my reach, I stepped and spun to the left. Both blades flashed out to my right side. Half a dozen hits found their mark as the flock drove right through my original location. The blood showered the ground, followed by an assortment of daemon parts. Many untouched daemons pulled up, as I continued my spin. Up they went, running for the safety of the sky. Tracking their trajectory, I had no doubts they were running to get help. Something inside me felt I had made a grave mistake in my tactics that day.

I struggled to focus on my own healing. Activating it should have been second nature, but the energy would not flow. I tried not to focus on the situation and found a point of serenity to open the pathways and allow the healing to activate.

Nothing happened.

My legs gave out, slamming my knees into the soil hard. The shame of losing to such a small number brought emotions to the surface, fueled by rage. They were not much larger than the smallest ones I had fought previously, but still they were about the size of a large man. My head felt lighter than usual.

"It figures," I laughed as the darkness took its hold. *Where was Malnuras? I did not even have time to look to the bluff. Was he coming?*

My vision blurred at the sight of my enemy taking more pieces of me.

A voice in my head coincided with the sound of my blades clattering to the ground. "You waited too long," it said.

Darkness came.

VI

Bigger and Badder

Never in my life had I imagined such a beast.

For something so huge and hideous, a measure of grace surrounded its flight. Four pairs of leathery hide wings beating as one synchronous heartbeat carried this monstrosity to its destination. I could see it had at least three sets of limbs. Two were for walking; the other seemed to be arms for grabbing. Huge talons sliced the air while it wiggled its fingers in anticipation. It was starting to go for the bait. Soon I would make my move.

The remnants of the scent gland I had salvaged from the smaller female made the perfect lure. The battle to retrieve the gland was the worst idea I had ever managed to use in my favor. Malnuras had been working with me on various tactics and tutoring me on my daemon lore for quite some time now. The plan was simple, or so it seemed. I was to lie in cover at a mating spot used by the daemons. Had I not trained the greatest warrior in Heaven, there would be no way that I could have even thought of assaulting such a beast.

The weave of the planes energy was strongest here. Any mating that took place near the nexus point yielded a higher chance of mutation. With my own eyes, I had studied the process. It was quite disgusting. Like the praying mantis of Earth, the male died in the process. The result was not just one offspring, but hundreds. Daemons mated constantly. A large infiltration was about to take place, so they needed greater numbers to swell the ranks. Gestation for the species was brief, requiring just a few days to birth new daemons.

Neither of us had anticipated the arrival of several females in the previous fight. In his experience, they never went to the same spot. Fights usually ensued for the right to use the nexus point. The presence of the other two females remained hidden until it was too late. Although I walked away from that battle, I bore horrible scars that would take time to fade.

My mind returned to the present.

The male landed and walked forward to where the scent gland lay buried. I had to guarantee he would land. My tactic worked. It clawed at the ground with its huge talons the size of large sword blades. While it was stationary and busy, I got a better look. Its long dragon-like body was rather disgusting to look at. How this thing could be so graceful in flight, I did not know. Large knots from old wounds covered its back and wings. It had no scales either, only thick, ugly skin. Even from a distance, the smell was enough to make me wretch. I never would have imagined that one of these monster's best defenses was to assault my ole factory lobe. Learning the anatomy of my enemy did, however, make me more efficient at dispatching them.

I had one distinct tactical advantage: speed. This thing moved so slowly on the ground that it was virtually ineffective. My agility on the ground was superior. I looked forward to carving him open, but had to wait for the exact moment that he uncovered the small hole. It was to be a small distraction. My hope was that it would give me enough time to close the distance where the dance of death could begin.

The daemon removed the camouflage placed over the hole faster than anticipated. The sheer size of its hands made short work of my trap. I sprang into action. My strides lengthened as my speed increased. I would be on my prey within moments. A roar announced my ruse failed.

Its large head swung left then right, buying me the extra seconds I needed since the bait failed to hold his attention long enough. As the gigantic head came to my side of his body, a buffet from his four wings nearly knocked me over. I turned my body and spun to my right with both swords out trying to use centrifugal force to keep me on target. My swords came in a low upward arc. They bit flesh hard. First blood fell to me, a small victory.

I had its undivided attention now.

I began to weave and strike, trying to cripple its wings in order to keep it on the ground. With the ferocity in which they beat, the creature's wings added to the damage with their own force. In flashed my swords as I spun out of the way of its lethal claws. My reaction was not soon enough. A voice broke my concentration.

"Tathlyn!"

Who in the world was that? My movement faltered a fraction of a second.

My anticipation of the creature's next move came a moment too late. I dealt with two sets of claws and his taloned feet now. Dodging one pair of claws moved me into the path of the other. A mistake soon realized.

My swords parried nothing. Redirecting these monstrous talons was the best I could do. It had faster speed with its hand-like claws than anticipated. Its feet were slower, but they had all that weight behind them. I had to keep moving and stay out from under it as it tried to herd me into its kill zones.

"Tathlyn!" The word came louder.

Its coordinated attacks were proving to be too much. I had underestimated my opponent. I could hear my master's voice in my head, scolding me for losing the tactical advantage. Why he was saying someone else's name was wrecking my flow. I had to refocus. His analysis started to enter my mind, as if he was speaking. Yet the voice was off. It was even deeper.

Strange.

If it was not my teacher trying to get my attention then who was it? Why now? I already knew his assessment. The creature's blind spots should make it an easy opponent. Taking advantage of those blind spots was my goal, but this damn voice in my head was throwing me off. I know both He and Malnuras could mentally speak to me.

That still messed me up.

There was no clue in my head what Malnuras really was. I was sure that Mathias was an angel, though...which made sense, for angels were very powerful. He thought me to be asleep one time when he took off his armor...Pretty sure I saw an outline of wings. So it made sense to me this was a racial enemy to him. He had a clear advantage over me, though: thousands of years of fighting under his belt and being the best swordsman and warrior that Heaven had to offer. I often wondered why they chose me for this task instead of someone like him.

It was mankind's destiny to save itself. My opinion may not be the same on that, but question or debating with Master proved painful more than once. He had a very martial way of proving his point, which I soon learned was my point after our "discussions" ended with me lying bloody on the ground. We would respectfully disagree often.

I learned to stop whining about it even if it was just a question and made a habit of asking him with my weapon in hand. In Earth's culture, this would have been a sign of disrespect to hold steel when asking a question to a superior but his answers were in the form of lessons. Memories of those past years brought a smile to my face. My Master helped mold me in ways that gratitude could not repay.

I had drifted again. The voice came again louder this time. "Tathlyn!"

The monster's roar pulled me back from nostalgia. My movements had been automatic. I had to stop letting my mind wander while I fought. I needed to be more than present.

Minor cuts began to add up. They might have only been nicks, but there were tens of tons, if not more, of mass behind those claws, and my own blood flowed freely from the lacerations. Even though I could regenerate wounds in a short time frame after the battle, my instincts told me the threat was great. With each attempt to "parry" performed, more of my life's essence escaped. I began to panic a bit and realized that some slight sensations in my extremities were beginning to fade. There had to be some sort of poison or nerve agent on the claws. It was no wonder that these creatures were the biggest and hardest to kill. They only had to strike a few times and wait. As my heart began to race beyond the influence of adrenalin, my lightheaded stature grew.

"This is it, either Malnuras is going to jump in, or it is curtains," I thought, trying to send just that to him.

My focus began to wane. My strikes became less effective. My strength faded, raising concerns…that I staunched before panic set in. My options closed fast.

A thought hit me. *If I can heal after a battle, why not now during the battle?* I began to refocus my sword on defense, while my mind was searching for tranquility and peace within. For several moments, I dodged and avoided attacks while attempting to stop my own bleeding and re-knit the damaged flesh. My eyes felt heavy as I fell into a rhythm, trying to stay alive. Weights felt attached to my upper eyelids. They got lower and lower. Finally, a surge of energy hit me.

Healing energy pulsated through my limbs, driving back the fatigue that was taking me. The tingling sensation of flesh rejoining caused an itching on my skin. My eyes no longer felt weighted and the adrenaline rush returned. I was about to wonder if the poison was going to get counter acted when a sudden furiousness returned to my arms and my timing re-synchronized my blades. I deflected the talons that came dangerously close to hitting something vital other than flesh and began countering the attacks. It worked. Why had I not thought of this before? Why had my teacher not mentioned it? The answer eluded me as I changed my focus to biting my blades deeper into my enemy.

The battle was not going my way. It was ironic to a small degree. Careful planning had gone out the window in the first few seconds of the fight. I suddenly remembered playing chess with my grandfather. His strategies allowed him to perform several attacks at once in several locations on the board. Even with the one victory achieved against him, I was a move or two away from losing that game.

Interesting how a game taught students strategy. Maybe I should have paid more attention. My mind snapped back to my own battle again as both sets of claws slammed into the ground on either side of me with such force that I came off my feet. A blood curdling scream came from the creature's mouth. I felt momentary terror. My muscles froze and contracted as if one giant cramp hit my body at once. I fell to the ground, twitching uncontrollably. The panic turned into fear and fear into terror. I could not move.

The ground around me fractured and loose dirt and stone showered me. Gargantuan claws pulled free from the stone. Debris rained down on me, pounding me with earth for several seconds. Whatever had healed before was now bruised and broken again. My weapons barely stayed in my grip; only sheer willpower kept them there. Despair rolled over me like an avalanche. Not being able to move meant the battle was over. The terror was in full swing now.

The ground shuddered with a terrific heave of energy as the grotesque creature slammed its full weight on me. A monster had never crushed me before today. My frame compressed and every nerve fiber in my body cried out in pain. Pressure spread across my nervous system in waves of incredible pain. My weapons were in front of me in a cross guard pattern and the blades bit into the flesh across my chest. The beast crushed the life out of me. Darkness was moments away.

A voice, as clear as if my teacher was next to me, echoed in my ears. "You are limiting yourself. Let go of reality. It does not exist here my pupil." Tears flowed freely from my eyes making mud out of the dirt where my face lay half buried. I openly wept and began to scream at the top of my lungs. Fear turned to rage. Every sinuous strand and tendon flexed and tore. My muscles protested greatly at the approaching fate.

Words repeatedly rang in my mind like a beating drum. How could he stand there when I was about to die? My death would be more horrible than any other ever seen in a movie, read in a book, or seen from my literal history lessons. I heard tendons snapping in my arms and the weight fell on me even harder, forcing a crimson cough to fill my mouth. The effects of no air took the rest of me gradually. Seconds felt like minutes. Every section of my lungs filling with blood forced the remaining air to bubble out from the punctures. I expected to hear a final crunch and an explosion of pain. Instead, warmth on my face suddenly appeared. I anticipated seeing the monster's maw open before me. I opened one eye and looked around. I was on the hillside sitting next to Mathias.

"Okay, this is new," I said.

He pointed out over a valley and spoke again. "Tathlyn."

I opened my other eye and turned my head. A forest clearing looked familiar. The monstrosity was on top of me. It was hard to believe that somewhere under it was my body dying. The creature had both of its taloned claws on me, like it was doing pulmonary resuscitation on the ground, only it was not hard to deduce what was under his large claws. It was grinding me into the ground.

A slight horror factor enveloped me over the seriousness of this mess. Then it caught my eye. The smallest of ironies or acts of defiance could sway the odds sometimes. Protruding ever so slightly out the top of its hands, I could see the two small tips of my swords. I smiled knowing even a gnat can be troublesome.

"Well, at least I am not going to die without messing his hands up." I felt a slight smack on the back of my head as Mathias's hand returned to his side. I did not even see it move to start with, only to resettle at his side and back into his lap.

"Look again," he said.

"At what? I am dead." Another smack with a bit more force, yet I reveled in the fact it was about one thousandth of what he could do. Even though I knew my view and outlook at life was now different from his, he still stood over me and commanded that respect like a parent. I looked back at the scene below me and took it apart piece by piece. A big nasty daemon crushed me under its paws and my swords stuck through its flesh. Then I noticed not only was it motionless, but also there were no sounds of it screaming. The flying daemons hovered motionless in flight around the larger one. Time stopped. "Did you do that?" I asked expecting him to swat me harder this time.

"No. I am not here right now, remember?"

It was true; he had left me some time ago on a mission he said was very important and did not concern me. My recent success in obtaining the female scent gland had me consumed, so thoughts of my master leaving had faded in my memory. He truly was not here, and I really was about to die. Yet time stood still.

I was the one stopping time somehow. Where this ability came from

I did not know. I did not learn it, nor was it passed on to me.

"You are over thinking this. Look at the fight and close your eyes, tell me what you really see," said Mathias.

I looked back and started to go over it again, replaying it from the start in my head. Each step taken, block attempted, or redirect executed moved in slow motion in front of me, as I was watching a video of myself. I saw myself leap and reposition with each attempted strike. Then it hit me when I saw myself under the paws of the beast and the pressure began to crush me.

"What are you forgetting?" he asked.

It hit me harder than the weight of the beast. *I had forgotten to turn on my defenses!* They not only lessened the damage taken and slowed the attackers' weapons down, they also repulsed the weapon back out of my personal space...even the daemon itself. Malnuras beat that into my head for days on end. I had just received my new rune days before this battle. Not activating my shield before entering combat *was* the true error.

The second aspect of it was shorter in duration but meant a daemon could not enter my personal space. Its fast moving claw attacks had enough momentum to get through the defenses, but my shield reduced the speed and force of the attack. The rune was strange looking, resembling a pattern of energy swirling around it. When activated the energy pattern expanded out from me about two feet. It kept me from their swarm. Even if a blow managed to hit me, deflection would occur with tremendous force.

The downside was it took a lot of energy out of me to turn this ability on, which meant I could only use it sparingly. My energy had to recharge in between uses. Logic descended on me. Turning the shield on now would push the daemons hands off my body and allow for potential escape.

The voice came again...This time it was my own voice saying the name.

I am Tathlyn.

I looked at Mathias with amazement and he was not there; neither was I. Pain exploded in my chest as the pressure snapped more ribs and tore more flesh. What little breath that I could draw came slow and labored. Pushing with all my might upwards, my energy flowed with the exhale. The bubble of the shield came into being, exploding outward, and surrounding me. Immediately the pressure on my chest subsided, and the daemons hands repelled away from me. Their position above me interfered with its view of me as it pressed down harder.

I imagined its surprise as it could not see why its paws and claws were forced open. My blades kept pushing as the weight diminished. Hoping it did not know there was now a space between us, I relaxed my mind and let my healing energy flow freely. My ribs decompressed and returned to their place one by one. It hurt as much as having them broken, but having the bone no longer piercing my lungs felt as good as the flesh rebuilding itself. Seconds later, I found myself healthy and healed but in the same situation. Tons of daemon filth was still on top of me. It would be seconds before it came crushing down again in another attempt. This creature had four legs plus the two arms so it did not normally walk on all six legs. I twisted the blades so the edges faced away from each other and, with a mighty yell; I forced my hands wide apart, taking the swords in opposite directions. Flesh separated and bone cleaved as my arms extended. Resistance meeting the blades ended as they extended. The daemon had a lot of its weight on its "hands" and its center of gravity shifted. Falling forward it pulled its stumps to its torso. Fingers with nasty claws fell around as the creatures weight came forward.

I rolled back and away from the hole that had almost become my grave. Backing off, my swords spinning gently to loosen my arms and wrists up, my eyes fell to my foe. I tried to gage its next move. My tendons were still a little sore, but functional. The healing energy did its job for the most part, but it would be a bit before I could do it again. The creature had regained its balance and was roaring at me with bulging bloodshot eyes. Trying to create a false pattern, I moved side to side as it advanced. The creature came at me again, wings flapping. Surprisingly agile this time, it spun, trying to catch me with one of its many flailing appendages.

With renewed strength, I rallied my cause and tried a new approach. Taking two steps, I vaulted myself atop the beast, avoiding the wings that were still trying to buffet me out of range. My footing shifted as the daemon tried to shake me off. There was no time before it started to roll back to its hind feet with me fighting to move with its shifting body. The creature reversed its direction in attempts to throw me off balance. I steadied my aim and struck with both of my blades right where the wing connected to a large shoulder muscle. Instantly, dark blood sprayed from a deep cut. A spasm rolled through its body.

Again I struck, this time hard enough that the only thing holding the wing in place was a large, fraying tendon, which I made short work of with my third and final strike. The great wing severed and flopped to the earth; its lifeblood sprayed. Black ichor gushed from the angry wound on its back. Up it reared, causing my footing to shift and one of my embedded swords broke free of my grip as I fell down clinging to its leathery hide. Gravity shifted again as it came down on all fours. One of its clawed hands reached back to grab me. Above, its head craned around, trying to spy my location.

I could now see I had not cut as many fingers off as I had hoped for each hand clearly had many. Only the smaller side ones were missing, but this thing had at least eight per paw. My grip released right as its front legs touched down again and slid me towards my other weapon, now lodged in its muscular, knotted definition.

In came the talons from the beast's wounded hands. A blow like no other launched me backwards and off its back with tremendous force, just like a car hitting me. Landing hard, I rolled to my fee. Around me, the dust and dirt flew in every direction. It was hard to see without getting dirt in my eyes. I felt heat.

Diving into a roll backwards, I managed to avoid the business end of its mouth. Its teeth made a snapping sound as they clamped down on the air near my body. Regaining my feet some distance away, I sprinted to the left towards the side missing a wing. The distance came easily as it was limping some from the blows previously rained down upon its feet, moments before it crushed me. Again, I leapt to its great back and assaulted its second set of wings. I wanted to make sure it could not fly.

The great leathery sails were not easy to hit. As my feet touched down on its mighty back, my attacks resumed. With balance regained, my blades bit deep on the second wing located on the same side as the first. Again the flow of blood exploded forth, making footing difficult, but manageable. Its body rolled to its right side as I moved in that direction. It must have known another wing was my target for it rolled to that same side in an attempt to crush me. As its weight shifted, so did my attack. The left wing was now folding up behind me as it pitched to its side. I turned and jumped, thrusting both blades out as it continued to roll.

I found my mark. The clean cut showered me with viscous fluid that fountained into the air. Falling to my right, I noticed I had cleaved the wing completely. It was bucking now. His remaining two wings buffeted. Still, he could not dislodge me. My grip held me securely. The beast rolled to the right again, but I was not quick enough. My body hit the ground, knocking my breath out. It was a struggle to roll out of the way of the impending doom with no breath, but finally my feet touched the earth, and I leapt skyward with all my strength.

To the daemon's surprise and mine, I landed on it again, this time on its belly. Now between four taloned feet, the threat slightly lessened. Reversing the grip on my blades, I went to work. The beast roared and convulsed as my stabbing blades bit repeatedly. Flat on its back it lay, with me running all over its underside slashing anything and everything I could. It continued to swat at me with its taloned feet. I ran toward its head to get at its throat in hopes of ending it.

That was a big mistake on my part.

I did not see the clawed hands coming. Both of my swords were in a downward motion when the shadow fell upon me. I barely had time to redirect them to the sides to meet the incoming threat. The steel bit as the trap collapsed on me. My blades slid to the hilt before my arms compressed back towards me, and I felt my right wrist fold backwards on itself to keep hold of the weapon.

My ears rang as the air clapped around my head with a tremendous bang. I would have been on my knees from the experience except I found myself between the beast's hands like a bug in a Venus flytrap. It did not care, and as it squeezed it pressed the swords deeper into its own hands until I was almost flat against both its palms when it began to apply insane amounts of pressure. A throaty laugh, like a gurgle, came from the daemon. The pressure squeezed tighter then suddenly let up for one second.

I managed to roll to the side in the midst of its claws and had my feet against one palm and my shoulder on the other. I cupped my broken wrist in my hand while leg pressing back to keep from being crushed.

The weight was greater. I thought getting smashed on the ground was bad, but the difference was I had been flat on my back. It felt just like being in a vice grip. With my swords in each of its hands, I squirmed as it tried to grind me between its palms.

Focusing on my wrist, I began to try to heal the broken bones and snapped tendons. It was almost too much; my mind faltered on the task. I felt the tingling begin in my wrist. The pressure on my legs and spine increased. My head began to spin with pain, overloading my nervous system. He ground me between his massive paws, and he had twice the force now to exert. Time felt like it stopped for a moment; although I was still aware but not like before. The bones reset for now; however, the damage was severe and my healing powers weakened. The tendons reattached finally when I felt its hands shift.

The daemon roared.

Instinctively grabbing for my swords still embedded in the large clawed hands of the beast, I turned the blades and held on. Its giant hands pulled apart. My grip tightened. One of the blades came free while the other stayed in. Using the momentum, I put my foot against the palm of its hand next to where my blade pierced and pushed up. It tore free.

Gravity released. I was free falling...but not to its torso again. Its breath engulfed me. I knew right where I was falling.

In all my life, both here in this world and home, I had never been so disgusted. In a pool of rotten saliva I landed. The teeth in its huge maw stood my height. Its jaw collapsed. The fluid level rose. Instantly, I felt the saliva go to work on the skin on my legs. I was thankful that its breath that did most of the damage. It could have just exhaled holding me in the pressure cooker against all those teeth; however, the thought of drowning in even acidic spit was not appealing. Then again, getting swallowed was just as bad.

Teeth began to grind. With all my remaining strength, both blades thrust out in front. Darkness fell. For a split second, the thought of death felt close again and peace was there. I felt strangely tranquil. It was not my day to die. There were too many things to do and thousands of more daemons to kill. A vision of home appeared in my mind for a moment, and I wondered if my parents had any idea what I was doing.

Light appeared slowly in the distance. It was as if the gates of heaven were parting to allow my admittance. My senses returned. I wrenched and twisted my blades in deeper. The fluids flushed as if it was swallowing steel. The light got brighter.

I closed my eyes. Intense wind surrounded me. My steel bit deeply before impact tore them from my grip. I had just lost both of my swords.

The end must be near.

My eyes opened just in time to see the ground rushing up at me. "Oh, you have got to be kidding!" I said before impact...covered in daemon saliva. The image of a giant spit wad came to mind. I lay there on the ground, afraid to move from the pain, my skin frozen and split in places from its breath. The blurry face of Malnuras leaned over my still form.

He smiled. "What do you have to say for yourself?"

I winced. We both laughed. It hurt to laugh because the skin on my face was splitting. I fought to regain my feet but stood teetering.

"It is dead, go get your swords!" he said, walking away.

"I am Tathlyn...my Teacher." My bow almost took me to the ground again. His answer surprised me.

"I know."

VII

The Big Picture

"It is not the destination that matters but the journey."

I loved that quote because of the infinite wisdom; it was so basic but powerful. When Master returned to me, I was happy to see him. Malnuras nodded to him as he walked into camp with his armor glowing bright in the morning sun. I bowed.

"It is time," he said, turning and leaving as abruptly as he arrived. A portal was waiting just outside camp. We left and travelled to a city in the wilds. Upon setting up camp, he turned to me and said one word: "Attack." We sparred for days, only stopping to eat and rest. The fights were brutal, and he cut me often. He did not wear his armor so my blades found flesh often as well. From me, he received only scratches, as my control was precise. He was not so kind in return. The battle must have been poetic to behold. Several onlookers passed by and watched for a time. They kept silent as to not distract, but we both knew they were there. I could feel them.

I was like a contest of wills...which I lost.

He took me to the edge of the town to a market place to buy food. We sat down off in the corner outside. He was good at dramatic pauses, making me wonder what he was about to say. We ate a modest meal and discussed many things. The food was superb and made of some local game that did not seem like it should be edible, but it was rather tasty. It did not taste like chicken. We ate some local fruit that was overly sweet, but the sugar rush it gave was amazing.

He began to speak and I listened intently.

"Since the dawn of mankind, the daemons have been trying to form permanent gates from a dimension you might refer to as Heaven. There is more than one habitable planet in the universe. Yet Lucifer has his eyes set on earth. Perhaps it is because this is where he first made contact with mankind as their creator. We really do not know his reasons."

"God chose to make many races, but humans were special. He placed humans on this planet so that your souls might learn what he could not teach...something that only experience can provide. He gave men the basic knowledge they needed to create tribal societies. As mankind reproduced, God sent down new souls from his kingdom to fill the newborn."

"For many thousands of years your race flourished. Small tribes came and went due to sickness or war. People died and returned to the creator with tales and stories of the lessons they had learned. But man was slowly influenced by an outside force and through his own actions was not able to return to God's plane of existence because of sin."

"Evil began to creep into man's heart from the moment he came down. Yet they continued to come. During this process, a great deception took place. Lucifer is actually a deity but of lesser power, for he rules the daemon horde. He amassed enough power that he was able to infiltrate the maker's realm in the disguise of an angel created to serve. It was his presence in the heavens, which caused man to doubt and falter. His power was also strong enough that he was able to cloak his identity, from God and many others. For thousands of years he hid and watched, and manipulated man. Man's evil grew and Lucifer must have been overjoyed to see the reaction to his presence."

"Fascinated with the corruption that mankind had suffered due to his influence, Lucifer decided to try to find a way to bridge the gap that spanned the two planes of existence. Many more millennium went by. God had made a pact with his creations after he had to destroy many of them with a great flood. If mankind were to follow God's example of living, they would be able to return. The pact required a blood sacrifice to be made for any and all wrongdoings perpetrated against God's will."

"Lucifer saw this as a weakness on God's behalf and was trying to find a way to exploit it. In his excitement, he began turning other servants of God against their master. Large meetings soon began to take place and a wave of dissent swept through the heavens."

"God found out about the plot. He learned the true identify of this corruptor and realized it had been Lucifer's doing that had affected his children on Earth. God banished him from the heavens, but not before Lucifer had amassed a sizable following. Armed with what he had learned so far, he watched and waited."

"Eventually, God created a copy of himself to be his son whom he would rule the heavens with and allowed his consciousness to move freely between them. As he watched the beginning of new civilizations unfold, he realized that he would need to save his people from themselves. The previous arrangement was not efficient. He sent himself in the form of his son to the planet to be a sacrifice so the way home would be locked open for those that chose to return. Man had become something beyond his control. The free will he gave them became their undoing. As soon as the event unfolded, man was free and simply had to choose to follow the creator's teachings."

"Lucifer simply watched from afar..." I interjected

"You may know this story from your bible. That is man's version of the account, however different it may be. Lucifer saw that blood mixed with magic, or the arcane, could open portals on a more permanent basis. His minions slay themselves for his glory. Sometimes they get enough blood and magic going in the right place to open a portal, which is how they enter. However, this is a small part of whatever his plan is. His main goal now was to harvest as many souls as he could and enslave them to serve him. Even if he never fully succeeds in flooding your plane with his minions, he seems to have some sort of satisfaction at one or more of his minions, even if it is only a handful, running around wreaking havoc amongst the populace. For anyone slain on your plane by one of his minions, he still gains power from it."

"In the beginning, it started small at first. One or two creatures would slip through; killing all crossed its path until God sent an angel to hunt them down. Soon the crossovers became too numerous or the numbers were too great for your average angel too handle. He created a special being. You know it as the Sasquatch. Magical in nature, they have the ability to cloak themselves to avoid detection. They are immortal in the sense that they do not die of natural causes, but they can die in battle. This is usually the case; they fall in combat."

"They also have the ability to mask the daemons as they exit, so the fights were usually undetected by the human eye. Large magnetic disturbances and geological events are some of the results of the energy displacements. Sometimes the weather changes in certain ways, like the rain suddenly turning to hail or a small whirlwind of air forms; you call them dust devils. The irony on that was not lost since it was masking a daemon. Electronic devices also may fail, creating a gremlin like effect. It's funny that Gremlins do exist, but they do not affect electronics."

After listening for some time, I spoke. "I don't see anything that would pass for technology up here Master. How do you know about it?" He simply gave me a look and I closed my mouth. I may be a tough fighter but he was still my master and I tried to be respectful always to him. He continued.

"When the larger deluges take place a volcanic eruption often accompanies the rift due to the tremendous force that involved in the fabric of space being torn as well as the magic needed to mask the effect. These battles last for days, sometimes weeks where the Defender must close the portal and hunt all the creatures that have skipped by. Along with the daemons and the physical repercussions comes the nature of evil in its purest form."

"This is displayed when someone who is mentally healthy suddenly breaks from his normal behavior and goes on a killing spree. The evil can affect anyone anywhere, not just near the rift. It literally ripples outward. Soon you will be able to see this and be able to track it back to its origin and close the portal. Whilst doing this task you will have to fight any daemons coming through and any still guarding the rift. Unless the event is apocalyptic in nature, no more than a dozen or so come through at a time, but they do not all stick around, and the hunt begins. They attempt reconnaissance too."

"The problem is sometimes many small portals opening all over the world and it can take time to find them. The Sasquatches can feel the portals and find them quicker sometimes before they open because the process to open is a slow one. The connecting bridge roots in this world like an anchor. As the energy builds, the perverted aspect of its creation is what will draw you to it...just like the current Defender."

"In the western part of the continent you lived on, where all the volcanoes are, is the hotspot of the planet. The other is on the other side of the ocean that your continent shares. The mountains next to that ocean are also problematic; although, it pales in comparison to the region you are from."

"Originally there was several. Only God knows the number he created. As the millennia crept by, only one survived. He is now a shadow of his former self as the years of battle have depleted him. So the need for a new plan has been in the inception phase for years."

"The last major rift caused a small volcanic eruption in the Cascade Mountains. The Sasquatch was responsible for closing it. This final act has left him weak, weak to the point he no longer knows when he has cloaked himself or not, without serious meditation. That is why you saw him that day. That is why both of you saw him. Now that you passed the test and accepted to replace him, you are no longer a threat to him. The driver of the car perished. Your friend, however, hunts the Defender and every day he comes a little closer to being able to see him at will. His hatred and lack of understanding have made him dangerous. You may have to intervene if the situation becomes critical. The Defender is the last of his kind. You may have to deal with your friend. It is for the greater good, although any ideas you might have will be given serious consideration."

"You have been given the same abilities as the Sasquatch. Runes that will allow you to detect these openings in the fabric that separates the two realities will develop and grow stronger in time. Hunting daemons through many means of detection after you close the portals will be your second priority. When you find a portal, open or not, you will be able to cloak the daemons as they come through. This is an area effect, and covers a very large area. Your weapons, as you know, can come to you at will so you will not have to worry about being armed. Most of these daemons you could kill with your bear hands if you needed to. The ability to mask yourself will also be at your disposal soon. If a daemon leaves the area, and finds people, it will be bad."

"A portal may not be open when you arrive, so cloak yourself, and then watch the area and wait. It may take hours for them to form, but when you get an urge to go somewhere that you cannot control, it is a portal form-ing. You will be able to teleport there. The rune attunes to the fabric or veil that separates the realities, if that destabilizes, you will know. If there is more than one, it will take you to the one that is farther along in its failing. The horde knows that the Defender always shows up so they have been working on ways to hide the energy transfer that creates the tear until the last possible moment. You may find yourself in the middle of a battle where people will die. They also can hide themselves from you to some small measure. It will take time for you learn their tricks."

"When will I get this rune?"

"In time. Do not be overwhelmed my pupil. The Sasquatch chose well when he saw the tenderness in your eyes. He told me he had never seen such compassion. He is tired and is looking forward to spending time with his maker as he has been performing this duty for several millennia and is the last survivor of his kind."

"Who is his maker?" I asked.

Silence.

Mathias quit speaking. I sat there in shock. Hearing the full truth about what I was to become had a certain weight to it. I swallowed hard and tried to think about my responsibility to the people on Earth. I was to be the first of my kind. However, the most serious trials still lay ahead. Failure was not an option, but I was not the one making the rules. Lucifer's influence was out there. I could feel its tug on me even from here.

"So how did the daemons get here, Master?"

"They invaded so quickly that God had to defend the city. That is the main reason why he cannot save mankind on Earth, and protect the souls in Heaven at the same time. Lucifer is after the souls as much as he is after getting to Earth to kill and consume human souls. He is still assaults Heaven forcing God is doing nothing else but focusing on its defense. Lucifer will never get through as long as God is there maintaining it."

Another long pause.

"In fact, he waited until God was watching his son crucified for the sins of the world. He struck at that moment. The people of earth think God turned his back on Jesus because of all the sin that was upon him. The truth is, the horde broke through into Heaven, and all he could do was wrap his arms around the city. Because Jesus is part of God, God was weakened, at that moment...To have part of him destroyed meant for a fraction of a second, he was incomplete."

"With the sudden insurgent of daemons, the balance of the realm of heaven taxed God so greatly that his power level dropped severely. He may be complete, but the presence of such an enormous horde means that all he can do is shield Heaven. Helping those on Earth or answering prayers is nothing compared to what it used to be."

"It is amazing, Master, that God has been able to protect Heaven even with the realm under siege." He took a draw off his water. A distant look fell upon his. A great sadness washed over his countenance.

"I will tell you more about that later," he said.

"Is there something on Earth that will allow Lucifer to breach Heaven's defenses," I asked, thinking aloud.

We sat in silence.

My training felt like it was approaching a milestone. The studies had been grueling as the classroom was a battlefield. Mathias returned to his duties. It was not so much a goodbye, but "good luck" that he said to me after returning me to the camp. I stood there pondering things and finally went to the fire pit to pull up and study my favorite Samurai. Malnuras looked up from his book, gave me a nod, and returned to his studies. The evening passed in silence.

I reflected on my path ahead. My skills grew beyond what Master taught me. I found the ability to leap into a fight from a great distance to be an awesome tactical advantage. They never saw me coming. Mathias could do this too.

My swordsmanship surpassed any warrior from history. I used to think Master held back to avoid hurting me, but after much observation, I realized mine barely surpassed his. It was not an obvious difference. He was just as fast but still stronger. But my ability to foresee moves gave me an edge. Sparring became a flurry of deadly, complex moves. I used two weapons, whereas he used a sword and shield.

My swords were amazing and to say they were an extension was an understatement. Earning a sword is an honor. To receive two of them means my esteem had to be as that of the generals. I imagined somewhere there was a forge with a smith hard at work making weapons. With the intensity of the assault on Heaven, the situation of defending God's kingdom took top priority. Sasquatch did not need swords. He had claws that were enchanted. However, my weapons could envelope in flames at a thought and that did a lot of damage to daemons. My swords grew in strength. Mathias told me that my swords together rivaled his. I playfully disagreed that they were better because I had two of them and he cuffed me. I did not have the heart to tell him I saw it coming, but I think he knew I let him do it.

Even though runes covered my skin, I could still take damage but it was hard to get something past me now. If a daemon managed to hurt me, I could heal, but at the cost of tremendous amounts of energy. This was not a reason to be foolish. My lessons reminded to be wise every day.

Teacher told me after I returned and asked about it, that my teleportation rune would form when it was time, on its own. Yesterday, I received a special adaptation rune. My own experiences and development could influence and trigger future runes as needed. So after the teleportation rune, which he explained was waiting for him to train me, came in, that the rest would be unique to my needs.

My training did not currently allow armor. This had taught me how to move and not rely on something absorbing the hits that got through my shield. I learned to do things that many of the other warriors in history could not do. Acrobatics, like many of the swash bucklers used, added an element that helped me master placement during fights and allowed me to redeploy to another location quickly. There were hints that something else would happen to me later.

I still had my free will. My mind was conditioned. I could not consciously do any evil. Though not perfect, I could not purposefully commit an evil act. Were I unscrupulous, my skills could make me a nearly unstoppable villain. I know saying never is a bad idea, but evil could never take root in my heart. I would miss my playful personality, but layers of conditioning changed that.

Soon I would learn to track the evil and locate portals. I was looking forward to learning this. Teleporting would be weird. My spirit was the core of all of my abilities. I did not yet understand exactly how it worked but in time, I would. Patience was my strong suit, so waiting was not an issue anymore. In time, they would teach me, of that I was certain.

It was a comfort to know that the side of good had a small advantage. Both of my mentors had faith in me. Master would beam with pride as if he was a father looking at his own son at times. It made me stand taller, fight harder, and listen. To disappoint him was unthinkable. My desire to honor them both directed my actions.

Many nights when I was sleeping, the conversations he had with

Malnuras still echoed in my memories over whether or not my skill would be enough to take on the task. Mathias did not have any doubt concearning my abilities, but of the numbers that might arrive at any moment while training in the realm. He sounded like a concerned parent would for the only human to get this far and live this long to achieve mastery. The previous candidates barely made it past the cave. Malnuras's faith in my ability to adapt always won out in those conversations. It made me feel pride.

My smile faded as a foreboding sense crept over me while looking towards the direction of Heaven.

"Why do you feel this way?" A voice like an airy whisper crept into my mind. I opened my eyes. Gazing around the campsite, I saw no one except my teacher.

"His confusion does not make sense," another voice chimed in.

I closed my eyes and reached out. *Two presences felt very close, so close they were within the camp, but I did know either of them!* Lifting my legs off the mat and thrusting them down, I thrust my shoulders instinctively into the mat. My feet touched down flat as my body followed upright and centered my balance evenly. Hand drew swords to the ready without a thought.

Nothing. Eyes panned the clearing. Nothing...Yet two distinct beings availed. A sudden intake of breath followed. My feet shifted as I turned...allowing my guard to pan with me as they turned to offer a view of the perimeter.

"We are awakened now. Do not be alarmed!" Both voices spoke in unison. My stance deepened, ready to spring into action. I closed my eyes again to pinpoint the direction of the intruders. Breathing slowed. My focus tightened on the campsite. The sense grew stronger meaning it was right on top of me. I sprung straight up looking above and my blades thrust into the sky...To my surprise, they were glowing faintly with an amber hue. There was nothing above.

I landed gently, still looking at the blades in my hands. The intricate designs, beautifully crafted, pulsed softly. Amber light glowed and pulsed from the base of the blade to the tip and seemed to lift off the blade at the end as if it was dripping upwards. Only wisps of energy rose, though, not like dripping water.

"What in the heavens...," My senses sharpened. The beings were in my hands. I was about to toss the blades when the voices spoke again. The feeling was soothing, something that was missed when they startled me from meditation.

"We are Enáretos Manía..."

"Righteous fury..." my lips orated immediately.

"Yes, you are correct," the swords responded in unison. "We are the spirit of your swords, manifested by your dedication and the fire that burns within your heart."

Ease drifted through my mind as the two voices began to speak to me about everything. They were inside my mind, as my ears did not hear anything aloud. It was like they had been asleep for thousands of years. The questions were unending through the night. I knew I would never be alone again. My heart rested.

In unison, the voices lulled me to sleep with a song.

VIII

Personal Revelations

I was troubled.

Ever since my master explained things as they were in Heaven, my mind worked overtime to process the reality of what he shared. Sadly, my mind was not at ease knowing the truth. The situation here in the realm of Heaven was dire. I could not change how it made me feel. Meditation helped little. I had to work through it in time. Time did pass. That was some time ago.

When I was not viewing the runes, I focused on living in the present.

My swords occasionally spoke to me now. Feelings, like filled with their emotions, communicated even more. They blended with me. My thoughts became theirs. Their feelings became mine. The final pieces of the puzzle fell into line to complete the psychic link. My master explained he did not know how things would unfold for me long ago, and I did not speak of it to him in the village the day he shared the bigger picture.

Since we spoke, my training had come full circle. In the past, I studied and mastered every known human weapon. Somehow, the mastering of all of these weapons came as easily as breathing. In essence, my weapons training finished a long time ago. Learning to apply the use of each weapon to specific circumstances was the next step. My raw tactics made most of the military leaders look like beginners. This education would never end because the horde was formless and shapeless. It was ever changing. Even

111

though most of the daemons attacked a predicable way, they came like a flood. No campaign against them had succeeded. The angelic commanders were good but could not adapt fast enough. They only kept the hordes from advancing.

The Sasquatch dealt with large numbers as a whole and still occasionally got over run. They did not train here with the horde as the training dummy. I was the first to get this far. That first day, Malnuras told me about the previous candidates' failures. How could everyone they brought here fail to accept their own death? Growing up, I expected to die at any time.

No pressure!

True tests, however, came not out on the battlefield but in my own mind. I had learned many hard lessons. Some of the lessons were how much damage my changing body could sustain. Many wounds had left their mark on my continuously growing frame. I looked my Master evenly in the eyes now when I saw him last meaning I was as tall as he was now. Malnuras was tall, but my youth with the proper diet had me gaining mass and size at an incredible rate. I stood over him by six inches now. There were no mirrors in the realm. Occasionally there was a glimpse of myself in a clear pool or my shadow would catch my eye. On Earth, this would take many years and steroids but would not come close because of the height. This height could not be possible even with science. My metamorphosis started the day I arrived and has not stopped.

Thoughts of that past became another life. Everything before was a blur as my calling was rewriting my memories. My role redefined each day in my own mind, as I honed skills. The application of those skills came easily to me, and adaptation was a second behavior pattern. I could analyze tactics and turn them around.

My meditation led me deeper into the study of balance by going deeper into myself. Inner peace that could not be broken, even when the waves of the horde crashed upon it, became my stride. These things guided me to serenity amidst a horrible fight, and balanced in my mind when a disturbance rippled my awareness.

"A presence approaches," a feeling advised me. I sensed nothing with my own senses and realized where the feeling came from. Soon I would be able to detect danger even farther away, as the blending was almost complete.

Smiling, I opened my eyes to greet my mentor. "I sensed your approach." Something smacked me upside my head faster than I could blink. A slight pain, accompanied by a ringing filled my head. I smelled fish. In Malnuras' hand was a scaly creature, one that I had learned to love to eat.

He was still a better angler. I tried. My patience wore thin sitting and waiting. The fish at this new location fled when I entered the water and were impossible to catch by hand. He enjoyed it, so I left him to it. I never tried eating some of the flesh of the monsters I had slain. Disgusting did not even come close to how they smelled.

We spent some time cleaning and frying up his catch. Overall, he had caught seven of them. The fish in this realm were bigger on average than of Earths fish, and harder to catch. They had scales that were like a suit of scale mail armor straight from the dark ages and possessed a higher intelligence. One could not merely fool them with a worm. A net or pronged spear was the best way, although spears were the less effective of the two.

There was not much conversation over the food. I was beginning to feel that my time with Malnuras neared its end, as he seemed to be treating me more as a friend then a pupil. The thought of this scared me sometimes as the realization grew in my mind. I felt ready to fight battles of a larger importance. My confidence was high and the chance of failure hanging over me like a dark cloud diminished. Part of me knew that I had to succeed, but another part of me wanted to be realistic. To be the first of a new concept of Defender made me a prototype. The chance of failure was equal to the chance of success.

I cleared my head as I finished cleaning up the cook pot. The remaining fish we wrapped in large leaves to protect them. They would keep for a day or two. With my appetite, they would not last the morrow. Malnuras had made his bed upon his favorite bluff and slipped into meditation for the third time that day. His solace was increasing. I was okay with it since my daily hunting routine kept me quite busy. When I patrolled the area around the camp, I grabbed any game that was unfortunate enough to be in my path. Today filled itself with reflection, as he put it, so the two of us had spent a fair amount of the day in deep thought.

Sometimes I missed his companionship. Often after a battle, I came and sat down next to him. In the years before, I sat across from him and hung on his every word. His vast knowledge of warfare kept me asking questions, which usually led to a point in history. New tactics always came from watching the failures of others.

Through all of my studies, daemonology was tremendously fascinating. Watching the legendary creature move and fight, was hypnotic for he did not move as a creature but a man. This ability captivated me most. I saw the different types of daemons, except the large dragon like beasts. None of those made it through a portal in any of my viewings. Size was a clear hindrance. They feared nothing.

Then there was the mystery around the Sasquatch. I studied everything the runes could show me. For a creature, although divine by right, to move as a man was not natural, even though it was bipedal. The moves that I had focused on were more like that of Chinese Kung Fu; Master taught me to move like an animal, learning many different styles. Long ago, Malnuras felt that this change would make me even more successful than the Sasquatch. He was right.

The ability to adapt was an immeasurable skill.

As I viewed my own battles just like the historical recordings, I could see the difference. As an animal, I could mimic the movements of the creatures and adapt. Bigfoot had only his brute strength and animal rage as his ally. He did possess the ability to heal, just as I, but he did not have the magic runes protecting him. He also did not use weapons…although he could teach the fundamentals. His hand-to-hand technique was brutal and strong. It was a style very similar to that of a bear, but with more speed. He would occasionally spin with his claws out, catching all within his radius. I smiled I saw the bear shape of Malnuras stand up and do that move too.

I moved over to where Malnuras sat and joined him. The breeze blew gently from the south towards the main mating grounds of the horde. I had hunted there many times. It gave off a disturbance and unnatural presence. The scent was pungent and thick, almost like dark viscous blood mixed with dirt, but in an ichorous form. From miles away, the scent caught my senses. I learned I could track this. It became a not so welcome link.

My first concern was the fear that my ability to sense them meant they could sense me. The number of ambushes I successfully pulled off, the upper hand was mine. They might be able to smell me coming, but only a fool attacked down wind. I was no fool. At times from our camp, I could smell them as they approached. It may have been that I had their scent and with my heightened senses could single them out. Perhaps the slaughter that occurred daily in the surrounding made the smell of blood thick as it hung in the air. My senses were constantly on alert. It made it hard to relax when I was studying. I kept expecting that there would be an attack at any moment. Thankfully, the wards Malnuras had put in place were reliable; and a good view and a good vantage was just a bonus.

I never took my edge for granted. Lord knows I needed one when the hordes attacked en masse. It made me chuckle at the thought considering it was Malnuras that allowed me to become the warrior. He had to have known.

"Can I meet God?" I asked one day

"Perhaps." I did not press the issue, knowing that a desire such a desire fell beneath all other priorities. Who was I to command God's attention? For me to consider anything else but protecting Earth seemed so far away.

Malnuras breathed out and deeply inhaled. I could tell he was about to speak because his breathing changed. I sat and waited out of respect, not wanting to interrupt his thoughts, which were plentiful. He shifted from his meditation pose to one of greater awareness. I did not doubt, however, that he was equal in both.

"Questions you have?" he began.

My desire to speak was obvious. "Teacher, since that you in the form of the bear that showed up to save humanity and the Sasquatch…"

"It was." There was a delay in the reply as if he had debated answering.

"So why did you not take a more active role in the defense of the people?" He was silent.

We sat in silence. I half expected to hear that he was too busy elsewhere. The answer rather shocked me. "I am not able nor allowed to directly interfere, except under the direst circumstances, as you have seen. My mandate is to let the Defenders do what they need to do. Even when the balance tips towards evil, God still holds back most of his angels. There are a few angels still tracking down the more troublesome of the daemons, but for the most part, the Sasquatch does the heavy lifting. There are far too many battles still raging in the spiritual plain. Daemons are trying to lay siege to Heaven. God needs his forces elsewhere. If he did not use his strength to beat back the hordes assaulting Heaven, there would be no Heaven for the souls to go to when they cross. Lucifer could just gather them up and take them."

"If he were allowed to do this, his power would grow tenfold in a matter of hours as he fed off the souls of the righteous. God's thinking in the immortal wisdom is that it is better to have man lose his life in the physical world than lose his soul in the spirit world."

"So we truly are on the same plain as Heaven! Is Heaven close?" Not that I felt Mathias would mislead me, for he would have no reason to, but hearing it from a second person cemented it. The concept of being this close to Heaven was so intriguing. Like a kid on the night before Christmas, my anticipation built. I had to know the truth as a child wanted to know which packages under the tree are for him.

"We are on the same plain as Heaven. Mathias has taught you this. Neither you nor Mathias can enter Lucifer's realm. The energy barrier alone would sunder you. I, on the other hand, might fare a bit longer with a few tricks."

"This is others hunt here. It helps thin the numbers. In time, when you return to your body back on earth, you will be there in unison. You can return to hunt here if you wish, from a sleep state. Your body will, however, take the damage you sustain here and be directly related to how rested you are. The more time you spend healing, the less pain and discomfort you will experience when you awake. This will take some time for you to get used to, but eventually, it will seem normal."

"Others hunt here?" He ignored my question and continued.

"However...time away from your station can be dangerous. Be warned and do not spend too much time away. I suggest."

"Is my body taking damage right now when I fight? That must be causing some unrest since you told me I am in a hospital bed. The doctors must be freaking out trying to solve the riddle. It would not surprise me if there is a priest in the room with me."

"Funny you should say that." chided Malnuras. "They ran tests of a useless nature. They could never understand the magnitude of what is really going on, and you must never explain it to them. They can never know the whole truth. The human mind has a hard time admitting this kind of evil truly exists, let alone understanding its true aims."

I took to heart what he said. It did not make much sense that the greatest minds on Earth could never know what I knew. It felt strange to be trusted on these matters more than the most scholarly. Scientists with this knowledge would be able to make leaps in knowledge in the area of astral physics, even quantum physics. The meta-physical aspect was a completely new science by itself. I had barely even heard of these sciences before my arrival. Now I could probably teach a college class on some of it. My ability to grasp and understand higher-level learning had increased greatly. The hunger for knowledge had yielded skill. It felt weird to consider myself highly educated.

"Do not despair, Teacher. Something tells me I will be too busy to have much of a social life."

"But you must!" This caught me off guard.

"How? I will be hunting at night and searching out portals during the day. How will I survive without some sort of job, Teacher?"

"Opportunities you seek will present themselves in due time. God will be with you and will help guide you on your path. Fear not."

My thoughts spun in circles. The idea that God would give me that much attention made me a little nauseous. The amount of mistakes in my previous life could fill up ten lives, even though most were childhood offences. Now having God's eye directly on me made me squirm. My mentality changed. I was more mature and even educated. In fact, I could not actually think of a sin committed since arriving. That worried me.

I sat in contemplation. Malnuras fell back into meditation. For quite a while as I sat there debating my piety, Malnuras was snoring. My old life was not overly religious, nor full of faith. However, I still believed God was there.

Yet here I was.

I stayed awake all night, deep in thought. The weight of the situation I stepped into hit me hard. How one man could make a difference in this war was beyond me. How could I possibly kill enough daemons to make a dent in their ever-growing population? According to both of my teachers, they bred rapidly. The magic involved in crossing over was the hard part for them. Conditions had to be exact for them to cross over and even more precise in order for them to gain access to Earth. I wrestled with this for some time. As I drifted asleep finally, poetic words of a different nature came to mind.

A glorious thing I have seen today,

When beauty so fair has touched me this way,

When she enters the room is aglow,

I want to share this tenderness so.

My eyes shot open. Where in the world did that come from? It was morning. My mind wrestled with those words that jarred me awake. I wondered if my subconscious mind thought of Sandra still. I lay there staring up at the colors of the sky changing hues when I saw stars again and glared at Malnuras for cracking me in the head with his staff. I realized what I had done and was about proffer myself for the disrespect, when he laughed making me feel even more nervous.

He shook his head. "Meditation of that level is excellent for the mind, but not to the point that you are unaware of your surroundings. I was calling you for many moments."

He was right. To lose track of time and my surroundings so easily was a mistake made by someone young in their journey. It was a step forward in my training under my own influence. My mind nagged as I rubbed the side of my face gently and felt a small welt forming. With the lesson now rubbed in, there was no reason to waste my healing powers. Where the poetry came from of that nature bothered me about as much as his dodging my question

When I leave, "Others" attempted to maintain thinning the numbers. The idea rolled over my mind. Who? Angels? My mouth finished the question. A long pause ensued.

Malnuras looked at me with a slight grin. He chuckled. I felt unease from him as he laughed and realized the desire to know faded. I stared at him. His eye twinkled. That usually meant something was about to change in my world. "At least I have my swords," was the only thing running through my mind.

"You will meet them in time, but for now...."

I stared at him with a shocked look, slightly irritated that I did not know there were others. There had to be something, or someone, perhaps many, assigned to do what I did. There was some comfort at this knowledge. It was important to thin the horde. My gaze stayed on him.

My senses tingled. We were not alone. Laughter echoed all around.

"Oh, that's dirty!" Distinctive outlines began to coalesce. Ten shapes appeared strategically around the campsite. I jumped to my feet, drew steel, and postured myself accordingly. My back was to the fire, eyes maintaining a panning gaze on the shapes. I expected this to be a test. Fire glinted off one of my blades and caught one of the shapes in the eyes; I saw a hand come up. I exploded into action.

This was going to be good.

IX

Toys

Excitement washed over me.

Standing unseen in the middle of an intersection, I watched daemons poor from a portal, allowing a small horde to infiltrate Earth. They did not detect me. A small group of leapers emerged to hold the ground on Earth's side. Normally, I was hard to miss, but they had not seen me yet. I had a few new toys in my inventory that I looked forward to testing.

Several days before, teacher and I met with a group of people that chose to defend the wilds of Heaven. They were Rangers, but what they really did was hunt daemons. Their attire was similar to mine. They had a cloak made of special clothing for camouflage, and boots that allowed them to move in silence. Their leader, Andrugal, took special interest in my role and offered to come teach me to hunt more effectively. I accepted the offer.

"Teacher, can I get some of these items?" I asked examining Andrugal's cloak.

"We shall discuss it later," he answered.

"I hope so, because these items would really help me hunt daemons." He pointed to the field where a loan daemon tried to sneak up on the group of us. I blinked and several blades flashed out of nowhere and killed it where it stood. I was envious.

I learned the Rangers' numbers were in the hundreds and they focused on killing scouts that came in small groups. Their purpose was sort of like mine; these people died in the real world and wanted to make a differ-ence in heaven. They staunched the tide of daemons that existed here. The meeting was brief, but to learn of the existence made me feel less alone.

There was a brief mention of another group, but because their meth-ods were not conventional, the Rangers advised against contacting them. They were wild and did not work well with the Rangers. However, the daemons that strayed from the main host died and never returned. There-fore, they could not carry back information on the location of these creatures. The men and women I met pulled the daemons to them to spring traps. When I asked the Rangers for more information, they fell silent.

One of them finally replied, "You will understand if you see." I felt left out of the loop but accepted that perhaps it was not the time for me to know everything. After all, my mind was on overload as it was. We parted company with each of us intrigued about the other's role. I looked forward to meeting them again soon.

A call came and the Rangers had to go suddenly.

Later that day, Teacher gave me several items to wear. He planned it all along I was sure. He almost seemed excited to give them to me.

My new attire consisted of a suit of heaven-forged cloth that was made of woven metal fibers. The fiber came from a special type of alloy that did not exist on earth. While it looked like cloth and had an artistic pattern, woven in intricate designs all over, it was simply not. It moved like comfort-able clothing and weighed almost nothing. Master instructed me long ago that not wearing any type of armor in this plain was tempting fate. Consid-ering all my training had been lethal to this point and death could have taken me at any time, why would they not give this to me earlier?

Most importantly, it could mimic basic fashions so on Earth, no one would know any difference.

My teacher told me the reason was so I would not rely on it for protection. The warriors of antiquity could avoid most blows, and he was right in his thinking for sure. He explained that it would adapt to my surroundings to help me blend in on its own. It resembled regular clothing. It was something to do with its enchantment. It could take the blows that I failed to block if my enemy got past my guard and past my runic defenses. We tested it right after I put it on. It was going to be about to trust the armor to prevent a strike from bypassing my defenses. Many lethal blows struck true. I had to know how it felt…to feel the shift in my balance as the blow landed and to compensate for it. "Never lose your feet in a battle," my master taught me. You cannot win a war from your backside.

I knew this from personal experience.

If the armor fell into the wrong hands back on Earth, it would be catastrophic. Just like the ship that crashed at Roswell, this technology needed safeguarding. That did not go to well for those aliens. Magic created the armor, but its physical design would keep scientist busy for years and would reveal more than they were ready to know. He told me to bond with the armor so it could change on mental command to my desired style. I got a dirty look when an hour later I was walking around the camp in blue jeans and a tank top…so I set it back to looking like traditional medieval breaches.

Double baldrics crossed my back for holding my swords securely. Adorned with runic designs, they too were of exceptional quality, though they did not contribute anything other than their purpose. I liked the feel of having my weapons on my back so I could draw them. Calling them to my hand felt like cheating.

My cloak allowed me to become invisible on command. Material made from a large chameleon type of daemon was the chief component. With the proper magic, the skin stayed alive. It smelled dead, but when I turned on the camouflage for the first time, the smell went away. Thankfully when off from that point forward, it did not smell dead. It gave off a slight shimmering effect bending the light just so slightly that the innate ability allowed a creature to vanish. When I studied it for the first time, the design amazed me. Movement had to be very slow.

Teacher told me to bond with this item also. It took longer, but when I held it in my hands and activated it, my hands disappeared, the ground shone through. It was as though anything touching it was simply not registering to the eye. My eyes could see as sharp as an eagle's, even they could not detect my hands when looking through. I had even discovered passing through small objects was possible. Trees and rocks that had been unaltered, if I went slowly, allowed me to pass through them, as long as my whole body was not inside the object. This function allowed the being that created it to allow me to infiltrate warrens of the creatures and kill them where they slept. From that day forward, the Rangers shared the technology with any one will to fight with them.

While I reflected on the events the day before, I felt prepared for my first real exercise without any support from my teacher or master. This was no longer a test by my guess. Dozens of daemons appeared. The portal destabilized for a moment, cutting the last one in half. He died gurgling while the others looked on and laughed. Even in my location, their voices carried a short distance. For a portal to open on the very edge of a town was rare. Mathias asked the Sasquatch at some point to tell him when a portal was in the process of opening. He wanted me to see firsthand how it worked.

I was back to Earth for this test.

It was a little strange to know that my body was here somewhere in the real world. This body manifested me as a corporeal being in the realm of Heaven. It would be crazy to see myself in a coma. I had been given an hour for the scenario before Bigfoot would be brought in to mop up if I failed. "No pressure," kept running through my mind as I stood there taking stock.

I watched in fascination before realizing that I had better make sure they remained hidden. Focusing on the lot of them, I reached into myself to tap into my internal energy and felt the rune on my forehead activate, cloaking all of them to make sure they did not appear to any unsuspecting humans. I looked for a sign somewhere over a business to see if I could spot a name. Glancing quickly here and there without taking my eyes of off my prey for too long, I tried to spot the name of the town. Because they were from another dimension, they did not coalesce until the portal locked open, allowing the rest of their essence to flow out of the portal. It was as if it helped part of them back, keeping them from being stuck there in the event they failed. It could also be a defense of the weave of energy around the planet. As the magic that brought them here strengthened, they would become solid. Right now as I watched, they seemed to act like ghosts. Knocking people over almost seemed like cow tipping. They were trying to touch anyone they could.

The cloaking formed a barrier that kept daemons in the area from seriously harming anyone, but only for what felt like a few minutes. There were a few people close by in a small crowd. They scattered quickly as soon as they saw a small dust devil kicking up the leaves.

They spread quickly around half of the block when the daemons started harassing their prey. I knew I had to move in fast. If they started killing each other and using some sort of ceremonial magic, a portal locked open from this side would be harder to close. The numbers coming through would be devastating. The daemons knew they had to establish a beachhead of sorts before they could sacrifice each other. They came here knowing they would die to achieve the goal.

Sadly, if the daemons succeeded in their magic, the barrier would falter, making it harder to hide the truth. The portal would draw the energy from the area, draining the energy from my illusion as well. I tried to argue this was not to my advantage when we arrived, but the response was not favorable as nothing is fair in war. Mathias said he did not make the rules that governed how magic and energy interacted. Therefore, my clock started before my arrival.

The townsfolk tried to run in all directions. People fell. Daemons tried to attack them. Then it hit me. This was the distraction! The daemons were very aware that the Defender would be here, only today I was alone. They meant to lure him away with a large host that feigned going after the people in hopes he would focus on killing the daemons to allow just enough daemons to stay behind to lock the portal in place with blood...their blood.

They did this in population centers to keep the Defender busy. I could barely understand the guttural language, but one of them spoke in some sort of incantation to start the process. The others began to taunt each other as if it was a game to see which daemon killed the most before they killed each other in the final blow to expand the portal.

Only today, I saw right through the rouse.

Plagues throughout history that appeared to have short runs and die out were the result of daemons. Daemons were chaotic and could barely function as a group so they tended to not follow the plan. There were numerous records in the last century with the increase of good record keeping. This sickness was the direct effect of the daemons "appearing" to take a host while still incorporeal, but they could not maintain this state for very long. A daemon would re-emerge inside the host. It was quite messy. The bodies burned in a pyre before anyone knew. Thankfully, the Defender was able to get there and remove the daemon in cases where someone looked at cause of death. The organs did not survive, sometimes liquefied by the blending of the two bodies. It was quite gross.

From just a touch, a human had a very good chance to contract an unidentifiable disease in which they died horribly. Lord knows what these diseases did to them, but I could only imagine how painful it could be. Thankfully, the protective barrier I could engage protected them from the actual touch of the daemon, but not from the kinetic energy. The anomaly affected them physically. It may not have kept them from bumps, bruises, or scrapes, but it kept them from death. If the daemons did manage to kill a human near a portal, that soul went straight through to someone on the other side, waiting to collect them. That soul made the horde stronger some-how; I could only imagine the benefits.

I moved across the street. Seeing one of the monsters stiffen as if he sensed my approach, I sprang into action. It turned only to meet my blades. There was a flash. The smell of burning flesh filled my nostrils as the heav-enly metal cleaved it in half with ease. Unnatural laws that governed its body on the other plain did not work the same here, but my blades worked, and that was all that mattered to me. Their design disintegrated daemon flesh eliminating clean up. Malnuras was a genius when he came up with the concept. Mathias saw to the forgers and enchanters.

What little of the blood remained, smoldered out of existence.

I waded into the first group. Three died before they realized their plight; I dodged back and forth making quick work of the first dozen. Dae-mons flashed out of existence quickly. They discovered me quickly.

Seeing my approach, the other twelve sacrificed half their numbers to open the portal. Four had died by their own kind before I reached them. I was visible now. Eight stood in various perches before me as they flew up and landed, observing and cursing at me in their tongue. I felt the rift lock-ing in place; my head ached, staggering my stride. The daemons saw my faultier and three more fell to their own, leaving five. The rift was about to lock open. I shifted my attention to closing it.

Such small numbers. This should be easy.

Too late, my overconfidence had betrayed me. A portal appeared as the two remaining turned on each other and one killed the other. I doubled over in pain, trying to focus my energies on closing the portal. It was a trap.

The last daemon dove through the portal before it slammed shut.

A voice in my head spoke "You were too close to it."

The other voice responded, "He will learn."

"Dark magic can affect you still. The portal is created by vileness...if you are too close, its mere presence will diminish you." They spoke together. The majestic sounds still caught me off guard when they spoke, especially together. It was a good lesson to learn.

Too close means pain.

I was on all fours. Embarrassed at what had just transpired, I rose to my feet and called out to Mathias for help. Within moments, I was at the campsite. Breathing hard, I stood up and walked over to him. Before I could speak, he said, "So you have a problem now?"

I knelt down with my head hanging shamefully low. I had not known defeat on this scale since starting, and it was not even a daemon action to cause it. Something told me that all my work had just been defeated as the daemon would be half way to his evil prince telling him of his discoveries. I felt an urge to take my own life. I drew a blade.

Malnuras's hand touched mine as I positioned the tip to do the deed; I knew it was a bit dramatic but truly felt that I had dishonored myself. I looked at him. "That won't work." I gave him a puzzled look. "Your blades have been designed so that they cannot be turned against you. You can try, but it won't even break the skin."

Therefore, I tried. He was not kidding. My painful look became apparent with a tear that formed. "There is no need for that," he said pointing over to the carcass of a newly killed daemon. "I told that one how to get back and waited for him. Your response time is too slow. Go back and we'll try again."

Mentally, I was back on my heels, bewildered at what I saw. The urgency was all a ploy to throw me off balance. Granted it gave me less time to plan my attack; they had not seen me coming until I was on them. Words would not form my thoughts. My teacher caught my look.

"Okay, I told that one you would be waiting for him on the other side and that he was to sacrifice the others to return. I helped from this end as well to guide the portal opening to me. You needed to see what it would be like to think you were in control. How did it feel?"

"So this was a test you knew I would fail?" I sat there shaking my head in disbelief. I knew "Teacher" was a master tactician but to risk this kind of exposure so soon was not like him. It seemed careless. My advantage would have been compromised had that daemon reported to the horde, and I would have been at a severe disadvantage until all the daemons with that knowledge had been hunted down. I wondered why he would take such a risk.

As I waited, Mathias walked in with a stern look on his face that faded to a smile. He was still hard to read, but that was actually a good sign. Perhaps the day was not a total waste

"Well?"

"Horrible. It happened just as you told me it would the first time."

"You needed to learn that things are not always as they appear. The agents of the enemy can live on Earth, disguised as humans, in certain circumstances. Be prepared that anyone you meet could be a daemon. Your senses have to be alert to see them, so never let down your guard." I was shocked at these words from Mathias and wondered when he planned to share this with me.

"Ever think of telling me this stuff?" I asked sarcastically.

"I just did."

I looked at him with wonder. He was in my head again. I always felt so violated. Even though he was playful at times, I knew he did not purposefully play games with me but when he withheld information, it felt like he was playing a game, or worse. I know the intent was not malicious but meant to instruct me in different ways. I sometimes grew frustrated of the lessons, but I accepted them for what they were. His lessons had not been as Malnuras's were. Even though I had taken many beatings from Malnuras, it was never an actual beating; it was always in the form of defending from his onslaught of blows. The lessons hurt.

Mathias, on the other hand, just flat beat me down in the past. He did this to teach humility and toughen me up, which accomplished both on many accounts. His teaching style allowed him to do with me as he pleased. There was always some sort of lesson that surfaced later. Sometimes weeks went by before the significance of his teaching became relevant. I did miss my master at times and the countless days spent with him had left their mark in my mind.

The training, the conditioning, and the skills he beat into me came out in my everyday life. At times, it seemed like every moment, I could identify something that he taught me and apply it to the situation. I felt gratitude every for all he had done for me. The tests had been, and were still very much real and the chances of dying high. I possessed the ability to survive, but there was no guarantee that I might not make a mistake that would get me or my teacher or master killed. The chance of that happening where they died was slim, but I could not take any situation for granted.

Now I had another angle to consider. The idea of daemons taking human hosts gave me chills. I had heard of possession before but this was not a just possession. They lived in and bonded with the hosts. I spent the next few days trying to learn what I could on the subject. There were only instances where the Defender fought off humans and in the process of defending himself, killed the human only to have a corporeal form of a daemon rise out of the corpse and try to materialize. Sometimes they fled and tried to get into a host in order to hide again.

I saw one scene where Bigfoot chased a daemon from host to host. On one hand, it was comical. But sad that those people died in the process. If I did not kill them all and keep track of them upon arrival, one of them might get away. This would cause other problems. Having to worry about the "seen" and the "unseen" made my stomach turn for the first time in months. The stakes had just gotten higher. Failing now was even less of an option. My jaw was set firmly on succeeding. I found myself clenching at the thought of failing. How to accomplish this escaped me.

Frustration mounted. A sigh ensued. "All would reveal itself in time," the phrase echoed in my head. I had much more to learn, and a new determination now awakened in me. I felt Malnuras's eyes on me and looked to him. He nodded. Bowing to both, my eyes locked on each of them respectfully.

It was going to take some getting used to. Was there a choice? My teacher always knew my thoughts. That did not bother me anymore. Greater issues seemed to be overshadowing the lesson. He knew my turmoil. Slightly comforted that I was not alone in my thoughts, I stood and drew my swords. A presence behind me stirred. It had been a few weeks since we sparred; my head turned to see him sneaking up behind me. I acted as if I did not see him until he swung his staff.

The defection was flawless.

His grin spread quickly across his lips.

"You will have to do better than that, Teacher."

Mathias drew his blade and looked at Malnuras. They nodded to each other.

X

They are here

The light that fills these fading eyes
Has always been my compromise
In the dark I made my stand
And bleed to meet the horde's demand

With each drop my life might fade
But in return lends strength to blade
Standing fast against the tide
No other course but to abide

All my life I have prepared
To stand alone without despair
Heightened skills have bought me time
I am the cork that holds the line

From those that passed in times before
Reinforce the mandate inside I swore
If I fail this day this hour
To the next I will add my power

I did not choose, yet here I stand
To turn the tide and save the land
I fight a battle to none exists
So they can have their crimson bliss

Breathing came in labored gasps.

Today's theme proved me wrong about many things as I ran for my life; this was the first time I had fled since my journey and training began.

Half the day was gone with only a few moments to relieve myself and take a quick drink before they caught my scent and I was on the move again. I could not believe how quick the small, wingless daemons moved. Something changed, which led me to believe that somehow my teacher controlled training events more than he let on. Their speed was faster and they could leap even farther than before. This was a problem.

The name given to the small ones translated to "leaping demons," which I thought was extremely accurate and highly simplistic. Admittedly, I laughed when Malnuras told me the name and what it meant. He cracked me upside the head that day with his staff and told me to learn respect for them before the week was out. The irony of that statement came true.

Now he fought for his life. Up until now, I looked at my enemies with hatred. Correcting my view was a lesson in academics.

I had no idea my world was about to go sideways. They found our location with numbers that measured in the tens of thousands, possibly more. Every size of every variety swarmed the camp, tearing down the barriers and the protections with ease. All Malnuras could do was say, "Run and stay alive!" then sent me flying over the hill with a wave of his hand.

He raised his hands over his head. Energy, like a white pillar, slammed into the ground with terrific force. The front ranks of the horde vanished. Several hundred daemons died instantly. The decimation was insane. A huge explosion rocked the area and a concussive shockwave rolled out from the impact point, killing more of the ground units and taking down several hundred flyers in midair. Thousands more came.

My vision blurred as the shock wave hit me in mid-flight. It sent me tumbling head over heels for what felt like an eternity. A cliff face stopped my momentum when my orientation was upside down. I fell yet again. This time a tree broke my fall reminding me of the tree back home. Now, I knew what to do and used the branches to rotate me so my feet found the main portion of the tree. The texture of its bark created friction, allowing me to slow my descent with minimal impact.

My feet burned through the shoes I had made from materials of the forest. The animal skin was a leather hide that had its own texture on the outside and the bottom. On that surface, we coated it with the saliva of some creature that was like rubber when it hardened. It used it to cocoon its prey and keep it fresh for later. Kind of like a spider wrapping its kill in its web to keep it secure.

This creature was a hunter. It ran you down then licked you all over while glands in its mouth secreted the smelly substance that I now wore proudly on my feet. I appreciated the substance right now, for the hide on the souls of my feel would have worn through on my slide down the trunk of the tree. I was grateful that we had done the project together, yet that turned to sadness as thoughts of him alone now flooded over me.

His last words of "Stay alive" rang through my head and heart. He never took the approach of telling me how important I was. The message was a hint, but never an outright statement, which made it easier to accept, in my eyes. It was not as if the world would crumble right now if I were to die. The Sasquatch was still there. He was still protecting the people and doing his job. My replacing him was the next evolution, not because of what he did or did not do, but because he had served the planet well. He deserved a vacation of the permanent variety.

An impressive light show lit the sky from over the hill. The thunderous explosions reverberated off the cliff behind me and returned, causing feedback that shook the very ground. I took a moment to survey my surroundings. Deep woods surrounded me at the base of a network of cliffs that went on for miles. Every few seconds the light in the distance flashed, followed by the shock wave that delayed my task of getting out of there. I had to either climb up or go one way or the other. Going up was bad because daemons had excellent vision, and they would no doubt see me scaling the cliff. If I tried to jump across, the sudden movement would attract their attention.

That left me two options: pick a direction and go. I knew there was a daemon warren to the south of our camp; luckily, my teacher threw me roughly north. I thought for a second about my chances. If the warren was empty and if passing by without a fight was possible, survival might also be. I knew better. Hosts that came from a direction generally lived in that direction. The odds of them coordinating an attack on our campsite when the glory would fall to the attacking group were slim.

My mind raced to remember daemon lore.

Daemons worked together but not until they were called by a higher authority. They all wanted to serve the greater evil, but earning stature still meant pleasures such as human flesh to eat or human females to create nasty offspring with, as a reward. I do not know the daemon version of the Nephilim, but it would not be good or pleasant to meet, especially since they could impregnate the female with multiple offspring at a time. Somehow, daemon seed found its way to the woman's ovaries and all the eggs in her body impregnated simultaneously. When the embryos matured, they destroyed the woman from the inside and released hundreds of spawn that grew quickly.

If a daemon had its own offspring to command, it became more powerful. They usually started their own warren and bred normally from there. This is how the power base established because the human chi gave these offspring special gifts. I did not know more than that about their overall hierarchy and ecology, but had listened to enough of the stories and had given attention to the information that both of my teachers had bestowed upon me. Usually the larger ones or stronger daemons pulled this off when the opportunity arose.

The decision was to head north. Moment to moment, choices of which way to go came up. Two separate creatures caught my scent and died quickly. I smeared blood and gore of the last one all over me. The chase was still going on. My decisions did not influence the battlefield. Mobility mattered. Normally before a training session, I would have to locate a suitable place to engage the host, and then lead them to it to fall back into the ambush that I both created and sprung.

Not today. Every time I found a suitable location, there was not long enough to set up anything. It was going to have to be a run and gun. Killing them while moving and to keep moving as fast as I can became my process today. My options were few and this was the best I could do.

My conditioning took over at this point. Winded, I kept going. My survival skills had me always looking at every possible avenue for places to hide to regroup. I knew what trees would not try to eat me and what berries to eat. All of that was child's play and second nature. I am sure I could teach Special Forces a thing or two when they went through the hell week or their SARS training. I was a master at survival. The problem was the train of daemons following me. They were getting closer every minute.

It is amazing what happens when you think you are paying attention, especially when not in your own area. The first trap was a surprise. I damn near stepped into the thing then heard a vine snap under some large leaves near the path. I jumped as high as possible and found another trip wire several meters in the air that broke with my momentum. Two logs tipped with metal plates and sharpened points, swung from the side. My eyes caught them at the last moment. My ability to slow my descent allowed me to time it perfectly. They swung through the area my body would have been below and the chime of the metal hitting metal rang out. Before I had time to react to the impact, a large net fell atop of me and somehow wrapped me up from all angles.

This was not on the agenda

The ground rushed up. There was no time to reposition my feet with a net weighing down. I managed to get a sword free, as the weight brought me to my knees and thrust upwards to slice a hole. To my dismay, only one strand cut. My limbs quickly became immobilized. Sudden realization hit. It was not just a net. Some sort of sticky substance coated me. I tried to saw it with the one blade already sticking through. The strand reformed as the blade pushed through. It rejoined after the blade passed. I was surprised that it did not stick to the metal. The net was made of living matter.

Four shadows fell from the trees above, so quietly they sounded like wind. Only my senses were able to detect the presence. I met this new challenge with a smile. All my protections came on. The figures approached and surrounded. With this giant net on me, it was hard to see. They had very bloated looking bodies and multiple limbs. Several acted like tendrils and the others attached to the net. Their faces had mandibles and three sets of eyes on what appeared to be a head. They walked as if the ground was a hot plate. They only left their appendages down long enough to shift their balance and lift the other one quickly, as if they feared getting burned. Their feet snapped back as they strode, only with no sound.

My hunters had found me, it seemed. I struggled to rise. The sheer weight on me appeared to be draining me of strength, when I realized it was doing exactly that. This material attached to the creatures was part of their body. The tendril wove into a net to trap prey. I felt a twinge of pain and was nauseated as they proceeded to drain the life force from me. Focusing hard and managing to push these daemons from me was not working. There was no way out, and they advanced. A chattering voice came from one of them. They spoke as they approached. This speech was new to me.

"Whut ees et? Et us beeg, vury beeg. Schmeels uf fud, leekks luk tucheer."

"Yiiis vury beeg, leeks tusty, it nut fluus nut nuur muvs on fure leeegs."

"Ees blundad un. Loung snee os teestad blundad."

"Tracheerri! Keell fure eet sutes wuth eets d'mon weeeze."

"Keell uit!" they chimed and the net wove itself around me tighter.

"Wait, "I cried out. "Whom do you serve? You called me a daemon. I hunt them, and there is a whole horde of them coming this way." It was getting harder to draw breath; my sword fell to the ground and the net lifted. They suspended me between them. Hanging flat now, I felt the tendrils weave in and around my legs and arms. It was really starting to hurt and to break any of the strands was impossible. I turned on my healing in hopes of lasting long enough to reason with them.

The sound of steel, as if drug along small rocks and hardened dirt, came from below. The feeling they were going to try to run through with my own sword came over me I figured anger would follow once they realized that would not work... The sound stopped. A tendril of one of the creatures had my sword suspended in front of it. It was looking at it curiously. The crushing weight and energy drain lessened for a moment. Some other voice chattered. It was not the language spoken by the people. The words were very animal sounding. There was more chattering and clicking, as if it was excited. The other began to speak, which made my head spin. This went on for a few moments. The constriction lessened, allowing my healing to do more of its work.

I could take full breaths now, but could not move.

The four of them continued chattering. I was in a death trap. My eyes panned around. This was a good place for an ambush, and I had walked right into it. I cursed my luck, or lack thereof, when suddenly there were more of them dropping out of the trees behind and all around me. A sickening feeling filled me with dread. They exchanged words and felt certain they were planning to eat me. They spoke a unanimous word. Next, I found out just how hard the ground was. Tendrils then picked me up and set me on my feet. As I gained my balance, dozens of these creatures surrounded me. I was in a bit of shock as the events unfolded before me.

One of them approached with my sword in its tendril. It was then that I realized the thing had twelve tendrils, yet walked only on four. It made no sound. With another one of its tendrils, it pointed to one of the runes on my sword. I looked and it was pointing towards the symbol they use to define the first human that has the title of Defender.

"Whut thus muin?" it asked, motioning to the symbol.

"That is what I am. I am the Defender. Teacher trained me to fight the hordes."

"Thusey Tuchier's," it said, and pointed to a small symbol that was very familiar to me. It was a small tree with a moon above it.

"That is Malnuras's symbol," I said and glanced around at the crowd of them that now gathered around me. "He is my teacher."

More excited chattering exploded around the clearing. It appeared they knew Malnuras and had respect for him. That made them an ally. It was the first good news I had in a while and was especially welcomed today. I pointed towards the distance. They all turned and looked, some of them cocking their heads like chickens pecking at the ground for food.

"Teacher is that way. Many daemons attack him." I was about to suggest we go save him when I heard their language roll through the crowd, all repeating the same word: "Kloschka!"

I looked where my finger was pointing and saw movement on the ground. Leapers were bounding towards me. More than I could count. The skies in that direction darkened. The horde had found me. I was about to ask for my swords back when I found them in my hands. Shrieks rolled through the population of my new friends, and they all ran to places of ambush. The one that spoke to me turned towards me.

"Wui huntee. Schtoy."

I was still getting used to the accent, but understood enough to know I should ready my weapons.

"Wow that's a lot of them," I said.

I do not know if it was a smile, but it recognized my words. "Give me room to move," I said to it. It nodded and scaled a tree faster than I could fall from it.

This is going to be messy.

Looking up, the nets wove together and then I saw a surprise. They vanished. Dozens of flesh woven nets formed and disappeared, spanning tens of yards between trees. I began to swing my swords and made sure engage my defenses. In the distance, the daemons approached.

"Damn, that is a lot," I muttered. This is going to hurt. I heard Mathias's voice in my head.

"Only if you think it will," I remembered he said to me before a particularly painful lesson. The first ones approached fast and slammed into the tendril nets. I could hear them scream in their daemonic language as their life force drained from them. The net opened and a bunch of husks fell to the ground. I suddenly felt fortunate my defenses had come on when they did.

Several of the flyers made it past the nets and dove for me; the leapers approached from the ground, rapidly. It did not matter if I was on the ground or in the air since the two were capable of both. My feet remained set for a sideways leap with both blades over my right shoulder in preparation. In they came. Out snapped my arms, taking several of them as they blazed passed me. The metal passed through hide and flesh with ease. The blades used their own momentum, which allowed me to conserve energy. I landed and reset my attack. The aerial ones farther back in the horde adjusted their trajectory while the ones up front streamed by with feeble attempts. I swung again and took the head off one leaper in the front of the wave, and took the legs of several others as they veered away.

Several more rapid strikes yielded dead daemons.

The dance of death began. Daemons on the ground came at me from all angles. Flyers flew away to regain speed for another volley of attacks; this gave me time to kill several more leapers before having to worry about the flyers. My blades struck faster and faster, like a whirlwind. Bodies piled up around me. I had to keep moving.

Still swinging my blades as a barrier of steel, I repositioned myself again. This time I began to feel nicks and scratches getting past my defenses, even though I was focusing on creating a barrier. My healing was on, and the wounds closed almost as fast as they opened. I found my footing and adjusted my attacks to be killing blows. Shrieking filled the clearing as daemons died. They fell with each strike. Ichor splattered the hard ground with a sound like infrequent rain.

In the distance, I occasionally saw my new friends killing daemons by the dozens. It was hard to see amidst my stride and the flow of my weapons. I had to remain focused to keep from letting them through my defenses. A few of the hunters may have died, but the amount of creatures they could snare at one time, kill, drop, and catch was staggering. I dealt with the leftover daemons. Their numbers still overran me. Yet I was one. They were hundreds strong.

Numerous cuts flowed on my arms. My healing slowed the flow of blood down to less than a trickle. However, I still bled. They still got through my shield, but it was one in a hundred...if that. Over time, it added up. A silent thank you for my training was on my lips amidst blows.

"You need to increase your healing," one blade declared while the other purred in agreement. It was true. Letting the damage stack up would overwhelm the rune. I started to gather energy from around me to lessen the impact on my own pool.

"We are alone out here; this race of beings cannot help you. They will only slow the horde down. These kinds of numbers will overrun them soon," Radu said mentally. He was right. The count of dead around me was in the hundreds in the opening melee. Anytime I swung, several died. The amount of flyers thinned for a moment and those on the ground suffered the most since they did not have to line up angles of attack. They just came on with teeth and claws in a continuous flow. The ground was slippery with ichor. It turned to mud.

The efforts of my helpers would not be enough.

Another reposition was in order. I leapt up and confronted some of the flyers overhead lining up their attack angle. It was easy to figure out the animal mentality of the creatures, even if they did have the same intelligence as an average human. My ascent took me up thirty feet where something impacted me. I had to react quickly.

One of the large ones with four wings swooped in and grabbed a hold of me. Three of its talons hit me hard and tried to sink in as it made a pass at a moderate speed. The impact was tremendous. I found myself flying toward a tree as large talons lost grip of me but tore my flesh in the process in areas that my protective cloth did not cover. Talons had bypassed my protections. The last thing I remember was hitting the tree and falling before blackness took me.

* * *

Sounds of battle, as if in a distant tunnel, filled my ears. I heard wind and felt it against my face. The pressure crushed down making breathing hard. Light peeked in through the cracks in my blinking eyelids. Trying to focus, I cracked one eye open even more and rolled my head to the side. I was airborne. A beast carried me. The stench of the beast was horrific and familiar.

My hands were empty. *Not good.*

I was about to panic.

Without weapons, I would be lucky to survive. No matter how long I fought, taking them down with rocks and sticks would take too long. With every beat of the creature's wings, the talons loosened and tightened gently. Hoping I could use that to my advantage. I began to memorize the timing. It could not glide, so it had to flap constantly; otherwise, it would plummet to the ground.

My healing was no longer active, being knocked out, and it took a moment to restore it. The runes magic coursed through me and instantly felt better. Thankfully, the daemon did not notice the wave of energy that rolled over me. At least if there was to be a fight, I would have my wits and my health. Held weaponless in the daemons claws, I prepared for the challenge.

In the distance, the battle raged; it could not be more than a mile away. My mind raced. On one hand, the large one was not part of the battle, so perhaps the creatures in the trees had a chance to win. Yet, on the other hand, I was alone and weaponless. I tried to run over scenarios that did not end with me eaten alive, and they all ended badly.

I was going to have to see how this panned out and decided to play possum for a bit longer; perhaps it would drop me if it thought I was dead. I shuddered as the thought rolled to the next conclusion. It might be bringing me back to its leader or to a nest to feed its offspring. I must have moved a bit too much because I heard it growl and start to squeeze me. Pain exploded in my body, and I groaned. It knew it caused me agony.

I actually heard it laugh.

Fighting to stay conscious, I tried to focus on my training. I began to cuss myself out internally while trying to focus to bring my defenses on. Why I kept forgetting about my healing left me to wonder how I was going to survive longer than a few minutes while protecting the planet. My healing powers engaged at full power. The energy released and slammed against the inside of the creature's claw, pushing against the debilitating energy the creature projected.

My healing powers burned the monster as it held me. I felt the grip tighten; it growled even louder and then roared. Its second claw wrapped around the first in a renewed effort to maintain a hold on me. The roar got louder as its discomfort grew. I could only imagine the pain the creature must be in when it passed me from its back claws to its front claw. Before I realized what was happening, I was in its mouth. I engaged my shield.

"Not again!" I cried out as I felt the creature swallow. Forced down its gullet, its saliva could not touch me because my barrier held. It took about three seconds by my guess to move from the mouth to stomach, and the smell made me gag. I floated in half digested bodies suspended by my shield. Several corpses of the new race of creatures just met were nearby so this thing was obviously not on their menu.

I felt bad that the horde had decimated the hunters. The responsibility for potentially wiping out that tribe was mine. I had no idea if there were more of them, but hoped the battle was going in their favor. Then the lights went out, for it closed its great maw.

Centrifugal force shifted as the daemon banked. Soon I hoped my fate would be obvious. Odds were it would digest me or regurgitate me for its young. I was not thrilled about my options. That anticipation of approaching death was worse than the act itself. The other issue was only a matter of time before hunger set in. I also did not know if the protection would shut off if I fell asleep. The theory remained untested. The sudden change of direction made me wonder if it was approaching its nest. The smell was atrocious.

The air grew thinner. Breathing in the gullet of a beast is no easy task.

My thoughts turned inward. Mathias's voice played in my mind, telling me about using my environment as a weapon. I recalled looking around while I let his martial sermon play in my head. Rotting flesh and small bones weak with decay littered its stomach. Nothing jumped out at me so I allowed my mind to roll over to another one of his lessons. My thoughts dug deep.

I remembered the day he gave me my swords and how exquisite they were to me. The beautiful lines that gave them balance and added strength to the blades' construction caught the light ever so gently. Crafted runes, so intricate, adorned the bladed center running vertically. The metal almost seemed alive to me. As they swung through the air, they almost sang their own song of death. When they impacted flesh, I barely noticed. The cuts were so clean it was as though the target was not there.

Their chatter of my swords always kept me company. I missed them now. The sound they made when in action was music to my ears. Their song was that of glorious death and righteous victory.

The beast's belly jumped again as if it hit something or changed course again. I was about to try to meditate when I heard Mathias's voice trail off in my head as it played one very important memory that I had forgotten. It was a thought that would change my thinking forever. I slapped my own forehead in disbelief. My misstep was epic.

Why did I always forget this?

The thought had not even cleared my mind when I felt the cold metal in both of my hands and a cheer escaped my lips. The stale air was full of acid vapors. They made it hard to draw breath as I in took the air for a yell. I paid for it with coughing. I was thankful my healing was still going strong.

I did my best to position myself on my knees in my bubble of protection. It took moments to right myself so I could raise both blades above my head. In one swift motion, I cut a terrific gouge into the bottom of the creature's feted stomach lining. It contracted as daylight spilled in past its teeth. Fresh air managed to make its way in and gave me added strength to balance myself.

The creature pitched wildly.

My swords fell again, making an even larger cut. Bile and stomach fluid drained into the soft tissue of the creature's underbelly. If this creature reacted like every other in regards to stomach acid, the fluid would burn like hell in its bowels. My cuts would make this worse, as it was an open wound and the acid should be hitting its blood stream, lighting a fire in its veins. I felt a shudder and a roar roll though the creature's flesh as my blades bit deeper. Air was thin even though I had gotten a trace amount of fresh air from the first strike. No new air was coming down to me, and I felt the first few stages of asphyxia start. The pins and needles started in my limbs. My healing helped, but no air meant unconsciousness, which meant the rune might not function.

My blades bit again, weaker than the first blow, but I continued to rain them down. The stomach fluid all but drained into the open wounds. Suddenly the lining floor rose up sharply, trying to smash me against the top. I turned my right hand blade up and left my other down while trying to maintain balance. Up it came again. This time both points met their respective surface and bit deep. Another shudder rolled through the beast's insides. Its stomach contracted violently in an attempt to regurgitate me.

I managed to maintain my pose while the blades bit deep yet again, and the rotting meat moved toward me. My mouth filled with my own saliva as if I was going to get sick too, but I choked it down, trying not to breathe. Rumbles inside the beast's belly made it hard to hold onto my swords embedded into its insides. The maw was open. Its roars of pain were deafening. It tumbled in all directions, trying to dislodge me.

I tried to get the timing of the tumbles down to re-sink the swords in for a better hold. Logic hit me. I did not want to be inside this creature when it hit the ground.

I changed my strategy and, with all my might, swung at the already deep cuts, further exposing the daemon's soft insides. The blade bit deep. There was resistance, which surprised me for the first time since owning the swords. A violent shudder rolled through the creature and it began to spasm. The blades appeared caught on something. I pitched my weight forward and felt them break free, snapping a rib bone or something off with it. Ichor flowed and the wails coming from the creature turned into gurgles. I felt weak and gave my all to one last swing, which rewarded me with sunlight and precious air.

I thrust my blades and my arms through the thick, leathery hide of the creature with all my remaining strength, cried out, and pulled my body through. Clean air whistled around me and felt amazing. The feeling was short lived, though, as the ground rushed up at me. The whistle sound that a plane makes when it dives filled my ears. Managing to pull myself free of the falling carcass, I launched myself out and up, away from the beast. There was no chance to slow my descent. The daemon concaved the ground creating a monstrous dust and debris cloud that settled over the area. It was only feet from me.

To my surprise, I did not black out; a break from the pain would have been nice.

I held my breath while waiting for the cloud to disperse and hoping for some wind to speed the process up. My body was fatigued and hurt. Time passed as I lay there focusing on healing. Something was wrong with my legs or spine; moving was impossible. With the movement of the sun being the only way to track time, I struggled to determine how long I lay face down in the dirt. At some point, I must have passed out or fallen asleep. My body lay on its side when my eyes crept open, but still hurt as if the distance fallen was farther than originally imagined.

Wearily, I rose to my knees and surveyed my location. Mountains surrounded me. Steep crags climbed skyward and snow on the ground showed signs of a thaw. The sun was high overhead, which told me that it was the next day. The heat felt good to my sore flesh. It was overtaxed keeping the creatures acid at bay. Plainly, it hurt to move.

The sound of water tantalized my ears. There might be a small creek close by. It only took a moment to locate the source, and I was on my knees instantly, ridding my face and hair of the funk that was clinging there. It must have been a lot because the downstream color turned brackish for several minutes. I needed more. Begrudgingly, I stood and stumbled farther downstream to look for a deeper place to submerge myself. With the sun overhead, drying off would not be an issue. My footfalls became rather heavy. I navigated the rough shore to follow the tiny stream. There was an uneasy silence in the surrounding desolation. Not a lot of animal scurried about, nor were there many signs of vegetation. The area appeared void of life. My pursuit of the stream finally revealed my prize; a pool that was a few feet deep, enough for me to submerge in. I gingerly waded in, feeling the cool water hit my skin and make the muscles spasm. The water turned foul. I hoped that nothing drinking downstream…if there was even anything downstream.

There were only a few hours until sundown and figuring out which way to go was my task. A sigh escaped my lips. I was frustrated. I hoped Malnuras was okay. Thoughts turned to those creatures' noble efforts to protect me. The dark water began to clear while I removed my clothes to cleanse. Some sort of scent saturated me. Around the pool nothing that gave off any fragrance. Nothing could counter the smell of it other than the bath. Several minutes passed and the water became less murky from the expunged filth. Once on shore again I took to cleaning my clothes and laid them on a nearby rock to dry. What little heat felt good and I basked in its rays while keeping an eye out for company, swords at the ready.

Sometime later, with my clothes mostly dry, I foraged the area for food. Some indigenous berries grew everywhere, but in this desolation, there was no luck just yet. I wandered for a bit, when in the distance, a sound echoed off the rocks and made it difficult to determine the direction it came from. I kept up my search but noticed that the sound was still present and growing. Everywhere looked, the paths seemed to all point one way. I deduced it had to be a known path, but could not tell what used it.

The density of the mountains made navigating any one direction difficult. The sound became more distinct and was a mix of many voices, possibly roars, and occasionally explosions of varying degrees. Our camp was in the other direction and was very far away. Therefore, it had to be something else. The large daemon that grabbed me must have been close to its goal. I felt like was heading towards some unfolding event. The thought of joining a battle excited me, and my energy levels climbed even though my stomach talked to me. Payback sounded good right about now.

The noise grew. It was definitely a battle. Sounds echoed off the walls of this small box end canyon. A way out presented itself, but it would take a bit of dexterous leaping to scale the wall. It was a steep cliff, nearly sheer from this angle. I maneuvered closer to the bottom and leapt. The timing was easy enough, allowing me to grab a few times as I backslid before my hands found places to hold. Temperatures dropped, and I did not even realize my skin tore from grabbing the cliff's stony face. After leaving a few bloody handprints on the rock face, my healing engaged on its own. Leaping again successfully, I grabbed my mark and this time my grip held. I repeated this a few more times and was able to crawl over the top ledge. Finally, the top was mine.

A small plateau greeted me with a smooth top that ran for quite a ways, leading into shadows as the sun dipped down. In the waning light, my vision still worked a bit. Normally I would be limited to moonlight or starlight. I took advantage while it lasted and increased my pace. My feet found a bit of a trail, which made traveling significantly easier. The path came to a natural "T" and the sound was coming from the left. My curiosity arose and I wanted to kill some daemons badly.

The faint scent of blood caught my nose. I was heading the right direction for sure. A chorus of voices now bounced around the walls and increased with each step. The hill came to a bend on the left then ran for a few yards back to the right. I had to climb about twenty feet. I chose to climb the last section. As I approached the top, the sound intensified to a fever pitch.

The mystery unfolded when I reached the top. My eyes beheld an unexpected sight. A city under siege. Fires erupted with objects and beams of energy exploding into a magic barrier, tearing at it with no effect. I stood transfixed for several moments, soaking it all in. Every blast lit the sky. Stones disintegrated as they collided with nothing, failing to impact the wall or the city beyond. Even at this distance, I could see movement on the walls and a host of daemons numbering beyond comprehension. If I had to guess by the sea of daemons, it had to be in the billions. A shudder ran through every fiber of my being. Never had I beheld anything so preposterously overwhelming. It was impossible. A tear ran down my face.

The city of Heaven lay before me.

XI

Siege

My jaw dropped.

The view was magnificent. It was a daemon horde that defied numbers, impressive in a frightening way. The masses spread over hundreds of miles. Line of sight allowed me to see to the horizon. The armies of hell gathered at the walls of Heaven. I would not have believed what I was seeing if it had not been for the flashes of magic and siege weapons pounding away. Gigantic golden walls several miles high with towers and other buildings behind them extended high into the sky. Smoke obscured parts of the city. Many of the towers looked to be miles high, disappearing into the clouds. Giant pits from missile attacks riddled the walls. Two millennia of hellish assault had not been kind to them.

The scene felt surreal. Master's description fell utterly short.

I could tell there were magic protections on the walls. When a projectile struck, a shimmer appeared like a rainbow effect of colors that scintillated with each impact. The striking projectile disintegrated, and an incredible sound shot across the field like an echoing explosion. Even at my great distance, it pounded in my ears. Those projectiles had to travel at least twenty miles.

There were no angels outside the shield. An orange glow would build for several moments, and then release from different points on the wall and from towers. They did incredible damage to the daemons and the

158

mechanisms on the battlefield. The orange beam made groups of daemons disappear in swaths. There were so many of them it did not matter. More simply moved up or attended to the devices when the current ones died. Any siege weapons hit shattered and burned instantly. Sometimes they glanced off, merely disabling them.

Some of the daemons' energy weapons appeared arcane in nature. There were no wheels attached, and they did not pivot or point in different directions from what I could tell. They stood fixed as if hard mounted to the ground. There appeared to be supports holding them up on three to five sides, depending on the point of view. A shimmer lit up around them as if they pulled energy out of the air before firing.

The purpose of these giant pieces of artillery unfolded before me.

There was a line behind them of smaller daemons that I thought at first were there to operate the weapons. I could not see the ones close to the walls very well, but the closest one to me was about a mile out. The line of daemons moved and some sort of apparatus on the weapon rotated down and picked up a daemon. It did not even look mechanical in nature, yet it articulated down and grabbed a minion. There was a dim flash of light. The air around it shimmered, and the daemon turned into a mass of goo and defied gravity; it flowed on its own up into the main body of the weapon.

It fired a bolt of energy almost black in color. This streaked towards Heaven and struck the shield in brilliant showers of color. The impact was deafening amidst the rainbow effect lighting up the sky.

I recognized other weapons, some made from a combination of wood and dark metal. The trebuchet weapons were hundreds of feet tall and

159

required thousands of daemons to operate. Large rocks manned were loaded onto the weapon very slowly. The arduous process was over in moments when the massive boulders hit their target miles away. There were thousands of these trebuchets all firing intermittently and some at the same time. The supply train for these monstrous machines trailed back towards me but disappeared below the cliff line below my visibility.

They had been cutting down the mountain.

The ringing of metal came from instruments breaking stone. I figured there were mines or quarries at the base of foothills below me. That explained the unending supply of stone to these weapons.

I saw a few large catapults too, but due to the short range, they were targeted by the wall defenses making them less effective. Several weapons burned in the moments I watched.

New siege engines made their way up from the back line to replace the ones lost which told me there had to be some sort of assembly plant nearby. As I watched, it gave me the feeling that every day the daemon host gained a little bit of ground, even if it was such a small percentage. Over time, that percentage would matter. Production like that had to be effective by now and it certainly explained why I saw no trees anywhere near the army or heaven for that matter. That meant they brought materials from somewhere else and put together here. Those supplied came from far away.

My thoughts began to run rampant. Was there something I could do to disrupt the flow of weapons? Even on a good day, my skills could not face an army. To engage even a few hundred with the horde so close was suicide. There were billions. Yet the siege engines seemed to cause all the damage to the walls and the shields. It might make some sort of difference. I decided to move closer and take a better look. Learning everything about this army and its strengths and weaknesses would be my best offense. Perhaps something of value would avail itself.

Following the ridgeline was easy. I was still hundreds of feet up and so far back behind the enemy's position that it took me quite a while locate my target. Using my cloak would make the time stretch and without a focus point, it would take longer too. I had to move slowly and crawl on all fours at times to avoid some daemons on patrol.

It occurred to me that nothing would come near this area. Wildlife and game had likely consumed. Even the insects were gone with food sources long been depleted. The ground was likely poisoned. Even the air was barely breathable.

Teacher taught me they used breeding to maintain the high numbers of troops. Individual fighters did not likely live very long. Were they eating each other in some kind of ritualistic sacrifice? I was not sure. That was disgusting to think about on both accounts. The horde lacked food and had too many mouths. However, in the end, they grew their own food...by eating each other.

Chaos.

I continued across the top of the ridgeline, moving slowly to not attract the attention of any sort. My familiarity with the ridge grew. I had to double back several times to work my way down and several times had to stand perfectly still so wandering daemons passing within an arm's reach of me without notice. I killed them quick, striking from behind with speed.

Since my weapons tended to kill on the first shot, there was not much noise, simply bodies.

Then I found what I was looking for. From a good distance, one of the big flyers approached my location with something large in its grasp. It did not take a genius to see it was a tree. I lost track of it below the ridgeline and knew there had to be something down there worth spying so crept forward to the edge.

A bush caught my eye with some berries on it, so I scavenged the little morsels before continuing. I felt refreshed even from so few nutrients and was thankful the daemons had missed them for one reason or another. They might not even eat berries. Soon the aftertaste left a tainted flavor in my mouth, and my happiness was gone. Daemons tainted what little food grew here. It affected the plant life which mutated.

Being invisible allowed me to walk right up to the edge and looked down. Below me, was a huge workshop buzzed with activity. It had to have been the main building. Due to my angle, seeing inside was impossible, but the flow of workers going in and out of it was a constant stream. There were many smaller covered buildings scattered around the main one. It surprised me they would care about the sun or the weather for that matter. The horde showed no kindness nor did it have a reputation for it. An assortment of smaller stations had workers operating them, and it appeared these were also small fabrication stations. Around the assembly area, there were catapults in different stages of assembly. Several forges used the branches from the trees. They would burn hot but not as good as coal. Sap would add to the heat. It would take more than that to get a good burn to forge metal.

The large flyer dropped the tree, and immediately creatures that seemed humanoid set upon it. I did not see any slave drivers forcing them to work under the crack of a whip.

That is when I noticed it. They had features that were not human. This group all had huge clawed hands with razor sharp talons, and they shaved the tree of its branches in moments and removed the bark from it equally fast. The branches got drug over and thrown on a fire under some covered section and the bark was gathered. There was a war machine production going on. The whole process amazed me. The process was efficient. The workers cranked the work out rapidly. A brand new catapult rolled off the production line right in front of me. The need to move closer arose to see what else was here. Over the edge, there was a gigantic cave carved back into the mountains roots. I looked left, right, and shuddered, and saw there were a few of these factories right here over the span of what I guess to be about two to three thousand feet.

If I could take out the factory somehow, many of the creatures would die and production slowed, but also killing a bunch of hybrids would be a bonus. It obviously took specialists to create the materials so taking them away would be a blow to their process. It was the best plan I could muster on short notice. My thoughts cranked around in my head.

An idea hit me.

I turned and looked to the mountain behind me and saw many loose stones and boulders at the base of a cliff. Farther up, the granite face showed many cracks in it, probably due to the quarrying of its stone. There must have also been a vein of some sort of metallic ore for all the important parts needed a forge for the braces and supports. The spot was ideal for an ava-lanche, but in order to do it, I would need something to break up the cliff face several thousand feet above me. My swords would take too long and the noise would draw too much attention. It was also taking too long. I needed something that would cause an explosion. It was then the realization of my task hit me.

One of those energy weapons pointed towards the cliff could possi-bly do it. How to accomplish that was still a mystery. My scent needed masking in order for me to go examine one and I would have to see how to get it to turn when firing. In addition, when the firing process initiated I hoped there was nothing to stop it. Next, there was the task of harvesting something from a daemon in order to disguise my scent.

A plan formed in my head.

Finding prey was easy. There was a lot to choose from, so I waited until another daemon wandered close, broke its neck, and cut it open. It did not take too much; the thing stunk so badly, my confidence was enough. I rubbed the ichor on then leapt off the cliff. After dropping like a rock for several hundred feet, my descent slowed at will. My feet touched down right at the base of the cliff. I waited and watched. My cloak reeked. They did not even look my direction. The nearest of the energy weapons was about a mile. They had the range so they kept them farther out. Something told me there was a fragile aspect to them. I looked forward to examining them.

Moments passed. My presence caused no alert to rise. It was time to move. My pace was a crawl, some steps larger than others were. It was slow and steady. I did my best to avoid any other daemons moving around for the first part. They had areas where they stood ready if the city were to break. Farther up, the flyers of all sizes staged. Large rock piles provided shelter from the energy blasts the city fired. Here the shock troops gathered in staging areas. Contact was heavy. Caution was imperative.

My efforts found their reward when I found a line feeding the weapons energy. They moved slowly, which was perfect for my pace. At times, I swore they could sense me but they seemed to be in some sort of trance. Perhaps this was not a choice. I kept moving.

The slow walking in the zombie daemon line had taken forever before I stood near the device. It looked organic in nature, as if it's outer skin was tough but still flexed as it pulsed and was a dark brown, which is why I thought it to be wood. The firing portion of it looked like a cigar except there was a lot of surface texture to it. It was about six feet long and about as big around as a basketball. The weapon stood about fifteen feet high. Pulsating light, very dim, rolled over the surface and the skin rippled again as it reached down and picked up a smaller daemon standing in its line. I realized the arm was actually an appendage of a creature, and it was actually alive and not animated. Large feet grew into the earth to hold it upright; large bulbous places rested near the ground. It consumed the daemons it picked up.

The creature sent out some sort of pulsating signal that must be overriding the daemon's free will. Pressure came off it and the air around it felt heavy. Malnuras told me about synaptic control once. This creature used that. I realized the smaller daemons had no choice but to line up to die.

It made me happy to know they ate themselves but sad that it barely made a dent if at all.

I studied how the legs supported it. They appeared muscular and gripped the dirt. Thoughts cutting a leg off to make it topple in hopes that it would spin around and point backwards before it collapsed grew. The lack of guarantee that it would fall the way I wanted it to lead me to believe that all I would be doing was drawing attention to the area on a gamble. However, if a leg detached, it would topple. My goal was to grab the head and force it to turn right as it fired. That made the most sense. I studied the timing the consumption process took. It would work.

I looked back at the cliff and gauged how high the weapon needed to aim to cause a slide. The creature grabbed a daemon, consumed it, and the process started. It took about to the count of seven from the point it absorbed the energy of the creature it ate and then released the energy. Memorizing the timing was crucial, and I sat and counted as the process went from beginning to end several times. The chain reaction formed from the essence of the daemon before it expunged the energy. I was nervous while thinking about how to do it. The time was now.

Without further delay, I found the leg supporting it near me and looked for some sort of footing. If I did not get it turned in time, another attempt could take too long resulting in a confrontation at the most inopportune time. The second option did not bode well. I waited. It fired. I watched as it picked up another daemon and turned it to goo. The liquid found the breach and flowed inside the creature. I swung and chopped the target leg off and pushed it so it started to topple then jumped up. My legs wrapped around its trunk and my hands grabbed the top and tried to twist. Tendons popped and snapped as it resisted, twisting around towards the cliff. The stress of the top turning tore the outside skin material and ichor sprayed. The creature fell over and I turned the weapon far enough finally and held. It fired, cutting a swath in the cliff face with an explosion but nothing near what it did when it hit the walls around Heaven.

Ichor oozed everywhere and I was covered head to toe, from the initial spray. My cloak still protected me and to my surprise, once the fluid covered me, it disappeared into my cloaking. I stood motionless for a moment to observe the effect before moving off slowly. There were not a lot of places to hide or be not in the way of the ensuing chaos that followed, but I managed to find a tent of animal skin to put my back against while watching the results of my effort. The cliff struck stood strong. Nothing happened and no stones fell to create the desired effect. My first attempt failed.

No daemons came running.

I decided to go for it and moved to the next weapon several hundred feet away. Some of the daemons moved towards where the one just destroyed lay. Some of them laughed, some argued, and a few fought. Chaos formed and for the first time, I thought there was a possibility for success.

I already knew the timing. To force the top around was tough; perhaps if I cut two of the legs before spinning it might be easier. It is not like I needed precision cuts, but twisting the head of this creature may have diminished the energy. I did not know if it was alive in the sense of thinking for itself. None of them moved around or do anything but grab, turn a daemon to energy, and fire. The decision was final. Positioning myself next to a leg, I waited until nothing was looking and sliced it clean. The creature shuddered. My second cut was faster than the first. To free up my hands, I dismissed my swords with a thought.

As it started to fall, I grabbed one of the cut legs and pulled it towards the cliff face. It fought me; all my might was barely enough as if it knew what was about to happen. In the end, it turned without protest. The base of the creature did not attach to the ground, so the topple factor was accentuated by the twisting. The fall was perfect. I grunted while pulling hard and was amazed that the other daemons here did not notice me even cloaked. My speed had to be slow to stay hidden. For them to see a leg held up in that way must have looked strange. Released energy hit the ground with more force than the last. A large explosion rocked the area. Cracking stone echoed off the cliff faces.

I let go of the leg. It spun back the other direction before finding equilibrium to settle. Ichor flowed from the wounds in spurts. The creature groaned and let out a call, a very loud call. Around me, several loose daemons looked for me. I did not dare move. Those looking on began to move over, some of them swinging their claws as they came, testing the very air as they strode, and looking for me. The number of daemons coming my way grew. They had me surrounded and did not even know it. Medium sized flyers began to show up. The risk increased with their presence.

More cracking echoed off the walls.

I was afraid to breathe for a moment. My second attempt had failed again and I was not going to push my luck. It was just then that a large four-legged daemon resembling a dog approached, snapping its oversized maw.

I did not want that thing to bite me. It moved in leaps right at me rather quickly. The darkened pupils of its eyes seemed to be looking right at me. If it could see me there had to be action. I stepped towards it calling my blades. I had no doubts it could see me as it tracked my movements by adjusting its own. My cloaking had failed.

"It sees you." the voices mentally spoke the obvious in their dual tone.

"It is just a large puppy," I said back. "We will succeed."

"Or you will die and that would be sad."

"Quiet, I need to think."

"No, you need to act," they declared.

This creature was huge. It stood twelve feet tall and its head was nearly four feet wide. Powerful shoulders like a pit bull controlled its heavily muscled legs. It had spikes protruding from the ridgeline on its back. They looked like bone and fluid oozed from them, no doubt poison. Black talons on its feet looked equally un-inviting. I closed the distance to kill this thing before my position was any more compromised than it was.

It leapt the last distance. My feet shifted to tilt my body to the side. I could see its right front paw, claws extended out in an attempt to open me up. As I rose upwards from the powerful thrust of my legs, I deflected with my first sword and countered with my second. Sparks flew as metal impacted claws, my second blade bit rather shallow. Considering the force I swung with, my surprise was great. The impact lessened the distance we both flew. I landed short, turned, and re-engaged. So did the creature

My eyes fell to the wounds. They were not as deep as expected. In this camp, how could it be anything but a daemon? Otherwise, the cuts would be worse. The irony hit as it came in fast, and it feigned and dodged, avoiding my blows. That scared me, for it denoted intelligence. I tried to compensate on the second pass when it charged leading with its teeth...my body barely got clear. This thing was faster than the small daemons. The fight would be close. I could win quickly if the others stayed out of it. I ducked and rolled. My daemon protections would do me no good here.

Sparks flew. My parries redirected its front claws again, followed by the teeth. This creature was so fast with its jaws it reminded me of the monsters I found at the river long ago. My blades bit but the damage appeared superficial. They just were not biting hard or fast enough no matter how quick I was, and I was fast. It lunged in again. I blocked and countered. My blade bit deep. It shrugged it off.

"This has to end this quick." A chorus of voices chattered in my head urging me forward. I turned my healing on only to hear, "Why the delay?"

*"My friends, do you mind? If it is not constructive, then silence your-*selves."

"Sorry, we are trying," they said.

"Try harder and remind me sooner. Is it unwise to commit halfheartedly?"
I replied, repositioning myself.

In it came.

I took the hit to get in close.

My blade found its eye; it burst as the tip penetrated.

One claw struck my unguarded abdomen. It had taken my bait, but the price was high as the tremendous impact rocked me. The claws did not penetrate my armor or skin, but broke a few ribs. Breath came labored at first. I was hurt, but focusing past the pain. My continued movement suffered as the rib reset over the next few moments.

"End this now," they replied in chorus.

The creature pulled back, pawing at its wounded eye like a dog, whimpering and snarling at the same time. It put its paw down and looked at me with its remaining eye, trying to focus on me. I stayed on its left side as it circled. Mere seconds had passed since the first exchange. Smaller daemons looked on and got ready to pounce en mass. My eyes fell back to the overgrown puppy as it let out a roar and dove at me headlong. I sucked in a breath and leapt in the air flipping in a barrel roll over its head. Both swords flashed out as I rotated around, finding my target. A flash of ichor ejected from its flesh as my swords scored two hits, taking its remaining good eye. It roared. My smile turned to pain as I landed. My ribs protested. I hissed.

My knees tried to buckle and I reengaged the cloak and winced as my strength left. I did not want to stick around as this creature thrashed around wildly, reaching out in all directions. The attempt felt like a failure until a cracking sound in the distance ran from one side of the cliff to the other end miles away. I smiled. A thunderous roar followed as mountain cliff came down with utter devastation. The ground shook so hard all fell to the ground as waves of energy rolled through the ranks.

An avalanche of rock and dust headed towards the manufacturing area below. A large cloud of dust blocked my view as it hit. The impact was deafening. Debris shattered the building and buried all within at least a mile. Clouds billowed forth, taking visibility from the destroyed area. With the mission accomplished, I chose to move laterally, away from the mass destruction. My creeping walk slowed even more as my path carried me against the tide of the daemons rushing to the afflicted area. Each step brought more pain. I refocused on the healing rune again and felt a little relief. Waiting for the rib to pop back in place, I could not risk making noise for fear of discovery in such close proximity.

That thought did not even finish when it popped.

I winced and sucked air rather loudly, but there was too much chaos in this part of the camp; they were not looking for me. My cloak engaged, but it could not muffle the sound. The camp had no end to it, except where it hit the mountains and ran toward the city walls. Due the size, my path took me into an area unaffected by the destruction. I adjusted my angle toward the ridgeline several miles out of view of the cataclysm. A few daemons rushed about in this area almost running into me. Even though I could slowly move through stationary items, if something hit me, they would feel me.

At least my ribs felt better. With no time reference to how much time had passed since the cliff came down, it was hard to gage how far away I was. Some creatures in this part of the camp headed back towards the ruin. Most of them remained in staging areas.

The sun started to go down now. Moving in the dark in this camp would not be easy so I picked up my crawling pace to a normal walk. I would appear more like a shimmer but with the waning light, the concern was minimal. I picked my way to the edge of the camp where the cliff rose up hundreds of feet and looked up. The top was beyond my sight, so a leap would be a bad idea. There would be many handholds on the way up and spotting them too difficult.

The risk was great, but to wait would be greater. I picked and chose visible handholds that were solid and obvious. My ascent started. An uncomfortable place to sleep was the reality of my situation. There had to be a ledge higher up. The darkness fell quickly but illuminated every time a projectile impacted the walls of heaven. My teacher's wisdom would be welcome as I climbed. His words repeatedly played in my head. Survive! Suddenly, my hand found an outcropping that went back a ways. There was enough room for my body. Heaving myself exhausted over the edge, I lay flat for quite some time.

The night, lit by the bombardment of heaven felt surreal. I started to feel like the composer of the national anthem for the United States did with the sky illuminating over and over. It was not quite the "rockets' red glare" but was close enough. Rainbow effects scattered across the skyline. Some went fast. Others were much slower as the colors mixed and changed. There was always the boom in the distance when the shield absorbed a hit. The vibrations traveled through the ground and up the cliff. Distance did not matter.

"Are you seeing this?" I said mentally. "Can you see this?"

"We can sense it." The lower voice said.

"But through your eyes and thoughts, we can see and experience what you see." The higher voice added. I still did not know which one was which, as they both did the same thing and both said the same things.

"It is so beautiful," I whispered. "Like real fire works!"

I missed home for the first time in a while. My mind drifted. Thoughts of the holiday parade when the Fourth of July came into my mind. I wondered what month it was at home. Was it raining or cold? Did the fate of the world change? Was humankind still on a downward spiral? Were they worth protecting? Were what few friends I had safe?

Friends. The word felt strange and far away.

They made all of this worthwhile. Not the people I did not know but those in my little world. Their safety mattered...though they could never know or possibly understand the expanse of the universe, a universe with issues of its own. Heaven was holding on, barely...God, although his power infinite had his hands full.

My reflecting faded. Suddenly an itch in my mind...The kind I would get before something wrong crashed over me like an ocean wave. I felt I had to be some place. A burning sensation on the back of my neck hit me with an electric jolt and burned my skin. It reminded me of the feeling of receiving runes. I reached back and felt a raised bump on my flesh forming. The area was sensitive. Another rune began to form.

"That's bizarre," I said as the urge to leave increased significantly. A sudden thought of Malnuras came into my mind, and I wondered if he was okay. My vision blurred. I felt sick. I could not shake the thought. The little food left in my stomach was on alert. Fire spread over my skin and enveloped my whole body like flames rolling over my flesh. I wanted to cry out when the weightlessness took over. A fire appeared in front of me, very blurry.

Gravity returned.

Was I hallucinating? Did my mind just shift? The smell of blood was overwhelming. Yet, it was not daemon blood. Crimson with the hint of iron caught my nose. I felt my eyes flutter as I drew in deep breaths. The euphoria played with my mind. Senses became acute. Intoxication overwhelmed me as the need for battle took hold, and I searched for a target. Bodies of daemons lay everywhere in twisted shapes and forms. The corpses were in various stages of damage, from scorched to nearly disintegrated. Some were piles of ash in different stages of losing their cohesive form. Their powdered forms drifted away in the gentle wind.

I was not on the ledge or dreaming.

Somehow, I had just been teleported or transported to the scene of a fight and within seconds, realized it was the campsite...our campsite. The fire pit lay before me smoldering. Panic rose in me as I survey the area, magic flattened the. My last memory of the area was from afar. Fire fell from the heavens consuming a small portion of an incredibly large host. The evidence that it did not bode well for the host was evident. I looked around at the carnage with an open mouth. The very ground was burned so badly there was not even a smell of turned up dirt.

Total devastation surrounded me.

I was both shocked and impressed at the same time for it extended in every direction for thousands of feet. Stones melted. Concern rose as my eyes shifted around the area. Where was he? I began to move around the campsite try to find some sort of sign of him. Emotions swelled for the first time in years. The proverbial lump began to form as I began to breathe rather labored, fighting my reactions back to their origin.

Debris littered the area. Trying to take it all in, I wandered around looking at the remnants of my sleeping mat, the cooking pot, and a small chest with a few of my personal effects. A pile of debris seemed strange. What I thought to be a pile of stones with a burnt tree resting on it was in fact not stones at all. Something was off. Crossing the wrecked clearing, I raced over and threw the fallen tree off with ease. Horrified at the mutilated form of my master, I felt my emotions swell, as if ready to explode. He had fallen where he stood; his robes covered in soil and clotted blood looking like stone.

"The teacher..." my swords spoke aloud...this time in unison. "How is this possible?"

My knees met the ashen soil. An inhuman cry escaped my lips. I pulled him into my lap and fell back on my heels. Tears flowed. All the days of his tutelage flooded my memory as I looked upon his broken body. The lacerations were so horrific that the caked blood had absorbed the dirt kicked up by the battle. He was unrecognizable, his body limp and lifeless. Despair took me quickly. Then I heard a sound. I looked around the clearing. Nothing stirred. It came again. A slight groan had escaped his lips.

Somehow, he was alive.

XII

Retribution

No...no...no...no.

This cannot be happening

Fear crept in. I fought to control the one thing a warrior should be able to master. Looking down at the broken body of my teacher stirred more emotions than my mind could process. I was not prepared to deal with this situation. The very thought that this could happen was unfathomable. Malnuras often took on hundreds of daemons without breaking a sweat. His skill with a weapon was exceptional. The practical application seen in the fire pit allowed me to see situations he could not recreate. Seeing how he leveled the area with magic brought a completely new depth to my teacher.

Even with my limited knowledge of the arcane, I understood the concept of magical power when referencing a being's ability. I had studied wizards and sorcerers before. With raw power and a strong mental fortitude, this kind of devastation was possible. How it worked did not really matter to me. The effects of magic on a battlefield convinced me. Even if the power or abilities employed were minimal, throwing magic around in a battle made enemies falter unless they too had access to the arts. I paid attention during those lessons, because learning about them was important because the enemy had many tricks.

With his ability to deftly wield a weapon and use magic in his favor, I concluded that Malnuras must have been some kind of hybrid. I smiled for a moment, forgetting the pain in my heart. He was always full of surprises.

His wrist registered a faint pulse. Hundreds of cuts caked with dirt and blood covered his body. I gently rubbed the filth from around his eyes. Unsure of what to do, I decided to use the water skin to clean him up. Setting him down gently, I searched for the skin. It took a moment to locate, and, to my surprise, it still contained fluid.

The scorched outside of the water skin was brittle. A reminder the entire area experienced holy fire that teacher pulled from the sky. I tore off a piece of my clothing off, moistened it, and began to wipe away the dirt. With each wipe of the cloth, his blood flowed again. Within minutes, I was frustrated because he was bleeding again. This was not acceptable. How could I stop him from bleeding out?

We had herbs for healing that could help stop bleeding. He had a satchel on him still that contained such items. It was empty as if it had either been scattered around the camp or used up. There were a few shavings inside but nothing close to the amount needed. I had a hard time seeing. Every few seconds things got blurry. Was it possible my vision affected by teleporting? Why were my eyes not working? I rubbed at them in frustration, and continued feverishly working to clean Malnuras's wounds. After a few moments, it was obvious tears made it hard to see.

Emotions this strong rarely plagued me. Tears occasionally came, but never accompanied by these emotions. The sensation was very weird and distracting, especially since it obscured my vision. My frustration grew and the tears flowed even more. Focus was just outside of my grasp. I refused to lose my teacher and friend in a battle that he should have been able to win alone.

My memories slipped back to the day it happened. The numbers I saw coming that day were way less than the bodies and piles of ash as far as my eyes could see. He must have faced numbers that were greater than he imagined they would send. The mass of the horde was as impressive as it was terrifying. That did not change the outcome of this battle, though. He was at death's door. What could I do? He was slipping away right in front of me.

Pain from the emotions made my chest hurt.

The air was very stale. It was as if the oxygen burned away. There was a taint in the air. Smoke blanketed the area and made it difficult to look around the camp while attending to Malnuras's situation. The answer eluded me. Hope faded. The attack obliterated our camp. Getting mad would not help. My emotions danced one the edge of undeniable rage. I put pressure on an area of a particularly nasty cut after cleaning it. The crimson kept flowing. Knowing it was his blood shut my lust for battle down right away. My failure hovered over me like a dark cloud; his life force faded. His blood further fed the dirt on which he lay. No more attempts to clean wounds would be wise. That would only accelerate his death. The issue settled itself. I could not save him.

Memories spilled into my conscious thoughts. My arrival here in this world opened my eyes to so much. Earth and Heaven were no longer mysteries to me. I thought back to my early lessons and how badly Malnuras defeated me, with almost effortless ease. It was more like getting your ass kicked by a single finger that kept poking holes in your body and actually causing wounds. Never did I think that such grace and skill could exist in such a dichotomy of a creature. I knew now he was not fully man. He neither moved nor behaved like any human. Nothing could be proven one way or another. At this moment, his secrets did not matter. Saving his life was all I had. With each passing moment, I felt is life force waning.

The blood on my hands mixed with layers of mud and grime. While the dirt was just a coating on the outside, but my failure was too much to carry. Why did the pursuing horde target him? I had to find a way to exonerate myself. Even though keeping my teacher alive was not my mandate, letting him die would be detrimental. His absence would do far more damage. It did not even matter that I made a small dent in the siege works anymore, or that I had first-hand intelligence of Heaven's plight. It would all be for nothing if Malnuras fell.

He stirred.

"Teacher, can you hear me?" I put my hand on his face to clear away more of the grime. A moan followed by a cough. I watched his body tremble. Was this a ray of hope?

"Tell me what to do. Tell me how to fix you. I do not know how." I noticed one of his eyes creep open and the pupil itself rolled back up in his head. He tried to focus on me but to no avail. My frustration grew, turning to anger again. Why did he send me away? Why did he not let me stand with him even if it meant my end?

My hand cleaned more dirt and blood away from his face when I felt an irritation on my skin in the area of one of my runes. It pulsed for several times before I noticed the sensation originated at a specific rune. The itch turned to pain, and it felt like another rune carving itself into my skin. Energy flowed from my core and rolled out to my hands in waves.

Bright light almost blinded me as my hand began to glow. A searing sensation on my healing rune spread over the entire area. Pain intensified. Energy continued to flow. Heat emanated from my hands like the heat rolling off the campfire; my skin began to burn. The light turned from white to blue. A void started in my abdomen and began to pull from my other extremities as it headed toward my glowing hand. Pins and needles hit me everywhere. I cried out. The pain got worse. Everything blurred.

Balance failed. My knees buckled. Cold sweat poured from my skin. Energy siphoned from me, much like the creatures I just met. Pain gave way to numbness. My senses reeled. Serenity took over; my surroundings spun.

The urge to vomit hit me but I kept my food down, probably because there was little to nothing in my stomach. I had to hold onto my core strength. My eyelids felt heavy. They crept down, trying to cover my eyes while I fought to remain conscious. Limbs shook. Reality felt like it shifted and becoming something else.

The battle to hold myself up was lost. My strength failed. Face down in the dirt I fell.

Blackness.

* * *

Dirt tastes different from all over the realm. My unique perspective on this qualified as an opinion in my eyes. When I was younger, dirt got in my mouth often. It had a unique taste that you cannot identify...although not something that I would recommend personally. This mud, ripe with the spilled blood of daemons, tasted disgusting.

The very taint of daemon that was saturating the ground got deep inside. It was just like rotten food mixed in with food that was not rotten. You can tell it is there and even taste the foulness or the mold, but you cannot see it directly. I gagged and tried to breathe without getting more of the vile dirt in my mouth. My motor functions were not working thus raising my head away from the nastiness was not possible. I just lay there, trying to minimize my exposure.

Moments passed. Beyond that, it became difficult to maintain consciousness. My strength was still gone and showed no signs of returning. At one point, sleep took me. When my eyes opened, disorientation made the ground spin beneath me. I felt like someone had kicked me in the stomach repeatedly. Suddenly I remembered Malnuras and fought to roll myself over. It took everything to muster enough to force my muscles to cooperate as I dug my hands into the foul earth and forced myself to rise. Gravity gave me the final boost I needed as my vision cleared.

Malnuras's was gone!

Did he die? He was gone. I could see the print in the dirt where his body used to be. The camp was silent. Light ash fell like snow from the clouds. The sky looked gray. The land wore it like a blanket. Unease came over me. My eyes panned the countryside to see if there was some sign of my teacher. The thought of something or someone wandering into camp and stealing his body seemed unbearable. Perhaps his body vanished. My lessons had shown me this was possible with some creatures of myth. Looking about at the ashen landscape, I saw no immediate clues. I tried to imagine what the life of such and individual would have been truly like. Sure, I had seen the campfire runes that showed me a lot of Malnuras's involvement. It did seem odd to me that I did not find him in bear form. Perhaps he only used that form with the humans he did not wish to frighten. Maybe he did not have to change into the bear. Maybe he could not cast magic in that form. My mind raced in too many directions at once.

I closed my eyes and focused on finding my center. Failure weighed heavily still. My mind relaxed, clearing itself of uncertainty. There had to be something I could have done differently. It was the typical guilt that a warrior feels when his honor is tainted. Although this had happened to countless warriors, it did not make it any easier to deal with.

One deep breath...then another...what to do? Malnuras and my master Mathias were everything to me here. We had only visited one village. No one really knew me. I had no ability to go anywhere other than where my feet cou...

I caught myself mid-sentence. It hit me sideways like a sledgehammer swung by a drunken Minotaur. Somehow, I had teleported myself to this campsite. Two new runes adorned my body. One of them brought me here. My body had somehow created it. The runic network was adapting..

"Find your master." How my swords always seemed to speak the obvious as if reading my mind was taking some getting used to. As if they could read my mind. Yes, we had a telepathic link, but how is it that my swords gave me logistical advice? Realization came to me that my swords were not just an extension of my body, but also an extension of my mind. They could think on their own. I would never be alone again.

"Do you know what happened?" I asked aloud, obviously angry at their silence during the loss of my teacher.

"We also have an unconscious state like you, when our energies are depleted. We shared in your plight to save you from further harm," they responded. "We know nothing of what has befallen the teacher. Find your master."

"Then I thank you for your efforts in this. I apologize if I snapped at you both."

"Nothing needed." said the lower voice. "We share your concern."

I had to get to Mathias.

Meditation was a skill I had learned early on. The ability to focus my energy on a singular task, object, or skill had been the aim of much of my training. It was difficult at first: trying to calm myself and find my center. Many failures had happened, before I learned to block out the ambient noises of myself. The smallest sound could derail meditation.

Once I learned to get past myself, the ability to block out the sounds while remaining aware of them was the last step. No warrior wants to be surprised. Sneaking up on me was bad for one's health. Well in truth, I never really could hurt Malnuras, even if I wanted to. It was almost like a trigger in my mind. Even when he found a way past my defenses, it was never as bad as it could have been.

In return, I just could not hurt him. He made it a point to try to sneak up on me. When he was successful, I still acted, for its better to act then to react. My action was to tap him with a hand, not to strike him hard. This had been our game for years, and I had finally mastered it.

I had learned to control pain using meditation and focus, and every injury was another opportunity to practice this technique. Malnuras taught me that being able to focus the healing energy while hurt made the healing happen stronger and faster. I used this focus to execute my next move.

I sat with my eyes closed, drinking in the surrounding landscape of sounds. My thoughts came into focus on each individual noise around me and then added it to the list of safe noises that I could ignore. No creatures moved here as the scorched earth scared them away. The predominant noise was the fractured earth still shifted due to the amount of magic fired off in the immediate area. Everything settled. When destructive magic happens, the soil can heave in protest. Magic may be normal, but it is still not natural. Most that wielded it had an affinity for nature magic as well as the true arcane…both equally deadly.

The sound of falling ash was the smallest noise of all, but because there was a lot of it coming down it had an orchestra of sounds all to its own. It sounded like rain. There was a small comfort in that realization for I enjoyed sitting in the rain to meditate when possible. It added a challenge to the aspect and the focus was more intense. Even though it was not the same, as soon as the sound association processed, I was able to cross that off my mental list as I fell into meditation. My focus was Mathias.

I started with his face. The memory of meeting him the first time and how chiseled his features were, like those of a Greek god. He had

185

strength in ways that I did not understand at the time. His very stride was that of a man that could kill you with his mind effortlessly. He had taught me that battles began in the mind...win or lose. I began pulling in all my remembrance of him. A cohesive thought finally formed. His voice came forward for me next out of the sensory aspect that my memory recalled. My master impressed me in everything he did.

I remembered hearing his voice the first time. It did not even sound human. The harmonics that made up his words were in perfect rhythm and cadence. Even for a warrior that had seen countless battles and had seen wonders and horrors, his voice never changed tempo unless he chose for it to. He controlled his excitement and recollection of his achievements whenever he spoke. There was an authority in his voice, and you hung on every word, for it was soothing at the same time. It reached into your soul and showed you a platter of confidence, yet it made you work for everything and handed you nothing. It inspired fear and confidence at the same time. Thinking of it now brought a small twinge that I had to force back. I did not realize how much I missed him.

My focus intensified as the pieces started to come into full view. His presence saturated my senses. He towered over me in the beginning, for my growth took a while to complete. Like a giant of legend, he cast a long shadow. The fondness I felt made me want to bow as if he were royalty from some distant land. Yet he led men into war, which is something that dukes and barons do not do. I still remembered seeing him swing his blade for the first time and the ease with which it passed through the leg of his target.

My thoughts narrowed to one word. *Extraordinary!* He was an example to me on every level of the type of man to strive to be. I smiled and opened my eyes. The singular picture in my thoughts began to grow and my focus shifted from pain to purpose. I stood and turned around slowly. His presence was everywhere. It enveloped me, growing larger and larger. It felt as if we both occupied the same space. Something was pulling me in the opposite direction than Malnuras had thrown me.

I paused and released my thoughts of Mathias for a moment. I returned my focus to Malnuras. Memories evoked emotions, yet I did not feel the same response as before. I felt nothing. That worried me greatly. I had no sense of where to look for him and no idea where to start. It was as if he were dead. Could he be? Why would he leave me here? I could not let those thoughts creep back in.

My goal was clear.

My mind shifted back to Mathias. Within seconds, I had the feeling that my master was back. The feelings were strong. I did not know what to do next so I locked in on wanting to be where my master was. This feeling of elation built within me, and the teleport rune started to heat up. The sensation intensified to a climax, but nothing happened.

I started to despair and felt doubt grow in my mind like a throbbing sliver. The focus began to bleed off. Trying not to get angry or let my emotions control me, I concentrated on a new idea.

I had not imagined me actually going to him. No sooner did the idea form than I felt my vision blurred like before. My balance shifted and I was off. This time, however, it was instant. There was no build up from the rune, nor was there any pain or nausea. The campsite simply vanished from sight. I could see nothing. My hope grew.

Solid ground appeared under my feet. Air moved rapidly around me like in a vortex, but it did not tear at me the way a tornado would. Air-flow stopped. My eyes focused and my ears adjusted to the sounds of battle. Called from their place on my back, my swords instinctively hit my hands.

My eyes panned my surroundings. I found myself atop an enormous wall. It was several hundreds of feet wide and had crenels on each side of it. In front of me, great golden buildings disappeared thousands of feet above in the clouds. The architecture was incredible as if I had stepped back in time to gothic designs that adorned every building in certain periods of history. I was in awe of such a sight, but my focus was on my mission and did not allow time for distractions. To my left and right, I heard the familiar sounds of the horde attacking. My eyes panned. Winged "men" and "women" were engaged in battle with swords all around me. They wore beautifully adorned armor and the weapons glowed with some type of energy. Combat was intense. The horde's foot troops seemed temporarily contained to one large area. The locust daemons died by the hundreds, but the numbers were too great... In they swept like a tide.

The energy field was right in front of me, changing colors like a rainbow. I had just seen this very same field not long ago. *This time I was on the inside.* I glanced around and saw the towers on the wall also disappeared into the cloud miles above me. I gasped as the magnitude of this structure assaulted my senses.

I stood on the fortified walls of the City of Heaven. Daemons killed angels by the hundreds every moment. My mind stopped. Everything inside me froze. Hell invaded. Heaven buckled beneath the onslaught. Impossible!

The horde had broken through the protective shield.

XIII

The Wall

With flaming blades in motion, I scythed the first of my attackers clean in half. Three more met a similar fate in the next few strokes. All died in a bloody mess faster than they could turn to engage me. The bodies burned from the holiness in my blades. Even the blood burned away.

I was just getting started. Daemons were getting a foothold on the wall, like a beachhead when a country invades the shores of another. They held a small section of the wall. That was all they needed to allow the fliers to get into the air. The blood lust took me to a place of controlled rage. Vengeance drove a righteous spike of fury into my heart. They had taken Malnuras and now Heaven was wide open. Nothing could make things even. Tens of thousands of them needed to die today to begin to cover the debt. My swords could not move fast enough. There were a few surprised looks from the winged beings when I strode up next to them and stole their kills.

I fought alongside angels!

They bore a strong resemblance to pictures I had seen as a child. The Grecian physique chiseled to perfection adorned with wings, ornate golden armor, and a beautiful weapon wreathed in flames. They were almost as tall as I was with little variation in height. Long lochs of braided hair of all shades, very Norse-like, fell upon the back their plate of armor. Most had great helms that also had a winged pattern on them. Several sported shields while others had two-handed weapons, like axes, spears, and mighty swords. All were amazingly graceful and warrior-like as they threw themselves methodically at the horde.

Sporadic glances around me revealed I was the only dual wielder. My weapons sang a deadly dance. Dozens more daemons died and I was catching them two and three at a time. The controlled rage turned to strategy. Hundreds of daemons fell by my hand in the first minutes. Cheers erupted as the masses fell. The momentum carried me. Faster and faster my hands went. The horde was not thinning by any means.

I hoped there were some wizards working on that shield. Someone had to repair it while the combatants dealt with the insurgents. "Why was God not defending the city?" I thought. Perhaps something happened to distract him, or maybe the horde finally hit the walls of Heaven with enough force to punch through. I knew the answer to that question was not relevant right now, but it mattered. The question occupied my thoughts for several minutes while I cut swaths of death through the nasty creatures closing in all around me.

I had not even turned my own protections on. In my rage, all I wanted was for them to perish, and I did not care what happened to me in the process. It took several hits on me and some major blood to flow and fill my boot before the realization hit home. My stubbornness hurt me more at times then the enemy did. There were allies around me to protect. Training was over. Today counted.

Bodies of angels littered the wall and started to pile up.

Medium sized fliers formed the core, but mainly ground runners of the small to medium variety were swarming. The Defenders appeared to stand strong. Hundreds of the flyers flew out into the city and disappeared every moment, but I was not paying attention to them. My foes all around died by the thousands as the forces of Heaven marshaled and we advanced. I could see the breach now in the distance; it was far away and very, very big.

It took several hours of fighting before I got close enough to the breach to realize that it was not what it appeared to be. The horde weakened the shield enough to allow magic to do more than simply creating an opening; it allowed the hordes to enter. It was a true portal and it was bigger than I imagined it could be. Siege weapons continued to pound and weaken the city's shield. Small openings, the size of my fist, were fluxing open and closed. Occasionally a stone projectile from outside would pass through. It was getting dire. With the horde pouring through and the projectiles smashing away at Heaven, I had all but forgotten my reason for being there. Mathias had to be somewhere close.

He was nowhere around. I could not risk disengaging to look for him. The attack was too intense. Chances were we would find one another in the middle of the horde and end up in a back-to-back fight like I had always imagined. Even alongside each other, the chance of failure was feasible. Eventually, those defending would tire, and the invading numbers would be unending. My faith in the skills of the angelic hosts renewed as I saw the ferocity in their fight. I had seen warriors lead with valor and command men with ferocious courage.

I found myself barking out commands to form lines and stand fast.

The portal was about five yards across and it flowed like a waterspout fully open. They poured through faster than could be measured, hundreds every few seconds. My skill at gauging the size of a host was good, which scared me. It was as if hell opened up on Heaven through a fire hose, which simply kept flowing.

The horde owned the sky.

Arrows and bolts would occasionally kill a daemon on the wall, but mostly the Archers focused on the sky. Angels tried to fight them in the air, but gangs of daemons descended upon them before they could get very far. The archers were far more effective in taking them out in flight, for they aimed at the entire cloud of daemons blanketing the sky. Dozens of daemons fell with every volley. Flyers increased every minute the portal spewed forth reinforcements. The tide was starting to turn in their favor.

A thing of beauty floated across the sky. Her sword glowed with gold light, and her wings beat heavy and strong. She wore the purest of white garments, fluttering behind her like snowy fire. I did not see any armor. Her blue eyes locked on mine, and I could see the concern on her face. She flew down to the wall to join the battle, unprepared in my opinion. At once, a giant clawed hand plucked her from the air. It was one of the large wingless daemons. The monster bit her head clean off and screamed. It threw her body at the line of archers in a distant tower, hitting several. Another angel fell at my feet, headless. Two more dropped nearby, their wings gone. My heart raced.

Heaven was losing.

On the wall, angels fell in uncountable numbers. Even though more filled their spots on the line, the fight was dismal. We pressed to get to the breach. I never thought I would see an angel get its wings torn from her back. It took two of the medium flyers to grab it and make a wish. A sickening rip sounded out before there was a shower of red. The angel did not fall but continued to fight the best she could. My stomach turned to see her bleeding out. Such beauty covered in gore. She killed one of the flyers that had one of her wings. The second fell from my sword. Her legs began to buckle and I grabbed her arm.

"Fall back and get some healing," I said trying to not to sound as if I was giving an order to an angel.

"My Lord, the healers were the first to fall."

"Wait, you mean to tell me they hit the healers first?"

"Yes my Lord."

"Can you heal yourself?"

She nodded. "It will take some time, but I can stop the bleeding."

"Go then. There is no reason to lose your life if you can live to fight another day." She begrudgingly started to walk away and fell flat on her face. They ripped her apart when a sudden wave of attackers surged forward. My body wanted to puke and fought back the pain from witnessing such evil. Until now all of the carnage I witnessed was against me. Even though the creatures in the forest died, I did not witness much of it. Angels were dying by the hundreds. How many could Heaven spare?

My attention turned back to the horde. I could not believe what I heard. The enemy not only breached the shields, but they managed to target the ones who can keep the guardians fighting...healers. Their gift was to give their life energy to the wounded. Depending on the skill level of the healer, each one could help dozens. Healing was all they did. Then they slept, and could do it again the next day. Something was seriously wrong. I needed to find Mathias fast or I felt we would lose this battle. Time was up.

Next to me dozens of daemons imploded and turned to dust. A flash of light and another group went down in a large swath. My eyes focused on decorated and prestigious armor suddenly visible. A blade, glowing bright, flashed out taking dozens of the denizens again. I could feel the heat just like when a fire roars to life. Its reach was incredible. Fire leapt from the end as it rose and fell extending the killing zone by several feet.

An officer of some kind stood a dozen feet before me wearing ornate armor and a winged helm. His chiseled features were obvious from under his helm that looked Spartan by design. His wings tucked in tight allowing his movement to be fluid in tight ranks. Behind him was a host of angels dressed the same. A new legion arrived that looked like battle hardy veterans. As the leader strode up to me, another strike took down an even larger group that simply vaporized. He nodded to me.

"Where is Mathias?" I shouted.

"Who?"

"Mathias, he is my master...I must find him."

His hand raised and point towards the center of the breach. All I saw was swarms of daemons flying now where the fighting was heaviest. Somehow it did not surprise me to learn the location of my master. My destination was clear. The horde surged suddenly again and the portal tore open farther. The uncontrolled flow turned into a deluge filling the skies. A wave of daemons slammed into the veterans and decimated the ranks as if breaking on sand. The angelic formation folded in on itself as they turtle shelled. Still outside, the commander stood before me still swinging his mighty blade at the tide in utter defiance.

"Turn around and fall back, you are going to die." Blood flowed freely from his wounds.

"This is what we do, my Lord." With that, he and these men threw himself in to a swarm of daemons and began to take them apart by the hundreds. It did not matter. Their sacrifice was tragic, but in war, people died...throw enough bodies at the machine to win. Most of the time it was sheer numbers that won over strategy. Spinning several times with blades out wide to clear my area, I turned my attention back to where Mathias was said to be and advanced. Daemons re-engaged me, a wide swath formed as they fell to righteous fury. Strikes rose and fell rhythmically with each step. I almost did not feel any resistance anymore when my blades connected with a target. Like a knife through butter, they passed unhindered. It was a bit over stated but now that I was actually doing it, but the statement to be true.

The top of the wall was slick with angelic blood. Angels continued to fall, adding to the mire of daemon ash blended with heavenly blood. The duet in my head spoke.

"Unleash us. The time is right." Amidst my swings, I inquired what my companions meant. An image filled my head of a flaming arc of energy decimating even more of my foes, extending off the tips of my blades like the blade the veteran commander had. Each swing felt as if time stopped and the path of destruction was incredible. The fallen were beyond count. Focus rushed forward in my mind. My blades had a request to empower them.

A vortex of death surrounded me.

Energy flowed up the blades. My hands felt like they were in an oven. I knew that feeling. Something was about to change. The same effect seen on that veteran officer's blade leapt from mine on my next attack. A primal yell came from my lips as the pain in my hands reached its max like before. Thankfully my blades did not slip one iota. The daemons engaging the angels around me turned to look giving the host time for a few free shots.

My next attack cleaved many of them in two; an arc of energy shot away from the blade as it cut and I watched in surprised satisfaction and this energy continued through several ranks of them. A hundred easily died with that swing. The next felled even more and opened a swath several yards deep. No bodies remained of those just killed...holy fire decimated them before they hit the ground. Renewed vigor came over me, and I fell upon my foes even faster and harder.

In front of me a wall of daemons crawled away from me in an attempt to retreat. Stacked at least four high, they moved like the tide crashing on the beach. The form rolled away from me. Few left behind died without effort. Suddenly the horde in front of me thinned. A wave of energy knocked them aside. A suit of bright armor unstained by the death, appeared, and disappeared as the battlefield flowed. The color was a blend of gold and blue. Not a speck of blood touched it. My eyes hurt to gaze upon it for more than a moment. I did not know if it was how it caught the light or the power contained within. I lost sight of him again and fought hard towards his direction.

Hundreds of the large ones were all over him. It was clear the main host broke through. The tide parted again. I could see it...this portal was massive. I found it odd that the largest of the multi-legged daemons came through last when they could have wreaked more havoc had they been first. Perhaps the smaller ones were harder to control, as they were more animalistic than the bigger smarter ones.

"Or Fodder!" the duet chimed in response to my thoughts.

Daemons disintegrated in front of me, felled by Mathias. His mighty swings felled several of them, but they did not go down as easy. They took the hits from the great sword he wielded as if he was swatting them with its flat side. The blade was not the same one he carried during training. It was twice the size and flashed as if made of energy itself. Yet he could not cut these down as he had the lesser before. The host parted as if something pushed through from behind. Several large monsters appeared with thick black blades, standing easily over ten feet tall. He engaged them without hesitation. They parried his attacks almost with ease as the blades did not break and turned his attacks aside. More appeared and surrounded him.

My master was in trouble.

His stance suggested he was trying to withdraw. As I approached, fighting my way through the shifting battlefield, something caught my eye that I had never seen. He had majestic wings...huge and beautiful. They shone brightly as if they exuded power and occasionally extended, bashing the horde away. The angels I had fought along did not command the same kind of presence-that is when I truly realized what he was and smiled.

Mathias was an Archangel. Even under the threat of being overrun, he gracefully backed away where anyone lesser would have lost hope. He parried and attacked in the same strike. I had never seen this move before. My jaw dropped in awe seeing him unleash. Several of them went down, but the hundreds advanced with more coming through the portal. The next wave arrived.

They were even bigger than the ones we were fighting.

I moved towards him, studying his movements to anticipate his retreat, carving my way in that direction. The large daemons tried to parry my first few attacks. With their eyes wide with terror, they fell by the dozens now with each swing, black swords cleaved and broken in half. The carnage inflicted upon my foes was unfathomable. Today was to be the day that retribution balanced the ledger.

I got within several yards and called out, "Master, it is Tathlyn, fall back to your left and I will meet you."

"What are you doing here? You should be with your teacher!" he hollered over his shoulder as he spun a few times to give himself some room before falling back the few yards allowing me to reach him. A small lull in the tide gave us a few seconds. I was not wearing a helmet, whereas he had to flip his up and gave me a bloody smile. "It is good to see you, but what are you thinking leaving your teacher?"

The sensation rolled up to my neck and back to my hands, adding to the rune already forming. Mathias raised his eyebrows as I made a funny expression. Air expelled from my lung as the energy released into my blades. I swung hard at the same time...they simply blew to pieces and continued to combust as they hit the ground...leaving no trace. My jaw dropped and so did Mathias's.

"That's new!" he yelled as he began to engage new targets.

"I know. It just happened. A lot has happened today." I felt a twinge. A lot truly had happened today. My mind raced back to what cause all of this, and I thought at that moment that I had seen a lot of the horde coming as they darkened the skies. The horde attacked the strange creatures with the tentacles for arms. Their method of catching and killing was unique. To round out the day and my getting swallowed and then finding the siege of heaven from the other side and seeing the horror that stood at its gates. I did not know where to begin with him, so I started at the end.

"Malnuras is dead or missing." I choked on the words. This was painful in ways that I truly could not fathom at that moment.

"What? What happened out there?"

"The same thing that happened in here happened to us out there." My flesh seared hot causing severe pain and I growled to quell it down. It moved to my forehead. The heat was intense. My knees buckled for a moment, and then I realized this was the moment. I did not want to look back today in regret. My feet stayed strong and my arms continued to fight as this new rune formed. I wanted to curse the timing of it but knew that events triggered the changes so I bit my tongue and kept swinging. It must have been a few seconds of silence as we both continued to end daemon lives and move closer to the portal.

How I even attempted before in training had to be my teacher's influence. That day in that town where the daemon fled and Malnuras called me back. It was puzzling. I felt the rune near completion as my gifts adapted. A voice chimed in my head, the duo of swords always spoke at the most in opportune time, but the wisdom was usually mind blowing.

"It was an illusion," they said. The pieces finally fit now.

"Huh!" I said, rolling a few more heads.

"What did you say?" Mathias barked.

"Nothing. Just a realization."

"Can you close that thing? It is a portal designed to penetrate into Earth and they managed to open it here. How did they pull that off?" he asked, causing me to shoot him a quick look. My head nodded slowly before the words came out. I did not know why the answer was yes until I finished a double swing attack that cut even deeper into the ranks of the horde. My new rune was the final piece of the puzzle that allowed me to do so, but I had no idea how. As my blade rose and fell, I looked through my memory for the knowledge of how to approach the task ahead. No sooner had the idea hit my mind...did I find it. Just as fast as I could think it, the dark edges of the rift starting to destabilize like a flat piece of paper on a pond and a whirlpool formed beneath it. Only the whirlpool was the rift and it started to fall in on itself near the edges. Slowly at first, little rips in the fabric that held it open formed first and the hole simply got smaller as it folded in on itself.

We kept fighting. Daemons continued to crawl or fly out of the portal. The flow did reduce significantly as the opening shrank. It allowed me to get a better look beyond the opaque curtain. To my surprise...my eyes adjusted to the dim light on the other side. A huge winged daemon with a huge nasty sword gazed at me. He was about twenty feet tall and was disgustingly muscled with what looked like pestilent flesh. His skin festered with nasty wounds…vapor rose from them. I could not even tell if there was a gender and almost did not care. Huge horns adorned the head like a crown of bone that had blackened tips dripping some sort of fluid. One large horn protruded from his head like a bastardized version of a Unicorn. The huge wings looked leathery and incapable of sustaining flight, but I knew better. They could fly with disproportionate wings.

It stood behind a rock pile. A smaller daemon on all fours stood atop of some human. Arcane like symbols were scratched and scrawled on the stones and gave off tremendous energy. The smaller daemon fed on this poor soul. Its toothy maw formed a smile dripping with blood as it looked up at me. Blood ran from open wounds on the humanoid, down the rocks into pools that spread out from my vision from there. A sudden shiver hit when I realized they were using blood magic to open this portal into the same plain, something not thought possible. I lost sight of the ground as the portal got smaller and the burning sensation on my skin increased. My energy flowed throughout my body towards the portal now. I could see it plain as day. It was still hard to maintain focus on memorizing what I saw.

I leveled my sword at the large daemon in a challenging gesture. A garbled, throaty sounding voice hollered out one single word, "Amduscias." and pointed to its own chest as if bragging its name to me as the portal closed. The folding of the fabric became exponential as it fell in on itself, and within a few moments was gone with a small popping sound. I stood there for a moment processing what just happened when a few daemons tried to attack me and but my protections repulsed them. I turned my head and looked at them with what felt like a burning hatred. They were no longer using themselves as a sacrifice to gain access to places. How they found a way to do so and open a portal in Heaven, which God himself protected, was unfathomable.

After thousands of years, a breach in Heaven's walls finally happened.

The small measure of achievement in closing my first portal dissipated as the memory of the humanoid haunted me. The view of the poor soul on the rock pile clung to my heart, making it heavier than ever. A hand on my shoulder pulled my thoughts back to the present. I looked up and caught the smiling eyes of my master. He extended his hand to me and shock took hold for a moment. No one made such a gesture to me since before for I was a student of the two men in my life, not equal. This was a gesture of respect. I hesitated while looking at him, not realizing it was dead silent around me.

The tide turned. With the portal's closure, the larger, harder to kill daemons began to fall faster to the regular angels that now formed a ring around my master and me. They crashed up the angelic host and broke while the power of heaven began to weaken the horde's might. With cries to the almighty they fell on the invaders with renewed vigor.

My master stared at me. I took his hand and a deafening cheer erupted around me. Voices from all around in one accord began to chant something that I did not realize was my name. My eyes fell upon the faces of those on the wall fighting not for their lives but for the very existence of the promise of life after death. I saw smiles that were beautiful and delicate, not just the warriors of heaven covered in daemon blood. Just when I thought my shock was over, Mathias, still holding my hand, raised it up high and hollered something.

"The savior of Heaven! The Defender has arrived." A host of angels all bent a knee, and silence followed. Not even the fighting on the wall near or far was heard for a moment. Thoughts escaped me. Standing there with my hand raised by my master, I was speechless. My mouth found no response as the angels began to rise still nodding and bowing to me. I did the only thing I could think of and placed my fist over my heart like a salute in Roman time seen a hundred times in the fire pit. Moments passed as those alive, behind the line of engagement, policed up the dead. The battle pressed forward, sweeping the walls. Angels reclaimed the skies, hunting the tens of thousands of fliers now trapped. The energy weapons on the walls turned inwards; vaporizing them mid-flight as panic ensued.

Watching the airborne carnage take place, my eyes caught the splendor of the city for the first time. Surreal was the view as I stood overlooking the city. It was true. The towers and buildings were made of gold. The light glinted off them like a rainbow when I realized that was the shield reflecting off them. I walked to the edge, and a mile or so down, I could see the streets crowded with little dots. They moved about their afterlife with no real concern, considering there was an invasion at hand.

Time passed. Angels thinned the horde. They dropped down from the sky like the helicopter leaves from a tree back home. They spiraled as they fell. Many turned to ash, leaving a trail as their bodies broke apart. The cities defenses, both angelic and arcane, completed their task. Losses were staggering.

"Not what you expected?" a familiar voice said. I turned suddenly and was looking at a man that looked and sounded like Malnuras, but with a different demeanor. He wore armor, but not like the angels on the wall. His breastplate was made of cloth like mine and had pieces on his shoulders that looked as though they held the garments in place. His bracers were gold, decorated with angelic symbols. The decorated hilt of a sword peaked over his right shoulder. I studied his features, amazed by how much he resembled Malnuras. I felt a twinge, as if looking at my teacher, and bowed low.

"The wall is safe. The portal is sealed," I said, standing. "I just got here a little bit ago, Teacher. So many ha..." He raised his hand as if to cut me off from speaking and turned away. I knew that lesson so I fell silent and waited for further instructions. He, however, did not speak; it was as if he was listening to something and was simply keeping me quiet so he could hear. In silence we waited. A few moments later he turned back to me. Mathias stood at my side, silent as well. He did not even appear as if he was in a battle because his armor did not have any daemon blood or bits on him. He glowed.

"Tathlyn, your presence is appreciated and turned the tide in the city's favor. We have a situation that has come to our attention that we need to have rectified." He did not show much concern in his voice or expressions, but the words he used carried a lot of weight with me. I stared at him and tried to get past the resemblance to Malnuras.

All I could say was, "Who are you?" I felt a pressure from his gaze, unlike any other intense stare. My mother used to give me that look when I was in trouble or when she really wanted me to focus. This had something else to it. Perhaps it was his resemblance. Maybe it was his position, for he was obviously important. He had a presence even bolder than my teacher and a commanding stature even more robust than Masters was. It struck me perhaps they were brothers or maybe because they served Heaven that they came from the same family. I did not know what to think, but I noticed he did not answer my question. He just stared at me. My unease grew a tad as his eyes bore into me.

"I do not have time to explain myself to you, Defender. I need you to be somewhere now. Do you not feel the matter pressing?"

He meant what he said. No sooner did he speak the words and my energy surged. It was the same feeling from before when I focused on finding my master. The need to be somewhere else right away arose. It hit me with such a strong feeling that I had a hard time focusing on his words. His lips kept moving. I had to play the words back mentally while he continued to speak. He had said, "Malnuras is in trouble." That was all I needed to hear.

"You need to get out there and find him before it is too late. No one else can do this, for the horde now has our scent. It has access to so much more that this entire city will fall if you do not succeed." He looked into me so deeply it was as though he knew my thoughts. Nothing felt sacred. Malnuras had never done this. I felt violated until memory reminded me of my oath. My life and thoughts were not my own anymore. I served Heaven. Shrugging the feeling off, I dropped to a knee with head bowed.

"What are your orders?" I felt a hand reach under my chin and lift me up with but a finger. There was not even any pressure and I came off my knees, not by my own doing.

"Tathlyn, if you do not go right now, something horrific is going to happen that is unimaginable." I glanced at Mathias. He had a grim look on his face. He knew something was indeed wrong. Just then I felt the city was starting to vibrate. A sound like the air splitting cracked like glass that had been hot suddenly filled cold water, only it did not break. The air protested. An event was about to take place.

Right above the wall, near the same place where previous portal existed, a hairline fracture started to form in the shield. It started small and slowly worked its way down towards the top of the wall. With every inch that it sliced, the sound got louder and louder...then deafening for a split second. A tremendous explosion rocked the top of the wall, killing all the angels within hundreds of feet. Sound deafened us all. The blast almost reached where we stood. Time slowed. Mathias raised a horn and blew it as he charged forward.

I began to follow and felt a hand on my shoulder stopping me. Glancing behind, I saw the man shaking his head. He mouthed the words, "Go to your teacher" repeatedly. When the sound finally returned to my ears, a trickle of blood came from his nose and eyes as he drew his sword. I tried to pull away one last time and felt a grip on me that was admittedly stronger than mine was. Our eyes met and he shook his head.

"Find Malnuras." Both of his hands were on the side of my face. Information spilled into my mind. Images, too blurry to focus on flashed in my mind. My legs buckled, but the hands held fast. Slow motion caught up to me as the wall exploded, and a huge hole appeared after the dust settled. The horde flowed out of it in such numbers it darkened the skies. The urge to engage my mortal enemy gave way to the desire to be somewhere. A familiar image popped into my head. A pile of rocks covered in blood.

I recognized this image from minutes before, only there was a recognizable human, obviously fed upon by some denizen, and overseen by that huge daemon. I felt sick as the reality hit me. They used Malnuras blood to open the portal to this plain, and not just to this plain, but also into Heaven. That was his body. The back of my neck burned as if the final part of the rune finished carving itself into my flesh. The pain did not even matter to me anymore. Energy gathered at my fingertips and gathered inwards from my extremities inflating me with power. There was lightning in my veins.

This sensation assaulted my senses. Muscles spasms cascaded through me. His hands were still on my face, filling me full of information and energy that ran right down to my core. It felt like floating. I balanced on my toes now. My mind was ablaze as it received the last of the images. The last image stuck in my mind as the hands fell away. I watched this clone-like person holler, "Go!" one last time then to face the horde flooding into Heaven. Above me, dots came from towers in the distance like birds from a nest or aerie. It was like watching bees coming from a hive but in turn the skyline began to darken as thousands approached to meet the influx of daemons.

My vision changed to what was stuck in my mind: total devastation. The walls of Heaven were falling, for barely half of them stood. The mighty towers still crumbled. It was a play on seeing Heaven for the first time. Little black dots swarmed over the ruins. The task was clear; this would be the result of failure. My stomach surged as this clear picture settled.

The second image that I received was chaotic at best and spilled back into my mind, helping me to focus on the pile of rocks. Somehow since words would have taken too long, this man had dumped images directly into my memory. He did it in less time than it would take to speak to them and try to explain the sense of urgency. I continued to pull my energy in and the rune on my neck activated. The image blurred and swirled like a drain in a bathtub that had its plug pulled out. Like poking a hole in a gallon of milk, or popping a balloon, something was draining God's power. It was inevitable what was going to happen, and he made it very clear to me.

An image of Malnuras holding his hands over his heart flashed. At first I did not see it but there was fluid running out from between his fingers very slowly. Behind him, there was an image coming into view, but I could not see what it was. The energy hit its crescendo and I felt my head explode in pain, blurring my vision. How could I focus with this swirling chaos to sort out? I felt dizzy, weightless…for a fraction of time, until my feet hit the ground without my knowing they had left. Air rushed back into my lungs. A burst of light made it difficult to refocus.

Countryside greeted me.

The coarse grass crunched under my feet as my weight shifted, returning balance to my control. Fresh air was a nice change from the death and carnage on the wall. The smell angels' blood was very strong. It was a relief.

I stood gathering my bearings and shook the disorientation off. Behind me sounds that, at first, seemed muted and diminished, caught my ears.

Birds fled the direction I faced. Their squawks alerted me back to focusing on my surroundings. *Death was closer than before.*

My mind exploded with thoughts from my blades. Like an alarm going off, they sensed a threat greater than I had ever felt, a feeling now grabbed my heart and squeezed. The daemonic words they screamed in my head were almost deafening even though nothing was audible. It took me several moments to reign in the maelstrom of panic I felt. I fought to calm my emotions. An eternity seemed to passed before the fear and excitement became manageable. It came down to one cohesive phrase.

"Tathlyn, he is here."

"Who?"

"Amduscias. The general in charge of hell's assault."

"You saw him through my eyes did you not, on the wall? Where was this fear then? You are metal...how can you be afraid?" I felt a twinge come from the blades as if they chastised me. "Why would he leave the horde?"

"Can you not feel it?" they chimed in their melodic duality. Even though it was still a dulcet voice, their pitch changed to a deep and dark cadence. "He is one of the worst. There is a reason Lucifer chose him."

"What would that be other than he is an evil monster unwelcome on Heaven's doorstep?" I asked.

"He is a fierce leader and commands loyalty. He uses music to entice legions to follow him to death. His enemies cannot hear his songs."

"Wait, could that be how those smaller daemons line up to be used as energy for those weapons assaulting Heaven? Do they use his power to enslave?"

"Yes," they replied. "He normally loves an audience and performs when commanded by those he serves."

"All the images I have seen when I studied daemonology did not show him having wings. Are we sure it is him?"

"Do not believe everything you see, Defender."

"I will keep that in mind," I said turning.

A small city lay behind me.

It reminded me of the one that I had been to only once before with Mathias where we had some food and spoke about the big picture. We had eaten at a small inn with service outside. The food was very good. I remembered thinking that it was strange there were no guards. The village was open and friendly. This place was bigger. I could hear noise in the distance but it was quiet...too quiet. In fact, I did not see anyone. I decided to move closer, being very cautious. With blades out, I advanced toward the structures, which appeared deserted.

The architecture was Roman-like, bearing many similarities. The people obviously had skill in crafting, for an artisan crafted the stone and someone moved them into place. It had to be a difficult task. The road was not paved with cobblestones but slate like tiles with a texture that allowed rainwater to run into a gutter, which meant some type of water collection or sewer. My master mentioned there were several in which souls could choose to reside. If people chose this life, they would live forever unless something happened and they died again.

It was strange to have a village so close. When a soul's body died again, it would pass to Heaven in the same plain of existence. Why not live in the city of Heaven? Why risk the horde finding the city? The thought perplexed me as I approached.

The sound grew as I stepped around a building. Several people gathered in a central area, as if holding a meeting, but their speech was in whispers. I immediately thought, "This cannot be good," as it would make slaughtering them too easy for the horde. Concern raised alarms in my mind because my focus on Malnuras had brought me here. They forced the people to gather here to hold my attention.

It was a trap.

I did not catch it before. The people had terrified looks on their faces and attempted to conceal them. I first noticed it on a woman in passing. She avoided looking at me. When she did make eye contact, with her fake waves to the people pretending to be coming and going, things became more apparent to me. I started to pan the square when I realized there were all sorts of baskets around it. Several hundred hastily placed. They were not small baskets; they could hold something large.

I heard laughter. Baskets exploded and out jumped more than four-dozen of the medium flyers followed by hundreds of leapers. There must have been holes under the baskets for it was like watching a clown car unloads. They just kept coming. The townsfolk died as they scattered in all directions.

I cannot say I was surprised. It was a masterful execution of a plan that the horde must have felt would throw me off guard. They lured me here and set a trap. Dying screams filled my ears as I stepped forward to engage the ground units. It was time for them to pay. The shadows cast by the flyers overhead grew fast as thousands filled the sky from all around. I heard the laughter again.

My blades were right in fearing it.

The sound of it pierced my heart...but instead of crippling me with fear, it unleashed the righteous fury inside. Energy leapt from the tips of my blades without my having to command it.

The time to settle the score was nigh...

XIV

Vengeance

The light that fills these fading eyes

Has always been my compromise

In the dark, I made my stand

I bleed to meet the horde's demand

With each drop, my life might fade

But in return lends strength to blade

Standing fast against the tide

No other course but to abide

All my life I have prepared

To stand alone without despair

Heightened skills have bought me time

I am the cork that holds the line

From those that passed in times before

Reinforce the mandate inside I swore

If I fail this day this hour

To the next, I will add my power

I did not choose, yet here I stand

To turn the tide and save the land

I fight a battle to none exists

So they can have their crimson bliss

214

A battle cry came from me like a bellow to greet the ages and proclaim that Tathlyn had arrived. Both of my swords reached skyward as the scream of righteous vengeance escaped my lungs in primal fury. Energy rolled forth like a blanket consecrating the very ground on which I stood. I was in full command of my focus and emotions. The horde in front of me froze for just a moment as my will hit them full on. Not a muscle flexed or moved without my command to do so and I felt all my defensive runes activate and the protective energies flow over my body like a second flexible skin.

The warrior had awakened.

Mathias told me some time ago that there would come a day when every action, thought, and impulse would come together in one cohesive moment. That day would be the day that hell knew of my arrival. Today was that day. The power felt in every muscle was divine in its inception and righteous in its execution. My senses reached out to the entire battlefield. It was as though the thoughts and intentions of my foes lay wide open to me.

My enemy faltered. I could taste the fear rolling off them. It felt sweet to my senses, to know that my presence struck fear in the heart of creatures that lived off hatred, and the torment of others. Such creatures willingly gave themselves to the greater evil. That action in and of itself did not make sense, for evil is selfish and greedy. Right now evil feared me. My mind tingled with a euphoric feeling, creating an intoxication of sorts. I found myself laughing as my swords swung again, cleaving five in half and taking the heads of a several more. The energy released from the swing and decimated dozens close behind those.

Legacy of the Defender

My defenses dampened the attempted strikes against me. The occasional claw found its way through my blades to be repelled. Most of the daemons could not even get close to me, as my protections deflected strikes as easily as they touched me. I was starting to sense the frustrations of the horde. They wanted me dead, badly.

Thankfully, the poor souls in this area had scattered. A few of the daemons chased them for a while, but hatred for me pulled them back like a magnet. They knew I was their mortal enemy as much as they were mine. Hundreds of them returned from side streets to engage in the fight only to die within moments. More failed at attempts to get through my defenses. I spun a few times, extending my steel as they re-engaged as a whole, their intention to overbear. Normally that would fell the strongest warrior or at least score some mortal wound on a lesser fighter.

They did not even touch me. My whirling blades bit through wing, skull, and flesh with great ease, dropping them or driving them back. They tried it again. I repeated the move with even greater efficiency, killing even more, but one of them scored a minor hit on my right leg as my blade passed. He had lunged in. Even though my timing was perfect, his was better. There were hundreds upon hundreds surrounding me. The odds mattered not. Claws rang against steel as I slashed at the medium sized daemons moving in on me. They provided a moderate challenge. Right hand high to left hand low, my hands gaited back and forth like extensions of my will. Daemon arms swung with furious abandon. My blows continued to reign down. I counted four parries before I found an opening on the last daemon, cleaving it head to groin with such force that I cracked the stones in the courtyard without even hitting them. The sheer force that released as my blade passed through with all that energy exploded in a tremendous burst into the ground and knocked a few of the small daemons down. Stone showered in small bits around me.

My mind was present. With each passing moment, I observed footing, positioning of targets, and every other incremental nuance of the battle. I could see everything. My training had taught me that each move set up the next move, and that move led into the next. It was a game of chess where staying several moves ahead of your opponent was is how the game worked. With a focused mind, my targets disappeared. Then it happened.

They stopped coming.

"Do not let them regroup. They will come again stronger," my blades spoke in unison.

I took pause and surveyed the square for a moment. It was a mess, littered with daemon corpses falling to ash. Bodies of several hundred villagers mixed in. I did not have to look to see the horde killed them. Hundreds flew around the area, circling in a taunting gesture. They dared me to engage. I wanted to holler out and say, "Look at the courtyard! You are losing!" The words would be a waste. They would die soon enough. One last look afforded me a glimpse of the big daemon as it walked behind a building and disappeared from sight. I sprinted to catch up, crossing the square and rounding the corner with a burst of speed.

One daemon hid there. I took his head off without breaking stride. It hit the ground, its eyes repeatedly blinking while I moved past. For a second it reminded me of Morse code and I wondered what the message would have been. "Thank you for killing me quickly." My grin remained as the head bounced behind me on the stones.

The building was at least thirty feet long and two stories with a pitched roof covered in tiles. One of the tiles hit the ground in front of me. It shattered into many pieces. A quick glance revealed a small leaper daemon up there cowering. It had tossed a tile at me, no doubt more of an insult, as it knew it could not stop me. I did not even bother looking again but reached the end of the building and rounded the corner in a defensive stance. Ahead, the monstrous daemon walked casually away. It had some type of domesticated animal in its hand that was crying out as he squeezed.

A sickening crunch followed by laughter.

Even at this distance, this thing was huge. Compared to one of the dragon-like daemons it was not as large, but it still towered over the largest of the common flying ones. A curved weapon hung at its hip. My studies had taught me that any creature using a weapon was intelligent on some level. I began to size it up mentally and went over engagement tactics in my head. Something told me not to charge. My fury was building and I kept fighting the urge to ignore my instincts. Breath came slowly. Energy flowed to my core for a moment then released, flowing to my hands, feet, and head. I drew nearer to the Leader.

All my runes burned as I got closer and my defenses automatically engaged. Thirty feet from him...there was a flash of movement...out of the shadows came four shapes. Large wolf shaped creatures that had a stride just like large gorillas, came at me from all sides. I tucked and rolled back to my feet, engaging them.

Laughter exploded from the rooftops. The horde wanted a show. The large daemon sat down on the edge of a small building and began to eat the animal in its grip. That distraction cost me. One of them lunged and tried to swallow my head. Its teeth almost closed on my neck.

My defenses held the razor sharp teeth at bay, but I kept the shield compressed enough that the beast still had ahold of me. I felt another grab my legs. A tug of war ensued. The energy required to keep the defensive shield strong was depleting me fast. I pulled on my reserves to replenish and bolster the shield's power.

A disgusting pop pervaded my ears...sinew tore and snapped. My defensive bubble expanded and the monster's jaw tore open, dislocating in the process. A spray of ichor fell on the shield and rolled off. The beast dropped me then fell away pawing at its face. The other lost its grip on me as well, nursing some chipped teeth that snapped. I was on my feet effortlessly in seconds and attacked...leaping at the one with a broken jaw. Both sword tips sliced into the skull and sunk to the hilt.

Then the unimaginable happened.

My attempts to free them failed. The beast convulsed and threw its body around. Not wanting to lose my weapons amidst a fight, I held onto the hilts with a vice grip. Flopping around in a death throw, the creature's motion was so violent that it tossed me as if I was not even there.

Other daemons landed blows against my thighs and legs. First one, then three in a row, struck. A few of the claws got through the shield and hit my calf. Skin split and moisture spilled out. The armored cloth had a small breach. Searing pain ignited my leg.

My leg burned from the inside. Poison seemed to be the standard for these creatures. I had to maintain focus on holding on and gripped for my very life. The daemon threw itself around, slamming us against both a building and causing damage to itself in the process. The wall collapsed. My shield took the impact easily and spread the kinetic energy evenly across it. Healing slowed and my shield drained my energy heavily. The effect of the poison crept in.

Several more thrashes attempted to dislodge me. The horde howled at the creature's display amidst its death throws. It had to be amusing, as it felt like a bull ride to me...one that I had never experienced. Efforts to turn the blades failed. They refused to budge. I would have to kill the beast or be at full strength before I could remove the rest of the horde. The thought of letting go and calling them to me sounded feasible, but the thought was impossible as long as were wedged.

Locking my grip, I shifted my focus inward and imagined the poison flushing out. The rune began to heat up and the energy flowed out then down. It felt like a battle was raging in my blood stream. Not wanting to close my eyes to increase the meditation focus I needed to deal with the poison, I kept trying to track where we would collide next. The swirling chaos of this beast's movements took me in a direction I did not anticipate. My grip failed and the world spun as I went through a wall, followed by another one, which buried me underneath it.

Choking on dust, my bearings eluded me. "The bell definitely got rung on that one," the words seemed so bold in my mind that I felt I was watching Mathias spray painting using a daemon's heart and ichor to paint the word "Clang" on the wall. It was all in my head, of course. The weight of the wall hampered my movement. The amount of rubble was unknown, as I prayed for a few seconds before they began to claw at me. One thought followed me to its conclusion.

I did not have my swords. My grip failed. Anxiety set in and I fought to drive it back. This was that moment that would define me for the rest of my life, no matter how long or short. I chose to hold for a moment and refocused on the healing to take place. Eternity had a new definition. The beasts began to dig through the pile above me. Weight on me shifted each time they cleared debris. My shield was off! Did they knock me more senseless than I had realized?

The weight pressed down on me...but it was bearable. A burning in my veins told me that the poison was still present. My mind let go and focus returned. The small pocket of air choked me with dust. This would have to happen without the benefit of breathing. Dark water flowed over stones in a stream...the image leapt into my thoughts. Its waters flowed clouded and rough. The barely visible plants swayed back and forth like a rhythm. I had some air in my lungs. It would have to suffice.

I imagined the water began to clear. The thought came as I imagined the pollutant upstream running dry. The bottom became clearer by the moment. Life returned to the water. Frogs and fish chased water striders and other small creatures. Balance had returned.

Energy flowed. I felt the poison recede and warmth flow internally from the inside down to my toes. It was just starting to feel like my body floated when the rune activated and not a moment too soon. The weight above me lessened. My shield came into place on its own to my surprise as if my body knew it had to turn it off to heal fully. That would not surprise me but was truly unexpected and for that, I was thankful. Rolling to my back was a little hard but I managed it just in time. I saw two sets of jaws coming in at me, and each one of them grabbed an arm and managed to bite down hard enough to secure me. I could not move.

Embarrassment set in for a moment. The events ran quickly through my head. I looked at my actions from at least three angles while being drug from the rubble and displayed almost proudly from the maws of these two stinky and fetid smelling creatures. The dead one with my swords in its skull twitched on the ground. The other one was injured and laid quiet, spilling ichor on the ground from its multiple wounds. It must have succumbed after I went through the wall. It also was not moving. The smell was awful. Had I not been in the stomach of the biggest one nothing could have smelled worse.

I started to laugh at the irony as my canine restraints of the daemon variety paraded me forward to the large daemon. Even with my tremendous strength, I could not break free. It was the first time anything had ever pinned me down. I tried to kick them in the sides, but they held on tighter. Somehow, the protective field around me was not working very well, and I started to feel pressure on my bones from teeth. I tried to turn my healing back on as the pressure turned to pain, and I felt the teeth start to crush but not break the skin. It had to be the armor holding them back from puncturing the skin, but the pressure was very painful.

In my mind, the image of being drug forward towards this creature played out. I was embarrassed that somehow my foes had gotten the best of me. A smile remained on my lips as I chose to be stoic in the face of this denizen. It felt as if I were doing an iron cross like a gymnast on the rings, only no skill was involved and it was not a demonstration. My pose was rather pathetic and beaten. With chin up, I looked the large daemon right in the eyes and gritted my teeth with a fully clenched jaw. The pain got worse.

Weakness settled over me, slight at first. My position no doubt led to a loss of circulation. I was fading. My training gave me a tactical advantage. I knew that my strength alone would have been enough to break free of the hold the overgrown daemon dogs had on me. The poison neutralized in my blood. How was my strength still waning? This did intrigue me, but it was not until my healing shut down on its own and my other failed completely that I knew there was something else terribly wrong. I cannot say it was an unfair fight, but this one had the upper hand when all of my runic abilities collapsed.

Fear found its way to my heart and wrapped its icy hands around it. The monstrous daemon chuckled as it stuffed its mouth full of whatever was left of the creature it had captured. Not only did it belch loudly, but it also sprayed me with half eaten particles. My eyes closed when I saw it heading towards me. The smell nearly made me gag. More laughter ensued. The daemon leaned against a building, half sitting on it and dislodging tiles with every shift of its weight as it fell over from laughing.

The creature roared with deep, throaty laughter.

"You must feel proud," I found myself saying.

Could it even understand me? Did my words register to this monster? Its gaze fell upon me giving chills that crawled up from my core and wrapped themselves around my neck. My airway tightened. The fear was real. This thing scared me more than a large six-legged beast that flew, a beast ten times the size of this one.

His giant head panned the clearing. Viscous drool dripped in long cords from its maw onto its chest. The largely formed plates there were natural and pitted, probably from such behavior before. His demeanor was arrogant as he surveyed the carnage of the city. There was hardly any damage to the city, but a dead populace put a damper on any hopes the inhabitants could recover.

Another chuckle rolled from its fetid mouth. It sat there looking at me. Anger and hatred radiated from it. For a second, I felt sorry for it. It only knew death and destruction. It caused only pain and agony to other sentient beings. That was not a life for anything to live. I had to remind myself that it was a daemon. Evil comprised its core. A moment of sadness washed over me. That changed when my eyes spotted a pile of rocks off to the side, near of the building on which it sat.

A corpse in rags lay atop the pile. Their colors were unrecognizable. Blood covered the mass. I was about to look away when something caught my eye. The arrangement of the rocks reminded me of something.

Malnuras had been on a similar rock pile!

My control was gone. Rage burst forth. All the time spent training on controlling how situations affected my judgment did not prepare me for this. My expression reflected this...for the large daemon looked straight at me and broke out into laughter. What could only be a smile crossed its twisted face. A spasm ran down my spine and my stomach felt like it was in my throat. Nausea was present when my eyes fell upon the body of my teacher...then shifted to his killer. Righteous fury returned to me as if God himself reached down and touched me.

Fury turned into vengeance. I had to kill this damnation and I needed to do it now. The sum of all my skill and determination may not be good enough, but I called everything forth. It felt like my heart was a cauldron bubbling over onto a raging fire. Pressure inside my head increased. Just when the stress was nearly unbearable, the creature spoke. My bones froze at the very sound of its voice as its spoke perfectly in a language I could understand. Its forked tongue waggled and there was not a hint of an accent.

"You should save your strength human. You are going to need it for what I have planned."

My look of shock must have been priceless for it made a pouting gesture with its face. My response was stuck in my throat. I stared in disbelief. More laughter rang out across the empty courtyard. Whisperings in the daemonic tongue echoed across the rooftops. I tried to count the individual voices I heard but lost track at about thirty-nine when it spoke again.

"What, nothing to say? Your teacher did not have much to say either. He did, however, taste delightful, and I savored every drop of his blood. I never thought that I would get to taste God's flesh. It was delicious."

I felt myself puke slightly in my mouth. Did I just hear this thing correctly? Did it say God's flesh? My thoughts raced over the last few years or what I felt to be years. The statement did not make any sense that God would be out here when Heaven was under siege. His power did keep Heaven safe. But was this possible?

Logic did not govern my thoughts for the few seconds after that statement. I was truly confused. If this were God, why would he allow this? How could the hordes stand up to God? His power should be enough to wipe out anything that attacked him. I was just about to call the declaration bullshit when I stopped in mid thought, just like a logic program screeching to a halt when it realizes it cannot calculate pi out to infinity.

It made sudden sense. Heaven fell because this daemon had a small piece of God. Without it, God is not whole, and the horde was able to punch a hole in the defenses of the city...the safe harbor of souls for eternity. I realized when this thought hit me that my mouth was still full of vomit. I was about to swallow it to speak when an idea came forth...one that I had used before. This daemon was still flesh and blood.

I felt myself grow weaker. Something needed to happen right now. Tactic after tactic played in my mind while this filth droned on about how it was going to torture me in ways a human, even one such as myself, could not tolerate for even a few moments. Nothing in my memory came to mind except the words "uh oh" written on the wall behind me in my own blood. Despair was about to take root when I heard a voice, plain as day, in my head. At first, I did not believe it. Again, it spoke.

"Call us," a faint whisper said.

Before the sentence even finished in my mind, my weapons were in my hands and in one motion I thrust them both right into the soft pallet and into the brain of the daemon dogs that had successfully soaked my shirt with

226

drool whilst holding me captive. The metal bit flesh and I turned on the flames while twisting the blades, proving my point to these creatures. A hushed sound followed by screaming emanated as I tore my blades free and fell to my feet. I looked at the large daemon in front of me that was staring in disbelief. There was no hesitation. With minuscule energy left, I launched myself at its head with only the need to get close. The contents of my mouth found their target, right in the creatures' eyes.

I swung hard at its head.

It rolled to the right at the last second and I felt my sword bite something that should not have given any resistance. The daemon had a necklace on with a large medallion hanging from it. As my blade struck true, a searing light, in slow motion escaped from the cut splitting it in two. A minor explosion went off right under the daemon's face. My landing was hard as this shock wave of energy hit me before my feet touched down. I went ass over elbows onto my face. A rumbling sound came from behind, followed by multiple crashes and screams. Several of the small fliers and leapers that lined the roofs died as well.

Even with the pain exploding in my brain, I had to smile as the horde continued its chorus of pain while they died. I managed to find my feet. Blood flowed from my face at a scary rate as I realized a large splinter of wood poked through a cheek, nearly severing my tongue. Blood flowed down my throat. Instinctively, I reached up and pulled it out, almost collapsing in the process. More splatters of blood hit the ground and the woozy feeling hit me hard and caused me to stumble. The fear I would actually pass out was a reality for a moment, when a familiar feeling surged through me. My healing rune had just activated.

Shocked is a hard word to use when you know something is supposed to be true but when it happens anyway, sometimes the self-doubt or the disbelief in the way things are can still catch you off guard. Just seconds before, none of my abilities worked. My strength had been gone along with anything else that I tried to do at that moment. I could barely leap twenty feet up to slice at the creature, let alone spit my distaste in its face. Yet something changed just when it needed to, allowing me to not only free myself, but also kill two major daemons, leveling the field somehow just enough.

Turning to face the daemon, I noticed it toppled backwards into the building it had been sitting on, and just regained its feet. Half of my strength had returned with more coming back stronger by the second. That is when I saw it.

The amulet was on the ground. Crackling energy rolled all over it and lit the ground up with lightning-like blue arcs. Blue arcane energy was enchanting the item and had failed when I caught a piece of it. It now had a bright glow about it and looked like it was failing.

I charged to finish the job, not knowing the outcome. I sang a battle cry I had heard several times from my lessons. The roar of the horde was deafening as if they knew that what was about to happen was bad for their cause. Three steps came and went so fast in those seconds. I was before the item and swung. Down came my blades. Right before they connected, I noticed a human finger protruding from the medallion. My blades connected and a vibration, as if I had hit a stone, rolled up my arms. My teeth rattled. The necklace survived, only moving a bit.

Motion caught my eye as the daemon pulled itself from the building. "No, you fool! Do not destroy it! Father will not be happy." It reached for its sword as my sword swung again. The same effect occurred. This time I felt fluid squirt from my eyes as the shock collided with my head. He parried the blow. Getting frustrated, I commanded my swords' energy to turn on. With a rush, the crackling arcs flowed down the blades.

Time slowed. I could sense the wind rushing the length of the blades as they sliced the air. It howled as if the blades protested the friction of the air rushing past. The daemon tried to intercept the attack again. I changed my position with a role to the side. The sudden motion in front of me flashed and my swords met resistance. He stopped me again and moved to engage. A sickening feeling came over me as the daemon stepped up. I felt the metal of the blade in my core, and I heard a protest come from my mind.

"UGGGGHHHH!"

The daemon swung at my head. As it came, I looked at the swords and at the blade coming in a downward strike at my head. I moved to side step and did so effortlessly, as if moving ever so slightly ahead of this large creature. I glanced at the ground and shifted my feet, noticing the specks of dirt and the grain in some wood that lay near me. My feet slid on command as the huge weapon came down to my right. A burning sensation ignited on the skin near all of my joints as if a rune was forming in every spot. This one hurt more than previous runes because it was everywhere and happening all at once.

Even with the pain rolling over my skin there could be no hesitation.

My blades responded and struck downward to redirect the huge blade towards the dirt. Barrel flipping sideways to my left, I passed over his blade. The concussive force of it striking the ground rocked the area. The timing was perfect. My feet found the ground on the other side. I raised my blades to deliver another blow. My attack was uninterrupted by my opponent's huge weapon. Energy gathered in the hilt and as I swung and shot toward the tips. The air split as they raced toward my target.

A sound crackled as if my weapons broke magical and physical barriers. It came from the metal as they raced towards my target. Nothing could prepare me for what happened next. My protections came up faster than ever before...without me telling them to. My blades passed smoothly through the metal-like material surrounding the protruding finger inside the medallion.

A magnificent flash of light followed, and a sudden rush of air exploded in every direction. I barely had time to cover my eyes with a sword before it reached me.

Energy raged around like the gale force wind of a tornado. With impaired vision, sight past my hand was blurry. I watched, as the large daemon did not fare so well in this release of energy. It flew backwards. The blast sundered it as if the two were connected. The broken building in front of me disintegrated before my eyes as the blast hit it after the giant beast split the strongest wall into pieces. The whistling sound in my ears diminished. The creature's location was lost in the chaos. Earth, rock, and wood rained down over the area for several moments while the haze of war covered the area, obscuring my senses.

I reached out with my mind for daemon presence. Nothing was behind me. Ahead of me, I felt nastiness telling me the big one survived. I was actually happy about this because I wanted to carve Malnuras's name into his hide while it was still alive. The icky chills pervaded my mind. The desire to charge right in was strong, but I had to collect my thoughts while the battlefield settled. Taking a moment to observe my surroundings would be wise. My feet sunk into the ground and it felt sick from the death here. The loss of life had been staggering on the human side. From the news received before arriving, and how funny Mathias was acting, the reality hit me. Part of God had died here under torture.

Rage wanted to rise. I fought to turn my emotions into righteous fury to draw from its power. My stomach dropped as if falling from a cliff. The smoke and dust blew past me and drum beat like wings beat the air in front of me. Something big was airborne. The ground vibrated with each gust of wind. As the air cleared, the daemon stood in front of me. It was obviously hurt.

"Did you think it would be that easy?" a gurgled voice spoke. "Now you will know why Father sent me to deal with you!"

My lips cracked a smile. Finally, it was a one on one fight with a worthy opponent. I caught myself, as that thought became words and passed my lips. "I challenge you."

I had just issued a challenge to Lucifer's son by my guess.

My peripheral vision worked overtime to watch for a flank by any of its minions. Nothing moved. I was alone. Today the warrior would face his final test. My swords pulsated with energy, and for the first time in my countless battles, that energy came from me. Without intending to, I spoke.

"I am Tathlyn, Defender of the Earth," I heard myself say.

The tips of my swords touched my forehead in a salute. He mocked me with a gesture in return.

"Amduscias, commander of legions, son of Lucifer." His perfect English mocked me as he bowed.

It was time to make Lucifer childless.

XV

Amduscias

Ferocity dominated the exchange of blows.

This daemon prince, Amduscias, attempted to enact vengeance upon me. Several moments had passed before I knew *it* was indeed a *he*, for at first glance it was not determinable. It took interpreting a reference made in anger about a father punishing a son for me to know for sure. Sparks showered the area and the clash of steel created thunderous claps, releasing energy from our two weapons. Eldridge fire crackled up and down his blade and created heat to such a degree that it would burn me if I got too near the sword.

My protections held. Energy returned to me just moments before, when the rage had transformed into righteous fury. Whatever diminished me had something to do with that amulet. Smashing it was my best move...this pissed the daemon off even more. I was sure he could be defeated until his dark rage boiled forth with such unholy saturation, that being in proximity made my bladder try to empty...and I did not feel fear the way other men did.

The thought that I might be in trouble arose.

The daemon was beyond angry. Each strike gave me an image of a hammer striking the strongest crystal. Small hairline fractures began to form and my shields were battered so badly that concern of failure set in. Sword versus sword, I outclassed him, but his sheer strength wore me down bit by bit. Eventually, my will to keep the energy flowing to my protections would diminish.

I was now on the defensive, working to keep him from striking my shield while planning my strategy. The problem was I did not have a clue yet. His rage should have been easy for me to use against him, but somehow it made him stronger and faster. I kept looking for an opening but was having little success. His attacks took too much of my focus. Keeping this up would be the end, and in my mind, my edge eluded me.

Going toe to toe was fruitless. The surrounding terrain became my answer. Ducking and dodging into buildings could bring me fractions of time to reposition myself before the walls or roofs came down. The buildings had open areas in the center allowing the smoke from the fire pits to escape and allowed access to the roofs. From there I could score some hits on my foe. After a few strikes, I could leap through a hole to the roof, allowing me to strike at its head easier. Problem with that strategy was clear. Hidden daemons lurked above. Going through an open hole was risky.

I tested my theory. Racing into the central area of a building, the beast crashed through right behind me, destroying it in moments. Its walls were too thin and too weak to keep the creature busy on the outside trying to get in. The second structure proved even weaker as I raced to get out before it collapsed.

The third building was much bigger than the other two. As I leapt up through the smoke exit in the ceiling and landed on the roof, I noticed very thick stones in places around the rooftop acting like buttresses. My body fit behind one such stone in a crouch, hiding me perfectly.

He came through the building swinging his sword upright like before and the roof disintegrated into tons of falling material, many large chunks landed where I would have been. Just like I attempted to do with him, he tried to lull me into a predictable rhythm. I felt the remaining section of the roof below my feet shake as if a train came through. Debris blasted the area. Stones the size of bricks exploded against the roof crenels. A floor beam punched through right next to my head causing the stoned wall to crack. The creature almost exited the building but turned first to look for me. He was in place. I leapt and swung both blades with everything that I had targeting his head.

The air cracked like a whip as my blades descended on him. For a moment, it looked like I had a clear shot. His pupils went wide as he tracked me flying through the air in a Kamikaze fashion. Victory seemed eminent. I felt the weapons' charge stronger than ever.

My swords were a foot from his head when his sword came up parallel to the ground and deflected my blows right into his other hand. Metal bit flesh and passed clean through. His body turned to the left as I passed him on the right and fell down into the dust-filled area that had once been a building. My feet touched uneven ground causing me to roll or risk breaking something. He howled post-strike; I took a small piece of him in the exchange. I heard the smallest finger from his left hand squish as it hit the ground follow by a small shower of daemonic ichor.

My other blade glanced off his forearm plate with a shower of sparks, falling around me as I rolled. The rush of wind was loud as his sword chased me to the ground, further crushing the debris of the building into smaller pieces that showered me. I found my feet and was on the move looking for my next tactical stand. Small fires started from cooking embers scattered about by the daemon prince's reckless pursuit added smoke.

Impact came from behind. Blinding pain! It was hard to run and not give him my back as a target. I had to move fast which meant not defending other than weaving. Something impacted my shield as I leapt over another pile of wall remnants. He had closed the distance. The force flipped me head long and I tucked and rolled landing hard on an intact wall, its angle leaning away from me, which caused my roll backwards toward the Prince, dropping me right as his feet.

A well-placed kick, most likely unintentional, took my wind away. I felt ribs crack as the shield buckled. I cried out.

"That will slow you down, little man! It is only a matter of time before my sword feasts on your flesh!"

His statement worried me a bit. I was air born and going through a wall and a window. The wall caught me just enough to spin me head over heels causing my landing to be the kind that would make any gymnastics' judge snicker for just a moment, even if they felt pity for the contestant lying there writhing in pain. However, this was not a friendly competition. The image of a panel of judges in my mind faded by the third bounce, and reminded me of the mortal danger hot on my heels. Still wincing, I rolled across sharp rocks, feeling my knuckles lose skin with each revolution of my body. My healing rune taxed my energy stores, as it must have been trying to re-knit my ribs while I moved…flesh wounds would have to wait. Again, the giant sword hit the ground close to me, sparks and debris hit my face.

Fluid ignited from a broken clay jar. A small fireball erupted right in the daemon's face and flash burned my skin on my right arm as I rolled away from it.

Expecting to be ablaze, I sprung to my feet landing in a partial crouch, then dove over his blade as he pulled it free. The flames enveloped his sword, fed by the flammable liquid. Heat washed over me as I passed over it, landing somewhat gracefully and firmly. Solid ground was not a guarantee anymore with buildings crumbling all around. A spin placed me behind the blade with enough room for me to dive through his legs. Thrusting both swords upwards, I pierced the flesh in his hamstring. He roared as my blades sunk in a few inches. Ichor flowed. I twisted and withdrew, preparing for another strike when his left hand, although missing a pinky, backhanded me in the chest. Stars filled my eyes. My knees met the ground hard as he spun to face me with a downward strike that had my death written all over it. I did not see it until the last second. It took everything I had, and a lot that I did not, to parry his attack off to my right. Even though it was just the tip of his sword, it found flesh, passing through several inches of my quadriceps. Blood rushed out.

I yelled.

Fire ignited my blood stream, causing great pain. I threw myself out of his reach, trying to suck it up. My body landed several yards away with an unskilled roll taking me into a large stone building, but not one of brick and mortar. Someone carved the entire building out of solid rock. Amidst my distress, it was obvious as my gaze fell to my surroundings. There were no seams from stones stacked up to form walls. The stone bore no marks of its creation. It was smooth. I crawled past shelves lined with clay pots by the hundreds. Now that the battering had stopped, what little energy my reserves had engaged my healing rune.

"You had better hurry, your leg is bad." The melodic tones whispered internally.

"I know. You do not have to remind me."

"The trail of blood is impressive. Shall we boost your healing?" they inquired with a measure of serious now.

"Save your strength for hurting the monster. The rune is engaged."

"Your energy is very low, Tathlyn," the lower voice said.

The ground shook and sparks flew behind me. A quick glance and none too soon, revealed his large hand missing the pinky coming in the small doorway trying to grab me. All I could do was fall out of his reach breaking several clay jars in the process. The water felt good as it pooled around me before the fluid dynamics kicked in and dispersed it evenly on the floor. I lay there wincing with each breath. My ribs already felt better, but the excess damage overtaxed the rune's ability to heal.

I realized the daemon could not get at me. Images of some comic monster fishing its hand into a small hole to get at its prey came to mind. It hurt to laugh. *He was pissed.* Occasionally the room shook. Sparks erupted near the entrance where his sword and claws struck the entrance. I was too weak to strike at him, but I had to keep him further engaged to give me time to heal. His attention needed to be on me to keep him from desecrating Malnuras's body further. To think that a small fraction of God had been essentially "killed" still messed with my head. Knowing the cause brought my focus back. The fault may not be mine, but it was my burden to bear, none-theless.

Heaven needed his body back.

My blades whispered to each other in my head. A sense of urgency flowed from them into my thoughts. A tranquil image appeared...a favorite. My teacher and I would to sit overlooking a valley and discuss many things. Those times relaxed me. In many ways, he was a father figure because he raised me the rest of the way. Those moments lived fondly in my mind and soothed me. The urgency, still present, urged me onward to complete my mission. I pulled my injured leg in and sat in a meditative position...just out-side of the daemon's reach. Full meditation would be impossible because I needed to occasionally hit his hand with a sword in order to hold his atten-tion. Its screams and roars of frustration outside only added to my sense of relief, for my plan was working. It had to look like the fight was over, so each strike had less and less strength behind it. It took some time, but I found my center

Daemonic laughter erupted when he realized after several moments that my strikes had no strength behind them. That calm, soothing voice he tried to lull me with when I first saw him was gone. His verbiage was now full of racial, human slurs; how he would have his way with my mother or had already and how I was his bastard child. I began long, deep breaths, clearing my mind while occasionally but non-rhythmically hitting his hand to create the illusion that he had won and that I was giving up. Eventually, the flat of the blade was all I gave him before finally stopping. His hand re-tracted.

Silence.

Like the calm of a hurricanes eye, the violent speech stopped. My blades sang quietly in my head. Their voices offset the negative energy radiating in from outside. Inner peace descended on my mind. I began to reflect on the battle as Malnuras had taught me. At that moment, energy surged up from the ground and inward, boosting my healing rune. It flowed in and everywhere inside me. Cursing began outside.

"Are you dead yet, little man? Do me the honor of crawling out so that I can enjoy your flesh!" He droned on an on in different variations of the same concept.

While he spoke, I felt restored and refreshed. I had not a clue where the reserves came from when the voice came from my blades. "We used our energy to restore you properly. We will be weak for a little while and silent. Use it wisely." As the sentence ended a disconnected feeling came and the sensation of being in tune lessened.

"I told you not to," I said.

"There was no choice; you would never be able to gather energy with him near. You need to default to our wisdom from time to time. We may be here to serve you, but we also must provide you with council when needed." There was a long pause while I adjusted to their presence lessening. They felt far away.

They were not kidding...I am on my own and it was time to move as soon as my healing finished.

In the center was a well with a wall around it to keep someone from falling in just as any water supply would have. The roof was about thirty feet up and had an octagonal opening; showing evidence that water entered from there. I glanced around and realized that the room acted like a cistern as well; water on the roof flowed down into collection points as well as down into the well. Catching the rain was important, and it rained a fair amount.

My ribs solidified, making breathing less painful. The muscle around them began to repair. The gash in my leg muscle closed completely. I felt the flesh reknit itself. I had the feeling of worms crawling through the tissue as the fibers found their attachment points and reconnected, even stronger than before. As my strength returned, the energy in the room felt tainted. My blades were not kidding. Amduscias was death incarnate. Only about a handful of moments had passed, maybe only ten seconds, when I felt the threat level outside increase and my senses tingle with danger. I opened my eyes to see that wicked sword coming into the building through the doorway.

Exploding into action, I leapt up to the hole in the roof and grabbed hold of the side with my left hand while gripping both swords in my right. The daemon's sword hit the wall where my body was moments before. Vibrations shook the building, one of them hard enough to break free of my grip. A blade plummeted into the well. Not stressing, I reached my leg up and put it through the hole to take some of the weight off my left hand, and let go. Hanging upside down, my hand was free to call my sword. As it appeared, a whisper made me chuckle.

"You are not the only one that can lose a weapon."

Timing had always been my specialty.

I waited until his weapon passed above the well, stabbing where my body had been. While jars shattered everywhere and sprayed the room with debris and fluids across the floor, my hand and leg released, dropping me on my target. Both swords struck square in the middle of the muscle on the outside of its forearm and sunk to the hilt. I twisted hard on both. It roared, shaking the building *and* the heavens. This started the sequence of events. My hands twisted again and I jerked hard.

Its gargantuan hand opened...releasing his weapon. It dropped with a clatter on the top the well opening, the giant hilt resting precariously on the outside edge. The stone chipped with some minor sparks jumping around the blade. He screamed as I pulled my blades free ungentle like, slicing tendon and muscle. Ichor sprayed from the grievous wound. If I had not pissed him off to this point, this latest blow had done it.

I deftly jumped over his hand and fished the weapon clear from its reach with my blades. Energy of unfathomable evil, an unimaginable source of pain to this realm, danced like electricity on the daemonic metal. *I dare not touch flesh and grab it.* Whatever that energy was, it was not kind to humans. Part of me wondered if it healed the daemon Prince. He barely took any damage from my swords, weapons made to hurt his kind. It may very well have life draining properties.

The list went on and on mentally while I scrambled to deliver this weapon where it would take many minions to retrieve. It was quite a balancing act, but I managed to feed the tip into the well and lift. A satisfying clatter rewarded my ears as the instrument of torture plummeted deep into the well to a watery cell.

His hand fished for me. Howls of rage accented the clawing of metallic like bone comprising his claws. Sparks showered the area, as the creatures other hand tore furiously at the stone. Small chunks occasionally broke free...falling to the ground with a resounding thud. The voice was in not even understandable as it spoke its vile curses at me. The language was something never heard before. I heard daemon speech several times and even knew a few phrases, but this was foreign. Part of me figured it was maybe a higher language, perhaps the daemonic equivalent of nobility. I laughed at the idea, but stranger things have happened.

The creature's roars made my skin crawl. He really was beyond angry. If he held his attention here, I might have a chance. With a fury, I began to carve his flesh. Continuous futile attempts to grab me added to his rage. My blades kept cutting and lacerating his gigantic hand until he withdrew. The building shook with such force, it was a debate if it could keep back the tide of his fury. Carved out of the solid stone and it still shook like an earthquake. Suddenly he fell silent. Moments flew by.

There is power in his voice. Why did he stop speaking?

The silence broke when he walked around the building, occasionally slamming something into it with some last act of defiance to get at his sword and me. The walls continued to shake but did not crack. I gave silent thanks to the building's architect. Then he laughed. He must have found there was no way out for me from his vantage.

I waited. He kept his rage on overload. After a few more moments, it was time to leave. A leap took me through the opening in the roof. My cloak activated before exiting. The stone accent on the roof gave me a place to pause and watch. He was not in sight. My ruse had failed. Spying the next rooftop, I leapt with ease and landed gracefully. Freezing in place, I waited.

"He is close. Do not be too quick to think you are clear," spoke my blades. *"He is hiding now."*

"I am waiting," I responded silently.

It was time to resume retrieval of my teacher as soon as a clear path presented itself to Malnuras. I had to find a way to lessen the breach on Heaven's walls. Mathias was right, I could not fail, or a daemonic host that outnumbered them beyond my ability to count would consume the souls of Heaven.

The ground gently vibrated with each step he took, but I could not pin point his location. I stole glances from around my small protective wall, knowing the word "protective" was like referring to a plastic bag keeping a rabid dog from a bloody steak. My position may be above his walking height, but he did have wings...lest he gained the drop on me when I was looking the other way; whether or not he could see me was unknown.

My teacher's body guess was about three building away. This meant risking a leap, even while cloaked. Standing still, I could remain unseen. Moving slow would be a gamble. A leap...I had no clue.

I could not engage him toe to toe, even unarmed, no matter how good of a swordsman I was. His strength was more than a challenge, but add in his abilities as a prince of darkness, he out matched me. It was not a matter of trying to kill him, but a matter of getting away with Malnuras.

I crept to the edge, looking carefully in case my nemesis could cloak as well. I looked for slow depressions in the ground. From this height, however, it was not easy to spot them. The sheer size of his feet you would think would give him away, but that same size also displaced mass, which meant he was lighter on his feet. Nothing moved saved a few birds returning to the area. Silence prevailed.

Another leap took me to another crenulated structure to hide behind on top. The game of cat and mouse continued. My breathing paused, I and knelt perfectly still listening. The occasional tremor and a throaty gurgle rolled through the streets. His location was still a mystery. Another jump was required to reach a rooftop two buildings away. I looked around for him while in the air, and could not see anything. That worried me.

My landing had been flawless. The target was the remnant of the building closest to the rock pile. Sadly, there were many piles of rubble. The prince destroyed so many of them in pursuit of me that he leveled the area right around where I needed to be. Dropping my stance, I could see the road below in full view. The pile of rubble used as an evil altar was below. Malnuras's body lay to the side from the explosion when the amulet detonated. Burns on the body were severe, and added an element of non-recognition to the body. I would still recognize him, though, even in this state.

Convinced it was clear, I jumped down and paused. Any motion or vibrations in the ground would be easy to spot this close. This was open ground now...zero cover. His body was so close that the smell of burned flesh filled the air. Burned blood covered the remnants of the makeshift altar. It made me want to gag. I felt sick seeing him that way, but there would be time for tears later. Focus was my game now.

The last few steps happened faster than I wanted. I bent over his body looking at his broken frame, lifeless and bled out. The burn marks were severe in places and not so much in many others. One whole half of his face remained unburned but still bruised from beatings. I glanced around to make sure it was clear and moved close. Something caught my eye as I knelt down slowly and carefully rolled him to his back. One of his fingers was missing. The realization hit me hard as I turned to look around on the ground. Several minutes passed before I found what I was looking for.

They had used Malnuras's finger to create that magic item and power it.

The amulet lay a dozen or so feet away, right in the middle of the road. To walk over there would cause the rubble to shift in plain sight. Just then, slight movement from my right made me freeze. The prince moved slowly. His presence on the road was apparent, but I could not see him until it was too late. To my surprise, the ability to cloak was not what he was using. I watched the area for several seconds and realized that a pattern that looked like the building was indeed taking slow steps. What I saw move was the tiny drops of ichor falling from its hands. I could barely see his outline. His approach slowed so the ground slightly vibrated. He was maybe twenty feet away now.

He could chameleon himself!

DAMN!

I sprang to action landing next to the amulet and scooped it up. He moved so fast and was on me before I could move away. No sword was in his hands but he punched me in the face so hard something cracked, and I flew backwards, flipped once, and then landed on my feet. Blood gushed from my nose and pooled on the ground underneath a cracked beam. His tainted stench amazingly still got in my nose, even with my face busted. My healing engaged as I rolled to the side to dodge his flawed hand trying to rake me. The landing was not perfect, but it kept me from taking more damage. My head tried to swim, but there was no time to be dizzy. I regained my balance and dove again to create more distance. The bones in my face started to knit back together right about the time the swelling hit, forcing my right eye closed and taking my depth perception out. A quick duck and spin under one of his huge hands brought me to sure footing, and I pulled the remnants of the finger from the amulet and tucked it into my belt.

He did not even make any sounds. No grunt or groans. His rage was pure.

Then he was on me. I drew my swords to parry his hands and cause some damage anytime he tried to swing. In came his left hand in an over-handed hammer fist. I deflected it to the side, but it cost me my balance and knocked me the other direction, opposite from where I needed to be. The body was about ten feet away and to the left. I realized that I would not be able to defend myself and get Malnuras out. It left only one option.

In came both hands in an attempt to grab me. He was faster somehow and I was slowing down. His hands missed again as I dove headlong through his legs, extending my swords right at the last second to take him in both thighs. My efforts rewarded a howl of pain but slowed my speed enough so that when I landed and grabbed Malnuras, I did not have time to get the shield full on before his hand penetrated my defenses and clocked me in the head from behind. I collapsed over my teacher's body. The fists began to rain down upon my defensive barrier. I knew that a daemon prince could bash his way through because my shield strength weakened right away.

My eyes crossed from the devastating blows. At this rate, I would not have enough energy to maintain any defenses and teleport us to Heaven. The blackness filled my thoughts. My sight had a red hue to it suddenly. Blood vessels had burst behind my eyes and blood flowed from my sockets. While unconscious, my defenses would not stay on. I needed to buy some time. I positioned my legs so I was on one knee and lifted Malnuras to my chest with both arms, making sure to have a good grip on his body. I lessened the energy going to my shield so it was only inches from my body and bolstered my strength to leap. Right as his last strike lifted for the next incoming one, I leapt, propelling me skyward. A glancing blow from his hand altered my trajectory.

Gravity let go of me...for a moment. I let my shield collapse, focusing all my thoughts on Heaven. We started to phase us out when Amduscias slammed into me. His mighty wings had carried him after his prey faster than I could leap. Arms closed in around us. Ribs crushed and lungs punctured. Muscles tore throughout my body as the vice-like grip of this monster smashed the body of my teacher and me together. Life essence fled my body like air escaping a balloon.

My eyes saw blackness. Weightlessness greeted me. I looked down at this image of our bodies in this monster's embrace. He had me crushed like a vice in his mighty arms. The strength alone from a creature this size would be huge, but add in dark power and it is no wonder it had me looking down upon myself. He had won.

I heard Mathias's voice in my head.

"Look."

"At what? I already did."

"Look closer. Your energy has not abandoned your body. It holds onto a shred of life."

I looked back at my body. Amduscias had just landed, dropping my (soon to be) corpse. He was cackling. I could see the wispy aspect of my spirit...a few tendrils trailed back my body.

"Your point, Master?"

"You are not dead yet; you can return and finish the teleportation. The power your ability uses has not dissipated yet, so you can finish, but be warned you may still yet die and it is going to be the worst pain of your life."

"I think you were the worst pain of my life, Master. Anything else is child's play." An image of him smacking me in the back of the head came to view. He was right; the connection between my spirit and my body remained. I focused on my broken form and began to feel the agonizing pain, but something beckoned me to return. The sounds my ears could hear, trickled in, making the draw stronger, the daemon's breath and laughter were close as he leaned in to gloat. My spirit drew a little closer again and my view from here blurred. The hatred felt for this creature and how ending its existence would validate my purpose was all it took. I found myself pulled forward.

Opening my eyes to this pain was not something one could prepare for. I could feel ribs through my lungs, muscles tore, and my spine felt crushed. Breath would not come. Paralyzed and unable to cry out...I was helpless. My eyes could only open half-mast. The creature held me in the palm of his hand now and looked at me. His mouth opened while raising his hand. He intended eat me.

Sudden thoughts of Heaven rallied my focus. I really wanted to be there. Energy inside of me flared to life. The last piece of the process fell into place. He started to push us into his mouth, Malnuras, and myself, smashed together. Recognition came a moment too late, as he must have felt the energy coalesce. He pulled his hand back to look at what was happening. Last thing I saw was his face go blurry with a surprised look, and he roared at the top of his lungs as he hurriedly tried stuffing me into his mouth.

We were gone before he finished his action.

Floating again. The pain this time was so intense...I felt numbness set in. Darkness swirled about me. It felt like falling this time. The stars in the cosmos came on like a light switch. My eyelids crept open as they struggled to focus. I looked up at moving clouds. The rainbow pattern of the shield protecting the city far beyond the clouds came into view. We made it.

Everything hurt. Hands, many hands carried me and healing energy flowed slowly into me. Vertebrae popped back in to place as the spine began to move back to normal. Cool air filled my lungs. I could breathe. My chest rose as my lungs filled deeply and exhaled hard. Muscle fibers rewove themselves.

"Father, he lives!" I heard an angelic voice say.

"It is a miracle of the highest favor. Father has blessed him."

"He has lived up to his name. He has honored his father."

"Of course he lives," I thought. *"He's right here...*Wait what did they just say? My father left when I was but a child. What does he have to do

with any of this?" I tried to pick the voice out and track the sound of it with my eyes, but the motion around me was a flurry. Many hands continued to touch me and heal me further. However, the damage had taken its toll on my mental state. A swift tiredness wash over me that bathed me in peace and closed my eyes. Light descended all around me. The need for sleep beckoned.

"The Defender chose him for many reasons," I heard a voice say that sounded like Malnuras. "One of which is the resilience to bounce back from death."

"My student has surpassed the teacher it appears," Mathias chimed in. "Let him rest. He has earned it. He will need more than healing magic to regain his strength and recover from such grievous wounds."

"He saved Heaven."

"Indeed. He made his father proud."

Focus was impossible. I gave in.

XVI

Portals

Moonlight fell on the surface on the land, illuminating everything in an eerie glow while casting many more shadows in return. The world was silent at this late hour, far too silent than it should be. No critters dared stir where thousands of sounds usually filled the night with their orchestra of nature, all playing the same song in different sections like a real concert it seemed. Tonight the forest knew something was about to happen, and all those critters hid and stayed quiet – all the way down to the strange crickets that crawled here.

This was the third day of my hiding like a fugitive. My instructions were to wait here and, under no circumstances, leave the area. So it felt like hiding out or hiding from something. I was never much for slinking around. It was hard to not feel kind of dirty, like I was up to something, especially here. A foul stench hung in the air that I could not quite identify yet.

The soil was dark brown to red in places and a murky purple color in other areas. Even the rocks had streaks from the taint that was millions of years old and infected the stones. I had smelled foul odors before and this was a close second to offend my nostrils. All of it smelled almost like...I paused. I almost had it, but then the thought escaped me. My mind began to run through all the smells I had experienced in the last few years. No familiar smell registered. It felt it was coming out my pores and had fully permeated my nose and lungs.

My minded drifted back.

It was hard to imagine what had happened to me in the last few weeks. Upon waking up, I was staring into the face of my teacher, only it was not really Malnuras. It was another of the faces of God. He was one of millions that had a different embodiment. Each managed the aspects of Heaven. Feeding the people, listening to them, and granting audience with God occasionally were among their tasks. It was strange to think people here ate since they were just a soul. I guess the desire to feast did not fade even with a perfect body that would never get sick or die. Daemon hordes attacking Heaven to consume your soul was not covered by that clause.

The story of the after is when a soul dies they go to be with God in Heaven if they followed the tenants of that faith. What they did not know was you could choose where to go or live, but your soul had to be manifested in a somewhat of a physical form. A daemon could hurt you still, and then consume your essence, leaving you just a husk. You would not exist anymore. In God's plan, he did not account for Heaven being under siege for thousands of years. It was not a short sight on his all-knowing ability. Lucifer was sneaky and caught him off guard. Death is what allows souls to leave Earth when they die, and the blood of your body is what activates the portal to allow your soul to go to him. I had to chuckle that God was so busy maintaining protection of his occupants that he had to turn his back on everywhere else. Not many prayers found his ears nor did help from On High come around much.

So to open my eyes and see another version of God standing over me was unsettling and unexpected. Sure, he had all of Malnuras's features and even his memories, but the voice was different enough but still the same. The mannerisms slightly changed. Yet, it was not my teacher; and to think that I had been living with part God himself for many years. He never told me anything that would have led me to even see that. It was hard to not feel lied to, but I understood that he had to keep it secret. If word got out that he was God, any time we visited a town outside the walls would raise questions. People who had chosen to live outside the city of Heaven would have no real memory of it. They lived in a place of their choosing. Not many wanted to leave the afterlife.

They did not get visits from any of God's faces.

Yet some held onto the idea of life and chose to exist outside of Heaven's walls. Villages and cities were all over the realm; none within several thousand miles of Heaven. It was doubtful that the horde knew they were there until recently. The city of Heaven held the attention of the horde for several thousand years, until now. That last village was proof. The horde consumed them all. A moment of remembrance was all that I could afford right now.

Those who tended to my wounds mentioned that the walls were safe and the shield was back at full strength. They called me the "Savior of Heaven" when greeting me. Everyone knew who I was and so many people wanted to shake my hand or hug me. This was a utopian society without a care in the world, until they saw it was vulnerable. Their underlying fears were now all over their faces, with a good reason to feel this way. They did not feel safe. It would take some time to restore.

It was strange to me that the man escorting me around had no name.

They called him Father. His face was known everywhere as the face of God. I wanted to call him Malnuras, but the need to do so went away in the first few days. He was also very scholarly.

He spent many hours explaining to me how things operated in Heaven. God's power provided everything for the people. They did not have to work for food; someone provided for those who felt the need to or simply enjoyed the experience. The city did not have any waste, as the food eaten looked like food but was really made of energy that nourished the spirit. Anything the mind could desire was available. You could eat and never get fat.

My food was organic, for there were thousands of people that had their own gardens and grew food for the simple pleasure of watching life grow. I needed real nourishment. Someone slaughter several cows in my honor. There was plenty of meat at every meal. My strength returned in time. It was tasty.

One question played on my mind that I did not know how to address. After teleporting back to the city, while my consciousness faded, the words, "My son has surpassed his father," played over and over. Confusion was prevalent. Mathias's voice spoke in reference to me. The statement made no sense unless he thought of me as his son after training under him for many years. However, several times there had been a strange occurrence. Several conversations I shared with him happened as if he had been there with me during a potentially failing moment. A conversation I heard only in my head.

Had I actually been communicating with him? Was there a telepathic link with my master? Was he indeed my father? The man my mother claimed to be my father left when I was barely crawling, so my memory of him did not exist. They chose me for this position because of my compassion and the desire to protect life. Was there more to it?

I pondered this for days when Mathias came to visit me. He had a guest with him. The look on my face must have been priceless to find myself face to face with the Sasquatch. It or he did not say much but did give me a nod. It was awkward to me to be as tall as he was. When I shook his hand, I heard something in my head.

"You will replace me when you return."

It almost was not a voice, but a feeling coming across between us accompanied by a very male presence. I nodded and he stepped and started to shimmer from sight. The hope of more conversation degraded with a look. He was not much of a conversationalist. Several of the sessions at the campfire had shown him teaching the people, but perhaps that instruction was very rudimentary or basic. I blinked. He was gone.

So that is what that looks like.

I stood silently. My eyes locked on my master. He smiled at me for a slight moment and there was a proud look on his face. To my surprise, he took a knee and bowed.

"Hail to the savior of Heaven," his words came rather stoic and firm.

"Master stand up, please," I urged.

He rose up gracefully and bowed.

"Why the formalities and titles? You know I did what I was trained to do."

"No, you are wrong.   We designed your training to protect Earth...not to save Heaven. Yet you managed to do both, bringing honor to yourself...and to your family."

"Master, what do you mean my family?" I asked, feeling hesitant and confused.

"You are Nathanael's son."

"Are you Nathanael?"

"I am."

My stomach knotted. Emotion welled up behind my eyes.

"Why do I address you as Mathias?" I stammered, fighting back disbelief.

"My given name is "Gift of God." You may know it as Matthew in your world. The pronunciation in your tongue would be "Mataeson" when God created me. When I earned my name and became Yahweh's General in charge of the city's defenses, my name changed to Nathanael and Mataeson became my surname. God allowed me to marry, giving me the hope of having offspring to give my name. I became an Archangel. I married another angel, Millennia ago, and stayed with her for hundreds of years. When she died, I mourned for a hundred more...before allowing myself the chance to take a mate again."

"So how did you end up with my mother, and why was I left with her to be raised in Hell?" I felt my voice crack.

"I decided to look for a human wife since the city was not under immediate threat. I started spending more time on Earth. Eighty three years later, I met your mother. The simplicity of attraction won. I fell in love with her and married her according to Earth's tradition. We had a child born of our love. You started to show angelic tendencies right away. This scared your mother, and I owed her an explanation."

"Once a child is created, a decision has to be made for that child to be human, living in one world, or Nephilim, a resident of both worlds. Your mother, when she learned who I was, could not handle the reality of it and chose to have her memory erased. Sadly, this process can cause severe depression. Your mother chose to drink heavily to deal with it and married your stepfather who mistreated you. For this, I am sorry."

He lowered his head.

My thoughts floored me. Here was my actual father. My mother had never been very forth coming regarding anything, other than he left months after my birth. He was an Archangel in charge of the city's defenses. The awe factor went off the scale, and I found myself embracing him tightly.

My father is an Archangel!

For several moments we embraced. Tears openly flowed. I did not care. This was more joyous than any victory. All the brutal lessons taught to me by my real father and the days I cursed under my breath meant nothing. His lessons had made me the warrior I am, and according to his own words, I had surpassed even his skills.

"I wish we had more time, my son, but something requires your attention. I have written instructions on this scroll. All of the details are there. Your training is over. It is time to join the war and fulfill your role," he said, smiling and putting his hand on my shoulder.

"That day in the village when I told you my name...You knew didn't you?" I said.

"Yes. Tathlyn is the name I gave you as a child. I had hoped it would come to you...and it did."

Warmth hugged me like a blanket.

"I will do as you ask, Father." I smiled. It was nice to hear he had faith in my abilities. He turned and began to walk away when he stopped and turned back.

"So now that you know who your teacher really was, had you not re-trieved all of him, the shield would not have been able to heal...as it is the Father's sheer will alone that keeps the horde out. I do not know if you real-ize how close we came to losing the city. That would have caused a cata-clysm to the universe."

"What do you mean, Father? Would Heaven have been destroyed?"

"Not just Heaven. The Heavenly Father would have started every-thing over."

"Oh..." It was all I could manage to say as my mind failed to wrap around his words. Nathanael walked away. I was sad at seeing my father go, but a strange peace came over me. Somehow, things made perfect sense.

I got to meet two important people today.

I closed the door and went back inside. I smiled knowing my father was proud.

Familiar voices whispered in the recesses of my mind. They spoke umongst themselves as if trying not to disturb me. My blades carried on a conversation in hushed tones. I sat and listened for a bit while arranging my thoughts and feelings about the recent events. A reference caught my attention. The need to interrupt the topic was too strong.

"So the two of you knew about my father and you kept it a secret?"

"It is true," they responded. "Nathanael has kept the two of us around for quite some time. We served under him."

"Wait...You served under him? What do you mean?" I asked.

"We are the souls of angels, fallen in battle. We chose to continue our service for the greater good by occupying and blending with weapons to increase their power. This honor bestows upon an Archangel added power. We did not know whom we would bond with when the time came. It gave us both great pleasure and has been an honor to serve you."

A long pause ensued

"What are your names?" I asked. "And I do not mean righteous fury."

"Sabathiel," the left hand said. "Communicating and creating divine light was my station. Divine light is what the City of Heaven uses to defend its walls. I create the flames that engulf your weapons when your energy is fully charged. That energy converted to divine light. By destroying me, another angel would have to be trained to replace me before any more divine light weapons could be created to defend the city."

I was stunned. The honor given to me was greater than I could have imagined.

"Radueriel," the right hand responded. "I use Heavenly Father's divine energy to create new angels. I fell before the invasion of Heaven. Father was in the process of creating another to replace me before hell breached the realm of Heaven and the assault on the city began. Father had to turn his attention to defending the city."

"Our divine sparks were given a chance to continue to serve. Usually, this was one of the Archangels. Then you came along, proving to be worthy and surpassing all expectations. God granted the honor to use us in the creation of your weapons to Nathanael. Your weapons were crafted soon after your arrival and stored in a vault, waiting for you to be ready."

"You honor me by sharing this," I said, enamored by their story.

"You may call us Saba and Radu for short should you need to address us individually. We felt it was time to tell you but were unsure of the timing."

"You chose well, my friends. Reflection on the events that have transpired helped me place this in perspective. Now we must go on a mission for Father. Shall we find out what it is?" A warm vibration came from my blades in agreement. I grabbed the scroll case and opened it. A gemstone fell into my hand. Upon contact, it flooded me with images. I knew where I had to go. The location was vividly clear.

After packing some food, I took the time to meditate and reflect upon the day's events. Time passed as my memory recounted and absorbed learning about who Nathanael really was. The memories were crisp and clear, as if my mind gave extra processing power to remembering them.

My arrival at the location was uneventful. The heavily forested area was full of leaves beginning to turn with the onset of fall. Even though the realm was not on a spherical planet, it still had a sun and the four seasons for those that chose to live outside the city to identify with.

It was very hard to believe that so many years had passed...and the years were definitely longer than at home. Nathanael told me once that years here were about fifty percent longer for someone choosing to live outside the walls. This affected me because my body functioned normally like a human. That meant there was five hundred and forty something days passing here but inside, Heaven time did not pass at all. I tried to count the exact number of days once, possibly last year, or the year before that.

A creature hit me hard on the head once. I lost my memory for a few days and lost track. It was a valuable lesson, one I intended not to repeat. It has since been coined the "not blocking with your head" lesson. It worked well. Since then, however, I had lost track again and stopped. I really had no clue how long it had been. Whatever counted as fall or autumn was in at its full height. The leaves on the ground made sneaking difficult. I had problems moving about silently, whereas my foes did not. Because it was autumn, there was no other way. My mind refocused. I never stopped looking around when reflecting, but it was easy to chase the rabbit and stay in a meditative loop.

The silence as I panned around was eerie. The night before, the area was a slight bustle of activity. Most of the creatures did not exist on earth. I knew what to stay away from; all of them. Especially when you watch a bird attacked by what looks like mosquitoes and its bones are all that remain in moments. My protective barrier was up when they tried to eat me. Using my swords to ignite ability to burn them away was more than satisfying. I swore they cried out in pain as they burned then burst from the superheated fluid boiling inside them. It was disgusting that they existed at all.

Other species here could not be identified either. I was not any sort of an animal nut, but I noticed the same principles did not exist here. There were other monster type creatures. Sure an actual daemon in the physical sense that could fly made sense. Large ones that looked like some sort of mythical creature like in the movies I could fathom. Bipedal creatures with multiple limbs, in uneven numbers, placed in non-symmetrical places on its body, had me believe that this place was the home the misfits of evolution.

I even saw a bird with its head located between its legs. Watching it walk was strange. How it did not hit itself in the head with its knees made me scratch mine. It had to walk bow legged. This was comical to watch until you see it eat a critter almost as large as it was and fly away afterwards.

It was hard to fathom things worse or even more different. It took years before these strange creatures started to catch my eye. Training kept me focused for so long that unless I was fighting it...it did not exist. I was used to daemons, though. Their ichor stunk so badly, the desire to vomit faded over the years.

Suddenly something was not right. A subtle noise. A slight buzz kept reaching a crescendo followed by a small popping sound. All this was barely audible at first. I thought it was a forest sound for a few minutes and perhaps the cautious nature of the forest had taken over. The volume rose slowly and increased in tempo. I stood up and peeked around the large rock my back touched. A steady popping sound echoed around the area. Changes in the air pressure worried me...but I could not see anything moving. No motions caught my eye even with my extra sensitive abilities to perceive the "not so there." I could only hear it. It made a bubbling sound kind of like what happened when you blew into a straw in your milk as a child.

It continued this rhythmic but not consecutive pattern. I gazed into the moonlit night, reaching out with my mind as well as my ears to find the source. Something caught my eye. In the distance coming down an incline, a summoner daemon approached. These were particular nasty daemons. I had faced these once. It moved towards something...clueless to my presence. My senses still could not pinpoint the sound.

I turned on my cloaking and moved slow, trying to get a better vantage point that offered me more information on what approached. My path took me to more difficult terrain. Stepping around in this area created more noise as the leaves crunched with every step. I moved slowly, very slowly to avoid detection. My footfalls still made noise no matter how slow I moved, but moving was necessary.

A desired vantage point was only a few more steps away. I steadied myself and watched. My instincts told me to wait, but the desire to kill it before it could summon more of his minions was strong. It became harder and harder to resist attacking them...so I entered a waking meditation to check my urge. With steady breathing and focus the urge fell into check.

Patience Tathlyn, patience.

I remained hidden and watched. To my horror, my breath created trace amounts of steam in the night air. My cloaking did not extend out far. I prayed that this did not give away my position. It would be embarrassing to fail a mission based on it being so cold and having a dire need to breathe. My focus shifted to slower breaths making them longer and deeper. Only time would tell if they would find me or not. The sound came from the direction opposite the daemon. I closed my eyes and listened, reaching out with my senses.

After mere moments, my senses pointed my internal energy and it was definitely towards the summoner but off to the left. Still unable to see anything, I began to feel crazy knowing there was something there and having no idea what it was. I decided to stay cloaked and swing wide around the area the sound was coming from. Moving in and around some of the larger boulders and rocks, I kept my eyes on the direction the summoner came from. It was tall enough that he stood out.

I fought a wounded summoner some time ago and he was still tough enough. Some beasts and monsters are stronger right before they die. This type of daemon killed angels even when outnumbered. It was not very hard to remember that encounter. My father Nathanael (back then he was simply Master) and I had waded in to a group of daemons not knowing there was a summoner around the corner. The smaller ones died quickly, which was normal. Suddenly there it was. I saw Nathanael engage it full on and scored some critical shots before the monster rag dolled him. A series of fast blows to his head and torso and down he went. He did not move and I feared he was dead. Had we prepared, the fight would have been much different. But not knowing the summoner was there, or how tough they were, was a factor we had not considered.

I knew for a fact that Nathanael had bested two summoners fore. They were harder to beat than the big six-legged ones with four wings that spit me out like a spit wad. I still shuddered at being in the beast's mouth. This one was smaller by far but still twice my size. It was faster and used a huge crooked sword that had an eerie green glow to it. The wounded one came at me right away after it appeared to kill Nathanael. Logic did not guide my hand. I came off a high guard like a giant scorpion's tail.

My motions were a blur to me that day, and I got a lucky shot in. Tactics did not win the day. I went from high to low in my stance and apparently that threw the daemon off. It also misjudged and both of my swords found its abdomen, right under the armor plate. They bit flesh and sunk to the hilt as I turned the energy on and yanked them free. They might be immune to fire on the outside, but on the inside, it was still flesh and my blades cooked its insides like they were sausages. Soft flesh boiled internally in seconds and burst the abdomen cavity. Entrails covered the area, me included. I wondered if I would ever get used to that.

When I turned around, Master was sitting up and shaking his head to get the blood out of his eyes. I was overjoyed at the sight of him looking well and felt a bit stupid that it happened. With our skill levels being equal now, the only thing that separated us was he had more experience of course. Creativity was the answer. This day, we simply got jumped and lucky all in the same time. Father was surprised by my victory and thankful that I had paid attention and did not freeze up when he went down. That is something that happens to most students when their Master falls before them. I went the other direction and became positively enraged, slaying my enemy.

The truth was, I lost it...and that is not how a warrior acts.

My rage allowed me to strike my target, but skill did more than imagined.

As my mind returned to the present, I promised myself the terms of engagement would be of my choosing. Summoner daemons were quite disgusting...with no obvious gender whatsoever. There was no reproduction.

They created another of themselves over time. Thankfully, this gestation cycle was long, for these things were the toughest.

It stood nearly twelve feet tall, had the normal number of arms and legs but three wings. The third wing extended to help them turn tighter and was smaller but articulated. It had spines that could extend on every one of its joint that moved and some in places that did not retract. Attacking one of these things head on was normally suicide. Nathanael never had time to go over the tactics I needed to defeat one when the win merited on luck. The only thing he said when I was helping him off the ground was a good strike to a shoulder area reduced its effectiveness.

In hindsight, that was cryptic advice.

As it approached, the first thing I noticed was the armored carapace on its shoulders. I did not remember seeing that on one we killed. This one was definitely nastier. The fear it emanated washed over me. Serenity and balance replaced the desire to unleash on this abomination without the benefit of tactics. Normally I had the urge to charge right into the fray, but as it stopped and chuckled, I was totally calm. It seemed to be very pleased with itself at this moment. It began to wave its arms around. Energy began to coalesce in front of it and I felt strange. Suddenly, a small twinge got my attention.

The last time I felt this was…wait….

I never got an answer out of my father regarding this feeling. In fact, every time I brought it up, he changed the subject. Being so tired of asking him, eventually I forgot and the question slipped away. It was just a twinge, but the lingering feeling was there. I had no idea what was going to transpire or how, simply that a summoner had come. There was a pinching sensation in my mind that ran up from my core.

Ignoring it, I moved my position further right of this ugly daemon. Sure, they were all disgusting to look at, but this one was grotesque. My cloaking held, for it would have seen me without it. As my vantage point changed, there was something shimmering in front of the beast. A faint line hung in the air about eight feet off the ground. It looked almost like string that danced as it fluxed. There was a black tinge to it, but it was opaque. Swinging even wider brought it now into full view. It hit me like a ton of boulders falling on my head like in the cartoons.

This was a portal, or the starting of one.

How could it open from here? I had a ton of questions that no one could answer up to this point when I watched the daemon start to move his hands and arms in certain motions, tracing symbol in the air. As I watched, those armored plates over the shoulders lifted up and energy that looked almost like smoke reached out and took a hold of the portal. It stretched slightly. The daemon made some sort of sound and out from under those plates flew a bunch of smaller daemons different from a normal locust daemon emerged. They appeared and started to grow, making these horrible screeching sounds. A chorus of daemonic language echoed in my ears and it began to hurt. The pain grew. The summoner began to glow. He started to shift back and forth like he was there one second, then gone, then back again.

I stood in amazement and wonder at what it had done and what it was about to do. Suddenly the frequency of this shifting increased in speed and started to make a whirring sound like a flutter. There was a flash. When my eyes finally adjusted, two began to phase in behind it. A curse came out of my mouth. For a second, I thought the smaller ones might have heard me. They were growing rapidly and flitting about. I finally had an answer.

This is how they worked!

"How do I stop this?" ran through my mind. This was not good when it was just one of them. Now two more of them gaited in. The smaller ones were almost full size now. I analyzed the situation. Nothing came to mind. Uncertainty flowed to all corners of my thoughts. What if this was another attempt to gain access to the City? The two new summoners finally solidified.

I cursed again. Father held something back. I thought of calling to him mentally but knew this was mine alone to handle.

Great. Taking one was hard enough, now there were three.

Now the trio of them started the process of stretching the portal open. The same thing happened as before. They opened up those plates on their shoulders and tendrils of energy shot out but instead of connecting to the gate, they connected to the one standing in front connected to the portal already. The tendrils attached and something new unfolded. First thing was all of a sudden the smaller daemons started to kill each other. Ichor flew everywhere and the portal open about an inch. The main summoner was now iridescent. I could see his form still but it was almost fully opaque and the energy drained from it into the two behind him. They in turn had a bunch of tiny little daemons erupt from the same areas as the shoulder plates had covered. They both began to chant something and energy began to build even higher. My stomach was upset. I started to wince a bit but could not take my eyes of this event. I had to learn everything I could.

Those two began to glow and the process repeated. The smaller daemons all began to slaughter themselves and the two newcomers phased in and out for seconds before a major shift, but this time it was four. Tendrils came out as they solidified and the plates opened up to release the next group of small daemons. This process seemed to be repeating itself about every ten to fifteen count and I started to do the math. Soon there would be more than I could imagine.

I looked down at my swords, already in my hands without even a thought. The incredible feeling from holding them made me smile. Confidence to take the whole host on by myself became a reality even though Malnuras's death shook me at the time. Reflecting, this event travelled across all my training making me realize one thing.

Everything happens for a reason and becomes a lesson.

The voices came into my head. Without even thinking about it, I responded internally.

There are now seven Summoners.

Remember the wall!

There is something was to be said for being a smart tactician and I was learning and processing every second this new information. My thoughts consumed me for a second and I tried to remember everything that happened on the wall. I ran over lesson after lesson in my mind as fast as my brain would let me review. The words he said about the shoulders. Those huge plates were like a breastplate on a warrior only ten times as thick. I looked at my swords. Even on a good day, piercing that kind of armored covering straight on would be difficult.

Then I remembered the flames. They could carve deeper. My mind finally opened fully. The last one cooked like a lobster.

I smiled. I could do this.

Energy rolled into the area from all around. My insides twisted in agony. It was hard to stand. The seven from before glowed bright, connected with each other. There was a flash and I expected to see fifteen if the ratio held true. To my horror, I was both right and wrong. My eyes fought to adjust. Standing behind the summoners was one of the big ones with four wings and six legs. I knew I could not take the summoners, the minions, and one of these big nasty dragon-like daemons. Whatever happened, the battlefield could not stay the way it was, so I watched the scene as it unfolded in front of me.

This changed everything.

Right after the dragon-daemon arrived, it did something I did not expect. I assumed some sort of stance and began to grunt and roll its abdomen. The dark colored flesh rippled like a wave. This went on for moments and was followed a shower of fluids that exploded from the belly of the beast. It went everywhere and it stunk. In this fluid, there were dozens of the flyers lying scattered over the area. They began to move. The summoners glowed even brighter.

I lost count of the bodies that were starting to stir in the horrible fluid when it hit me. That was the faint smell I had been dealing with all three days except this was so putrid that my stomach turned several times. My seasoned skill in slaying these creatures by the hundreds and their ichor covering me is the only thing that kept me from making noise by donating my stomach to the ground.

I was hurting. This was worse than the day at the portal. The smell reached right inside and grabbed me by the base of my spine. I was pinned in place. It took sheer willpower to stand. The medium daemons now stood and began moving around. It was some sort of embryonic fluid. This rotted the ground just like negative energy itself in physical form. Disgust turned to anger.

The medium daemons then took to the air, swirling in a chaotic formation like bees around the big one. They gained speed and maneuvered around. I glanced at the portal. It was now more than five feet across and growing. I was in trouble.

I predicted, if they killed the big one, it would open the portal the rest of the way and complete the ritual. My pain leveled off. My arms felt weighted as if held down by chains. I felt hopeless as if about to fail. I had to act...I needed to act. This had to stop. I needed my blood lust. Where was it? I had to break the hold this weakness had on me. I wanted to cry out but doing so would get me killed. My own teeth dug into my tongue and crimson began to flow.

My arms shook. My legs felt like roots not wanting to break free of the ground. Yet I lifted them...one step forward...two steps...then five. Sheer force of will was moving my feet. I could hear Father's words ringing in my mind. Slow motion took over. The flying host of hundreds was in a passing formation and was about to open up the big female that birthed them. I heard the words in my mind.

"You have to hit them in the shoulder!"

Looking at the closest Summoners, I realized something. The plates lifted and the tendrils of energy came from the exposed area. I could see strange looking flesh in a hive like formation with little honeycomb patterns. There were tendons and strange looking organs. It really was vulnerable there. There was no protection with it lifted.

My feet left the ground ten paces away. Momentum carried me across the forty feet. Swords were out wide; this exposed area was my target. There was enough of the creature still in phase and my swords found their mark. My blades bit flesh right under the open plates on both sides. A blinding flash erupted.

Time exploded.

A crack like thunder deafened my ears. I was already flying off some direction, blinded. My skin was of fire. Nerves head to toe felt the impact. A vortex swirled and pulled me towards where the portal was forming. Seeing through the flying debris was difficult but I managed to see the seven summoners were gone, probably consumed right away and many of the flyers were gone.

Impact!

Hitting hard, my body tumbled across the rocky surface before taking a knee. The maelstrom of energy tore at me for several more seconds before it died to a lulling wind. Dust filled the air. I could barely see anything. The vile dirt, muddied by the daemon fluid, got in my mouth. My teeth were caked Gagging was breathing. A large shadow in front of me...that I thought was the coalescing of the dust into a small vortex...now went up in to the air like a small tornado.

Reduces its effectiveness? That is funny.

Did the summoner daemon best father that day, or did father fake it so he could see my response in dealing with something that he knew would be a challenge? All I could do was laugh while the earth fell all around me.

The wind slowed. All the dust and dirt fell to the ground.

Debris continued to rain down, taking most of the darkness out of the air. I realized the shadow was not the dust or dirt. It was the flyers coming right at me with a big six-legged dragon daemon in a full run as they swarmed around, blotting the large one out. I could hear their teeth chattering with excitement and their guttural speech sounded like a daemonic chorus, only it was every musical key all at once. Almost like the sound of bees coming.

Bees would be nice compared to this mess.

Since I had learned to fight, a certain amount of refinement came with the power. The knowledge of one's achievement makes one think almost like a scholar or in a similar fashion. It dawned on me that facing such odds was fool hardy. Standing upon the walls of Heaven I saw millions, but I stood with angels that numbered as many. The word escaped my lips and the first wave came in high and from the right. I could not count the incoming horde, for its number defied logic and blotted out the bright moon.

"Shit!"

I happened to glance behind me at the portal. It remained, but reduced back to a rift. Then it began to grow again. The fabric flexed and flapped like a sail on a ship getting wider and wider, moving faster and faster. I could see movement on the other side. Light started to pour through and bathed the area in a warm hue...much like the unnatural light of a florescent bulb might cast in a room. A white room now, sparsely decorated came to view.

The horde flew back a thousand feet or more by the vortex and was still dozens of moments out. I took my eyes off them to afford a better look inside the rift, as this was a unique opportunity. I peeked in a little further and, to my horror, found a hospital. There was an occupied gurney there.

Fury hit me. They were going to attack a helpless place. Instinct told me to close this portal and face my greatest battle. Time was running out. The sky was now black, for there were so many incoming flyers that it blotted out the moon completely as they came. There was not enough time on this side to close it from here and defend myself at the same time. I knew what needed doing. I had seen the horde at Heaven's walls. I had estimated millions of legions there in the siege. This number that came at me was only a fraction of that army, but who knows what I could not see. This was a force meant to establish a beachhead on Earth. The assault on Heaven had, once again, been the distraction.

My instructions were vague. Father did not tell me I would be witnessing a portal opening, or dealing with those beings responsible. Now I knew what he meant for me to do. I pictured the Summoners and the acts to follow. I focused on my Father and called his name out in my mind. "Father, here it is, this is what we needed to know. Use this information well." Energy left me as the message went out. I hoped he would get it. They now knew what to look for in the daemon ranks to staunch the tide of the portals opening to Earth.

If I jumped through and used it as a choke point, then that would buy me the time to close it? I should be able to teleport back. The portal was only several strides away. Nearing the opening, I gasped in shock at what I saw. *The body in the bed was mine!* I dove without delay head first through the opening. If my body remained unprotected, they would win.

This just got personal.

Light began to fade. I envisioned the portal collapsing as tendrils of energy latched on behind me and began to fold it up like paper. The energy flowed from me out to the edges of the fabric. Like before, invisible hands began grabbing that portal's edges to pull them closed again. I felt the bubble finally pop as it collapsed in on itself.

My body began to dematerialize. Panic arose. Darkness swallowed me. I swirled into the void. My essence flowed in circles. Ahead, two lights speed towards me. The closer I got the face of a beautiful woman appeared in each portal. Her blond hair glowed as if sunlight made up each of the hairs. I felt myself slam into something soft. My mind went blank. Beeping in the distance sounded like an alarm on a machine.

What just happened? Where was I?

Part II

XVII

Rude Awakenings

My eyelids crept open.

Darkness, my ally for ages, fled at the first sign of light. Blackness remained behind and surrounded me like a tainted sweater. Dark and pungent odors filled my senses, as if evil itself was just there and I was its meal. I felt submerged in some sort of fluid that secreted out of my pores. It gave me the creeps. My body hurt head to toe and something was not right. Painfully, I raised my head. Bad idea! As my eyes came into focus, a splitting headache followed. After a few moments, the images came into focus.

A hospital.

What am I doing in a hospital?

The clean smell of bleach and sanitation drifted about. I painfully panned the room with strained eyes. There were pictures next to the bed. My mother, Jason, and Jesus, all in different frames, thankfully, because that would have really freaked me out. *Okay weird combination,* I thought. Then it hit me...my mother and Jason were older. Hell, he had facial hair, my mother did too, but it was not that noticeable. I sucked in a gulp of air as I tried to sit up. It caused a spasm. That is when the priest sleeping in a corner chair caught my eye. My head began to throb even more and weightlessness made everything spin a bit. I was descending backwards into the pillows before long.

Images swam in my head. Pain shot though every nerve in my

278

body. I heard something that sounded like when someone flat lines on a heart monitor. BEEEEEEEEEEEEPPPPPPPP! Everything was so confusing. My response was to close my eyes and moan. "This must be hell!" The words sounded more like croaking. It did not even sound like English.

I heard shouting coming from somewhere nearby. More noise followed a crashing sound. My thoughts continued to race. Suddenly there was someone next to me. A gentle presence masked in strength...female. Her scent was subtle. Kind of a sweet smell but there was something else unidentifiable. Firm hands held me down as another set of hands checked what I could only assume were vitals. A slight pinch in my arm, followed by a warm dizziness, rolled over me.

My eyes opened to confront my assailant. She was beautiful, almost angelic. Long blonde hair pulled back tightly. The brownest eyes I had ever seen next to that pinup model Jason had...what was her name again? I thought about it for a moment. My then mind raced back to the woman before me. Was the concept of a hot nurse a fable? *Maybe this was Heaven.* To my right, my eyes lazily turned and made me jump; another woman looked me over. She had a huge nose, squinty eyes, and black hair, all mounted on a very large, round head. Her face started to twist and melt away. I began to shudder and tried to crawl away. Vice-like hands gripped me. I could go nowhere.

"Hold still!" she said. "Dammit Eryn, hold him, he's convulsing!"

"I have him, and no, he's not convulsing, but you startled him," the goddess spoke in return. The mere sound of her voice made me calm a bit. That warmth running through me was increasing more and more. "This must be what drugs feel like," my voice uttered.

Silence gripped the room as eyes locked on mine and looks of surprise ensued.

"Did he just speak?" said a male voice from across the room. "Sweet Jesus, I better call his mother." Footsteps clapped out of the room and down the hall.

I panned the room then back to the beautiful blonde. She held my gaze for just a moment and smiled in a caregiver kind of way. There was warmth about her. A depth in her eyes suggested to me that she had seen many horrible things.

How would I know that? I am only sixteen.

My mind overloaded with images and memories. I tensed up and closed my eyes. Memories of pain and suffering mixed with violence. Had someone been reading me stories of such horrors? A creeping darkness pinned me to the bed. There were images of creatures crawling out of a dark spot that was fading. They began to swoop on me, taunting me as they flew with great speed, and all I could do was throw up my hands and cower.

"What the hell am I seeing? Make them go away!" My hands guarded my face and no matter what I did I could still see them swirling around me. Voices, so dark and guttural, spoke and the gestures were obvious. When they spoke, some viscous fluid dripped from their mouths that, disgusting in color, was almost black like a putrid vileness. Whimpering was all I could do...I waved my hands in front of my face to fend them off.

I heard that soothing voice again. "Shhh, you are hallucinating. There's nothing there. It's okay," she said softly.

Before I could think, I replied, "No shit!" even though the images did not appear any less then real. They were real enough and kept coming at me, but I noticed they never touched me and they began to fade with each pass as a white light bathed them from somewhere. The room returned to view. Waves of nausea hit me. They crashed against my head. My stomach knotted, each time causing my body to shudder with each pass. I must have been convulsing more than imagined for my body was practically lifting off the table every time one hit. This lasted for several moments. Strong, gentle hands on me managed to hold me in place.

"This will pass, but it will take time. Try to relax." An image of Jason with his goatee jumped in my head. He looked so much older. I felt an eyebrow painfully rise on my face.

"How long has it been?" the question finally moved its way to the surface of my thought and found a way to my lips.

"I think you should wait until the counselor comes in, I wou…."

"How long, dammit?" I demanded as the anger in me started to rise. I tried to sit up, but her strong hands held me firmly in place.

"Strangely…six years to the day," the doctor chimed in after removing the stethoscope from my chest. "You have been in a coma for six years, Dieter."

Six years…what the hell? Where did he come from?

"Call me Dietz," I interjected before her words sunk in. "Only my mother calls me Dieter."

She smiled.

"Did you hear me, Dietz? Six years!" she repeated this time with a softer voice. The words processed but did not fully take hold, for it made no sense what she was saying.

"Wait," I thought, "the accident. A car had hit us both, and then I hit a tree."

Images of Jason on the hood of a car with a mangled bike smashed on the bumper flashed through my mind. It was out of control and my view faded back as the car swerved off the road. The look of terror the driver's face before it flipped over was the last thing I remember before darkness rolled over my vision like a black cloud of smoke obscuring everything. Thoughts of the lake swirled before me bringing the feeling of the pretty girl's lips upon mine. I must have made a funny face or something. The nurse tried to not laugh, but a kind of stifled snicker happened, and she cleared her throat.

My mind raced again but this time it stopped on one stabbing question like someone turned the wheel of fortune with my thoughts being the topic: *If it has been six years, then why did I hurt so damn bad and not just have a dull ache?* I paused and swallowed what little saliva that had begun to gather to moisten my throat. Another breath followed. They got easier, the deeper the intake as if my oxygen was cut short, making me weak all these years.

"So why does my body hurt so much if it's had time to heal?"

The murmuring around the room was inaudible...but I could tell there was another voice now that must have joined the noise. The bed began to raise me to an upright position; the nurse stepped back when it hit its zenith. The first thing I noticed was her figure. Damn it looked good. I started to undress her with my eyes when a man stepped forward blocking my view. He must have done it on purpose because he completely blocked her out. My eyes refocused. *Figures.* I was not staring that hard… I can barely focus… maybe that is what it looked like.

"Dietz, this is going to be hard to understand, but I want you to hear me out before you respond, okay?"

I nodded my head the best I could, my eyes transfixed on his horrible tie he wore that had caught my attention soon after they refocused. His voice was rather pleasant and made me relax a little bit more.

"How are his vitals?" I felt hands checking my pulse. A bright light shone in my eyes that made me wince. A beeping came from next to the bed and some equipment that must have been monitoring me was visible but remained blurry. My pulse was steady. A calm image rolled across the screen. There was a pause in the room. I closed my eyes to rest.

"They seem strong, Doctor. I'll go get his doctor, and I want to make su…"

"No need, I am here, stand aside," another male voice commanded as it approached. I felt the other presence move aside. I heard this new voice enter the room and footsteps approach. A hand on my chin, rather firm, lifted my head slightly. I opened my eyes and saw an older man, mid-fifties by his look. Graying hair blotted his head and dark brown eyes. He was clean-shaven despite his horrible haircut, or lack thereof.

"Dieter, I am Doctor Cooper your attending physician. How do you feel?" He turned to the monitor and looked at the nurse. "His vitals are good, this is remarkable. How long has he been awake?" A bright light shined in my eyes. I winced again and blinked a few times to try to shrug off the intruding light.

"Minutes," the nurse responded. "He just awoke. I can't believe how strong his vitals are now because a minute ago he flat lined." She tried to whisper the last word into his ear, but I caught it.

"Did he now?" the new doctor said. "Well young man, you are truly a wonder." He turned to the nurse. "Get him some food and monitor him. Something simple. We don't want to shock his system. I would advise taking it easy for now. You'll have some questions for us soon I imagine. We will have someone speak to you in a bit and tell you what has been going on once we are sure you are stable."

Words came to my lips. "Ok...can I get some water?"

"Sure...Eryn will you?" He nodded as he moved over the grab the chart off the end of my bed and waved another man out of the room that had been at my side moments earlier. He attempted to whisper and I was surprised that I could hear his voice so clearly. "Try not to tell him too much up front unless he shows signs he can handle it. This is truly amazing." The hushed tones continued as they exited the room and a glass of water with a straw arrived held by the beautiful nurse. I took a draw off the straw and swallowed. A small wince hit my face for it even hurt to swallow.

"Easy now," she said with a smile. I managed to smile in return as my head slowly dropped back. Six years. It was not fathomable. My eyes locked on the nurse's for a few seconds before they closed. "I'll get you some food. The mac and cheese is really good and should be soft enough."

"Ok," I responded, not knowing if eating was possible though it sounded good. Pondering how long it had been was hard. My entire body hurt. Any small movements racked me with pain because of my efforts. I decided against moving for now and closed my eyes again. *What the hell was happening?*

The next few hours passed in a blur. When asleep, my dreams were the better part of horrific. Shadow-like creatures ran around me in a field somewhere. The smell was disgusting and indescribable. My body was in some strange position...one that could not have been comfortable. It was like what you would see when someone's body lay broken on the ground. Things were not right with this pose. Several times I sat up ready to scream but was too weak to do so. I paid dearly for my sudden exit from the dreams. Pain racked me each time.

Several nurses paid me many visits. On several occasions, they jumped more than I did when my exodus from a dream was sudden and startling. A few laughed...but the others felt very threatened or timid near me to start with. It added to my growing confusion.

The pretty one came back only once. That was disappointing. Something about her drew me in. Something felt like a magnet. It was not just because of her beauty. Something about her made me curious why deep in her gaze there was so much sadness behind the smile. She did not speak on this occasion, only jotted quickly on my chart and left.

I could get used to looking at her.

Movement caught my eye. They were back...the little bastards. The shadows flitted across the walls and around the room. They moved so fast I could not track them. Like waving a flashlight on a wall, they flowed over top one another. My body tensed up and the heart monitor went nuts. God it hurt to move. What in the world was happening?

Into the room burst several nurses, the pretty one, and the not so pretty one. I was already swatting my hand in front of my face. The biting was new. I was trying to knock these shadow figures off my arms and legs to no avail. I could not move fast enough. "Get them off me...please! Help!"

Strong arms grabbed hold of me. Pressing me to the bed firmly, their nails felt like little teeth in the mouths of these creatures. I screamed and thrashed about trying to get away. In they came. The nurses helped me down. A large one slowly crawled up my chest. His eyes burned with hatred. Spittle ran down his chin onto the sheet, scorching holes as each drop landed. It opened its mouth wide and leaned in. I screamed.

Light exploded into my eyes. The door to the room flew open. More nurses flooded in. My lungs wanted to explode from the panic attack I was suffering. What was real? Where did reality start? I cannot take this. My head felt like it was erupting out of my ears. A gentle hand touched my forehead. Warmth began to spread through the tumultuous waves of fear that held my mind captive only moments before. The light that had felt like it was searing my mind was an ambient glow from the closed blinds mixed with the dimly illuminated light next to the door.

The only shadow I saw was backlit by a radiant light. It felt like I gazed upon an angel for just a moment when the light dimmed and my favorite nurse's face came into focus. It was her hand upon my brow gently stroking my hair back.

"I am having such horrible dreams. They are so real it feels like I am losing my mind. Then just when I wake up, the shadows come at me. I can't take this anymore."

"You are safe," she whispered. "I have you. The doctor is on his way. He will be here in just a moment."

I wept quietly. Slow tears started a journey they did not finish. For each time one crossed my cheek and was about to roll off, her hand tenderly wiped it away. Several moments passed. Her soothing gestures were the only thing I felt or heard. Silence blocked out every sound in the room. I did not even notice the others had left. She sat there for some time while the bustle of nurses and doctors came and went. My eyes never left her. She gazed at me while her hand caressed my face.

I fell asleep.

XVIII

Darkness

"Dieter, my name is Dr. Price. I am the onsite psychologist. The staff and I have been monitoring you for years now. You have a condition that none of us knows quite how to explain, but there are theories." He paused for a moment to flip through some files in a large box. I could tell he lost his train of thought...or perhaps did not have a cohesive one.

Okay, that was a scary start!

"How are you feeling?" the pretty nurse asked, pressing the balloon as the blood pressure sleeve tightened on my arm. I looked at the cuff, at her, and back at the cuff.

Feeling? I thought. *How am I feeling?* The walls of the sanitized room looked pale. There is an I.V. embedded into my upper arm. A monitor of some kind intermittently beeps while I try to sleep. A half-eaten sandwich and a plastic cup of green Jell-O, and a cup of ice chips that I attempted to eat just before the doctor arrived taunted me. There were other machines with numbers and displays. More tubes. My lower back throbbed, and the pillow under my head felt stiff. The nurse finished another round of vitals and left, not taking the time to repeat the question. I leaned my head back and closed my eyes.

I was so grateful to her for the tenderness earlier. My lips could not even muster a smile, but my eyes did manage a squint at her that probably looked like a drunken attempt at a wink. The last few hours had been touch and go on my sanity. Without her there, my chance of survival would have been severely diminished I felt. The door closed behind her. My mind drifted.

"Tell me what you remember about the dreams," his voice casually probed.

I looked up. The psychiatrist was back. Perhaps it was my attention returning. I was concerned he might have actually been talking for a few minutes before I snapped back to...Doctor what's-his-name. I searched for the right words to begin describing my scrambled thoughts and found myself falling into a deep hole in my mind. The words bounced off me repeatedly, like a pinball falling back to the flippers because they held no sway over gravity. Just when I thought I wrapped my mind around an answer, the words fell away again slowly...only to pick up speed and then poof. This visual image happened several times, in the few seconds it took him to ask again. Then I found myself asking my own questions internally – a process that seemed to last for hours. The answers were being elusive.

What *did* I remember? I remembered darkness; lots of pain, and being scared… terrified…that is all. No matter how many different ways the psychiatrist asked, the three elements arranged themselves differently every time. Deeper depths availed, only if my psyche allowed. To tell him more might begin a journey that was more than a pursuit of the truth. I worried about what else I might see. The reality was no matter what truth I told him, things would not go well for me.

My thoughts turned to what had happened. If I spoke about that day, he would think I was nuts. Confusion set in for a moment while I took a breath. There were memories of blood...lots of blood, but the color was too dark – and too red. How I knew it was blood was unknown to me. However, I *did* know. It felt like a shadow cast over my eyes like a veil kept me from seeing anything more. The fear was prevalent, and the muted color made it worse.

How dark is darkness really? Some call it blackness. I like to think of darkness in another light, beyond just describing different degrees of light. You hear the term "That is really dark," or "The darkness in his heart." To me, darkness means something beyond evil, or miscreant. Malevolence is another good word, but even it does not quite hit the mark. Malevolence is a choice. Darkness just exists...everywhere. In the physical, the clinical, and the crusade-like judgments. Darkness simply is.

Darkness has a way of measuring the shadows that steer us one way or another. I may not be the only person in history to refer to the evil nature of man as dark, but my understanding was felt to be greater than most. I did not yet know why. The comparison of blackness to the purity of the night would not allow the two concepts to relate. The simple purity of the night hid all the complexities of the heart and soul.

The soul is like a canvass; everything we do adds color for good or ill. In the end, we have a picture detailing our lives, good and bad, light and dark. These colors camouflaged themselves when one stood in the darkness. We simply existed.

Up until now my canvas had been plain, not having seen or done anything horrific. My head would not fully wrap around this concept and forced me to take pause as images of my child hood raced forward. Drunken so-called "parents" made up the extent of the atmosphere I knew. As I walked around inside my mind, wondering what kind of picture I painted...my own question lingered on the horizon of my thoughts.

"Was the artistry of my deeds worth seeing?"

For most of my life, I had felt like a large cloud hovered over me. The cloud cast a shadow across my young life's canvas. I wondered how God viewed my life. Was he proud of my actions as a good child? Did it matter at that young age what kind of man I *was not*? Let us face it, the Dark Ages aside, teenagers nowadays were nothing compared to what they had been during the dawn of man, when you were a soldier and killing by fifteen or earlier. The necessity to stay alive stripped common sense from my generation. Survivors lived on the streets or in neighborhoods where they carved respect out of their enemy's skin.

This cloud followed me always, but it did not physically exist. Still, I felt its presence hiding me from the world. Sometimes it seemed as if the cloud influenced every decision of mine somehow.

Since childhood, I had felt an evil presence in my life. Ever since my parents split before I was six months old, I never felt like I belonged anywhere. Life took a tragic turn. My mother remarried a rather unpleasant man named Larry, who had already raised his children. He took no interest in me. The abuse started at a young age.

It took me years to put my finger on it – that the cloud I felt started with him. The fear I felt was explainable. Maybe it was just my gut reaction to this feeling of darkness. Something inside me might have hatched and wreaked havoc on the unsuspecting world had I allowed his example to mold me.

The darkness was invisible to my mother. There was no doubt in my mind that if she knew about it, she would ignore it. She saw the abuse, of course, as it was right in front of her. It seemed at times that there was something more behind his eyes. I vowed never to be like him.

Children are fragile only if you work too hard at protecting them. Do not get me wrong, I would have loved to avoid the pain physically. At the time, I did not realize that physical abuse actually built mental toughness too.

Looking back, I was not a fool either. Staying out of my step dad's way was much easier on my wellbeing than if he caught me in the open. That was the biggest reason why I preferred the night. Hiding was easier. Gazing outside with the lights off, I noticed the gentle illumination from the streetlight in the driveway. Sitting quietly, I could take in the world without the world knowing of my existence.

Sleep eluded me often even when exhaustion was just over the horizon. My thoughts turned to the outdoors during my teen years. Exploration became paramount when I met Jason. We used to spend a lot of time in the woods or walking the roads to some unknown destination, sometimes without saying anything for hours. There were also times we ran from tree to tree pretending an assailant gave chase, or that we were the hunters on some quest to find some mystical monster newly created that day. I do not even remember the name of it to tell you the truth. And through these adventures many times the only light we had was that of the moon. It always bathed everything in an eerie glow, almost iridescent at times, adding a certain element to the hunt.

At night, the woods seem to come alive. Although I have only been in the city a few times, night is not the same there. Sure, Jason and I were afraid sometimes. Each sound we heard, whether it was a twig suddenly snapping or some animal calling out, added to the ambience we tried to build together. I never admitted to Jason how scary it was at times. There was a dark swamp, and to this day, I always felt there were eyes on me, looking out from the mist that seemed to shroud the water like some sort of protection from prying eyes. We could never see in, but whatever it was could see out.

When I got scared or worried, it made me that much more aware of our situation. We were alone by choice, and we liked it that way. We never truly felt it. There was never any proof to back up our feelings so we did not go there that often. We saved that for special occasions when something bad happened. It was a method of forgetting your problems and just staring out at the water as if being called by something or someone. Yet out there, it made sense to fear the unknown.

Jason used to tell me stories of living in Seattle. He used to tell me how after 5:00 in the evening the town flipped over and another breed of human walked the streets. Sometimes this breed came into his neighborhood in spite of how rough the neighborhoods were. The nineteen eighties saw many changes to Seattle. He lived there until he was thirteen. That is when we met. Therefore, he had more time spent in a truly hostile environment than I did, even though I lived in one, too. That explained why he was so tough. His parents enrolled him in karate with hopes that he avoid fights up or get beat down living where they did. It was some place called Rainer Avenue South; also known as Rainier Valley.

Apparently, that is where many of the gangs were, so he had to learn to survive in a racially challenged neighborhood, where no matter you're your skin color, there was violence spread evenly if some one crossed to the wrong side of the street. I never had a problem with the concept of separation, if it kept people from killing each other. We all bleed red; some people just have a problem getting along with anyone, regardless of race or culture. Let them live apart then. Unfortunately, the concept never works and there are always incursions onto rival turf. That is what most of the fighting was about. Especially if your parents were idiots and did not even think about the consequences of where they lived and how it would affect their kids. Jason's parents at least gave him a fighting chance. It was the fact that he could fight that eventually led him to my world, albeit much later.

He was good at fighting; hell, he could kick my ass. We used to spar on a regular basis. I was clearly no match for him and he knew it. At times, the thoughts arose that he used to do it to try to toughen me up. Survival had become a way of life to him so he would get a crazed look in his eye when we horsed around. That made me nervous.

One day Jason finally told me a story about a bad scrape with some friends before we met. There were three of them, all from his karate school, so they had some training. Still, it was not enough. When you have three to one odds, training helps if you have had practice in the tactics needed to survive the odds. Only Jason walked away. He never spoke of it again, but I understood now what he experienced. He had seen death first hand and it changed him. The pain he felt from it surfaced and ran along the lines of his generally smiling face. He always thought things were funny, just not that day.

I can see it now in our combat lessons. He positioned himself as if he was outnumbering me. The attacks always came from different locations around me. Yet his teaching worked. My confidence was shaky most of the time, but as soon as I got a little cocky, he would smack me down. It was at these times his inner demons would surface when he was losing the upper hand, which was rare. It never lasted long, and always turned into an ass kicking. He never went full on with me, but he lost himself enough times. From this, I could defend myself to a point, but I could never strike.

My first year with him as friends taught me a lot about defending myself, but I lacked the experience needed to lock it in mentally until the time came to defend myself for real. However, I went to a private school and did not have to worry too much about fighting. That was until my ninth grade year and a bully eight inches taller wanted to get into a tumble. He was a doughboy and had no speed, no form, and no strength, relying on his size to intimidate me. I tried convincing him he could be hurt without trying to actually hit him. The show of force was good until I walked away. He hit me from behind. After I regained my balance, he was sorry he laid hands on me. It was luck, not skill, which helped me prevail. Looking back, it could have gone either way. His size was his advantage as my speed was mine. Winning a fight at school did earn me some respect. Soon after that, I finally expressed my interest in martial arts to my parents, but they shot the idea down.

To them, it was only mind control. They were too narrow minded and set in their ways to consider anything that did not "glorify" God. That line of thinking always made me laugh, and the anger I felt because they denied me lingered just below the surface. It did not make sense that it was not from God. Did he not send his people to fight his enemies? Shortsighted people frustrated me and not knowing how to defend myself was foolish.

My stepfather had Special Forces training. They trained him to kill. What was wrong with my desire to have all my teeth still when I graduated? They did not see it that way...even boxing was not in my future. I was mad. They denied me anything that would help me defend myself.

Lessons from Jason continued while managing to sneak martial arts books from the library to read them cover to cover. My skills improved drastically. "Go outside," they would say whenever I was trying to study fighting. Without Jason, it was never as exciting. Trying to learn katas in the sun was grueling, especially if you are trying to hide what you are doing. Mother wanted me outside to get exercise. She had no idea how hard I was working inside.

He begged me to sneak out one weekend. *I did not dare.* Sneaking out from home was bad for my health. I did obey the rules on this one. It just was not worth the risk of not being able to spend the night over at Jason's, or vice versa. When we did hang out it was usually at his house. My parents were too protective to allow me any such freedoms, so I never dared any such attempts while at home.

Jason's parents were lax. Whenever I stayed over, they let us roam freely. He was responsible, but I was a good influence on him morally, so there were never any constrictions. In return, we never gave them reasons to mistrust us. At night, we stayed later at the lake or we rode our bikes crazy distances. Out of all of our time we shared, we enjoyed walking the woods most of all...suddenly everything changed.

I paused, startled. *Had I been speaking aloud this entire time?* The doctor looked bored, and I realized he had just finished asking the question. He sat and waited for my answer. My internal conversation had taken only seconds. Yet if I told him the truth, he would have me committed. We stared at each other as I repositioned painfully in bed. He got bored with my silence because he stood up and turned around, moving the chair off to the side and back against the far wall.

Funny, in my mind I had covered from start to finish. I was a geek, a bookworm, a wimp, and probably a coward because I backed down from most confrontations. Thanks to my stepfather, fear of someone hitting me prevailed. Perhaps had the beatings been worse there would be less fear. Maybe I would have been tougher.

Nothing prepared me for what he said next.

"In the past six years you have sustained a series of injuries I'm afraid without leaving the comfort of your own bed. We placed someone in the room soon after the incident happened." I could see a puzzled look on his face.

"It started with claw marks appearing in various places on your body. The nurses and doctors thought at first it might have been your family leaving marks on you by accident. Your mother was very upset and passionate about your recovery. It crossed our minds that maybe she was trying to cause pain to see if she could wake you up. They monitored her visits, and she made no efforts or gestures to harm you. Yet the markings continued. Initially, no one ever actually saw them take place. They were seen at varying intervals, at first." He paused, but I did not interrupt him. This was all crazy to me, but something held my tongue.

"We brought in the church to observe you and see if there was any sort of presence here that might be attacking you. They ruled out demonic attacks quickly. The priest felt nothing present and did not see any marks that were similar to demonic possession. This went on for many, many months, about fifteen. We were close to ruling it out when a large amount of blood came from a wound on your back. They classified it as a puncture wound. I saw the blood soaking the sheets right in front of my eyes. When we rolled you over a wound opened up right in front of me. Then several more appeared. We could not patch you up fast enough. Blood...given right away, saved your life. You were going to die while we stitched you up."

I began trying to move some of the muscles in my back to see if I could feel anything of the sort. My entire back still hurt. Further movement aggravated things greatly. I needed to slow down. Movement meant pain.

"This repeated so frequently that we had to leave you on your stomach to monitor your condition every day. I thought it was strange that it was only on your back that the marks appeared at first. It showed no signs of stopping. Slowly they began to appear all over, and there was no pattern to it. Nothing made any sense; the church came back to evaluate you, and they still could not detect any evil forces or demons at work. You were not convulsing during the attacks. This stumped all the doctors and scientists. Then one day they suddenly stopped."

The doctor paced the room in front of me. He walked over and poured some water into a cup, took a long drink while watching me. It was bizarre. The chaos beheld was great. My mind drew blanks.

I just sat there staring at him and him at me. I was starting to feel like a freak. Movies from my childhood played mentally. They were the kind of movies where something unseen attacked someone, but there was always some way of detecting it. Granted those were movies.

He drank his fill and began again. "Several weeks later, it started up again, only this time it was broken bones, torn muscles, and crushed vertebrae. Then there were wounds to suggest something larger was somehow hitting you from beyond who knows where. You were getting the hell beat out of you somehow, and we could only watch and attend to your wounds. Your story stayed quiet save a few church leaders and scientists who came to participate in a comprehensive study. Many different churches sent many different priests to try to find answers. Eventually, they all left. However, the Catholic Church stayed and began to perform exorcisms on you. Nothing worked. The attacks came and the damage was left in their wake."

"The science community brought in several different devices to see if they could detect paranormal activity. For weeks, machines that monitored movement, and several light spectrometers, decorated your room. Another device that measured electromagnetic fields found nothing. That is actually the one they figured would catch it. Nothing worked."

"Samples of your tissue were analyzed at the lab. Your DNA was tested and retested. There is nothing special about you other than elevated levels of testosterone in your blood. Why your body was healing and literally re-knitting was something some of the best could not figure out."

He was still pacing the room and was looking out the windows now. I could see his reflection and the mystified look he held close.

"After a year of dealing with these new threats to you, the church finally gave up and posted a priest here twenty-four hours a day. There were no answers, nothing logical anyway. They left the priest incase last rights or spiritual intervention was required. Even though your family is not Catholic, they stayed."

A sideways glance from him showed me he was not much of a believer. Faith was a joke to him. He continued.

"Then everything stopped again. We thought whatever it was had done its worst. Your body was healing at an amazing rate, except you were still in a coma. The church pulled the coverage from your room since the danger seemed to be past and visited once a week. All was quiet."

He paused and looked at me for a long time. I found the energy to interject something, but all I could manage to say was, "So that's it? It's over now?"

He shook his head with a very sad look on his face. I could actually feel his pain flowing from him into me from across the room.

"No Dieter, it's not. It got much worse. You began to show signs of bite marks from something whose teeth marks we could not identify. You showed signs of burns from acid. Hell, I could have sworn at one point you had been run through buy something large. Several times your nose was broken. They even had to partially sew your hand back on once!"

Legacy of the Defender

I raised both hands and looked at them. There was a faint scar on my right wrist. "But yet you healed remarkably fast, almost before we could finish stitching you up. So fast that three different doctors petitioned for permits to make you a life study. Your mother denied them when they did not offer or bring any financial aid with them."

He refilled his glass and returned next to the bed, and took a long look at me.

"You should have been dead long ago, but something helped keep you alive. I may have left out some minor details here and there, you are welcome to read the reports I have written," he offered with a slight smile that seemed very tired. "We will talk again after you have seen your family. I am sure you have a million questions that I cannot answer."

He began to walk to the door. A flood of questions came to my mind, but the only thing I found myself saying shocked me. "There was something there the night of the accident. I am having weird dreams that seem so real... about monsters... I..." He raised his hand to stop me.

"Had I not witnessed these events over the last four years, I would laugh and doubt you. At this point, anything might be possible. Get some rest we will talk soon." He left the room. His loud foot falls carried him off into the corridor to somewhere.

The nurse returned. She approached the bed with a sad look on her face. Moisture was collecting in her eyes. I was processing how to request that he call me Dietz and the doctor's refusal. What do you do with people that do not respect your wishes on what to call you? It was both irritating and frustrating on top of everything that was racing around in my mind. I

301

had even made it a point to call him something to irritate him to make my point and had hoped he would have understood. Sadly my efforts met resistance so the thought faded of winning that one with him. It was not worth arguing over. Her scent overwhelmed me. With her next to the bed, it was as if I was placing my nose on her skin. I took another deep breath. It was intoxicating

"I have been looking after you for four years now. Never have I seen such strength and recovery before, let alone so many times," she said.

"Eryn is your name right?" I stammered, having difficulties speaking to her for such beauty moved me beyond what words could bring to bear and loss of motor skills did not help.

She nodded. "Yes, Eryn Magnussen," extending her hand for a proper shake. I took her hand gently.

"How old do I look?" I asked.

She made a motion of looking me over before replying. "If I didn't know I would say thirty-something. Not bad for someone with as many wounds as you have taken either."

I smiled. It did not make sense to be able to mature while in this bed for so long. Perhaps it was possible to learn from dreams. *Was that even possible?* Could I really be capable of acting my biological age without adjustment?

"I feel...older," I said, pausing. "Please forgive me for staring at you. It was nice to have you to look at when my eyes first opened." She smiled and patted me on the arm.

"I hope and pray that whatever has done this to you is truly gone.

Lord knows you deserve some peace after six years." The look in her eyes told me that what she had witnessed had been traumatic for her as well. Had she been witness to what Doctor Price explained?

"Thanks. I am very tired, though. I am going get some rest," I said. She stepped back and turned to the door.

"The call button is next to the bed if you need anything," she said. She made a motion of depressing a button as she opened the door.

"Okay." My eyelids failed to remain open any longer. That feeling crept over me again like when first I opened my eyes and saw the creatures flying around me. Almost terror like, this creeping doom circled back in the room with me. The image was out of focus, but it smelled dark and earthlike, yet nothing was actually visible when my eyes popped open and scanned the room. I sensed something familiar when the aroma changed to a smell that reeked of darkness. The aroma seemed to be oozing out of my pours. Growing in strength, this presence caused my thoughts to shift into a dreamlike state. I became aware that a dream state had entered, merging the reality of my room with the reality of something un-definable.

"We'll talk tomorrow," she said and walked out the door.

My eyes snapped open one last time, not wanting to see the creatures.

The fact is, my memory leading up to the event was fine, but afterward, there were only bits. Those were hard to believe. What the Doctor told me may just have trumped what I held back. None of this made sense. It sounded even crazier. I had to get it straight in my own head before anyone else knew. I focused. The memory appeared and formed again. Just when I felt I could see it clearly, it faded as if something inside me fought to protect me from the truth.

I stared at the walls and the horribly bland pictures decorating the room. A slight chuckle escaped. It hurt, mainly due to fatigue. His question was more involved than he could imagine. It did not matter that there had been strange occurrences regarding my stay. With each breath, my eyes became heavier. At this point being stuck in the bed was no fun. It hurt to move. It hurt to breathe. My eyelids rose and fell to the rhythm of my own breath like a raft on the ocean. I always liked that sensation.

My eyelids finally fell. I drifted rhythmically toward a deep sleep. Like waves rushing to the sand and crashing, I felt myself slipping. Exhaustion pulled at me. A familiarity sensation settled over me. My dreams flooded with scenes of that night – the same one of which the shrink inquired. Visions emerged. I was moving again, even as I lay motionless on the hospital bed. Forces pulled at me. An image of the moon came to me. Yet it was not the moon of this world. The size, shape, and colors were all wrong.

XIX

Patience

My Legacy
(Written in the wilds of Heaven)

The growing pain I feel inside
Is tearing me up, I've no place to hide
Each day I rise the stronger it gets
Consuming my soul until the sun sets

I wish I could say at dusk that it ends
But that is where it truly descends
I have no real peace not even in my sleep
My soul goes to wander in darkness so deep

The demons they haunt me and torment me so
I get no reprise as I travel below
I cry, I scream for a moment of rest
But it continues all night, a never-ending test

I struggle; I fight to conquer the fears
Sweating my blood and crying my tears
But my demons they feed on my will and feed well
It's as though I am falling straight into Hell

The irony is that I battle the night
Sacrifice my all and fight the good fight
I guess you could say I stand against the tide
As I gaze at the maw, those jaws open wide

You can try to destroy me, but I will not compromise
I will not go quietly now that I realize
I will always fight you, to win back my inside
I'm human, I'm stubborn, and I'll swallow my pride

305

Legacy of the Defender

I know now the answer comes not from within
But asking for wisdom is where to begin
This I have done and the price is now paid
So I will go on fighting for promises made.

I wish I could say that the tides have now turned
But each day the fires consume what I learn
Anew I have started each day when I rise
I tear back my soul to my solace and shed my disguise

People say that rest is where we regain
The strength that we lose when we each face our bane
Since I get no release when I sleep day or night
I get all my strength from walking in the light

Under these eyes are the signs of my test
Bearing the mark of a soul laid to rest
When my life is over my sacrifice will show
I'm a soldier who fights what is hidden below

The light crept across the floor. Mostly hidden by the blinds, the sun peaked into the room. Its yellow hue showed softly as it set, concluding its business with my part of the world. What is it about light that makes it more intense as you cut it down? It is not like the beam is a laser. The light waves and particles do not combine forces. The blinds stopped most of the sun's energy, yet the beams in the room were blinding. Like a sword, the sun's light pierced the increasing dark room in a final assault before succumbing the oncoming night. *It is never good to hinder the sun. It always finds a way.* I pondered the thought for a moment longer. I never did like the daytime.

It was the evening of the first day after returning from my immobile prison of my comatose body. I awakened again after falling asleep twice in the day. Each one of my attempts, dreams of monsters or imaginary dae-mons appeared randomly during my lucid periods. I could not yet tell the difference between my dream state and my awakened state. All I knew was that the Sasquatch had been real. The Sasquatch had happened. Everything else remained cloudy. I have ever seen a real monster. Tall and furry while still man-like...the image was ever present in my mind. I did not feel fear when examining the memory of the creature. Childhood mythos of the beast did not help the instant fear one would think they would feel; however, the feeling of sanity is still part of this reality. Curiosity reigned supreme, though. Not knowing how or why, only that I would see it again someday, was the conclusion every time

As I lay in my bed and watched the light continue its journey up the wall, thoughts of the creatures in my dreams continued to perplex me. It did not make much sense to me to have the same dream twice, but so far it had been the same thing each time. In the dreams, I fought and killed daemons. Nothing more. I used incredible swords to do so. It was my singular task. Both of my hands flexed at the remembrance. *Yes, it was definitely two blades.* The invisible items in my hands seemed so real, even when I held them aloft in front of my face. Something felt to be still in my grip, a phantom feeling, in which something tangible lingered. So unique was the experience that my hands still felt energized and strong. Placing them on the metal tubing the hospital bed had on the side of it to keep me from rolling off did not even equal this present sensation. The cold stainless steel mimicked the feeling like the hilt of a sword and was the right size for a giant man, but did not fit right as I was. So strange this experience was. It made me feel strong; only to be denied. Yet the ease of holding myself up, my arms were just too weak for continued attempts.

Patience, Dietz. You just woke up from a long nap laced with reoccurring dreams. I found myself saying the first part of this out loud repeatedly, like a mantra or a chant. The sound of my own voice began to drone a bit and I found my eyelids heavy for a moment. I shook my head as the feeling came over me not wanting to waste more of my life. I personally had a lot of questions and a few new goals to achieve. One of which was to get over my hatred of the revealing light.

No, you have slept long enough, snap out of it.

I slapped my face a few times even though there was not very much behind it; in fact I barely felt a sting. The sound slightly echoed in the room but reverberated in my ears like the beating of wings. Strangely enough, images of those creatures appeared again and started coming at me almost like they were dive-bombing me in a clearing. In they came over and over and the flutter sound grew in intensity. Not being able to fend them off any more, smaller ones began swarming near my face making me start flailing my arms instinctively. I heard the heart monitor increase its beeping sound, keeping pace with my heart beat.

Beep...Beep...Beep...

Faster and faster it went. Pressure in my head began building like it was in a vice grip. My eyes were having an issue focusing around the room. Closing them did not help, and my breathing began to race. Wanting to run and hide evolved into wanting to challenge and destroy everything and stand victorious over my foes, only to have it swing back to fear and running. Both emotions slammed me hard until one of them emerged the victor. I wanted to fight and watch the blood of my foes spray all over the battle-field. Just as I became comfortable with this idea, suffocation and pressure began crushing me. My condition monitor was going crazy as my heart felt like it was going to explode.

Just breathe!

My eyes shot open. I had been asleep again.

The lights in the room were on a minimal setting to prepare for even-ing, although dipping, the sun was still bright. Wait, it was in the same place... it had not moved or seemed to reset. All I could think about was patience. The answers would come soon enough.

What was happening to me? The same moment repeated. The light moving, the hospital sounds...all of it seemed to be familiar in a way that made no sense to me...yet I had never been in the hospital before, at least never for a stay. Only visits to loved ones or friends growing up. This chaos swirled around me causing confusion, and made cognitive thinking difficult. My breathing became my focus for hours in an attempt to clear my head.

I do not know how much time passed as I lay there experiencing a sort of dementia or delusion. My sanity felt like it was being over written and caused doubts as to what was reality for a moment, when I heard a voice from the corner of the room. I blinked my eyes. I could see a man sitting there in black clothing.

"Dieter."

I lay there shaking my head as if it were a phantom coming to claim my soul.

309

"Dieter."

I tried telling myself he was a hallucination. The dreams seemed so real and I was starting to think they were a figment of my mind as well, so there was no reason that what I was hearing had to be real. Again the voice came.

"DIETER!"

I had enough. "What do you want? Stop bothering me!" I felt hands on my shoulders start to shake me.

"Wake up, you're dreaming."

More shaking.... followed by a feeling of dread. My eyes shot open. Wait? My eyes had been open. A glance around the room revealed a man sitting in the corner. Wait, Déjà vu? Was it that same priest?

"Dieter," he said. This time I saw his lips move. I finally felt like I was awake and the feeling of metal in my hands was there again. I wanted to swing my arms, but they felt so heavy. I just wanted to sleep.

"Dieter, I know you can see me. I assure you I am really here," he said.

I lay there staring at him for several minutes before concluding that he was here and that my mind was not playing tricks on me. The light on the floor caught my eye, for it had not moved much still and was nowhere near getting close to setting yet. I had imagined it repeatedly or it was a dream. My courage finally mustered enough to speak.

"Yes priest, I am here and I see you," I said.

"Did you doubt it? Truly?" he asked.

"You have no idea," I said.

"Well can you give me an idea?" he asked.

"Not really," I said.

"I think you can," he replied with firmness in his voice. "Tell me what you have been seeing."

"I'd rather not."

"Why?" he asked.

"Because you do not want to know what I have been seeing or hearing or dreaming or feeling!" I snapped.

"Yes, I do. Tell me."

"I can't," I said.

"Yes, you can. Tell me. I know you want to," he urged.

I was getting angry. It felt like the pressure in my temples was going off the charts. I wanted him to go away, anywhere.

"Tell me Dieter. I want you to say it."

"Why?" I demanded.

"Because you need to tell me, and I want you to say it. You need to hear yourself say it."

"Fine!" I shouted. "Daemons! Daemons! There, I said it. Happy?"

"They are called demons…Continue," he said.

"What? You want more. Okay, I smell their filth! I feel their presence! I hear their awful screams. And yes, I *kill* them. I fight them, and I kill them. Is that what you want to hear? It makes sense to call them daemons, I do not know why." I was nearly in tears from rage.

"Is it the truth?" he asked.

I sat motionless. Our eyes remained locked. I wanted desperately to say it was a lie, to deny any such truth could possibly be real about my life. *My life? Why?* I wanted it to be false. When the moisture made my eyes blink, I turned my face away.

"You can tell me, Dieter."

"Yes," I answered quietly. "It is really true."

Oh man, I suddenly thought. *That sounds bad.* I cringed inside.

The pressure seemed to release and I swore I saw him put something away. I looked over and he was just sitting there.

"There now, was that so bad?" he asked.

"Yes, it was. I did not wish to discuss it."

"Well, perhaps you should tell me when you first started seeing demons?" he said, looking concerned and trusting.

"I have never seen a daemon."

"You just said you had, Dieter. Why are you changing your story?"

"I am *NOT* changing my story." I raised my voice because he was starting to anger me. I felt as though he was trying to convince me of something and I swear the pressure in my head came back and felt as if something invasive was attempting to dig inside. An image of pages turning in a book came to mind. Hitting my palm against my temple repeatedly did not make it go away. He sat there staring at me shaking his head. His gaze, penetrating, crawled all over and inside me and something about it seemed off as if he was looking into me. Extreme discomfort ensued. He was making me mad now, and I decided since my voice still worked to let him have it.

"How dare you priest. I *just* woke up from a coma, as you are very aware and it is literally the first day. You are accusing me of seeing daemons just because I have had a few dreams about them and *said* they were real to such an extent that it felt like I *had* seen them." I paused to cough because even though my voice worked, it was still difficult to talk. "I have not even been awake from my coma for a day, and you are here accusing me of something that's insane. If you had some..." he cut me off mid-sentence.

"Listen, you little brat. I have watched over you and prayed for you for years now, knowing full well that the wounds you have been receiving were not the marks of Christ. Evil of the highest order attacked you and exposure to that kind of evil will taint you. You are going to confess your associa..." This time I cut him off, astounded at what I was hearing.

"How *DARE* you, you ass. How can you call yourself a man of the cloth? I was not even awake, and it does not make any sense to me nor can I give you answers. You need to get out of my room. *NURSE!*" my voice cracked.

He was on his feet now in may face. I could smell alcohol on his breath. "Some priest," I thought when he grabbed me by the shoulder and placed his hand on my forehead. I was too weak to fight him off and felt something against my skin. My head was swimming. He spoke in some unrecognized language.

"Exorcizamus te, omnis immunde spiritus, omni satanica potestas, omnis incursio infernalis adversarii, omnis legio, omnis congregatio et secta diabolica, in nomini et virtute Domini nostri Jesu Christi, eradicare..."

His voice seemed to fade even though his lips were moving. The room spun. I could not hear anything now. A fog settled over my mind, taking all my senses away. My body went numb, taking my vision with it.

A familiar smell tickled the senses. Something excited me...something from before. My will begged for it to stop for I could handle no more. He needed to go away before I hurt him. Even in this state, I knew I could tear him apart. Something primal was awakening. It would have been easy.

I saw the fog bank clear and a weird looking man approached me looking at me in a strange fashion. He looked like some sort of native or maybe was dressed like a native or a mystic. Perhaps he was a Shaman. Very strange markings adorned his face and hands. The patterns on his clothing were not identifiable. They seemed to move on their own. Something was at my back and this felt familiar. He moved with purpose right up to me placing his hand on my forehead and spoke.

"Crux sacra sit mihi lux! Nunquam draco sit mihi dux. Vade retro Satana! Nunquam suade mihi vana! Sunt ..." Suddenly he was pulled away from me still speaking, "libas. Ipse venena bib..."

As the mist parted, some unseen force pulled him away and then re-closed again, swallowing him up. A voice far off called my name. It was getting closer slowly. Sitting there covering my eyes trying to make sense of what just happened, my body began to shake. Fear gripped me and there was something in my eyes now. Trying to clear them, a viscous fluid was sticking to my eyelids making it difficult. Voices in the distance, a chorus sang out, but the words were not clear.

Am I dreaming again?

Many hands were on my wrists gripping gently but firmly. A voice called out my name again, muffled this time. Disorientation and dizziness took hold. Fluid was in my mouth and then all down the front of me. It was really thick and foamy. Panic set in when I felt my eyes open again even though I thought they had been. Foamy spit was coming out of my mouth. I was starting to hear more now.

"Start an I.V. drip of...."

"The tube needs to be in his..."

"OH my god we are losing him..." More murmuring, that I could not pick out, and a flurry of movement was all around. A mask was over my nose.... needles and nurses brandishing them. A cop? Someone brought in a cart full of hoses and tubes.... Something beeping like it was running a race.

"...curiosity...find that priest...have gotten far."

"....actually used a cyanide pi..."

I felt silence as if it was a physical state, followed by weakness, and could not breathe. It was like was drowning. Cold waves rolled over me in a pulse like fashion. I could hear voices still, but they were inaudible. Something smelled funny and I had this horrible taste in my mouth. I heard another voice, very bold and beautiful, as if there were multiple voices woven into one. Behind all of this the beeping was a steady *"Beeeeeeeeeep!"*

A muffled voice in the distance made mention of calling me something, but it used the word "it." Then all was quiet, save the steady tone, almost like when you pick up the phone but do not dial right away. The sound became faded as if it moved away rapidly. Serenity washed over me like a wave of energy like everything was going to be all right. I saw the color gold, a solid color, but a rainbow effect danced front of it in a shifting pattern. A shape started to coalesce in front of me and started to come into view. Suddenly a voice was in front of me. Something surged through me.

"YOU NEED TO FIGHT." A clap of thunder rolled in the distance. I felt moisture saturating the front of me. I was coughing and gagging. Another big breath and the room came into view slowly. It was full of people. Nurses and a few doctors were in various positions around the room. They all stared at me.

"Oh my GOD...Doctorrrr"

I was sitting up. Looking around the room, all of their faces fixed on mine. A more then putrid vomit was running slowly down the front of me; the horrible taste lingered in my mouth. Shocked looks greeted me and no one moved. I could compare it to an old Telecom commercial I had seen once. You could have heard anything drop on the floor. Thirst gripped me hard as I tried to swallow to clear my throat, but the inserted tube prevented such an action. A feeling of dread was in the room that was so heavy it felt like something was truly wrong. All eyes stared at me for another moment then like a coordinated dance sprang into action as towels, tubes, and other instruments seemed to be getting removed from me and other devices or tools where replacing them. The heart monitor was returning to normal while a nurse was taking a hold of the tube and suction in my mouth was evacuating the vile fluids. Cool water flowed several times then I coughed trying to get air once the tube vanished.

"Oh my God, he is breathing on his own..."

"Can I get some water?" I coughed out. "This taste is horrible."

XX

Aftermath

"At first I couldn't breathe," I said, beginning to recount my story. "Something felt like it was in my mouth obstructing my airway. I got dizzy. Pins and needles felt euphoric." *Why were traumatic situations often pleasurable?* "People talk about a white light and a tunnel. I didn't see either of these."

Words stumbled a bit as my recounting labored. The entire experience burned into my mind. I could see the memory, smell it, and taste it even, but finding the right words seemed to be an issue. I tried not to pause, even though it seemed to be adding to the drama of the moment.

She seemed to be hanging on my every word and processing my previous words. "Last time I remembered any sort of similar experience was when I went into the hospital." Laughing internally at the irony that this happened twice, I tried to stick to the task. The strange thing was being aware that my body was unconscious. How that was possible while maintaining cognitive thought was perplexing. She nodded her head keeping her eyes locked on mine

Yet here I was. Talking to this Goddess, I kept thinking. She had a look on her face like she was about to break down and pour forth with emotion. Her touch was so tender and nurturing as she checked my vitals and she took a lot longer this time. Seeing this woman smile made me forget everything that had just happened to me for a few moments. I was declared legal-

317

ly dead apparently for about three seconds before sitting up on my own. The priest failed... something not too soon forgotten.

"I felt water all around me. The sensation of floating was present but was not able to move, just that feeling of buoyancy and being fully submerged. The water around me moved gently moving. It was like a plant swaying in the gentle breeze. There was a slight feeling of tranquility, but nothing but blackness surrounded me. Burning sensations rolled over me like my skin was on fire. Heat seared my lungs. My body twitched violently, spasm's rolled all over, then stopped."

That part bothered me. The violent spasms felt so pronounced. Such a feeling was so hard to dismiss.

I looked at her. When gazing at those eyes, something in the pit of my stomach penetrated my soul. She caught me staring. A brief smile flared then she looked down. 'Sigh' if it were an emotion, encapsulated my soul. Life took on new meaning and the desire to pick her up and hold her though weak as a kitten was my current state of being. Had my strength been like that in my dreams breaking that priest in half before he even got that pill in my mouth would have been a reality, hell, before he even touched his cross to my forehead. She stood there patiently waiting for me to finish my thought that was almost lost due to the radiant energy felt from her gazed at me.

"This feeling continued as my dream like state unfolded. The violent contraction turned to tremors…then nothing. It felt like the ability to pan my surroundings returned even though I could not. A bright flash, like an explosion, erupted…then the air flow reversed. Next thing I knew my eyes opened to chaos. That acidic foam spewed up and out all over me. It was rather disgusting."

"All that happened in several seconds? That's mind blowing," she said scrawling something on my chart. Eryn had a point that admittedly did not make sense. All of that *had indeed* occurred in a very short time...yet it seemed like it was a lot longer from the perspective currently known, a lot longer. With nothing mustered to say I nodded in agreement. She was completely accurate.

Somehow time had changed and had lasted a lot longer. A long gaze followed and making me pauses. I must have been staring or something because she smiled and turned away suddenly. A sniffle barely audible came from her as she wrote on her clipboard. The scrawling of the pen in a ferocious manner was very loud for several moments then the metal clatter as she closed it. She dropped it in a holder on the end of my bed. A moment of silence hung. Eryn stood there facing the door. With a *sigh,* she looked back over her left shoulder and surprised me at what she said.

"You keep an eye out and try not to sleep. I know it may be difficult, but there is a strange feeling coming over the staff and the ward regarding you." Her voice reduced to a whisper. "That priest's actions really have every one worried as to why he would try to kill you even if there was some merit to his reason or logic."

"Let alone, why would the church sanction something like murder....oh wait the Spanish Inquisition? Did we forget about that already? I did not sleep much last night so I don't know how long I can remain awake but will do my best." I had too many thoughts creating pressure in my head.

A slight twinge of pain made my facial muscles spasm for a moment.

"I'm off shift; try to sleep. I will be back in eight hours. I offered to work double the next few days so I'll be around." She turned and looked right at me and smiled. "Just be careful."

She walked away briskly. The door closed. I was alone. *She has got to be kidding that I need to be careful in a hospital,* I thought. Then again, a priest, a man of the cloth....or supposed to be, tried to end my life with a capsule of cyanide. If that did not open my eyes that there was something wrong, no telling what would. I was at the mercy of others. My control of my own life was gone. My first priority needed to be to get it back. How to do this was still a mystery.

The clock ticked slowly as if to mock my plight. 'Twelve o' eight' Eryn would be back in the morning staying awake was my first mission. It was hard to believe that I had been dead five hours ago. What was harder to believe was in details of those few moments that lasted longer on the sub-conscious. Being dead for a few minutes must have felt like an eternity to the staff helping me before they finally gave up; then having me sit up on my own gasping for air.

Killed by a priest that got away clean. The police had not found him yet. He had eluded them. A citywide search was under way. I overheard the television in the hallway on my way back from having my lungs sucked clean. They used a device, like a vaccuum, made specifically for survivors of drowning. Even though it felt like they sucked your lungs out of your chest. There was no pain. It was strong enough to pull excess moisture but gentle enough that it did not damage the tissue. Afterwards, coughing for several minutes produced lots of the fluid, a by-product of the vapors to loosen the inhaled toxins.

They were worried that the scarring in the lungs meant I would have to live on life support in some closed, bacteria free environment, but when they listened to me breathe it was perfectly fine. This perplexed them so much that they took x-rays and would "get back to me." Swabbing even told them no surface tissue damage had occurred. The prognosis had several of the doctors perplexed.

Then there was my blood work. The doctors told me the amount of poison absorbed in to the blood was enough to kill a person several times over with cyanide. The Strange thing is the amount given to me was quite a bit. It was a fast, silent killer in the sense, which the victim usually could not speak due to the "foaming of the mouth." It tasted like almonds, burnt almonds. Talk about a nasty after taste that stayed with you.

The clock rolled to twelve o nine. A whole minute had passed in my massive internal dialogue. It was going to be a long night to be alone with my thoughts. With the speed my mind was processing; I would be out of things to think about without being redundant. My focus changed back to trying to replay the dream. The mistake did not become obvious until they re-opened to see 6:23 on the clock. Sleep had taken me rather quickly. A quick pan of the corners did not yield any evil priests. A sigh of relief escaped my lips.

The room was quiet.

Minutes passed. I began to wish Eryn would show up. Gazing upon her was beautiful in a way never imagined before. She was a woman, not a girl to start. She was mature and funny, yet serious and business like. It made me think about my surrounds even more now because worrying about her getting hurt in this new situation was a factor. Her safety was also a concern, especially if she stood between a crazy priest and me.

Thoughts poured in, reminding me of when my eyes first saw her, merely a day ago. Her beauty had caught me off guard. There was no way to be prepared for anything of that nature upon coming out of a coma. Nothing can truly prepare one, in my eyes, even in my self-reflection. The world had changed. More importantly *MY* world had changed. A slight feeling of doom hung over me now that someone had tried to take my life. Anger flared at the thought made me sit upright quickly. My strength was growing; it felt good to feel it return. My toes wiggled while contemplation of trying to stand became a mental debate. Deciding against it when the image of me falling on the floor came to mind, the torture of boredom set in. I had suffered enough traumas for one week and no amount of logic could take that away. One thought rolled into my mind again.

A damn priest tried to kill me!

Anger swelled again. My pulse pounded in my throat on both sides. Breathing increased. Pressure in my temples and my eyes started to cause pain. The desire to kill that bastard for what he tried to do rampaged through any remaining peaceful thoughts. Without realizing it, my hands beat the bed with closed fists striking the metal frame. The impact made me jump. It was a solid hit. I expected to feel pain. None arrived. In return, there was exhilaration hitting something. Again my fist struck again and again until they were bloody, and the crimson scent of my own essence drove me further into frenzy.

My actions drew in the night watch nurse and several of his friends. Before I knew it, with a great struggle, they restrained me. Even trying to be gentle about it the nature of what they had to do was forceful and hurt quite a bit. Several of them got a bit more than they bargained for before succeeding. The restraints they used were not easy to get on an unwilling participant, but that is where four of them became part of the equation. I felt the needles go in on both arms. A haze covered my mind, making it hard to move and a cool sensation hit my blood stream that took only moments for it to take effect. The image of an orderly, though blurry, caught my attention as the drugs coursed its way through. Hoping he was not going to hit me brought a sudden wave of fear up that to my surprise helped me calm down. The euphoria hit and pushed me through a door that suddenly appeared in my mind. An image or Eryn appeared and a phrase hit me out of the blue.

A glorious thing I have seen today,
When beauty so fair has touched me this way,
When she enters the room is aglow,
I want to share this tenderness so.

Pausing for a second and staring at the wall, I felt ideas begin to wrap around my creative thoughts. Never had any ever been composed in such a way let alone a poem or something poetic. The gentle words just flowed right out of my mind like a spring bubbling out of the ground. The certainty and intensity carried a weight with it that did catch me off guard.

My heart actually felt a little lighter at the thoughts of her poured out of me and into creation. I do not know what love truly feels like, but I smiled at this new warmth experienced. The words hit me again slowly. While trying to grasp the feeling of the words that came out of my mouth, a smile crept over me. The last phrase brought about a certain emotion but did not feel dirty. It was almost as though I had confessed something that had just opened my eyes to a whole different world.

I was falling for her and I barely knew her.

"How is this possible?" arose from my lips in my quiet room and began its journey to lunacy. Growing up, several people showed me that love makes you crazy and that only someone who was insane would fall in love. Yet, everyone I knew even at a young age talked about it like it was this elusive creature that was hard to find because it required two people to hunt it. Yet technically, you never found it. Love found you. Rolling to my side I stared at the wall that was perfectly smooth.

I thought about how a person's heart was smooth, like the wall. There were no crevices or imperfections viewable by the naked eye. From this point, it appeared to be flawless. No imperfections or openings existed. Yet if you poured water onto that material if would find a way through. I knew that microscopically it was porous material and that fluids could find their way through it. The longer it was exposed to that liquid, the more saturated it would become, allowing more of it to pass through.

Just like the human heart.

When love finds someone who is hardened, it is like moving into a hostile environment. They tend to armor themselves up even more to keep the emotional intruder from getting past the gates. Defenses build up naturally over time but tend to go into some sort of frenzy when it is apparent that someone may be sneaking inside to take a peak. It amazed me how much our own defenses that we have against words acted very much like a real fortification. Enemies often breached the gatehouse, but they were the first line of defense and sometimes the last place to fall.

Where was I coming up with these analogies?

Moments of deep consideration went by. The very depths of wisdom peeked through a door inside of me that I unknowingly sought after most of my life; and now that wisdom finally sought me out. Finally, I thought, perhaps now it will feel like I had something to offer.

Laughter.

Yet another pearl of wisdom out of the multiverse came to me from my first real debate, and I felt saner than I had ever felt in my life. Feelings aside for Eryn, one thought returned to me like a sledgehammer striking the bell in my tower harder than before. The residual gong resonated through my inner self.

The church tried to kill me, or one sanctioned by them, which means they knew something. But what?

One conclusion remained. Anything that happens is supposed to happen; this means that I was to be in a coma and supposed to awaken at this time. It also hit me that survival for something bigger had to play a part. Whatever that may be….and that priest would fail in his attempt to kill me. My guard would never to drop again, not matter the cost or reason.

How was I supposed to sleep?

Too many thoughts at once made my brain hurt. There was, of course, no sort of timeframe for me to figure out my role now. Silently my thoughts turned to God or the universe for guidance. There was something special about this situation. It was impossible to ignore now. I suddenly felt alone. Everyone around me was a stranger. The hospital called my parents; they were on vacation out of state. It would take time to drive back...Even though I felt ignored as a child; I knew my mother would arrive eventually.

I felt my eyes getting heavy. Images started to trickle into my head. In the distant sounds rolled over hills that now formed in front of me as if my mind simply brought them into existence. A ringing sound coming from a far off place echoed all around. It sounded like a battle was in progress. The chaotic sounds, like cries of pain, rage, and fear intermixed with the sounds of clashing steel. I found myself able to look around at my surroundings. It was a valley, very tight walls on either side and I was somehow moving through it.

I came to a small cliff. My hands reached holds and there was a sense of rising up as I scaled the wall. Strange armor adorned my body. It was not like anything I had seen and felt like cloth. With a certain amount of speed, I reached the top and snuck along near some rocks. My body felt very close to the earth, and it was very dark. I felt myself peek around a large stone to see a large army on the other side and down a mountainside. The army assembled in front of a great wall. By its shadow was some sort of castle or keep. Creatures shouted in a language I could not understand.

I looked at my hands again. This time I held twin swords covered in some sort of blood like ichor. The blades curved but not like blades I had ever seen. They were neither scimitars nor oriental blades; but something altogether different. The viscous ichor dripped from the leading edge and fell to the ground. The smell of it suddenly caught my nose and it intoxicated me by its odor. Brine like scent that had foulness to it whose origin escaped me assaulted my nostrils and right up to my brain. The feeling or need to attack anything that stepped near me came on strong. Suddenly, my blades passed through a monster leaving dark cuts. It fell and began to disappear. I looked closer.

The smell got stronger. Nudging it with a blade, I made the body rolled over. It appeared to be a small monster. I felt myself jump back in my mind, but my body did not move. It stood there prodding once at the creature as if to ensure it was dead. I

I shook my head. The image exploded leaving me with a smell in my nose that gave me that euphoric punch drunk feeling. The desire to fight, stab, and kill my opponents dominated me. I wanted to sunder shields and wreck armor. Yet no enemy stood near me to enact upon with my primal thoughts.

What the hell was happening? These are not my thoughts, yet they feel familiar.

Panic arose inside me as a surge of energy hit me that must have been adrenaline and I got out of bed and walked over to the room. Grabbing the doors, I tore the hinges away, ripping the door frame off completely. A roar came from my lips that shook the room. Orderlies fled down the hall and nurses ducking behind counters. There was no control.

A doctor ran by me and my hand grabbed him, lifting him high into the air. My actions did not belong to me anymore and the feeling of freedom saturated my mind. I could see him kicking and squirming as his eyes met mine. His face looked exactly like the priest. My hand cocked back to hit him. Rage washed over me uncontrolled as I felt energy release within me and saw a flash of light. Darkness followed and the idea came that maybe someone had hit me with some sort of strobe weapon to blind me. My senses reeled as the room came to focus.

I was sitting in bed covered in sweat. Fading light gave way to the clock on the wall whose gentle illumination did not light the room. It was ticking as if it were inside of my head pounding like water onto my forehead, creating echoes in my mind. Two thirty five barely showed on its stationary face. I had fallen asleep again.

Starting to get mad at myself did not help matters. Defense while asleep was already an issue…and now this. My hand began to itch. Scratching it made the feeling more intense. The wall was my focus. As long as the stir crazy feelings preoccupied me, there was no relief from the sensation. Soon, both hands felt it. I felt depressions in my palms, and I held up my hands.

There was a pattern here, which looked symmetrical in both hands. It appeared imbedded in my hand. It was as if I had been holding something for a very long time. My hands hurt from being in a seized state, like they had gripped something for dear life. I opened and closed them, trying to loosen them up. However, the feeling that something belonged there remained. The metal bars on the side of the bed seemed to be calling to me. Both hands grabbed onto the bed frame. A satisfying feeling of cold steel rolled up my arms and made me smile. The coolness not only felt at home, but also gave me a sense that something belonged there. Had there been someone watching, they would likely have thought I was a lunatic.

My recent dreams popped into my head. *Swords.* I was holding them loosely yet maintained a grip. I relaxed my hands and felt a shiver roll up my spine. It felt so good.

Huh?

I heard a noise and looked up. The door opened, and I was looking at Eryn, who was smiling as she walked in.

"You're early," I said, not being able to wait until she was near me.

She looked at me puzzled. "Its 8:05, Dietz" I glanced at the clock. It had just been half past two. I must have shown my surprise as the clock face indeed reflected her statement.

"Good morning. I see you are still alive. It is good to see you," she said.

I smiled, almost a little embarrassed.

"I have something to share with you," she said.

XXI

Taking Chances

Fear takes hold at the strangest times.

Something innocent sounds fine before you say it aloud, but to hear it spoken aloud changes the dynamic. Eryn sat down on the bed and smiled at me. I know that it was strange for her to do so, because a certain amount of professionalism needed to discourage the staff from forming attachments to patients. I could see the slight unease in her eyes as she did so, but it was almost as if she sensed something within me had changed. Or perhaps something within her was changing.

Her level of warmth was there, yet there seemed something new to it, a sort of tingling as she brushed my arm. Whether or not that was intentional, my face must have glowed as radiant as the sun. Childlike emotions became a lump in my throat. My speech failed and panic rose over me like a ghost, freezing my muscles and making it impossible to speak. This was not what I had envisioned at this moment as I was going to tell this woman I fancied her. Cruelty was a word that came to mind. There is no training you can learn that gives a man the courage to share his feelings with a woman. My only comfort was I knew I was not the only man to feel this way in such situations.

I swallowed hard, took a deep breath, and smiled with the confidence hoping for the confidence felt in my own mind. A dry throat was the killer of good conversation, especially when I just gotten the nerve up to say

330

something special to her. Never in my life had I ever truly cared about someone so soon. Only a few days had gone by since I awoke. Something in me drew me to the tenderness this woman had for me and left me defenseless. Words had to come out as if my very soul was bubbling up and the space inside of me had already expanded to make room. It was about to bubble forth. I was losing control. My hand found hers.

She smiled and looked intently at me. I took another slow breath and spoke. *"A glorious thing I have seen today, when beauty so fair has touched me this way, when she enters the room there is a glow, I want to share this tenderness so."*

Silence took the room. The sounds of the machines, the staff, or the birds that chirped playfully outside the window as they flew from tree to tree went quiet as if they knew what had just transpired. Eryn stared at me with a shocked look that changed to a blank stare. I knew this feeling for I was experiencing it now, yet mine was more like terror because this was one of those defining moments for a man.

She gasped.

Seconds passed as the tension grew. My senses tingled. She suddenly stood and the warmth left as her hand pulled away. I resisted it just enough to create a slight friction, but not to make it seem needy.

She rushed towards the door. The moment felt like a failure. Embarrassment flooded over me. Then she stopped. There was a long pause...her back was to me.

"Have I misspoken?" I asked.

She trembled...still facing away.

"That was beautiful," she said, her words flowed through my mind like the dawn reaching the mountains. A sigh escaped my lips as the anxiety of not knowing her response released. The feeling of weightless let go of me as gravity released me from its grasp for just a moment until reality gave me a painful slap. "I think there is something very special about you..."

"Here it comes..." I thought, getting ready to eat my own liver. My insides tensed up. She gazed at me with an intensity that could have made a wild animal take pause. It made me feel slightly uncomfortable for a second until she smiled again and the room truly brightened, or perhaps it was my heart beaming.

"That's not the first time you've said those words to me," she said.

It took a moment for her words to sink in.

Wait...what?

"I have watched over you for so long. I have witnessed you get wounded while you lay there helpless and no one had any explanations as to why. I have seen parts of your insides as you lay wide open, bleeding out and about to die. I have pulled my hand back from your wounds to swap out bandages only to find the wounds closed and you whiter than the sheets. I have seen tears form in your eyes out of the blue when I checked your vitals as if you knew my presence."

I was stunned. She continued.

"Then it happened. You spoke to me. I was the only one in the room. At first I thought you were just mumbling, so I ignored it. Then it happened again a week later. You said something else. I was right next to you when it happened and heard you plain as day," she said.

"Are you serious?" I asked.

"Yes," she answered.

"It has happened on and off for several years. I felt the messages were for me. The poems...were so tender. I could not bring myself to tell the doctor. There were times when you spoke for several minutes, as if you felt my presence. As if you knew me! Once you spoke about Jason. You wondered if he was okay. That was three weeks ago." She stopped, looking to see if I was processing her words.

She walked back to the bed and sat down again.

Her hand took mine as my gaze lowered. Perhaps being too close to a situation makes you miss too many things. I was dazed as the poem escaped my lips. In the movies, reactions in these moments always seem too exaggerated. She did not throw herself in my arms or kiss me. We sat in silence for a moment looking at each other. I was amazed at the strange calmness that descended upon me, telling me it would be okay.

"Now here you are awake, alive, smiling, and laughing with such a sense of humor and wit that I did not ever imagined existed in that boy who has become a man right in front of me. I was but twenty-two, straight out of college when I started my internship here. You were my first assignment. After my internship was over, I requested to stay here to see this through, no matter how it ended. Now here you sit, quoting me poetry." She paused for several seconds while her breathing trembled. "I know this is a lot to process. I thought it was just your body sensing my presence. But now I know the connection is real." She rose and walked away at a rushed pace. "I have to go."

I blinked and sat there frozen. The warmth left the room as if some-one opened the window. It might have been the door closing that stirred the air in the room, but the temperature dropped sharply and solitude followed. My hand found the remote, lowered the bed down so my body reclined, and began to play the situation over that had just unfolded. My mind did not fall into chaos as predicted, but instead, serenity flowed forth. I was happy at the outcome, but my lack of experience in the matter gave me no measuring stick to gage it. Contemplation occupied my thoughts.

In my coma, I spoke to her. What are the odds?

It was not hard to feel the elation that I did amidst these crushing walls with their white paint and long hallways that smelled of bleach water. My perception that hospitals were clean and had to be was still accurate, but it seemed a little excessive to me that this stench of bleach was there at every intake of breath. Sadly when it comes to the human condition and sickness, there was a reason for that sanitized smell to be so prevalent to cover up the death and disease that was rampant in hospitals. How I knew so much about that baffled me. It did not make those white walls any cleaner or fa-ther away from me. It felt insane, for the clarity of which I viewed my sur-roundings was quite clear. I was not going to get out of there anytime soon until they had their look from a medical stand point.

Add to that equation a crazy Catholic priest who tried to send me to the afterlife prematurely. I did not fully understand the concept of religion and faith from the Catholic standpoint. To learn they put so much emphasis on the mother of Christ being important, but the need to worship this icon did not make sense, although you have to admire the logic. One should always respect those that have the power to bring life into the world. I was okay with it from that view, save the fact that they might have supported the priests trying to end my life. Further research on this topic would have to wait. I had other things on my mind.

Sounds from the hallway snapped me out of my current thoughts. I could hear running in the distance. Code alerts came over the intercom. They were normally barely audible, but for some reason these were exceptionally loud. The codes were unknown but most likely meant that someone on my wing was about the buy the farm. Whoever it was most likely would not have the strange ability to heal that had experienced for the last six years. Numerous things in life had tried to kill me and my power had kept me alive. I added surviving a cyanide capsule to that list of oddities. What was next?

Childhood parenting does not exactly prepare you for the weirdness of the world, especially when it is so beyond what is normal in life. Going to school for twelve years, graduating, and going to college. It was so normal, but not for me. Find the career that you hope will make you a lot of money so you can find and support a wife, have children, and then watch them repeat the cycle. As exciting as the potential of all of that was, I realized that none of it would compare to the last few days of my life. The desire to have real blood pumping excitement had never been my aspiration, but someone targeted my life, the allurement to dangerous situations that I have heard people develop was now a curiosity. Danger was never something to chase, but a small exhilaration that had started to grow in the pit of my stomach. I wanted a piece of that priest. I wanted to hit him in the face. I wanted to watch blood spray from his broken nose as I hit him repeatedly.

I felt my heart beating in my chest like it was going to leap from it at any moment. My breathing turned into coughing as I fought for more air. Pain tore at my lungs. It was hard to believe how strong my feelings were. The desire to right the injustice delivered to me by the church over wrote logic. I laughed knowing I was not the first, nor the last to have that thought roll into their mind like a steel ball, knocking down walls made of inhibition. The coughing subsided after a few minutes with thoughts of being a vigilante teasing my sensibilities. I was not strong enough and probably would never be. It was a nice thought.

This amazing image of a very large man with my features, came to mind. He had broad shoulders and muscles that bulged much like that of a bodybuilder, just not quite as toned. I could see the definition under a thin shirt as he moved. The size of his biceps kind of made me laugh a bit when I looked at my own. This mental image of me was something that everyone does when there is a bully needing a lesson and it was foolish that this conjuration I had come up with was such a monstrosity. How my mind came up with this as a solution to my problem was rather intriguing. Muscle mass aside; this image had to be so large that it towered over even the largest football player ever seen on television. I tried to shrink the image to a more muscular version of me but could not.

"I guess you cannot visualize all that we can imagine, after all," I heard myself say. It was disturbing to me that phrases came out verbally with no control.

The door opened. Hoping it was she, my eyes shot towards the sound. Another nurse came in and grabbed my chart, her pen scrawling furiously on it. The clock caught my attention and it was a lot later than expected. Minutes turned to hours with me in deep contemplation. That thought rolled around in my head for a moment as she took my vitals. How was it that I was getting so engrossed in my thoughts that minutes were flying by? It was as though my mind had some serious holes in the memory portion of it and when falling into my thoughts I got stuck in these holes, until managing to claw my way free. These gaps in my mind did not allow for rational thinking. There were missing pieces of the puzzle. My so called daydreams were turning into waking dreams; they had now evolved into what seemed to be visions or memories. I knew I must be hallucinating, however. I would certainly remember being so tall. I was not a massive hulk of a man. My mind played tricks on me.

Thoughts changed. I was seeing Eryn's face now. She was smiling at me, like the first time my eyes opened and saw her. A shudder ran down my spine, and I wondered was it possible to fall in love so quickly with someone you barely knew. Was it a real emotion, or just a fantasy, that gave what someone needed, at that moment? Would it ultimately be fleeting in the end?

"The doctor will be in to see you in a few minutes."

Where the hell did that voice come from? I thought.

I realized my mind had drifted again. The nurse had finished her once over of me and was already walking out the door. I had hardly even paid attention when she came in, let alone when she was there touching me. This made me very nervous. I need to have my wits about me in case the "crazy cleric" comes back. It had a nice ring to it, but I was mad at myself now for letting my mind wander so much. Focusing on my surroundings was proving difficult. I blinked to moisten my eyes. They dried out from the long pause to wake myself out of this haze.

To my dismay, my view had changed and I was not looking at the ceiling. My mouth was dry. Terror tried to run through my mind, making me think that something had just happened again when papers rustled follow by the scrawling sound of someone writing or taking notes. I raised my head and tried to focus through the light that was hitting me in the eyes from the blinds. It was a lot higher than earlier. The rays cut through the air as if a slow reaching laser were extending its death towards me. Sleep had taken me again.

Okay, this was getting old. Finding slight focus, I saw the shrink sitting in the corner, engrossed in paperwork.

How sad that must be.

A life of filling out assessments for patients you do not really know. The guys think they get inside your head when all they hear is what you tell them. Feelings are hard enough to deal with, let alone describe accurately to someone. How someone could even think one could rationalize what I was experiencing was absurd to me. I knew I needed to escape soon before they found out that I was blacking out.

So far he seemed unaware that I was awake. My head lowered down with the effort not to wince or exhale from the weakening muscles still protesting. Silence pervaded the room except for the occasional slight sigh coming from him until I realized that was his breathing. He had stopped

writing now and sat there reading. A page turning confirmed it. My imagination ran amuck thinking about what was on that page. I decided to get it
over with and sat up after laying there for a few more minutes trying to collect my thoughts. He simply sat there reading for a few more minutes before
he looked up.

"Hey, Doc."

There was no reply, just a simple frown.

Moments passed.

"You know Dieter, after yesterday, you are very fortunate to be talking to me today. I should be closing your case as we speak." He looked at
me for several seconds before I saw him click his pen almost as if he was dis-
appointed. Some smell in the room suddenly caught my nose, but I could
not pin point it. Trying not to be too obvious, my attention continued to
classify the smell. The odor was certainly more interesting than his insulting
words. Might as well tell me I should be dead so he does not have to deal
with me.

The smell increased in intensity and there was no hiding it. I raised
my nose up and inhaled deeply.

It smelled like fear.

XXII

Dreams

"Can I stop there?" I asked.

Hearing nothing but my own voice for about an hour was getting tiring, especially while trying to recall the details of my dreams. My throat was sore from speaking. Doctor Price sat in the corner scribbling on a yellow pad. I did not think it was possible to write so fast, let alone legibly. His work reminded me of a stockbroker whose firm just told him to sell. I saw that in a movie once, it seemed like a sad life.

I had just explained to him the dream several times. The level of detail had to be limited because it was difficult to recall exact facts. The logic of having the same dream in context but having the details change slightly was frustrating. My "lack of cooperation" in previous sessions still frustrated him. It took me several days to come up with what I could tell him.

My dreams were less weird to me than the stories he and Eryn told me. I was too tired to read any files. It was easier to listen to them recount. My attempt to recall my dreams made me wonder if they somehow manifested physically on my body. He had to be thinking the same thing. If so, how powerful was my mind?

He stood shaking his head at times. Sometimes he nodded as he wrote. I swore I saw dollar signs floating above his head. I knew what he was thinking.

My new room was very much the same but no longer in the Intensive Care Unit. Muted hospital colors with a little personal touch adorned the room. I never cared much for hospitals. My recent experience made it even worse. I did not like being someone's experiment. The doctor seemed too "matter of fact." I doubted he cared about me; he just wanted information that might up his status in the medical community. At times his comments suggested he thought I might be involved in a cult. This offended me.

"Yes Dieter, that's good for now. I am quite amazed at your memory of these events. You're not ad-libbing any of this, are you?" He looked me over for any signs of lying. The way my mother always used to do. I decided to test the theory with him and fudged my numbers a bit, but somehow I do not think that mattered. He seemed bored and obsessed at the same time. That was quite the dichotomy to me...like he wanted to be doing or saying something else.

"If anything, I am leaving parts out. Up to this point in the story, I had killed at least five dozen flyers and twice that in bipedal daemons!" I replied, feeling a bit irritable. It has only been forty-eight hours since recovering from the coma and neither my mother nor Jason had been there to see me yet. It was odd for them to drill me so hard after only being awake for such a little amount of time. My happiness was diminished knowing Jason was out there somewhere without me. Feeling imprisoned was becoming my daily norm. I knew that even if I wanted to leave, my strength was not anywhere near the levels needed and in truth the desire to just lie there was overpowering.

"Why do you say daemon and not the word demon?" he asked.

"I do not really know, Doc. It just feels right to call them daemons. It is almost like they are so minor they don't really count or are not the real thing."

The doctor looked at me; his face softened into a smile. He really did seem like a nice man and that he cared to some degree, but I felt like a lab rat... a freak. I was having a hard time fathoming what the information in these dreams meant, especially dreams from my comatose years. The detail was astonishing. Why was I able to do this? It almost seemed like they were recalled events from my past. That was impossible, but the dream sequences felt so much like memories.

The doctor stayed in his chair. He was still scribbling some notes when the door opened. I felt the weariness lift from me a bit as Eryn walked in. As cheesy as it may sound, the room somehow seemed to light up when she entered. Granted she was wearing her traditional hospital white, which I know from a scientific point of view does actually brighten a room. There was something about her...almost a purity of sorts. I chuckled, thinking about the idea of an outrageously attractive woman still being a virgin and there was no way she was even thirty. Virtue aside, it was just not possible.

She approached my bed and began to poke and prod the usual places for my vitals. Silence hung in the room save the mad scribbling from the doctor. Her scent created a desire with in me that I found intriguing. It was intoxicating. I closed my eyes while she worked, imagining fields of flowers and her running through them in a spring dress. The sun was shining from behind so I could see her silhouette, moving rhythmically towards me with each stride. Suddenly I felt a little ashamed and opened my eyes. If I kept it up, there was bound to be a very manly response to these images. I shook my head to clear the fog.

"Stop moving, Dieter, I'm trying to take some blood," she said, trying not to yell at me. I suddenly felt a pinch in my right arm and relaxed a bit. Her scent was dancing on my mind in a more lewd fashion. Sensations I could only attribute to my body being more mature sent tingles all over me.

"All done, keep that cotton on for a little while. I know you hate bandages after last night." When I awoke that morning, the wraps were all on the floor. She put a label on the vial and dropped it into her pocket all the while looking at me with her big brown eyes. I could not help but experience boyhood crush symptoms when looking at her. A crooked, mischievous grin danced up the corner of my mouth. She obviously noticed it and smiled back. Shyly my head looked down erasing my smile. She turned to the shrink still sitting there.

"That's all for today doctor, he needs to sleep. Oh, by the way, Dieter, your mother will be here tomorrow." I did not have the energy to correct her again and realized there was slight enjoyment from hearing her say my full name. I had never liked the sound of my name before, yet hearing it roll off her lips was comforting. She smiled at me warmly. Her voice suddenly dropped to a whisper. *"Did I thank you for sharing the other day?"*

It was so amazing to sit and just talk to her the day before. Never had anyone shown so much genuine interest in me before. None of the previous girls had and certainly the girl at the lake had not. Thoughts about the changes my body experienced raced around and realization within that not only had many aspects about me changed inside but outside. This was a woman, not a young girl. She was a real lady and the level of attention and the depths of the conversations were different. As the comparison faded, I was still thinking about my talk with her and shook my head no. A wink flew my direction and she turned to walk away. She redefined grace and beauty when she moved. I could not take my eyes off her. A small sadness came over me the first time. I did not know why or what it was.

SIGH!

This woman, this creature of beauty, had my attention every time she came near me and yet again, I noticed my attention drifted with her presence. I sat upright in bed. She left without another word. Doctor Price rose to his feet and stretched. He gathered his tablets and books into a satchel and closed the flap. He too walked out of the room without another sound. Funny, I had imagined some sort of exciting conversation about learning more tomorrow; yet he simply left. It was sort of a relief. Sleep did sound good right now.

Mom! I almost did not want to see her because I knew she would probably lecture me about something from six years ago. On some level, there would be an argument. The time just did not feel right. I would not respond to her attacks. It was strange that my own mother would wait days to come see me. If I had a child in the hospital, nothing would keep me from going to them when they awoke from a six-year coma or anything of the sort. I could understand if they were out of town and perhaps that is what it was. It still puzzled me and my thoughts wandered back to the dreams. They were easier to understand than my parents were.

I rolled over and my mind kept replaying scenes described earlier.

The swords felt at home in my hands as if they belonged there. There was also something familiar about them as though they were a part of me somehow...an extension. I had heard stories from Jason growing up that people could get so good fighting with weapons that they became a part of them. It seemed far-fetched to me. How could anything not actually flesh become part of something else unless there was some sort of mojo involved?

My mind was definitely not at rest. I had left part of the story I was telling the doctor out on purpose. It seemed a little irrelevant to the actual dream itself. Although the fact that I was at *least* seven foot something in my dream and awesomely chiseled with a warrior's body was interesting to say the least. I almost seemed barbaric in many ways, were it not for the clean-shaven head. My frame in real life was not even five and a half feet being heavy to some degree before the accident, maybe thirty pounds or so, made the idea of being a towering muscle man laughable. My hand ran down my chest as I lay there; it was very lean from the atrophy. My ribs were pushing against my skin with not much to hold them there.

Physical therapy was going to suck.

Something sparked my memory from the dreams. Markings...lots of them were all over my body. There was no clue if they were scars or tattoos, but the ones on my arms were clearly visible. They moved on their own accord. Kind of like the symbols I saw in the campfire in my dream just for brief moments, rising up with the smoke.

The fire seemed so real. That old wizard character seen near the fire seemed to be doing things that appeared to be magic. Magic! I laughed and felt sore from doing so. As a kid, I had some big dreams, but none of them was ever this real, let alone being able to remember them this well. As my thoughts pondered that idea, a scent was now in the room. The smell seemed to be stronger when I rubbed my eyes. It was coming from me, copper and pungent, blended together. My arms were radiating heat.

That smell, it was coming from them. I do not know why but I touched my tongue to my skin. Blood. The smell was not human; it had to be from the daemons in my dreams. It smelled evil, as though darkness itself was rising to my nostrils. The same smell I remember experiencing when I woke up. I felt saturated by it.

My arms seemed to be sweating so I tried to wipe them off with my hands. The fluid on my arm was too thick to be sweat. It felt as if I was just smearing it in. The substance spread on my arms and coated them like oil. It was slippery and hard to wipe off. My eyes fell to my hands to see what was there. Panic rose inside me for a moment as dark red fluid coated them. Partially coagulated, it stuck to my fingers just like blood; yet too dark and thick to be human, let alone mine. My pulse was pounding in my throat. The smell of it was exhilarating. I was not feeling panic, but adrenaline and blood lust. A deep breath did not help as it soaked into my senses. It was going to be a good hunt tonight.

I froze. Did I just think that?

I found myself falling into blackness.

There was no ground, no sound, no anything really, just this void of all color or wind. The air was still. I thought that falling would have created some sort of wind. The strange part was now it was falling, but I did not feel that sickening pull of gravity as your stomach comes out your mouth. The surreal aspect was simply there.

My eyes could not focus on anything except the bed. Objects were out there. I could feel them. The sheets were moving still. I held onto the frame with was made of a cast iron or something dark but still metal and held on for dear life. Knowing it was a dream did not make it any easier for the senses to perceive. My eyes started to adjust to the lack of light when it suddenly appeared above.

I shielded my eyes with one hand and daringly had let to go from the metal bed frame. The intensity of the light increased. Suddenly the wind was tearing at my ears with gale force intensity. My eyes began to dry out as it was hitting them with intensity like a burst from an air horn. I was hoping tears would form, but they did not, in fact quite the opposite. The wind was hitting me so hard now my eyelids were having a very hard time maintaining the ability to blink and the desire to close them hit me harder and harder. My hand return to the safety of the rail I was holding onto. The bed spun and increased in speed; centrifugal forces started to push me towards the railing which I held.

Intense heat blasted down on me. Through the very small slits I allowed my eyes to open, the sky above me had turned into a vortex that was pushing me away from it. The wind whipped past me making it hard to hold on, while the bed continued to fall. Weightlessness tried to take hold and uproot me. Hoping that this would end, I issued a cry (more like a scream) and begged for it to stop. Nausea threatened my breakfast. I was about to get sick when the bed landed hard on stone. My eyes flew open as sparks lit up from the metal grinding on the surface as it skidded to a halt.

The sound faded and the swirling above me slowed down like a movie that was losing speed but still playing. Time dilation affected the sparks around me. Silence took the area, wherever here was. The sound of my own breathing, labored and heavy, became the only sound. It echoed off something because it sounded like a stone room.

I could not see clearly. No walls, no ceiling, no doors, or windows were in view. So whatever was out there remained unseen. I glanced around trying to find a measure of logic to what I had seen. Moments passed. Nothing appeared. No changes in my surroundings occurred. Just like the calm before a storm, an eerie peace washed over me. The echo stopped as if my ears no longer functioned. Motion out of the corner of my eye caught my attention.

I turned just in time to see a huge figure swinging two weapons at my head and I felt a slash through my throat. My hands instinctively went up. Sticky moisture flowed from a fresh wound. I was in disbelief. The large figure loomed in and I was shocked at what I saw. All attempts to breathe or speak became difficult; then a deep voice rumbled in my mind.

"You must be destroyed to rise again." I felt my head fall away from my body toppling end over end as it fell. The bed was still above me as I repeatedly lost sight of it. All faded from view slowly. Senses cut off completely as if something had truly disconnected my head.

I awoke to find my hands holding my throat and I could not draw breath. Adrenaline surged through me. Machines giving off alerts rang out. My vision was blurred and convulsions rolled through my body. A door to the room opened with a loud crash. Foot falls. Darkness was closing in and

I felt the pins and needles set in from lack of oxygen.

The last thing I remember were multiple hands seizing me. I do not know if I passed out or they drugged me. Everything went black.

XXIII

Jason

"And they tell me I'm scrawny."

The words hit me from a dead sleep. A man stood in front of me. I had been sleeping on my side since the atrophy, which made it hard to sit upright. It still hurt to focus quickly on anything, so it took a moment to adjust. The beard looked familiar; I had seen it just a few days earlier. At first I thought it might have been my stepfather. But wait, could it be Jason?

"Man you look like hell. What are they feeding you here?" he said with a knowing grin. That was just his way. I lay there rubbing my eyes to get a better look at him. He was dressed the same as always. His Levi's were faded and his plaid shirt untucked. Fashion never really held sway over either of us. I was happy to see he was still a non-conformist.

I took a long look at him. His brown hair, slightly curly and unmanaged, hung at various lengths around his head. I did not know what kind of a hairstyle it was, but my reaction was to burst out in laughter. My body convulsed for a moment in a wheezing cough, and he began to laugh too. He did not care; he never did.

"Man, you are a welcomed sight. I haven't seen anyone familiar since I woke up." My voice stammered, trying to keep the emotions in check. Even though it seemed like yesterday to me, I knew it had many years since we had seen each other. He smelled of the outside. The scent of flowers, trees, and many other creatures rolled off him in waves. I drank it all in. Something about it made me long to run outside and head for the nearest woods. His jeans bore the effects of his job. The desire to be free of this place suddenly rose inside me.

He must have seen my expression because he offered up an explanation. "I'm a landscaper," he shamefully replied. "I work for my dad since I have a hard time keeping a job."

The puzzlement returned to my face. Apparently, he was used to judgements for his profession. I looked him over again and smiled, still the same person. My thoughts spun like a top just released from its string. I did not know where to begin. So much time had passed, and he must have a lot of stories to tell. Of course, my interest would be in one topic.

"Have a seat." I motioned to the chair the doctor sits in. "I need to know something. What do you remember about that night?"

His thoughts replayed that night in his mind. The doubt, the guilt, all of it lumped into one expression: pain. He began to shift in his chair as if the mere thought of it brought him back to everything he had experienced. I could see his uneasiness. The silence spoke volumes.

"You never told anyone, did you?" I asked, knowing the answer but wanting to hear him say it. His eyes were pleading for me to not ask anymore question regarding that day. He had to know we both saw it. I continued.

"Jason, we both know what we saw. I remember. It saved your life. Why this fear of acknowledging it? We saw a Bigfoot, a Sasquatch!" There, it came out. Jason seemed to be hanging on my every word as I laboriously got them out.

Tension hung in the room; then I felt it wane finally. I had broken the ice. It felt like the torrential rain had been building up behind a dam inside him. It broke and the conversation flowed forth.

"I know what we saw. I awoke to see it standing over you. You were knocked out. It touched you. The folks that arrived at the scene must not have seen him, or it, whatever the hell it was." The worried look remained in his eyes.

His words did not make sense. I remembered the couple that found us. I could still see them. How they were there and failed to see what Jason saw defied logic.

"I didn't tell anyone because they would never believe me...living these past six years thinking it did something to you...and I have hunted it ever since." He put his head in his hands. The gentle rise and fall of his shoulders followed by a few almost inaudible sobs broke the silence. I knew how he felt.

Suddenly a word he had said hit me. He had been *hunting* a creature that no one could prove existed. A wave of pity washed over me and for a moment I thought he was serious. There was no way he could hunt the creature. It did not leave any tracks and no one has ever even found a body. I suddenly had a thought come to my mind out of nowhere. Could Bigfoot hide himself from the world? A camouflage perhaps? It was far-fetched, but would make sense since a couple stood right next to him unaware he was there. I decided to share my thoughts.

"Jason, what if there was more to Bigfoot than meets the eye?"

He chuckled for a moment and gave me the 'duh' look. I felt stupid for a moment then decided to rephrase. "I mean what if he could cloak himself somehow? Think about it. Thousands of years and no one has ever found a body. That has to account for something."

He nodded and slipped into deep thought for a minute or two while we sat there. He had taken his head out of his hand a few moments earlier to give me the idiot look. Apparently my theory held water to him and he began to nod continuously. The excitement seemed to mount in the room. He jumped up and began to pace the room. I wished I could pace. Hell, I could barely sit up. I felt a tinge of jealousy wash over me.

"What if it's magical like a demon?" he quipped, still pacing erratically.

"I don't think that's the case. It lifted the car off of you!" I piped in. Knowing full well what I saw, and feeling the need to prove it, I continued. "You know you were under the car, it lifted it right up and off you. Then picked it you up and brought you over to me. How does that qualify as a daemon?"

"Why are you saying daemon? It's pronounced DEMON."

"I think there is a difference...Moving on."

"You had a concussion. You didn't see straight. Why would it lift the car off me?" he responded, clearly not ready to give up his witch-hunt. "Maybe it was sizing us up to see whom to eat first?"

"That is ridicules, I...."

"Why, just because you say it happened does not make it the case. You almost died because it that thing." He was clearly getting emotional so I decided to redirect the conversation. I did not want to press the issue any further. He obviously had not had a chance to work through any of it since he was so hell bent on revenge. Years of hating have a way of twisting you. I understood this more than he knew because of my step dad. It was not healthy, but Jason would have to learn that for himself. No one can teach you that.

I thought hard for a moment on something else he could turn his focus to. His home situation was not much better growing up. Granted, that must have changed over time. "So why are you working for your dad? You used to hate him," I sad.

"Cause I dropped out of school and was obsessed with finding the creature. I was cutting classes and sneaking out even more than usual."

I looked at him with raised eyebrows.

"So you are you serious, you actually hunt him?" I asked.

"Yes," he said simply. I decided to drop it. I did not truly grasp why he was taking on this fool's quest. He would never find it. There was a long pause and silence threatened the room for a moment.

"I can't get a better job till I get my General Education Diploma. Besides, the old man pays decent and I can make my own hours."

"Cool."

"Yeah, it's not bad, if you don't mind doing laundry. I still live at home too. My parents might not like it that much, but they feel the need to watch over me. They claim I am unstable because I go hunting for days at a time. They do not know that I park my car off the road and walk back home and enter the woods there. I figured the scene of the crime is the best place to start."

We both laughed. It still hurt, but I managed to let go for a moment. The mood seemed to lighten; he continued to fill me in on what was going on in the world. There were so many wars to hear about. The Middle East was still brewing as it had been before my coma. The only difference was neither Jason nor I would have cared what happened over there back then. The Gulf War had been over for two years, but it never truly ended. Now that we were older it seemed to affect him more. I still felt young, but something in me tuned into what he was telling me.

We sat there taking everything in for several hours. The nurse brought in my meal at noon. I kept looking at the clock, expecting my mother to walk in at any moment. Hating to admit I might have been nervous, I changed the subject a few times whenever it steered around or close to the subject of Mom. It was strange that she was not there yet. One would have thought her son coming out of a six-year coma, especially a coma this strange and mysterious, would have brought her down that very hour. Harborview Hospital was not real close to home, but also not that far. I was nervous.

Five o'clock rolled around and Jason and I were not even close to being finished talking. We had covered everything from his eccentric girlfriend to popular new music. The transformation of rock 'n' roll into this grunge seemed weird until I listened to some of it. It was different but catchy. He let me hear some of it on his Walkman. It had a dark sound and I liked it. It was already starting to grow on me when the doctor came in.

He stood there silently looking at me. I had a smile on my face from talking with Jason. It had been a full day of remembrance of old times and schemes to come. I was really looking forward to getting back on my feet, literally. There was a darkness hanging over the doctor. It was as if he stood underneath a cloud in a comic, which seemed to follow him around the room. I was kind of surprised that he had not spoken yet. I looked at Jason and motioned for him to stop in mid-sentence.

"Doc, what's up?" I paused for a moment as Jason started to crack up before realizing what I almost said. My head shook slowly side-to-side with laughter, trying very hard not to move too much. Glancing up at the shrink again we both noticed he was not smiling. In fact, his face looked very grave.

"Did I fail one of my tests? I jested. I figured Jason would get that one. He was already laughing. I started to wonder if he was using drugs with how hard and easily he was laughing. The doctors' face stayed the same. I got a bad feeling suddenly. Jason took one look at me and realized there was something amiss. "Okay doc, what's wrong? I have not seen my friend in a long time. Why the long face?"

He took a deep breath and stepped over to the bed.

"I have some bad news Dieter, I am very sorry to have to be the one to tell you this. Your family was in a car accident on the way to the hospital. There were no survivors. I am sorry," he said.

I froze. Jason stared at me, as I looked the doctor square in the face. "What is this, some sort of sick joke?" My voice was yelling. I had no control. Everything shook. Each moment was more intense than the last. A primal rage tore open something inside of me. My chest felt tight and it was hard to breath.

"Doc, do something!" Jason yelled amidst the pounding of feet. My vision went blurry but not before I saw Eryn enter the room followed by the doctor who reminded me of Broom Hilda. Hands began to force me down in the bed. I fought back unintentionally. I must have launched someone across the room. A thundering crash echoed in the hall. It was impossible to focus. Light got dark real fast. The bed spun. My right hand held onto the edge of the bed...squeezing...when the rage got free.

An inhuman, animal-like yell escaped my lips. Energy released all around me. The only way to describe it is raw power. It tore from my very soul and burst outward in all directions. My right hand pulled hard and I felt the metal rail move and groan in protest. A snapping sound followed by a gasp.

"Oh my God, he tore the metal railing off the bed!" Eryn yelled. "Sedate him, Doctor!" I heard the railing clatter to the floor as my body raised from the bed; the nurses forced me back down. I felt a pinch in my one arm, then cooling sensation rolling up to my chest. Euphoria hit me sideways, and I felt myself disconnect from my body and it would no longer respond. I wanted to kill them all and would have tried had I been able to move my arms. The power was stronger than anything imagined. The desire to destroy everything in the room obsessed me. I felt unstoppable. I did not want to lose this feeling.

I was like a god.

XXIV

Misunderstood

Confinement was killing me.

Three weeks had passed; although I do not know how accurate my count was. I was in restraints, tied to my bed following my performance given after the ill-fated news. They were gone, dead. It was a sick irony. This happened the very day my parents were set to arrive. I was alone and did not know what to feel. It felt like only a few days had passed since the accident. I was experiencing sensory overload. Everything had changed. A small twinge of emotional pain let me know it was still there, locking me down. The irony hit me again as my physical restraints seemed to match emotional restraints.

I tried to look over the straps a few days before. Thick leather encompassed my wrists and had some sort of locking mechanism on both sides. There was no undoing them. They immobilized my head...but it could turn slightly. My feet had the same lack of motion. Apparently they felt I was a threat. My recollection of the rage was minimal, as though my very soul had disconnected from my memory of the event.

Every few hours someone came in with a bedpan for obvious reason. My robe was more like a poncho. It was clear they did not want to look at much of me either, except when they had to.

At least they were feeding me real food. Eryn came in three times a day to spoon-feed me. It was not very good food but it was edible – your

358

typical mystery meat with surprise. She supplied and I ate. The conversation took a turn, and she shared with me my actions had injured several orderlies. Although I could not remember, the guilt was heavy. Last thing recalled was the bed section breaking off in my grasp. Eryn told me that even though unconscious, my actions continued to hurt many of the staff. I felt shame.

It did not make sense that I was such a threat, or that I did the things that Eryn recanted. The strength part was about the only real aspect that I could quantify. Adrenaline was something you heard stories about as a child. Feats of strength that allowed a woman to roll a car off her baby or some craziness were always my favorite. At least it had a good ending. Apparently I was zero for two in the assault category now. Security stood outside my room.

Eryn's presence became my sanity. She kept it professional, though. Her previous warmth was missing. I tried to guard my feelings and emotions. I was not scared while I was near her, but she saw right through it. Not only was I worried about what was to come but also of how it felt when she was near me. She was so beautiful and funny that the feeling of being almost normal started to become part of our interaction...aside from my being strapped to a bed. Our conversations were light hearted. She asked me about where I grew up and what my childhood had been like. I did not have much to say, but her eyes spoke volumes. She might have been looking for possible reasons for the rage.

The truth was simple but unhappy. I spoke of my desire to explore the countryside with my closest friend. She had met Jason the other day

359

when things went sideways. He did not stay long. They told him to go home.

Her visits that occurred several times a day as she made her rounds gave me something to look forward to since Jason left. They barely let him in the first time he came to see me in restraints. When the door opened the day of his arrival, one of the orderlies referred to me as a freak. The comment stung. All I could think about was ripping another bar off the bed and clubbing him with it. The thought brought a smile to my face. Jason seemed to be more upset about it than I was. If he knew my thoughts, he might have been more worried. He told the orderly it was inappropriate and must have given him some sort of stare that made him back off because I did not hear another word...only the door close.

Jason came in and sat down on the only other piece of furniture in the room off to my right. He moved the chair next to me. We sat in silence, grim looks, and all. He was very disturbed by the recent events. I could tell he had not slept from the drifting look in his eyes. Silence continued for quite a while. Humor usually broke the tension in awkward situations. This was definitely one of those moments. Next I had to think of what to say.

"So what do you think of my new suit?" I jested. Silence hung in the room like a wet sweater. I pressed my luck. "I asked the doctor for a red one and threatened that if he did not give it to me, I'd use my own blood." I knew the last part was over the top, but it worked; he sat upright and stared at me intensely.

"How can you joke around?" he began, "Your mother is dead and you have no place to go! I even asked my father if you could stay with us.

360

He said no way."

"In case you failed to notice I am getting fed and have a bed to sleep in. I am the one in here, and if I can take it, you can take it."

He was right; perhaps I was not taking the events seriously enough. I was having a hard time focusing on anything. All I wanted to do was sleep. At least then I was in control. Granted I found it very weird that the same dreams occurred every night...of being a mighty warrior fighting daemons. Still experiencing bouts of fatigue, I fought to keep my eyes from closing. It was harder than imagined. Jason stood up and moved over to the bed. Grabbing my shoulders he started to shake me, slowly at first, but the intensity built as his rage floodgates overflowed. I opened my eyes and glared at him.

"Better! You have a pulse now. I am the one strapped to a bed. You are free. Snap out of it." He let me go. I could see the fire burning in his eyes as clearly as looking upon a burning field. Emotions rolled off him in waves. It was intoxicating. Fear, anger, and adrenalin, all wrapped up inside him crying for release.

He breathed hard trying to rein it in. For some reason, I wanted him to snap. Something came from him. It felt like pressure. I could feel him...sense him. This feeling rolled right into me. After a small pause to ponder what this could be, the thought formed. It was energy...flowing off him in waves. The desire to jump out of the bed, atrophy and all, and fight him arose fast. Next thing I knew I had torn free off my bonds with ease. The material ripped and gave way. Some of the leather tore and stitched seams ruptured. My arms still had the straps wrapping around them, but my head and legs were completely free.

Jason backed up until he was at the door. He stared at me in horror. A long pause ensued before he began to bang on the door. I finished ripping the rest of the straps off and closed the distance with an effortless leap from the bed. Within two strides, I was on him. I grabbed his arms lifted him off the floor. He called for help, which surprised me. Drunk on his fear and leaning in close, a throaty growl escaped my lips.

He froze.

It still had not struck home yet that I had torn out of straps rated for someone four times my strength. Jason did not know the meaning of coward. He certainly did not run from a fight. I was rather surprised that he had backed away from me. Let alone asked for help. The fact that I held him off the floor completely escaped me.

I looked at him eye to level for several seconds before I heard myself whisper "Sorry." Deep inside me, calm trickled over me. The rage began to subside. My arms suddenly weakened, so I lowered him, expecting to see his height difference. It never came. His feet were the floor so he *was* standing. Over the top of his head, the picture on the wall was in full view. My gaze looked down on him for the first time in my life. Somehow I was taller.

A surprised look...one of fear...crossed Jason's face. His weight shifted as though he would attack me. Then the door opened and a sea of orderlies covered me, all too eager to get some payback. Onto the bed, I was tossed. They added new restraints and replaced the old ones. There was no fighting. Something told me I would hurt them with further resistance. With the inner rage on overload, the desire to rip arms out of their socket was overwhelming.

To my surprise, I controlled it.

They were none too gentle with the straps either. It felt like a vice grip held me everywhere. I just lay there fighting to control the rage boiling in the depths of my soul. Once restrained, many fists struck my stomach followed by mutterings of "this is for so and so" or "That was for what you did to blah...blah...blah." The words fell on deaf ears.

I knew that somehow I could kill all of them without breaking a sweat. It was tantalizing. Shamed followed the thoughts. These men were scared, pure and simple. Their job was to deal with people like me. I did not intend to make their lives harder especially by hurting them. It was curious, that after they had hit me, the pain went away rather fast. A pinch in my arm told me the doctor had arrived. It was the scary woman, but her touch was gentle. I had managed a glance at her before they fixed my head in place. Whatever they administered was stronger than before. It blurred my vision fast but leveled off fast.

Strapped in once again...this was getting old.

Someone told Jason to go home. He was out in the hall cursing over what had just happened. The thought of punching him in the face made me slightly happy. He needed a wakeup call. This had to give it to him. It was not my desire to hurt him, but he acted like a spineless human with no opinion...incapable of making a decision. He was not the one tied down; he did not lose his family, nor was he the one torn to ribbons by some unseen force. Yet he crippled emotionally.

The drug rolled through my veins. The sluggishness that accompanied was not as strong for hitting me so fast. I tried to focus my mind to fight it. I tried to find a focus point to begin my resistance when a voice spoke.

"Keep this up Dieter, and you are going to be permanent here." The shrink had arrived. These people were too predictable. It had been a few weeks since I had seen him. One of the orderlies mentioned something about a trip, and then he was gone. Apparently that was the case and he had returned. He never did tell me where, but I can guess it had to do with science and my case.

"I hear you were a bad boy, Dieter. Violence will not get you out of here. Showing to me you can function in society will, however, help your case."

The door closed, trapping me with him. Out of the corner of my eye, he passed by me to grab the chair. It screeched horribly as it drug across the floor. He set his stack of files on top of me while he fumbled for a pen. I gave a small grunt. He left them there while he began to scribble something down. I could hear the scrawling of the pen. He stunk of spent nicotine and coffee.

Did these people not get it that people who do not smoke do not want to smell the aftermath either? I thought. But they never cared, none of them ever do.

"This rage you seem to be experiencing. Tell me what you think about when it happens," he said.

I laughed.

"This isn't a joke, Dieter. You have a serious issue here. The fact that you tore out of the restraints shows a lack of willingness to cooperate as well as the desire to do others harm, not to mention you're too damn strong for your own good. Do you think we can afford to risk the lives of our employees? Behavior like this could get you in much bigger trouble. And you lack the will power to maintain your emotions."

He had a point. I sighed.

"I do not feel or hear anything. There is no pain or anger. Something just takes over. Do you think I would give in to it if I could control it? You know about my childhood. It was calm and serene aside from an abusive stepfather that did not care if I lived or died, and a mother that chose him over her child. There may or may not be anger issues over it, but that has been dealt with in whatever way possible as a young adult. Jason was part of that sanity. He was my only and best friend. Is there rage stemming from that? Is it my body's way of dealing with this nightmare? You tell me!"

His eyes got big. He indeed knew about what had happened to me, but I think he just connected the dots in his head and the gears began turning in his mind. My interest in this meeting had waned an hour earlier, and I hoped sleep would take me with my eyes open. He droned on about my self-control. I proclaimed to not know why the reactions happened the way they did. My suspicions existed; none of the made sense.

The more I tried to relax and listen, the angrier things made me. None of this was my fault. They found me guilty like a criminal. Restraining me was a bad idea...they were threatening to throw away the key.

Respect kept me silent. Now was not the time. I had to play their game to be able to leave, but to where? With no place to retreat to my options were null. I knew that the state would take my parents' house to pay their bills. It happened when my grandparents died; very little remained. It was really quite sad.

My mind snapped back to the present. He continued speaking about working through feelings of anger. I finally closed my eyes and gave into the drugs. It felt funny that he shot me up then talked me to sleep. It worked. My reality shifted into dreamland almost immediately.

A fight.

A claw came right at my head as I ducked and thrust my weapon to meet its exposed rib cage, and a shower of ichor rewarded me. Somehow I knew that sleep had just taken me and glanced behind instinctively. It looked as though a portal to the previous room had closed. Yanking my sword free, I looked passed the beast as he slid free of my blade in a heap and fell the ground. It was a valley filled with rocks and corpses. Light flickered as if something passed in front of it repeatedly. I shielded my eyes for a moment and saw a whole host in flight heading right towards me.

The terrain around me was hostile and lots of misshapen rocky crags jutted out in all directions. Sure footing did not exist. Every step was laborious. Blood flowed down my shins from the dozens of times I stumbled. I did not even know where I was going.

Looking behind, my eyes caught the sky darkened with the approach of this mass of flying creatures. With no stable ground on which to fight, my options were few. An idea hit me suddenly, and my swords flashed out wide and in a spinning arc. Shards flew in all directions in an array of sparks and debris as my swords cut down the rough stone. Continuing to spin, I carved the stones down quickly. Moments passed. Around me was a place to stand. Glancing over my shoulder, I slowly turned to face the onslaught.

The flying horde approached without form. I could not gage how far out the main host was, but enough of them were not with the main group and would arrive in mere moments. I re-postured myself and felt warmth wash over me, emanating from my core, and then rolling outward. My limbs did not feel heavy. Blood no longer flowed from my legs. To my astonishment, my legs had healed themselves! It was a curious sensation. I quickly glanced down at my legs as a gentle blue glow faded. I felt my weight shift again, and the tip of the horde approached and flew within range of my blades. My arm swung.

I smiled. They were all about to die.

XXV

Changes

The pain was excruciating.

Fire head to toe, burned as if the very fiber of my being was tore from its roots and held over an open flame. Body convulsions tore at me. Lying flat on the bed was not possible. My back kept arcing to the point it felt like I would snap my own spine. I screamed. I finally gave in and let out a sob. I could not take much more.

I did not hear the key in the door, but several individuals entered the room. Their panicked voices were unintelligible with the exception of the occasional curse or metaphor for what was happening. Was my life's canvas now black? At one point, I called out to God to save me but there was no reply or release from the pain. Occasionally something in my arm, unlike the fire burning my core, provided momentary relief. I could not even form a cognitive thought amidst the madness. Every second felt like an hour. When would it end?

I must have blacked out at some point or perhaps they found a drug that made me sleep. My thoughts drifted, but it was not sleep. Everything felt strange beyond comparison to anything previously experienced. I remembered falling out of the tree outside my window once. If you have ever played pinball you would understand my experience with the fir tree. Near the top the branches were thin. You do not think about this as a kid, especially when it is a place treaded before. You get heavier as you grow. I enjoyed being up high in trees, sometimes just because they were there...other times to get away and think. I do not recall which reason had me up in this hundred-foot tree that day. There was a sickening crack and gravity did its job. It was a solid memory.

By my guess, I hit every branch on the way down. The bruises covering my body supported the theory. I was tender for days after. An hour passed with me doing a systems check before getting up. Having fallen out of trees before, the day took my desire to climb right out of me. In fact, I do not think I ever climbed another tree in that fashion again.

That event did not even come close to what I felt when awakened. My mind attributed that tree experience to a diminished version of what overloaded my senses. My head was not as constricted this time, but the leather shackles remained in place. There was a little more play but just an inch or so. The sheets were soaked. I felt the same sensation like before when I awoke from the coma.

My muscles hurt and my bones felt like they were out of place in every possible way. I tried slowly moving parts of my body and felt shooting pains firing off in all directions. My facial muscles locked in a frozen expression of pain. A beeping sound came from my left in the distance that sounded like it might some sort of monitor. The slow rhythmic beat lulled me in for a moment and reminded me of a song from a long time ago where the drum was actually a heartbeat. I had always thought that was a cool idea. The name of the song escaped me. It really did not matter though, my head felt so foggy. My mind floated.

Was it some sort of painkiller?

Legacy of the Defender

Although it was difficult to reason right now, I thought about what was happening and came up with a few conclusions amidst the fog banks in my mind. First, the attacks returned and this is what it felt like when conscious. Second, it was a result of all the damage finally catching up to my nervous system. I could not imagine it could all hit me at once like this, but I was open to suggestions in my semi cognitive state. The third idea was that I was in Hell.

I flexed my hands and feet a few times and felt the muscles protest and cramp up as if they had been in cold weather too long. The cramps became so intense that it felt like the tendon wanted tear away from the bone. Deep breaths helped me relax a little. They eventually went away but took several more minutes. A strange noise hit my ears, like ear drums popping at high altitude followed by a high-pitched whine. I raised my head and panned the room with my eyes half open. It took me a moment to see that I was not in a room in the psych ward now, but some dark place instead. It smelled horrible.

I gagged for a moment and felt bile hit my throat. The burning sensation followed. Spit took forever to accumulate to chase it down...it was then I realized there was a hose hanging close to my head. I did not smell any foulness to it and its position was accessible...*water*...a small kindness and very appreciated.

I managed to get my lips around it and began to suck as hard as my weakened state would allow. Thankfully it was water. Several minutes passed of drinking before things felt better and diminished the burning in my throat. The water was cool but kind of stagnant. I began to cough a little bit from the after taste. It then hit me that I could raise my head. Most of the times when sedated it was not possible because they fully strapped me in. It was very odd that I was not in "full nut bar kit" as nurses called it. There was no catheter or diaper of any sort on me.

The high pitch sounded again catching my attention. It sounded like some sort of power tool but was hard to say since I was not exactly adept at picking the sounds out that power tools made. It finally stopped after several minutes. My head was still pounding when it finally stopped so I called out.

"Hello?" I cracked.

Silence

I waited another few minutes and called out again. A bit more volume came out this time. My destroyed voice sounded horrible to me so I could imagine the sound it must have been making did not sound human at all.

"Anybody there? Orderly? Doctor Price? Anyone?" A clatter, something metal hitting something, echoed from outside the door. The handle turned and it swung wide. A man came in about a step wearing a plastic facemask swung up from his face. He had on an apron covered with blood. I smelled the crimson scent, it hit me right in the forehead like a sledgehammer, and my breathing quickened.

A squeaky voice assaulted my eardrums. It was so annoying I just wanted to get up and punch him so he could not speak again...ever. I was having a hard time processing the words when he spoke again.

"Holy shit! Who the hell are you and what are you doing down here?" I noticed a look of fear on his face.

"What do you mean *down* here?" I managed to say before my voice cracked.

"The morgue. Why are you in this room?"

My smart-ass humor really was pulling to the surface right now. I decided to be sort of nice. "Do I look like I have any sort of say in the matter?" There was a long pause.

"Yes?" came the timid answer. I lost my patience.

"Are you kidding me?" I wanted to start cussing him out but knew it would not help the situation.

"No sir I am not. I am the mortician. Please don't hurt me."

I raised my head and looked at him. He was actually shaking. "Do I look like I could hurt you? I am a scrawny little kid."

Silence again.

"Whatever you say." His voice shook.

That was a strange answer. While staring at him I noticed my feet hung off the bed buy a foot, probably more and just out into the air. My eyes panned up to my thighs and must have gotten big because he was starting to cower now and backed up. An attempt to raise myself up met resistance from the straps across my chest holding me down. This was finally enough. I raised my arm a little and felt the restrains as well, but I could see enough. My forearm looked distorted. I blinked my eyes and shook my head. This has got to be an illusion. I reopened my eyes and looked again. It was still blurry.

I looked him in the eyes. "Take this off...now!"

He shook his head no. I dropped my head back to the pillow. A throaty growl escaped my lips and I stopped for a second; it did not sound normal, let alone human. The door creaked and I looked up. He was gone and more shuffling was coming from down the hall as he apparently left the other room too. Anger was building. The rage swelled inside. My boiler was about to blow. I was tired of doctors and their tests. This was the last straw! They had me so pumped full of drugs that my eyes did not even work right, and now some little imp of a man would not let me go. On top of that they had me on some bed that was for a child. The intensity reached a crescendo and my body started to shake. The adrenaline hit. My arms tested the limits of the straps and I started to pull at them.

Something snapped and my arm moved a little. Not caring, I busted apart the restraints as they flexed again. I was spinning out of control fast and just wanted to hit something. The blood on the apron from moments before fueled the burn, and for some reason it made me want to hit something even more. Another snap gave me more movement. I did not care. My voice echoed through the room as everything flexed and pulled. My days as a lab rat were over.

A ripping sound filled the room followed by metal bits hit the floor. I was now sitting up; my arms were free. Heavy breathing heightened the enraged feeling, but it was not like before. There was no dizzy feeling as if my consciousness was fading. Looking around the room, it was in disarray. There were bugs on the floor both alive and dead with some sort of dead animal from a while ago based on the decomposition. The air was dank and heavier now with the metallic scent to it. Moisture also hung in the room, which most likely contributed to the smell. Far off occasional sounds added to the confusion...a clatter here, a faint bell of some sort there.

I could now move my upper body freely. The I.V. came out in the process of sitting up and a small trickle of blood rolled down my arm. As the drugs began to wear off, almost immediately the fuzzy feeling started to slowly lift. The feeling started to return to some of the affected areas. I took a deep breath. It felt very good to breathe deeply. Strength began to fill in the void inside me. With a quick yank, my feet were free and the task or removing the restraints the rest of the way was easy. It was very strange to me that the straps, especially so many of them would be so weak. The drugs had to have made me stronger or maybe it was the moisture in this room had an ill effect on the leather. I swung my legs over the side and found my feet touched the floor right away; there was not even any need to drop down.

I did not want my bare feet to touch this filthy floor. It was slimy and cold. As I applied pressure to the balls of my feet and gently rose to test my balance, my ascent was too quick and my head hit the low ceiling. The ringing sensation when you crack your head filled my ears telling me how the impact was. I ducked down and rubbed the top of my head furiously. Slightly angry at the lowness of this room I found myself pulling my fist out of the wall. The Broken material fell all over the floor and I retracted my hand making quite a mess.

"Glad I won't be paying for that, I don't have a job! Try to collect from me after you put me in this hole," I yelled, a little less angry now. "This must be from an old wing or something made for a child. Even the ceiling is very low. If this really is the morgue, why would that matter?"

Heading over to the door I opened it. Ducking was the only way to peer into the room beyond. As my eyes adjusted to how bright it was, horror filled my thoughts at what I saw and smelled. Tables upon tables lined the walls. Each one had a body on it in various stages of something. Some were covered with sheets stained with blood, some were just lying there naked, no sheet at all. The smell was something like an old folk's home, it just stunk as if old people do when they get to that age that they do not care and stop bathing. Urine mixed with decay assaulted my nose. A hint of blood was still in the air and made it bearable. I coughed a bit. The mixture was still hard to breathe.

He was not kidding. This really is the morgue.

I must have had some sort of shocked look on my face as I peeked into the room because someone watched me through what looked like a window and he saw me enter. As I walked in he appeared to watch me and move towards me. The largest man I had ever seen was looking at me. I did not hear any glass break and was ready to for this huge orderly to grab me. He did not move, but reacted to my movements. He just stared at me with a strange look on his face. I froze and waited for him act. He did not budge. Something looked very familiar about this person, as I stood fixated. My hand rubbed my throbbing head and the person in the window appeared to mimic. I touched my nose; so did he. This went on for about thirty seconds when I realized in shock that it was a distorted reflection of me. It was highly polished stainless steel fridge catching my reflection. The drugs must be really messing with my head. I moved farther into the room, observing my surroundings.

I took in the scents in the room. The smells, the blood, the other cleaning chemicals, and the embalming solution made a disgusting bouquet of aroma. All of it was revolting, but I was somewhat fascinated by the bodies. They all seemed so peaceful, yet frozen in the grip of death forever. When it is my time, going peacefully without leaving behind a mess would be ideal. A Viking burial had my vote. Put my ass in a boat filled with wood, and fire and arrow. It was simple and easy...no muss, no fuss, and no mess. Well, if you count sinking a boat in the ocean as not being a mess.

More glancing around the room revealed two doors; one looked like it went into a fridge, the other the hallway. The previous sound was probably the fan in the cooler being off balance or something. It rattled loudly; the guy working in here must be a whack job for all the bodies and the noise not to bother him. I walked over towards the door and felt searing pain in my forehead and a popping sound. My knees hit the floor. I could feel moisture and heard a crunching sound when attempting to regain my balance followed by pain in my knees. Blood run from my scalp line to my brow, then right into my eyes. Attempting to get to my feet brought more pain and wetness. My eyes burned when trying to keep them open. Remembering there was a sink right by the door, I made my way in that general direction.

I could barely see while hobbling over to it and it too...was low. That was very odd to me that everything was so low. It had to be some sort of children's wing converted to a morgue. Maybe it was an old school house, the ceiling, and the tables too. I turned the water on and grabbed a hand towel to wipe my eyes with after getting it wet. My scalp began to throb. I tried applying pressure to it while I rinsed my eyes out blinded by pain.

Sticking my finger on a piece of glass was an even larger surprise and made me that much more furious. The second and third pieces were insults to injury and dozens littered my scalp. I gingerly began to pull them out and the blood flowed freely.

I shifted my focus to my knees; more glass. Frustration began to mount when I glanced over my shoulder in the room, and noticed a light was out. The bulb had shattered and glass littered the floor. Logic finally settled in and I realized I had broken the bulb with my head. Feeling stupid, the cause of my injuries sank in. Deep breaths helped alleviate the growing tension that kept getting the better of me. Vowing to slow down, I grabbed another towel and cleaned my wounds. With the glass no longer embedded in my skin, cleaning went much easier and my scalp felt a rush of heat.

Just as I finished with my fourth towel, the door opened. It was the man with the plastic facemask. He was not wearing it now as he stood in the doorway. He seemed short. Other voices in the hall were getting closer and the sound of the footsteps approached. He just stood there in the door frozen again for about thirty seconds; then he pointed his finger at me.

The room exploded into action. Unseen hands yanked the man back as the room filled with what looked like soldiers. They filed into the room brandishing weapons and surrounded me in a half circle. I backed up and put my hands up.

"What did I do?" A bunch of little pinches hit my skin, I saw flashes and began to convulse. It felt as though my legs might buckle amidst the shaking but my strength surged, and I remained standing. Reaching up to pull out what attached to my skin on my torso, I noticed many wires. After grabbing hold of the wires, electricity flowed into me, causing my grip to tighten. I tugged. Flesh ripped. There was no pain. Pulses hit me over and over...I roared and yanked hard. Three out of the six men flew towards me and my other arm swung with the back of my fist. A sickening crunch happened as I hit one in the nose. He flew backwards and hit a table, knocking him and it over. A corpse fell on the floor as well, landing partially onto the downed man. Blood sprayed the room in slow motion as my other hand with the metal wires swept across the other two catching the first one in the side of the head and bowling him into the other. I could now see the word swat on their vests.

The last three standing lost grip of their weapons and went for their batons in one motion. They advanced on me. I growled and kicked one of them in the chest, sending him over a table and against the wall. The other two flanked and caught me each with a baton as my hands found their heads and slammed them together. A quick glance of the room showed it cleared of men. I looked into the hall. Red beams of light hit me in the chest. More men stood at the ready with guns trained on me, my hands slowly rose.

"It wasn't my fault, they attacked me!" I said quickly, still running things over in my head. I just downed not one but six police officers. The excitement was intoxicating, but I had no idea how it was possible.

"On your knees, NOW!" they demanded repeatedly.

The room had no other exits. There was no place to run. Moments went by slowly. I dropped to my knees expecting to wince from the pain, but I felt nothing. Police poured into the room surrounding me. The second wave to enter saw to the fallen officers. They carried the one with the broken nose out. I felt bad, but they attacked me first. Perhaps a judge would see it that way. More commotion from the hall way caught my attention as the officers tried to put cuffs on while cursing.

"Dammit Mike, the bastard's wrists are too big. I don't have any zip ties!" an officer shouted.

How was that even possible? I knew I was a little taller than Jason. The drugs must be affecting my hearing. My head was still foggy. A man in a suit stepped into the room. He had a self-important look about him. They referred to him as Sergeant. Apparently, I was important enough to send in seven plus officers to collect, which bothered me. Was I lost? Tucked away but not lost? "Sergeant" walked up to me and looked me in the eyes.

"My God, you must be over seven and a half feet tall...how long have you been lifting? I bet it's steroids you were after; it always is with you muscle heads. What did your parents feed you?" He paused.

I could have sworn I heard him say seven and a half feet tall. Something clicked in my brain and things began to make sense. The low ceiling, the scared man, the broken bulb, the low tables, and now hearing I am a giant.

"Officer, when I went to bed I was small. I woke up in that room over th..." I started.

"This is for assaulting cops!" Knuckles met my face. It hurt for a second as my eyes reopened to see him dancing around holding his fist in his other hand in obvious pain. Someone rushed in from the hallway; I did not catch who it was at first. My ears rang for a second. Dizziness still affected my faculties. I heard a voice.

"This is broken; you need to get up to emergency."

"His face is like stone!" is all I heard from him followed by lots of cussing.

"Get this one up there as well. He has a concussi..." Then I heard a gasp.

"Oh my God!" came a female voice.

That voice!

My favorite person in the whole world walked over to me with a look of horror on her face. She was trembling so bad she could barely speak. Her hand reached up for a second then pulled back suddenly. Tears welled up in her eyes. This had to be a mistake. Even on my knees I was taller than she was. Stopping about four feet from me she put her hand over her mouth, a sob escaped. I smiled. It felt like a year since I had seen her.

"Where have you been? What happened to you? All we found was a note saying you were gone and no one knew anything. All the papers had been filled out and everything." She was still shaking and raised her hand up to touch my face. So warm and gentle...my eyes closed. I could not speak. Her hand came away from my face. I opened my eyes and saw her turn to Sergeant.

"In case you are wondering this is one of our patients. He suffers from some form of abnormal growth. Someone signed him out. I just witnessed your men attack him without provocation, and I am sure there is a good explanation as to why he is here. So unless you want me to file a grievance against you for police brutality, I suggest you take your men and leave."

The Sergeant was in the hallway glaring at me. My eyes panned the room. There were still four guns trained on me. I knew I could take them if they did not back down... but they *were* police officers. I felt bad for hurting them but was invigorated that six armed officers fell to me with no training other than what Jason had taught me. She turned to look at him.

"Well? Do I need to make some phone calls?" she said.

"Come to the desk in the hospital and make your report. I'll be in the emergency room." He glared at her and walked away motioning for the men to fall back. The little man was in the corner looking at me from around the cabinets there.

My eyes came back to Eryn. She was radiant. All I could do was gaze at her. The officer behind me let go and stepped back after looking at his Sergeant. I reached out to Eryn and touched her face; my huge hands covered most of her cheek. The smile on my face spread ear to ear. She closed her eyes at my touch. Thoughts of how to explain this raced through my mind, but I had no idea what was happening.

"I am here," is all my voice could muster.

"I don't know what's going on, Eryn. I woke up about fifteen minutes ago by my guess and was restrained in that room back there." I gestured with my head. "I was alone and heavily sedated. This man came in when I called." I paused then looked at him.

"Are you the only worker down here? How could you not know I was in there? Wasn't someone coming in to check on me or anything?" He flinched a bit at her words.

"I only work part time and was told by my boss, David, to ignore any noises I heard back in here. He said they ran out of rooms and that a patient was going to be using that room under heavy sedation. I don't know how long you have been in there. Sorry, I panicked; I just wasn't prepared to see a giant in there."

I laughed and it was very loud. "You weren't prepared. Imagine how I felt, waking up like this?

"I don't follow sir." He hung his head.

I looked back to Eryn, who still had a surprised look on her face. "Can we get out of here? I am starving."

"We need to get you back upstairs. First I want to look at the room you were in." She walked over and opened the door. She covered her nose and coughed. "Oh my God, you were in here?" She looked in and stepped back closing the door. She pointed at the little man.

"Who are you?" she demanded.

He hesitated.

"Look you aren't in trouble but you did see what the cops did and how they handled the situation so I suggest you stay out of that room and do not talk to your boss or anyone else. In fact..." she reached into her pocket and pulled out a business card. "You call me if they give you any crap or the police harass you into lying about their actions. Can you do that?"

He nodded.

She looked over at a folded pile of white sheets, walked over, and grabbed one. She turned back to me and unfolded it like a sail, then threw it over and around my shoulders. She had a concerned look on her face and I could tell she was dying to ask me what they did to me.

"How long?" I asked. By the look on her face, it had to have been a few days ago. I cannot imagine they would be able to keep me a secret for very long. The situation still baffled me. I mutated into the monster. She tried to fit this sheet around me and was not having very good luck doing it. She kept losing one side or the other and was starting to get frustrated. Tears began welling up while she tried to hold it together. This side of her even with the weeks getting to know her had never showed itself. I took her hand in mine and with the other took a hold of the sheet. She pulled the other side of and made the two corners tie together just like a kid would try to make a cloak like superman.

She finished and stepped back smiling. "There, you look like a super hero now."

"How long Eryn?" I asked again. A little bit of irritation came out and she looked me in the eyes. I was still on my knees.

"Seven weeks and three days. I came into work; you were gone, and there was no information, only that someone transferred you to an actual mental hospital. The discharge order did not say which one."

I did not know much about the medical field and in truth anything other than the occasional television show or movie seen growing up but this did not sound right. There was always some sort of paper trail. Turning to the guy in the corner to ask him more about his boss, I noticed he had disappeared. I glanced past Eryn to see if he had moved but could not see him.

He was gone.

Just then the door to the morgue closed and another man walked towards the center of the room with his face buried in a clipboard and flipping through some pages. He suddenly stopped and looked up, first at

Eryn, then me, and jumped back.

"Holy shit, how did you get in here?" He backed up to the door looking back and forth between us. Something about his eyes was familiar. I could not place my finger on it. I had seen them over me before in a weird look on his face in some memory, still blurry from before. Taking a long look at him made fidgety. Perhaps he was one of the doctors.

"Relax, I am a nurse here. I am just giving one of my patients a tour." She held up her badge and pointed to the room in the back, "What do you normally keep in there and who is responsible for this facility?"

"What room?" he asked. "The fridge?"

She pointed back to the room I had been in while I was getting to my feet. I glanced back there. To my shock, there was a solid wall. All I saw was tile. Eryn continued to rake the man over the coals and I began to tap her on the arm. The man protested that he did not know what she was talking about and Eryn got more agitated. I kept tapping her on the shoulder and she kept ignoring me while laying further into the man. Finally, she got tired of my tapping, and looked over her shoulder and yelled, "What Dieter?"

My finger pointed at the missing doorway and shrugged. She paused and turned to look. The second she turned her head...clattering... and the man ran out of the room. I gave chase catching the door and ducking to get in to the hallway.

An empty corridor!

This dumbfounded me.

My head felt a lot less foggy than five minutes ago. Two men had now disappeared out from under my nose within three minutes of each other and now there was an empty corridor with no place to hide and a missing room. I ducked back down and looked at Eryn, she faced the wall where the room used to be and had her hand on her hip while the other touched her lips; trying to wrap her mind around what had just happened with the room disappearing. I do not think she realized this guy had practically vanished. I got to the door fast and he had just passed through it; there were no footfalls in the hallway.

He was gone.

A realization came to me suddenly...the priests eyes looked like that. A look of shock came over me. I knew that somehow he had come down here looking for me or he knew where to find me. This discovery rocked me to the core as I glance back to Eryn.

"Eryn."

She held up a hand with one finger up, meaning wait a minute. Walking over to the wall, she looked all around the area. She hesitated and put her hand out and against the wall section that had been a door only minutes before. It looked like tile that had been there for years and was filthy. She put her hand up against it and, to both our surprise, it went into the wall as if it was some sort of illusion. She turned her head back to me in amazement at what she was doing and then suddenly got a panicked look on her face. She was trying to pull her hand free and it was not budging. Something had a hold of it.

I was just clearing the doorway when I heard her make a strange noise and her hand popped free of the wall. She stumbled away, not looking where she was going. Running right into my arms, she cried and buried her face in my chest. Her sobs came more violently. I stood there trying to wrap my mind around what had just happened. I had no answers. Standing there in the morgue, I held her for the first time.

I found myself smiling for the first time in a long time.

XXVI

Visits

Boredom.

I sat in my cell for the better part of three days falling into my own mind. There were windows in this room that had a chain link mesh on the outside, unlike the previous room, to keep the nut bars from getting out. At least there was a view if you climbed up on a chair to look. So it must have been a minor "nut bar room" or a holding cell. Being so tall, I did not have that issue and could see outside easily. The room was sparse, but it had a partition to the toilet offering a little privacy. A chair and bed completed the ambiance. I had to laugh about the bed. It was too small of course, again, so the mattress was on the floor. Sleep did not find me often.

Three days earlier, Eryn took me back up to the ward via the stairs so we would not scare the employees or patients. She readmitted me to the hospital for testing. There were hardly any employees on shift at the time, but knowing the word would spread soon and the ward would be buzzing of my return made me laugh. I had allowed them to poke and prod me once again at their whim. This did not make me happy because I was starting to black out a lot when they took blood. It was hard not to feel like a pansy who could not handle the sight of his own blood.

The days were boring at best. The hospital staff took more and more blood as new reasons arose. A theory was forming they were trying to bleed me dry somehow so they could dissect me when fighting back was impossible. I dubbed it "Death by blood draw" and tried to get used to it. Granted, I think we were only on number seventeen.

The orderlies looked terrified. This was funny. I kind of liked not being a wimpy little kid anymore. They visibly sweat when walking in the room now. My height dwarfed them all by over a foot. A hundred pounds of muscle easily separated them from me. They had also heard the rumors that took down six policemen, when in truth it was six swat officers, without breaking a stride or a sweat for that matter. I could smell them before they even opened the door for some reason and could hear them approach twenty feet before they arrived. Discussions through the door were just as easily identifiable. Nobody has any clue how I got to be this size. I think it was my body reacting to all the attacks and growing its own defensive measures. That is the only idea that comes to mind. And even that sounds insane.

Many of their conversations took place down the hall, away from my ears. Fear of my rage seemed to be the top of the list. They said multiple times they did not want to go in the room if it was not safe. I found that ironic considering my hands never touched any of them since returning. They feared me now because they knew I was stronger and could fight. Their demeanor was wrong for the job in my eyes and that left a bad taste. Why do this job if you are not willing to deal with the patients, no matter how big they are? I had to admit, that made me smile just a bit.

The day I submitted myself for re-evaluation, Eryn told hospital staff to leave me out of the papers. They agreed to keep my presence quite, and the employees had to sign something that would keep them from talking. I was in a section all to myself. Just a handful of people worked in my area. It was a fair request in my mind. They honored my request after all I had been through and did not tell anyone what had happened to me. The police strangely had some influence and leaned on Doctor Price to keep this quiet. This surprised me greatly, especially after all those years of studying me. Would the science community forget about the scrawny boy in a coma? Could the church let it go?

I looked different enough that the police agreed that for safety reasons, a name change would be appropriate. Eryn filed her report and told them that my disappearance was not only against my wishes but against the wishes of my Doctor too. They needed to forget who Dieter was. I chose to be called a name that came to me one day while scribbling on some paper looking out the out the window. I missed the good old days of running around at night fighting pretend monsters with Jason. Life seemed so easy then. My parents rarely came to mind. A barrier in my mind kept that feeling on the edges of my reality.

When I came back to reality that day, the name "Tathlyn" appeared on the notepad bolded many times over then circled and underlined. I took this to be a sign of what to call myself. The police were to come to process my request for a name change soon.

So here I waited. It was ironic to get a visit from the sergeant that hit me in the face. I sat listening to some music when a knock on my cell echoed before it opened. A nurse named Meagan poked her head in. The staff assigned her to me about a week before my disappearance. Behind her, I could see the detail of two officers in plain clothes that were outside my door at all times for obvious reasons.

"Dieter...the sergeant is here." I returned from my thoughts and caught his stare. He was a hard man in his late thirties by my guess and well-built for his frame. He had the same suit on from the previous day, so a few jokes about police salary were bound to find their way into the conversation. I guessed him to be about six foot two, black hair in a crew cut, polished of his cheap "FBI" look he was going for.

"Forgive me if I don't stand up but all of my orifices hurt again from being poked and prodded," I said, looking away and back outside. He walked up and handed me a file folder. I thumbed through it while he started to speak. Ignoring him came as a playful idea, but he surprised me with his tone and opening line. It would take some getting used to, seeing my last name as Thompson now.

"Tathlyn, I wanted to apologize for our behavior the other day. As far as we knew a monstrous man had broken into the morgue and was desecrating corpses. Sadly, in my line of work that is usually the case." He held out his hand to shake mine and I was tempted to crush the other one to teach him a lesson. I refrained and took his hand gently. "We have never been officially introduced. My name is Sergeant Rick Kostas," he said.

He continued, "Eryn told me that you had some weird things happen to the two of you after we left. Would you care to elaborate?"

I was looking at the forms that I had to sign to make my name change official. They all seemed to be in order. I was no lawyer, but it did not appear as if anything was out of order, or that my life was forfeit. It simply said I was changing my name and the official paperwork was there with an identification card. There was no driver's license since I could not drive yet. The photo used was from the previous day. They took the picture right in my "cell" right after bringing me a five times extra-large shirt that was so tight breathing was rough.

The photo looked like a convict. Dieter was certainly gone for good. The humor of it made me smile. I had beaten up six police officers and technically gotten away with it, even though they started it. A judge would have flayed me alive.

"Define *weird*, Sergeant. Look at me. I am over seven and a half feet tall. They think I am still growing, based on the muscle and bone density. My strength is more than three men of my size combined, and my weight is just over four hundred pounds." I could not help it; I had to bring up something bad. "Not to mention those injured in that altercation were part of your SWAT team, and I did not even break a sweat taking them down. I am not proud of my actions, but it happened. What is crazy is my friend told me once, that I only have the equivalent of a green belt in Karate. So yeah, I suppose we can start with *weird*."

I continued, "Not to mention being attacked by supernatural forces while in a six year coma. And, of course, there is the face that I grew this tall and strong in a total of seven weeks. You have already read my profile." I paused to read his response. So far he was blank. "I am sure the doctor has documented my dreams of fighting daemons, and you have no doubt read my files. So what do you think I find *weird* Sergeant? How about if you tell me what *you* think is weird first. I need some damn answers." My jaw tensed and I noticed he stepped back half a step. I breathed deeply and calmed myself. I did not need more trouble at this point.

Typical cop posture though, with his hands on his hips. One resting on his concealed piece of hardware under the cheap suit jacket he wore. I could see it printing way more now that his hand was on it. The gruffness in my voice made him uneasy. He did not answer, which surprised me. I pegged him for a show pony police officer by the way he held himself upright, chest out, and chin up. *Could there be a broom stuck in there?* I tried not to chuckle. He finally spoke several moments later.

"Yes, I read the reports and the doctors' notes and am well aware of your past injuries now. I should by every account advocate for you to stay here based on the six men, all of which are in the hospital or under some care of some type. Officer Campbell has a fractured face. They say his brain might be bruised." He paused and turned to look at me and to my surprise smiled. "Yet you did stop when commanded. Someone who is completely unstable or hates the police would have kept going. You weren't having any trouble throwing us around, that's for sure. I was about to come after you with the full weight of the department, but then I read your file. Yes...you were five foot whatever and one hundred and thirty or so pounds. Your upbringing was rather nerdy. You have never been in trouble before. You also did well in school. These are not the signs of a raging maniac."

I looked at him sideways. "I fail to see the point, let alone why you are reading notes from a confidential session with a shrink. How is any of this relevant?"

He continued. "The way you fought, however, indicates you've had specialized training. So until there is an answer to that, I imagine you are going to be a mystery to me." He looked me right in the eye and waited. "I cannot risk ignoring this one. Someone taught you how to fight like that."

Laughable. I did not tell the doctor about Bigfoot. Jason did not either. Was that room bugged? They are not wondering why I had that strength when they told me my mother had died. That was adrenaline. I was scrawny, post comatose, and was not very strong to start with. Now that I have reacted and grown they are going to have some of hay day as soon as they get another scientific burr where it is uncomfortable or sensitive. I do not really know what folks say now other than *he* is even more of a freak.

To hear him say, "Something weird happened" made me slightly angry. Eryn had said something to him. Nobody understood this whole thing, especially not me. This was my life, and I had to accept and deal with it. To the mundanes that sit at their desks and have no grasp of reality, this was as good as it was going. The Sergeant was no exception to that. I decided to be candid.

"Well...what do you want to know? Or shall I rephrase it and say how much do you want to know?" His eyes looked rather deep into me. The coldness of his penetrating stare pushed deeper inside. He was looking for triggers to see if there was any dishonesty. With nothing to hide regarding what had happened the night of the accident, I decided to err on the side of caution and probe a bit more first. I tested his response.

"Tathlyn, I want the truth, you can talk to me," he said.

I laughed. "You really have no idea what you are dealing with, do you? Look at me. From five foot six to this...in two months? I have grown in muscle mass as if bodybuilding was my whole life. If you really wanted the truth, you are looking at it. I am a freak of nature. Or something super-natural happened. I had no idea. What does it matter what I say? You aren't going to believe me anyways."

I stood and began to pace the room. This was getting tiresome. I felt like some lab animal that was clawing its way out of a steel cage, but all he did was wear his claws down. This cage could not hold me. He knew it, and the only thing wearing down was the little patience of mine that remained.

Regret manifested in my mind for letting Eryn talk me into letting the doctors re-examine me. I should have just walked and let them look for a scrawny kid with a man's face.

The sergeant went to the corner and grabbed the chair. "I am not go-ing anywhere till you give me something I can use, Tathlyn," he said as he sat down, pulling out and note pad. Looking at me with un-patient eyes he began to tap the pen on the paper as if he were doing Morse code. The rhythmic beat was slightly annoying like water torture would be. A constant drumming would drive me crazy eventually. It was easy to imagine what would happen if my stay here became mandatory, leaving the use of force, as my only ally in leaving. How many of them could I take out? Getting shot would hurt for sure. Did I even care? The need to fight something or some-one burned deep.

It was too easy for my mind to get lost on this subject, especially since it seemed to be on my mind all the time. I constantly thought about fighting and using weapons to fight daemons. It was always daemons. Since more cognizant thoughts about my dreams formed, the longing for battle became a real desire. I wanted to engage daemons in combat and have them surround me, with no hope of survival. Yet knowing full well I would survive worked my tiny ego over hard. Why were there such confident feelings on the matter? I had no idea. Why the dreams seemed so real now and I could recall them now when I was awake did not make sense.

I longed for a fight.

The Sergeant droned on as the doctor used to in my sessions. I was unaware how long I zoned out again and wondered what type of nonsense he spewed. What typical cop lingo did he throw at me? Was he going to preach to me about civic duty to try to find who did this to me? It was hard not to laugh inside while looking myself over for he was still giving me the cooperation speech. I had to admit, my body was amazing. Each day when I looked in the mirrored non-glass surface they gave me for grooming myself, I thought about what it would be like to be normal size again. It seemed rather boring to me to not be the way I was. Freak or not, it was beginning to grow on me as well.

Silence.

I looked over at the officer sitting in the chair. He was staring at me. A look of impatience crossed his face. "Well?" he said, drumming the pen a bit more furious this time.

"Fine!" I said, "Repeat the question."

"You're kidding, right?"

"Yes, well no. You lost me at the part where I am supposed to help you with something you have no idea how to handle. Something that you think I know…which I do not. Do I need to remind you that when *they* took me, they doped me and tied me down? So you ask me what I saw right when I just woke up and hit my head to the point of needing stitches. I am just as lost as anyone about this," I said. For just a moment, it almost appeared as if the Sergeant felt bad for me.

"You never actually got stitches. I checked the records. There was no wound," he said.

"Hey, you saw the blood right before you punched me in the face. I know you saw it because I was on my knees and looked you right in the eyes. If the wound healed as you say it did, then you know that when I was in a coma, my body was healing at an insane rate." I paused and looked at him directly...looking for some hint of him getting it. "So, Sergeant, with all due respect, I was abducted. Perhaps you should be asking the staff that was here that night questions."

He glared at me for a few seconds. I could tell he was looking for any facial twitch or nervous tick that would tell him something. Having seen cops in movies before, it was obvious to me what he was looking for. A lot of Hollywood drama over did interrogation scenes, but the reality of them and the goal held true. This might have been a very loose version of it, but he was digging for anything he could use and it made me mad. Anger crept up inside me and a low guttural growl rose up in my throat. He heard it and shifted a bit uneasily in the chair a few times... then looked nervously at the door a few times before standing up. A good rule when fighting is never to be caught sitting down. Jason taught me that.

He began to pace towards the door. I did not move. My anger was apparent and the desire to smash something with my fists was obvious. Images of me pummeling him into submission began to play over and over. He had nothing that could stop me, I could get to him before is gun even cleared the holster. The urge was getting unbearable. I felt a moment of clarity open a small clearing in my head. "You had best leave Sergeant," I growled. "You are really pissing me off, and I would rather not hurt you."

He moved towards the door and knocked loudly. It opened and he exited at a rapid pace. For a moment I heard the buzz from the hallway while the door opened and closed. The locks fell back in place. *Alone with my rage.* I was growing tired of feeling this way after seeing someone who refused to see beyond the outside. My self-control was the only thing keeping him alive at times. As a child or teenager no matter how much my parents mistreated me, control was never an issue. I was having a hard time with rational thinking as the window in my mind closed and the rage began to build. My desire was to hurt something now.

An image appeared in my mind of a cave entrance; it was giving off a faint light as if I was in the cave and the outside awaited me, beckoning me forward. I could hear strange cries in some language that were calling to me, almost taunting me to come out. I heard a sound like scissors opening and closing in rapid succession, like a child furiously going at a news paper. I imagined making snowflakes with folded paper and a large pair of shears. The shears dripped with blood, and the paper was actully leather hide of some creature in the process of evisceration. I fixated on this image of these shears in my hand and was furiously carving on this leathery hide. Droplets of blood flung everywhere as the shears tore into the material. A sick sort of satisfaction surprised me as blood splattered all over my skin.

The leathery hide began changing shape and started to grow larger but had no form yet. It grew taller and taller by the second. In mere moments, it was taller than I was. My hands slowly stopped the scissoring on the shears. It simply kept growing and forming some hideous shape that was not recognizable. My fear started to rise. I could not identify my enemy. Logic hit me. I have fought things larger and meaner in my dreams.

In previous dreams, there was always a distinct feeling of overwhelming or over bearing by multiple enemies. They surrounded and outnumbered me by such odds that any normal warrior would have either perished or fled. Even a seasoned warrior would have counted the odds and decided whether an engagement was fool hardy. This time it was different. It was only one daemon and I was unarmed. In part, the surrealism of this dream was really starting to gain momentum, yet the logic side of it made no sense that I would be attacking a daemon with large shears. No matter how effective the tactic might be it made me laugh at the thought of it.

I watched in sheer horror as it grew taller and was now at least a hundred feet tall, towering over me. The shape began to form itself into a humanoid mass, but the surface of it was almost bubbling and boiling on its surface. Faces coalesced in the skin. They would scream out in pain then dissipate as fast as they formed. These sounds created in me fear and anger. I was not sure. They grated my hearing and caused me pain. Something popped in my ears and fluid began to spill out...running down my face. It dripped onto my shoulders. Anger and fear turned to rage as I started to back up, and the sheers fell from my hands and clattered on the cave floor.

Moments passed. My feet retreated from this enemy that defeated me without even attacking physically. I finally understood the concept of chess and the psychological aspect of defeating your opponent with your mind. I fell back in fear and watched the shapes continue to form on the surface of the skin as the whole mass started to solidify in a final state. Looking up, the face of this monster stared back at me. We locked eyes. To my horror...it was my own face. In its largeness, my mind failed to recognize that I was looking at a demonstrated evil version of me with thousands of daemon faces imbedded in its skin. Each face cried out to me in a chorus of voices in different pitches and tones. Some of them I actually recognized as foes I had faced in my dreams at one point or another. It was as though their very essence was a part of me now, writhing below the surface of my skin, and trying to exude influence over me.

My skin suddenly itched and then I felt pain. To my own horror, I looked down to see that a face was splitting my skin slowly as it was pushing its way through on my forearm. It began to shriek at me as it tore its way through my flesh. I felt a burning feeling as its teeth broke the skin and started to eat my flesh. Tearing at my own skin, I found myself screaming at the top of my lungs. The tall form in front of me was laughing in a deep guttural tone. I could hear and feel its mockery as the fight with this aberration forming on my arm continued. Tears formed in my eyes and began to run down my cheeks as my panic grew. I knew it was only a matter of time before this thing spread and infected another part of me.

Despair formed in the back of my mind and crept forward like some sort of sludge in a gutter filling with rain. Slowly it moved consuming my thoughts and I felt myself getting weaker by the minute. The strength in my hand began to fail as I started to lose control of the motor functions of my fingers. My heart pounded in my chest and the pressure drove up into my skull like a water hose spraying at full capacity at a fire that it could not put out. The strength in my hand waned, and I sank to my knees caving to the despair of failure. Eye sockets with malformed daemon eyes stared at me. Drool flowed out of its disgusting maw. The spittle ran of my forearm in a viscous blob that fell to the ground with a terrific splat. The large form in front of me faded from view, and I was on my knees looking into the eyes of this disgusting face on my arm.

No sound came from anywhere. Total silence enveloped me so my location faded from concern for a moment. The face coughed and showered me with its drool, creating irritation from the saliva that started to eat my flesh. Then it spoke but not in a guttural voice. It was clear as I could speak...and sounded like me.

"You think you have problems, wait till you're growing out of someone's arm." The look on my face must have been one of disbelief because it started to cackle a bit as it choked on more of its own drool. "What, you're too good to talk to me? Idiot, I am you or what you will become if you stay on this path of anger." My arm was speaking to me!

"You are not me," I said. "This is just a bad dream."

"Am I now?" I felt a stabbing pain in my arm and opened my eyes. The face rose out of my arm and sunk its teeth into my forearm to its gum line, if it actually had one. Instinctively I smacked it in the face.

"Hey, that hurt!" it yelled as it let go of the meat on my arm. "Do that again and I won't let go. I'll swallow it and you can feel what it is like to eat yourself for a change." The very thought made me ill.

"Why are you torturing me?" I asked, not expecting an answer.

"And here I thought I was smart back when I was you. I let hate consume me and I started enjoying the people around me getting hurt since I had endured so much. I got my wish, consumed by my own pain. It was only a matter of time before they killed me in battle after I failed to stop a breach."

"What are you talking about? This is a dream and you are not here. This is all in my own head." I closed my eyes and repeated these thoughts again and again.

"Stay on this path of self-destruction and you will find out soon enough, Tathlyn." It spat vileness at me as it choked my name out. I could not believe what I was hearing. As much as this cave brought its own disparity, seeing this thing growing out of my own arm was more than I could handle. Something inside my mind burst and tears flowed freely. I wept.

"I refuse to give into my own self-doubt now," I sobbed. "There are too many questions unanswered." I managed to choke out the words in between swells of emotions. I did not think I could feel any worse in a dream than I felt at that moment. My face tightened up so much that the muscles began to cramp up. I could not imagine my life going so wrong that my lack of faith would consume me. A maze of darkness seemed to surround me. A deadly circular cycle of self-doubt and fear trapped me.

Something pressed on my cheek; warmth. I opened my eyes and saw the floor below me. It was close so I must have been sitting down. I could still feel warmth on my cheek, and I noticed tiny feet in white shoes in front of me and looked up. Eryn stood with moist eyes and a solemn look.

401

She had her hand on my face and was gently rubbing my cheek. I looked her in the eyes and saw more tenderness than I could imagine. She had a softness about her that could calm the strongest storm yet strength to take it head on if she had to. Something told me she had wells of untapped energy.

"Hey you, I came to check on you," she said.

"Hey," I echoed.

"Why are you sitting like that?" she asked.

"Like what?" I looked down and noticed I was on my knees in a meditative pose. I shook my head, still feeling fuzzy from waking up. I suddenly realized that I had not been asleep.

Eryn gasped! "What did you do to your arm? Let me see it!" She grabbed my right arm. I looked down. My forearm was rather stiff and felt numb. The shape of a skull was now a scar carved so perfectly it was as though someone had used a scalpel like a detail knife. Its shape had a sunken eyes version of my face, but there was no color or ink. Simply a face representing mine in some twisted fashion. She was tracing over it with her fingers and I could feel the warmth of her touch transferring into me. The glow of her spirit as if it moved within me now became apparent. Such tenderness commanded my attention.

How could I sense this?

I sat there soaking in her attention but feeling confused by my growing affection for her. Meanwhile, my mind tried to imagine the ghastly image on my arm and where it came from; when suddenly chills ran down my back. An image popped into my head of a daemonic face that spoke to me.

"Do not forget. If you hold onto your past, those you love will die!"

it said. It vanished as fast as it popped up. I shuddered head to toe and jumped to my feet.

Eryn stepped back. "What's wrong Dieter?"

"Dieter is no more, my name is Tathlyn!" I said.

"Okay, Tathlyn, what's going on?" she said, noticing a touch of the strange.

"I had a really messed up dream, better yet, call it a waking nightmare. It was so real and I cannot even begin to explain it. It was surreal, almost too surreal." Her hand found my cheek. She felt like home, unlike any other feeling I had felt about living somewhere.

A very concerned look crossed her face.

"You do not have to tell me if you do not want to," she reassured.

"Or cannot," I interjected. She smiled at me, reflecting that everything was going to be all right. Part of me wanted to believe her. The other part knew something was terribly wrong. Something was so wrong that I could not explain the foreboding feeling inside me. I tried to fake a smile, but it turned into more of a grimace. I knew I was in trouble because I could not hide my feeling from her any longer.

"I have not forgotten about those words you spoke to me. They are part of me now." she said.

Hearing her say that felt like a punch on the chin from a dragon. I had no response. What I felt inside did not compare to how I was feeling that day. Things escalated quickly amidst the chaos of my life. My focus right now needed to be on figuring this out, but my heart would not let it go so easily.

"Eryn, there is something," I paused. "I do have something to tell you."

She locked eyes with me.

XXVII

Confessions

"So what exactly did that Sergeant say that got you so upset?" Eryn asked, looking intently into my eyes.

I could not help but get lost in her eyes for a moment. She had this ability to calm me down when she started talking to me like this. It was hard to stay frustrated. *She soothes me.*

"The room surveillance, are they listening to us right now and watching us?" I asked.

"No," came her reply with her very gentle voice. "They turn off the cameras and listening when officers show up to speak to a patient and since this is not an interrogation cell, they do not want their methods recorded. I don't like it, but today I don't mind."

That was kind of strange that they would not want their questioning recorded, but then again this was not the police station either. It made a little sense that they would not want to have things recorded of the premises and out of their control. I cannot imagine the lunacy the officers must deal with on the day-to-day dealings with the public. Then again, now that I was on their radar, they had plenty to talk about even though my situation was unlike any they had ever dealt with. I hoped this was the case. If my new life was a day-to-day routine, the world is in for a rude awakening.

I was not sure what I could tell her. There was so much that I knew was real and just as much confusion that I did not know where to start. So many un-answered questions remained; more than I could count. What was happening now? What happened then? Where to start was even tougher than imagined.

"You don't have to tell me anything you do not want to. Take your time. *We* have time." Her words rang true. I loved how she used the word *we*. I liked the sound of that. It made me feel good that someone seemed to have my best interest in mind since the doctors were trying to make life study cases out of me. This woman seemed to really care. I did not know how to respond.

A large part of me wanted to trust her with the truth...with every-thing. The other part wanted to not say anything at all and see where this led. I just did not know what to do or say, or if saying anything at all would be detrimental. My current situation was that I was getting closer to this woman to the point of having feelings for her. I had never really had a girl-friend. The girl at the lake the day that my life changed was the closest ever. A few childhood crushes happened, but nothing was ever serious. This feel-ing could be anything. It just felt good to feel it.

I gazed at her. She stood in front of me staring me down with a faint smile and accepting eyes. Her hair was out of her ponytail a bit; the part that would be the bangs was barely long enough to be in her ponytail, and she was always adjusting it. Boldly, my hand went to her face. She closed her eyes while my monstrous palm cupped her cheek. It was so small against my hand to the point of freakishness, but that did not stop me. I knew this woman cared for me. I leaned forward and gave her a gentle kiss on the lips. To my pleasant surprise, she responded and kissed me back.

I experienced something that I had never felt before in the excitement of my first kiss with the girl at the lake. It was a sinking yet lifting sensation...*giddiness*. Fear gripped me. *How to respond to this feeling?* Anxiety pulled me back. I did not know what to say and found my lips moving. "Sorry, Eryn, I..." Her finger found my lips and she pressed it ever so gently to them. Next thing I knew she was kissing me again.

It was classic to compare kissing to losing track of time, but it happened. I felt silly while my brain processed what happened. A kiss *could* say a thousand words but at this moment I think my brain processed about ten thousand in the blink of an eye. I could not imagine something so simple feeling so good. Time passed. Eryn was now holding onto me and her head was on my shoulder. We sat in silence for a few minutes... with me smiling like a schoolboy. I could not help it. My life had hope for the first time since waking. For this to work, taking a chance in telling her everything was paramount. If she did not receive it well, I would deal with it.

"What do you know about how I ended up in the hospital?" I began, not sure of how to approach what I was about to say.

"I know that you were on your bike riding home and that a car hit you and put you in a coma."

"A car actually hit both Jason and me. He ended up underneath the car." I paused, waiting for her to say what I knew she would.

"How did you end up here without him? Your wounds were so severe that I cannot imagine how he walked away without a scratch."

"Well, both of us were hit. I flew into a tree from the impact, which put me in the coma. Jason stayed on the hood of the car and rolled with it while it went off the road and turned on its roof. The driver took a leaning tree through the face, killing him instantly. That tree kept the car from crushing Jason." I felt her expression on her face change with her face firm against my body. It was a frown of some sort, but definitely not a smile.

"Here is the part you are not going to believe. We saw something that day that defied all logic and brought myth to reality." I paused, waiting for her to become unsettled or get nervous. She did not move. "It was a Sasquatch. Jason and I were so surprised to see it that we made jokes about it."

Her head came away from my chest and she looked me square in the eyes. I could see there was a sense of awe on her face. She stared at me for a few moments. Part of me felt like she was analyzing me while I watched her watching me. She expected a flinch or a blink, maybe even smile to show I was kidding. When my face did not change and I did not reveal any "tells" her face got serious real fast. Like a mime waving his hand in front of his face and changing his expressions with each pass, only there was no hand waving. I smiled nervously. She just stared at me.

"You are serious? You saw Bigfoot! A Sasquatch! Do you know how huge that is?" She turned her head shaking it in disbelief. "Man, what I would give to have seen that." I was rather surprised at the use of her words. She had never used the word *man* when talking to me let alone in this context. Then I reminded myself she did just kiss me.

She was overwhelmed as she began to babble about how amazing that was and how lucky I am to have been there to see it. It took her few minutes for to realize I was not saying anything. She paused and looked back at me with a snap of her head to where she was now making eye contact again.

"Was it scary?" she said, almost mocking me and must have caught that I was not kidding still. "Are you sure you didn't just hit your head?" Her smile quickly faded when she saw I was not amused.

"There is more; a lot more." I took a deep breath, tried to calm my nerves, and started again. "*He*, it, is the reason we got hit by the car. The car swerved to miss the creature and hit Jason and me. I blacked out because when I came to, *it* was lifting the car off Jason. *It* then brought him over to me while I was passing out from blood loss and going into a coma. I remember this all clear as it happened, just like it was yesterday. Then I blacked out again."

Eryn was staring at me with a look of shock. I could see that her eyes were moistening a bit. Her shock turned to sorrow and a single tear flowed from her left eye. The moisture reached its brimming point and overflowed the lower lid, allowing the tear to run free making a streak down her cheek. She smiled slightly. The sight of the smile returned warmed my soul again.

"And here you are now," she said after a moment of silence.

"Yeah, here I am...a freak of nature." I looked at the floor for a moment when I felt her hand on my chin. She held my gaze for a few more moments and cocked her head to the side ever so slightly.

"There is more Eryn...more that does not make any sense. I have these waking dreams now that are so real it feels like I am standing there. There are daemons fighting me. This happens more and more. It literally feels like there are two swords in my hands when facing these creatures, and I am using movements never seen before, not even in the movies. A normal person that is trained probably could not do them." I paused and looked at her. She remained trained on my eyes with hers.

"In the actual dreams, my skills are impressive. There are monsters that I assume are daemons, that are so horrific that I cannot believe I feel no fear. I get excited even as I am saying this at the thought of fighting them. I literally think about them when I am awake, trying to sleep, or sleeping. I just want to slay them. My viewpoint in the dream is never looking at myself but based on where I am standing and sometimes looking at the ground. My size is the same as now."

I glanced at her. She intently listened to me but had a questioning look on her face. She had to be thinking, *"He is insane."* Those thoughts ran through my own mind when this first started to happen. I brushed it off as some sort of posttraumatic stress but the more they happened, the more it made me question my sanity. In the end, I still felt nuts for even experiencing what my life had become. She seemed to be taking the information well, but I knew that she had to be thinking I was crazy.

"To top all this off, Eryn, there is the small matter of all those wounds I was receiving. How do we explain that? How can anything explain that? I know the church believes in stigmata, and that is why they came to examine me. I am fine with all that. Whatever...I just...I just." My words fell silent.

"You just what?" she asked.

I stared at the floor. A flood of emotion built inside me, like a volcano preparing to erupt. My shoulders shook. It was the first time I had actually listened to myself explaining things aloud. It was the first acknowledgment that something might really be happening to me.

Eryn stayed put. She said again, "You just what?"

"I just want to know why." I looked at her. My eyes began to moisten.

"We will figure this out," she said. "For now, just keep talking. Keep sharing. The more you talk, the more you will understand."

I stared at her, amazed. Did she understand me? Was she real?

"Talk," she repeated.

"Okay, um… Well, the church obviously felt it was daemon attacks on my defenseless body while I was in a coma. I was never much of a religious person. Daemon attacks don't make much sense, do they?" My recant must have stirred deeply, her memories of caring for me. She was crying now. I was not accustomed to drying her tears. Thankfully, I did not poke her eye out or something. For having large digits, my hands were very dexterous. The flow stopped after a moment and she put her hand on my cheek again.

"Whatever this is, Tathlyn, we will figure it out. I am really going to have to get used to this new name you have given yourself."

"Dieter is no longer. Whatever I am is yet to be determined, but he is gone." Hearing these words come out of my mouth was very strange. After sixteen years of answering to my name...that felt like a distant memory. I tried to imagine my future, but there was an insurmountable wall needing climbing. It was ironic that there seemed to be daemons on the top of the wall and flying above it. I found it ironic that they looked like the ones from my dreams. I knew this was just an image in my head. It just seemed like it was actually there, especially now.

Silence blanketed over the room like when a hero on television gets his bell rung and he cannot hear anything. The sound comes rushing back as he got his senses back. It was very similar to me as I sat there in this intimate moment with Eryn, except there was no explosion...just a moment of clarity that everything truly was connected. The answers existed somewhere inside my mind. It would not be easy since with no idea how to do it. As I sat there holding Eryn, it was hard to not feel that together we would be unstoppable. I could not explain this feeling. I only knew it to be true.

The door rattled like someone tried to open it without the key and Eryn sat got to her feet. She pointed up to the camera and made a motion that would turn them on soon. It was easy to forget they were watching all the time. She had to maintain that she was not forming any attachments, which made sense. Since my awakening, I knew now that she felt the same in return. Moments later the door opened and in came another nurse with something on a tray that looked like meds.

I glanced at Eryn and shook my head slightly. I did not want any medications. I looked at my arm still shaking my head. She saw my look and stepped forward towards the other nurse. "I'll take that," she said, intercepting her rather quickly. This startled the other nurse. She handed the tray to Eryn, glanced at me, and scurried out of the room. Eryn looked at the tray and frowned. Her reaction was obvious that she did not like the contents of the tray. She knew that I had only agreed to test if there were no medications involved. There was nothing wrong with me mentally and she knew it.

This was another ploy for someone in some office somewhere to try to gain control over me or make me do something. They had a reason to keep me. Eryn walked over to the door and unlocked it. She winked at me and nodded. Opening the door, I saw her slide the contents from the tray into her pocket very discreetly. She gave me one last smile and said, "I'll be back to check on you after I look in to whose order is attached to these meds." Then she was gone.

Alone in my thoughts again.

My senses were on overload after kissing and holding her close. My reaction to the way she treated me must mean I was falling for her. Nothing like this happened to me as a teenager. Feelings spinning out of control must have been hard for an adolescent. I at least had the benefit of the mature body, but my brain felt under-developed in some ways. There was confusion over my feelings. My anger over the treatment I had received was rather unchecked and not resolved. This was only part of the solution. Dealing with it would be the hardest part. I did not understand what was going on. Fear of the unknown was becoming my greatest challenge. Something told me that there was more at stake than my sanity.

My forearm itched. Scratching it subconsciously, I did not even look down at first. The raised portion of the skin where the mouth outline was still bothered me. It felt like a latent burn. My skin felt calloused with a leathery texture to it. The sensitivity of the area was incredible but did not register the sensation. The feeling was none other than a bug that had

413

crawled across the area; my scratches smashed it.

By the time, my eyes looked down the image from earlier had returned. I could see the maw, full of rotting, razor sharp teeth...mouthing the word "remember." It did this repeatedly and if it was stuck on repeat. Blinking, I looked again. Was the wound talking to me? Did they find a way to drug me after all? Still, the damaged area spoke. I watched it for several minutes, trying to learn something...*anything*...that could give me more clues to my current situation. It began to fade after a while and was gone, leaving a slight discoloration of the skin and a faint scar. I heard a whisper in my mind say, "Remember." This time the voice sounded like the chorus of two voices blended. They did not sound like a monster...but something dulcet. This created some complexities that pitted the dreams against something serene and calming.

While trying to focus on this event, visions of monsters flashed in my mind. I could only guess they were representations of the daemons in my dreams. The overpowering desire to do something physical hit me. At first I tried walking around the room, but due to my large stride it took me only a few paces to make it around the room and doing so several hundred times seemed ridiculous. After about fifteen revolutions, I dropped into a push up stance and cranked out several hundred of them realizing I was not even getting tired. My mind raced faster than I could move. I decided to try another route.

I sat down and slowed my breathing. Images still flashed through my mind like a slide show on speed. It was very difficult. The images were flowing by so fast and I found myself actually watching them and capturing them as they went. Only a fraction of it made sense, but it seemed to be images of some pre- Stone Age society, or tribe. They sat around a campfire talking to a large creature that remained out of focus. The fire was huge and lit the area in a rather large clearing quite well. People wore leather armor of some type and carried strange looking weapons. Just as I began to focus on the weapons, the scene changed to a battle that involved familiar creatures.

Daemons.

Now this was interesting...very interesting. Believing came easily for me since my perception of reality changed each and every day. These new events added to that belief.

The daemons attacked these town folk by the hundreds. People fell left and right to the jaws and claws of the small denizens. In the end, the people were triumphant over their foe. Bodies of the creatures littered the ground. The scene changed and there was a large shadow overhanging the people fighting. A huge claw swung out and fell multiple people at a time. It was horrific at first because it came so suddenly. I did not expect to see people falling by the dozens to this unseen threat.

Those left scattered. This attacker, a looming shadow, remained unseen. The only part of it, a huge curved talon, rained death, and terror down on the people standing to defend their town. All hope seemed to be lost. None could stand against this new evil.

Sadness washed over me. Tears began to well in my eyes. This was not fair. How could evil like this exist even in my dreams or daydreams? Evil of this nature created imbalance. Vengeance swelled inside me. It was very strange to go from one extreme to the other in a short period, but I al-

415

most did not know the difference these days. As the images swam by, the townsfolk continued to scatter into the smoke from the burning town. They ran from the monster; some only got a few steps before it cut them down.

A large figure emerged from nowhere. Covered with brownish fur from head to toe, it carried no weapon of any kind. My view from behind it detailed its broad shouldered with long arms moving with powerful grace as it ran right into the darkness and engaged the daemon. This newcomer's speed was amazing. It moved so fast as if watching a blur to a movie that had been sped up, only I knew this was not the case. The monster moved just as fast as he had been while attacking the town folk. Combat lasted for many moments. The fury of blows exchanged was unbelievable as this new furious humanoid, using its giant claws or fists, beat the daemon into submission and literally tore its heart out while it stood.

The daemon crumbled to the ground with a roar, expending the last of its foul breath as it collapsed with a tremendous thud. Dirt and dust shot out in all directions as the rest of its lifeless shell found a place to settle. Silence was small for a moment and then the only sound was the crackling of the fires. The creature that defeated the daemon was still partially in shadow for a moment. I could see its chest rising heavily to the rhythm of its own breath. It turned from the massive corpse on the ground and stepped out of the smoke. The image shocked me.

Bigfoot. I could not believe it.

This creature of legend and myth was now entering my dreams. Even though my body still sat on the floor of the hospital, my mind took me somewhere else entirely. My mouth hung open in shock and disbelief.

Thoughts raced. I should be surprised at this turn of events, but somehow a small amount comfort settled in. This slowly started to sink in. Bigfoot has been around for many thousands if not tens of thousands of years, helping mankind fight off these hordes of daemons spilling into our world...my world. I suddenly felt very protective of my planet and the pieces of the puzzle felt like they got a little clearer regarding at least why I had seen him that fateful night so many years before.

He walked forward with several large strides of his huge legs. He appeared to be looking right at me, even though this was some sort of day dream. I had no control over it. He walked behind me and headed towards the fleeing people's direction to aid them.

I shifted my vantage point, not sure of how interacting with this dream was even possible. Villagers started to reform their ranks against the smaller daemons. Bigfoot walked over, grabbed one of them by the head, and crushed its skull in his hand casually as he passed by. Black ichor squeezed through his fingers until he let go of the dead creature and flung it away from him. He shook his hand off to free it of the disgusting fluid; the droplets showered the area to his right as he engaged another one by grab-bing one of its wings, pinned it to the ground by its head and tore it free. I heard a sickening crunch and the creature's gray matter escaped its broken skull and splattered on the ground.

This assault continued. The villagers finally turned the tide by form-ing defensive lines and the daemon host was weakening. A feeling of relief engulfed me for the first time since the sequence started. It was weird to know this was a day dream and that I was along for the ride but could control my view point while this scenario played out. Just as I got the hang of it, the battle ended, forcing my mind backwards through a tunnel. The light got smaller and smaller until it faded and my eyes opened.

Did that just happen?

I sat there staring at my arm. My eyes were slowly coming back into focus. The scar previously there was faded, but the faint outline of the vicious face remained. The memory of it ripping its way through my flesh was real. Its evil looking eyes tracked my movement even though the flesh was perfectly flat.

My sanity came into question. Confusion kept hitting me like waves crashing on the northern shore of one of the Hawaiian Islands. I saw the footage of a long time ago. This image drove itself deeper into my mind with the power and intensity of those waves.

My pulse pounded in my head. I started to think it was going be a horrible headache when something released in my mind and the pain subsided. It felt like my last grip of sanity had just let go. I took a deep breath and relaxed. My mind started to calm down.

"Do not forget!" the chorus came like before, jolting me out of my one serene moment for the day. I laughed...gently at first. The waves of laugher started out slow at first then turned into all out hysterics.

"This must be what it feels like to lose your mind," I proclaimed with a yell.

Seconds later the door burst open. Several men poured in dressed as orderlies. They all had very serious looks on their faces and seemed to have a strong resolve about them. In fact, my gaze panned from one face to then next, and I realized I had never seen these men before. They closed around me in a slow circle. One of them had a syringe, the others...restraints.

I locked my gaze on him. He had a very weird look on his face, like he knew what he was going to enjoy doing to me. With a sudden explosion, the other men came in from the sides. I leapt to my feet...ready.

Grabbing the first one by the arms, I spun him into the second one. They both flew against the wall hard. The third man rushed in, grabbed my arms, and pinned them at my side while I regained my footing. My hands went out wide. I turned to face him. Something stabbed the skin on my back. My elbow found his face and his nose disintegrated into a shower of red as he collapsed, pulling the item out of my skin. The man in front of me took advantage of my distraction. My jaw took one as my head turned back to face him. Again the sting came, only this time his fist landed in my palm, which promptly wrapped around the tiny hand. My kick caught him in the chest with the ball of my foot.

He fell down choking for air and clutching his torso. Another sound came from behind me. Spinning fast, my fist flew. The face of Doctor Price appeared right before my fist connected with him.

"What going on here?" he proclaimed as my punch stuck with me managing to pull much of the power back. It still connected hard. He flew backwards and hit the wall. I glanced around the room; none of the other assailants moved anymore. Turning back to the doctor, I noticed he was shaking his head. This was certainly going to extend my stay. He moaned with his hands cupping his now gushing nose.

I cursed...walked over to his body and knelt down. He looked up at me with a bloodied nose. "You pulled that didn't you?" His voice gurgled as the crimson flowed.

Nodding, I carried him out the door. Several terrified looks flew my direction from nurses shying away until they realized I was trying to help him.

"We came to tell you that you are to be released," he coughed.

"Oh," was all I could muster.

XXVIII

Freedom

"So I'm finally free to go then?"

The words felt strange to hear after the reality of what had just happened. Four men had attempted to kidnap me in broad daylight. Such a bold move meant someone had their eye on me and must have decided that it was time to take me out. Doctor Price finished talking to the hospital security and had his nose full of gauss thanks to me. It could have been worse had the punch not been pulled. At least he was not pressing charges.

I stood in the room where the attack occurred. Glass and gnarled chain link mesh littered the floor. Blood stains decorated the walls. The in-room security camera went offline at the time of the attack. The police were on their way. The fleeing men left no trace. They simply vanished. It was another item to add to the "weird" file.

Doctor Price finished his conversation and instructed me to follow him to a room to talk. Conveniently, several of the bigger orderlies were working nearby. They were "busy" outside the room in case he needed them. After what he just saw, he knew they would do him no good. I walked in ducking the door and sat on the floor, ignoring the flimsy plastic chair set in place for me. "No back injuries today," I thought, remembering the first time I tried to use one.

"I will not miss this place." A few episodes of anger turned border-line rage a few times when I was startled awake by an orderly coming in to attend to me for whatever reason in the middle of the night. The doctor told them not to disturb me at night, but they rarely listened. Several of them know better now. Instead of being smart about it and alerting me beforehand, it was as if they had decided the dangerous approach would be better. Maybe even fun. I found there behavior suspicious, especially since they were warned.

I was, after all, in here of my own free will. They had no grounds to hold me involuntarily, but acted as if they did. Their instructions were to observe, but they were buying time, trying to find a loophole. Part of me thought, maybe there was a judge in the loop somewhere they coerced into a decision to hold me. After all, there was no way they could. They attacked me without provocation. The S.W.A.T. team helmet cams were proof. Eryn did her homework. I had to hand it to her.

Today was the end of my un-official period of cooperation. Rather than days, it had been weeks. I went along good naturedly. The situation was as much a mystery to me as to anyone else. My questions needed answers too.

The doctor looked at me over the broken nose I had given him. He did not seem angry. In his eyes was a look of curiosity and respect.

"I know we have had our differences Diete – excuse me, Tathlyn. Your situation is very unique, and it has been a privilege to be part of it. From a medical point of view, you are in perfect health. Your physical condition is that of an elite athlete. Your mental clarity is keen. Our tests show no abnormalities."

"Did you have something specific in mind?" I asked.

"Steroids tend to alter the mind and produce quick-to-anger responses. You've no doubt heard of roid rage. We have not caught on camera whoever has been slipping them to you all this time. Somehow, you were unaffected mentally. We also cannot find any trace of an anabolic agent in your blood work. It could be a new product. We suspect you have contracted a form of gigantism. There is no conclusive proof." He paused. I sat there seemingly un-phased by his comments. What could I say? I was asleep for six years.

"It's just a working theory for now. The other weird part is your Sergeant friend has ordered your records sealed and taken. What we discuss stays in this room. You were never officially here," he said.

I still looked at him without responding.

"Is any of this getting through, Tathlyn?" he asked.

"You mean do I understand what the hell you are talking about?" I started. "Actually, I do not. Is that clear enough?"

"Fair enough. As far as your wounds opening and healing on their own, I have no theory. Could it be an undiscovered viral strand? Sure. Could it be spiritual? As a doctor, I really don't have a comment. Off the record, I suppose anything is possible."

"So I'm a freak," I said, almost in a whisper.

"That's one way of putting it I suppose," said the doctor.

Whether or not he meant to pause for dramatic effect, he did.

"You have been evaluated Tathlyn, to the best of my ability. The rage you experience seems to have passed for now. I can issue a clean bill of health. The truth is, I don't know where we'd put you if we wanted to have you committed." He paused and looked me up and down the best he could with me sitting. "And I don't think we have enough extra-large orderlies to *make* you do anything you don't want to do." He smiled and brought a new tissue to his nose.

"Sorry about your nose, Doc," I said.

"It's okay. The bleeding has stopped. Besides, I am certain you could have killed me. Try not to hurt anyone, ok?"

"Will do," I managed.

"Oh, and another thing, with your file sealed and gone, there will be no more research or tests. This tied our hands. Whatever is going on with you, it belongs to you now."

He stood to go. I watched him. Who could blame him? They had done what they could. I could not really complain about my treatment. There were bound to be people, even groups, interested in figuring me out. At least they had kept the Press away. That is a headache I did not need.

Besides back fisting the first orderly who tried giving me a shot when I was asleep, I behaved myself. The staff learned a valuable lesson that day. *Deal with the giant when he is awake.* Besides, I had no way of knowing his intentions. Anything could have been in that syringe.

I drifted mentally. The doctor's voice was a soft whir. When I refocused, the subject had changed to my previously scheduled appointments, which they cancelled. He was interested in having me come back on my own. He wanted to check in with me from time to time.

Not a chance. Eryn and I would figure this out ourselves. She was the only person I could trust.

I nodded and smiled. How could anyone explain scientifically how I grew in the span of nine weeks? Seven of those had been in a vegetative state, and I had not only tripled my body weight, but it had been solid muscle. How could a chemical induced coma add muscle? I looked like a bodybuilder. My appetite was ravenous.

Maybe it is good that my files are gone, I thought.

I was in a coma for six years. In that time, I had been severely "wounded" dozens of times, with no apparent cause. Surviving the attacks must have made me stronger. The medical and scientific communities spent years trying to get answers. They loved sipping warm coffee and pontificating on their "findings" in all-day meetings. I had been their experiment. One of them wanted to be the one to make the official diagnosis. Get his name in a magazine. Win a prize. To them, it was a game. They had no idea what was happening to me.

And now, thanks to the Sergeant, my file disappeared.

I was having a hard time trying to figure out my dreams. Why so much fighting? Why so many creatures? My day dreams were bizarre, too. I found myself constantly tracing the outline of my new face with my finger. It was like an obsession. Something was more than missing. There were clues, but I was missing them. The dreams, both day, and night, overshadowed everything.

Many mornings I woke up smelling blood. At night, I would sit up certain that I had blood all over me. Every time, I was clean, not a spot of blood on anything. Then one morning I felt moisture in my groin area. Fearing I had become a bed wetter, I was surprised to find it to be blood. The

425

blood spawned a dozen theories, words I cannot even pronounce. It was similar to previous injuries, but the difference was there were no visible wounds before. The doctor ran tests thinking it was a nocturnal emission traced with blood, but he found no semen in the sample. I felt relieved that I could rule out bloody wet dreams as my problem. At last some good news for a change. I tossed it into the "weird" file and tried not to worry.

One day at a time.

Another different scent got my attention too. I do not know what it was, or what caused it, but it smelled of musk. I detected the scent on various people in the room at times. It was distant, but distinct. I logged it away for later. Too much thinking did me no good.

The doctor continued to drone on about not finishing his work. My own thoughts had me lost in the day's events. Who wanted me kidnapped? How could they have gotten away so easily? What would I do next time they tried? If there was a next time. They had already made three attempts. I had no reason to doubt a fourth was in the works. I was glad Eryn had not been there. I might have killed someone protecting her. She was the rock that kept me grounded. With her, I felt stable.

Getting to see her every day was about the only high point in my life during those times. It did look good that I cooperative, especially after beating up the S.W.A.T. team. Jail should have been the next stop. Eryn's quick wit saved the day. She had them worried about accusations of excessive force because of my size. Silly as it sounded, *"Hey, you attacked my freakishly massive boyfriend for no reason!"* Size discrimination. There is a concept. I was still surprised the charges went away.

Doctor Price finished.

"So that's it," he said. "You are no longer under the care of this facility. For security reasons, follow me and you will be escorted out the back."

My mind had faded completely. I barely returned to hear the last of his remarks. Standing up, my thoughts turned to a vision of myself running in the woods, hunting.

I had never been a hunter.

I drifted again, thinking about the vision, unaware of the room when the silence shattered.

Pain.

It was as if someone had hit me square in the nose with a board. My guard dropped defensive. I could taste of blood on my lips. My tongue instinctively wiped it away. The orderlies outside the room turned and must have seen the blood and my reaction to it. They scattered like cockroaches in daylight. Two of them bolted from the hallway through a door at the end. The other two ran and hid behind pillars built out from the walls.

Standing there with my fists clenched, my breathing got heavy as the adrenaline hit me. The smell of fear filled the room. A noise came behind me. Turning I saw the doctor trying to hide under a desk. Sound, like white noise, flooded my ears. Deafness rolled over me. The doctor's lips were moving very rapidly, and I was suddenly aware that he was yelling something. Buzzing followed by a slight popping sound brought things back to into focus. The doctor was indeed yelling.

"Stay calm, Tathlyn! Nobody hit you. No one even touched you. What the hell was that?" He was clearly scared.

I touched my upper lip and felt the moisture already starting to recede. It seems I had smacked my face on the upper entrance as I started out the door. I forgot to duck. Everyone in the room panicked thinking I would go into a rage. The doctor was under a desk. His behavior was odd for a grown man. I found myself wondering what had happened to him as a child. Had there been an abusive parent? The thought took me to my own childhood. I remembered every time my stepfather ever laid a hand on me. Deep down the hate was there, but it did no good. He was dead. I had nothing. I did not even go to his funeral. Anger suddenly rose and the desire to break something filled me. Something inside me boiled. I wanted to inflict pain like the kind experienced all my life.

My hands shook. It was rather rapid, almost like a vibration, but small and focused. A deep breath seemed to help. My nose pulsed with each beat of my heart. With each breath I took, the pain subsided. Then it stopped entirely. The pain fled, with no trace of soreness. No ache of any kind. I looked up and saw two orderlies peeking in at me. They were scared of me just standing there.

Minutes passed and a small crowd of orderlies and nurses gathered. Murmurings circulated. I could hear it all; no matter how quietly they spoke. Everyone agreed. *I was a freak.*

I heard a familiar voice. Eryn! She pushed her way through the crowd outside. She had become quite a friend. She approached me slowly. I felt a smile force its way to the surface.

"Hi."

"Hi," I said in a low, defeated tone.

428

"Did you try to hurt the doctor again?"

"No," I said. "My face hit the doorway."

I had to laugh. The memory of punching him in the nose was there. I looked over at the desk and could see him peeking out at me from underneath. He did look terrified. There was no blame. I felt more like a freak. I put my head in my hands and ran my fingers over my scalp. As I ran my fingers through my hair , I felt a lock come away in my hands. I heard Eryn gasp. I looked at my hands. They were full of my hair. I looked at Eryn. Her hand was over her mouth. She was shaking. She looked as if she was expecting me to lose it. I started to giggle out of sheer nervousness, not knowing what was happening.

"Looks like I will have to shave my head," I said, awkwardly.

The room was silent. Eryn tried to ease the tension with a nervous laugh. A few moments later the orderlies joined in and from under the bed I heard the doctor clear his throat. He crawled out from under his refuge, stood, and straightened his tie.

"Well Tathlyn, you handled that quite well. You have shown you can control yourself. I will escort you out." His voice shook as he spoke, but he tried to look strong even though he had been cowering like a child just moments before.

I stood up, letting the collected hair fall to the floor and moved towards the door. My eye line was above the door jamb. This would take some adjusting. Going in and out of rooms ducking was part of that equation. I could no longer afford any lack of awareness. Day dreaming or losing focus was dangerous now. My guard could never be down...ever again.

I exited the office and looked at the room that had been my home for many weeks. A hand took mine. It was small and warm to the touch; it seemed to vanish in my grasp. I did not have to look to know it was Eryn's, but knew what it meant. I smiled until the bright lights from the windows hit me, forcing me to shield my eyes with my free hand. My heart would do anything to secure whatever the bond was that was developing with Eryn.

It was a good day after all.

I stepped outside into the sunlight. There was trouble focusing in the brightness making me shield my eyes. Fresh air mingled with sounds both new and old. Eryn pulled her car up to take me home. Thankfully, it was a larger car. Anything smaller would have been pointless. With my size, I could not have fit. To my surprise, she walked around and opened the door for me. I smiled at her and my eyes happened to drift over her shoulder. She must have noticed as my eyes found my least favorite detective still sporting his cast he earned while grappling with me.

He motioned with his good hand and pointed his fingers at me first, then his eyes. It was the proverbial, "I am watching you." I laughed slightly and thought of how cheesy and cliché he was. He could teach a class on how to be a cliché. As I got in the car, my gaze fell upon him once more with a smile that turned into a cold stare. He looked at me for another moment before turning away. I knew I scared him.

Hell, I scared me.

I felt the car lower on the suspension forcing me to adjust the seat. Eryn looked at me and for the first with a real smile on her face. Yet it was more than a smile, for there was something there unknown to me until now.

430

Today, hope presented itself. I reached over and took her hand. A sigh escaped my lips.

"Let's go home," she said.

"Sounds good to me."

XXIX

Awakenings

It was not long after leaving the hospital that my first real glimpse of my coming path revealed itself. Everything was still cryptic and felt like layers of wrapping paper on a gift. Just as one layer came away, another layer appeared. I may not have been any closer to figuring out what was happening to me, but the consistent weirdness was pointing in a direction that scared me.

I was staying in a second bedroom with Eryn for several weeks. The connection we shared was not hard to explain. Aside from my attraction for her, she had a quality about her that she just cared about people. That was a rare trait too. No one else at the hospital really showed an interest in who I was or what I was going through. To them, the freak was loose on society.

Eryn understood me.

Even though she could not explain my metamorphosis, she knew an explanation existed somewhere. She accepted my sudden hair loss and appreciated the insane shape of my body. My mentality changed as new experiences redefined me; I was no longer an ignorant teenager. Fitting into social situations was awkward weeks ago. I tended to stay quiet for fear of looking or sounding any more stupid than I already felt. This just added to the weirdness that had become my life. Science failed to categorize me.

In a few short weeks, my thought processes gave me hidden insight. Clarity increased. All situations became tactical and strategic to me. My

432

thoughts often focused on fighting and combat. When I would go on morning runs near Eryn's house, I found myself analyzing the terrain as if looking for a tactical advantage in combat. How to approach these areas and what to do if a situation arose became a morning ritual.

This was my life!

Eryn shared a real interest in my thoughts and we spoke for many hours each night when she got off shift at the hospital. She asked me about what I remembered the most and what the "shrink" had asked me. Everything I told her was new and fascinating, but left me confused and exhausted. My dreams did not make any sense. Why was there so much violence? What purpose lay behind all the fighting? My guess was it had something to do with my childhood; at least this is what the shrink had said.

Each day, the strangeness of my life became harder to understand, but easier to accept. My focus changed to the small things I could figure out, like trying to acclimate into a society that had moved forward without me. It felt a little like what my parents used to say about things changing so much that they could not understand. Yet in the same sentence, they tried to tell me they had been there, that they understood. That left me even more confused as a child. Now here I was, adapting to my new body that had freakishly grown. This was like a bad Twilight Zone episode.

People stared at me as if I was a monster. Mothers pulled their young ones close and gave me a nervous smile when I looked at them. Sometimes if I smiled, they would visibly relax a bit but most would scurry away like rats after stealing some cheese, looking back the entire way.

It felt like I caused terror in the streets with my mere presence. I did not feel sorry for myself; it was not a pity party. Instead, the pity was for the people that could not see anything but evil when they looked at me. There was not a lot I could do. No disguise would change my size. Walking the quiet streets from Eryn's to the park each day, I realized this had become my new normal. My guard was never down, though.

Then everything changed.

The air was starting to warm as the morning sun rose. "Typical Washington weather," I thought as the first true rays of the sun touched my eyes. I was six blocks from Eryn's and striding quickly.

A gasp came from my right. Half-expecting serious trouble, I almost turned ready to fight, only to find quite the opposite. A woman stepped backward off the curb and fell down at the sight of me. I heard a sickening thud as her head met pavement. Somehow, she managed to hold onto a child. It was bad enough she hit her head. The approaching car changed everything. I took the entire scene in at once. My mind registered the driver as she fixed her mascara in the rear view window. It had a Ford logo, a green paint job, and thumping of loud music blaring from speakers. The dazed woman lay in the street helpless, directly in the vehicle's path. I saw the distance between them shrank rapidly. The child was silent. My body was both frozen and in motion. I made decisions without deciding anything. I moved without moving.

My feet sprang into action. Without even thinking, I was at full speed flying over bench length wise, and landed right near the edge of the curb. The car approached fast, and showed no signs of course correction to avoid the woman. Somehow, I cleared the stroller of another woman and was in the street before anyone realized what was going on. In one motion, I scooped the woman and child up and leapt straight up in the air. The car passed under me. Screams and gasps came from onlookers.

Landing on the pavement, I stepped over to the bench and set the woman gently down making sure the baby did not slip from her grasp. Moving back, I knelt down. Comments came from all directions. I felt dizzy. My stomach turned. A small crowd gathered.

More murmurs came from around me. The sound of a woman's voice to my left; she was making a phone call on a rather large looking device with an antenna. My senses snapped back in place, and I looked over and saw a middle-aged woman with a younger woman and a carriage that had twins aboard. The older woman answered the dispatcher's questions.

"An accident. No, not another car. No, nobody is seriously hurt, but..." she was saying.

I stood very still, not wanting to spook the crowd any more. I could hear folks saying, "She is breathing" and "Did he hurt the baby?" To my relief, the woman's chest rose and fell normally. Someone said something that caught me by surprise. A woman off to my right walked right up to me and placed her hand on my shoulder. I felt kindness radiate from her.

"I saw what you did just now."

Like a scolded child, I froze. Guilt and fear flooded me. Had I mishandled the woman? Had I harmed the baby?

"People don't risk their lives anymore," she said. "There aren't any more heroes."

I stared at her.

"Why did you do it?" she asked.

I was looking at the road. I felt embarrassed and afraid. She stepped forward and knelt down looking me in the eyes. I looked at her. She was nodding, and I heard a faint whisper from her. "It's okay. You saved them."

"That is not what I hear," I finally choked out the words. My voice sounded like a hoarse whisper. I cleared my throat. "She fell backwards and hit her head. I was just trying to help."

I raised my head up, noticed another woman taking the child out of the fallen woman's grasp, and checked the child over. The baby cried as she removed him from his mother's hands. That was odd. The baby had not even cried out through the whole ordeal. It only began to make noise when removed from the warmth and security of the mother's arms. This puzzled me greatly, and I began to analyze my actions.

Sirens.

I stood up and backed away while the other woman comforted the child. It struck me as odd that I had not even considered the baby in all of this. Failure set it. The woman calming the baby down turned and said something to the crowd now gathered. There were hushed conversations taking place all around. My feet slowly created distance.

"I can't believe what I am hearing from you people!" Began the woman, she turned and pointed at the woman on the bench. "He saved their lives, and all you can do is comments regarding his size or the fact that he jumped over a car." More hushed words.

She continued, "There is something really wrong here when some-one who doesn't feel like he fits in steps up and helps out and all you have to say is what a freak he is. You should all be ashamed."

My size became apparent as I rose.

I noticed a vehicle approach, lights flashing, and more sirens in the distance. The crowd had an uneasy feel to it. More unease washed over the crowd. My voice found its volume button and spoke aloud before I could think.

"I don't know how I did it. Would you rather I had let them die?" The murmurs died down to silence in a matter of seconds. I looked around. "Well?"

The ambulance had arrived. Two paramedics ran to the woman on the bench and began to check her for injuries. They both opened up emergency kits and started speaking to her, letting her know they were checking her over. One of them put something under her nose and she jolted awake and started to cry. Without looking at the crowd again, I melted away while their attention was on the woman. Perhaps leaving the house was a bad idea. That thought depressed me. My head hurt. I just wanted a quiet room to ponder what had happened. Part of me was mad that instincts reacted, but another part of me was still reeling from what I had done. It seemed surreal in so many ways; playing it back over and over would be part of my meditation today. The elements of what just happened started playing in my mind already. I shook my head and walked, muttering.

"Where the hell did all that come from?" What was I saying? My whole life was a giant disbelief. How could any of this be happening? Within minutes, I was in front of the house and inside before I think I actually blinked.

I just wanted darkness. Rage built inside of me. I wanted to kill something badly and did not know why.

*   *   *

My life was all about pondering these days. I always analyzed everything to try to solve the riddle of me. The events of the day weighed heavily. I questioned how the situation unfolded. Did I make the right decision? Was there another option? The answer always seemed to be that my presence caused the problem. I was the component that needed removing. The world was not ready for the new me.

On the floor in my room was my spot to meditate. It gave me a good view of the back yard and the bird feeder outside the window. The living room had a nice view out the back, but I felt safer in my room. Perhaps it was the cell in the hospital, which afforded me this feeling of comfort. A presence approached the door, and then a key fumbled in the lock. Eryn tended to come home when the world was asleep, including me if I managed to sleep. The door creaked open. Rising from my spot, I walked into the front room to greet her. It was rather strange to feel people approach, but made sense when I knew it was she. The sight of her made me smile, but it soon faded. Something was not right. Her hair was a mess and I could smell the sweat as if she had been running a race.

I locked eyes with her. Facial features betrayed her unhappiness. The blonde locks of hair were lightly hanging in her right eye. I moved to her the best I could while avoiding the low ceiling by the door and took her

438

bag from her. Without a word, my hand brushed the hair out of her eyes. "Rough shift at the hospital?" I asked with a slight grin creeping across my face. She clearly did not appreciate the humor. The slight glare made me step back.

She looked at me for about five seconds before her posture changed. She just pointed finger at me and said, "How could you?" I was a little confused. I had not done anything that I knew of that cold have possibly have left her mad at me.

"I do not follow, Eryn? Did I make a mistake?" I turned and set her bag down on the table and turned back to her. She was smiling and had a slight grin but was shaking her head now.

"The next time you see fit to be a hero, call me, or come to work and tell me." I was confused for a second then remembered why I sat at home all day; the woman that hit her head ended up at the hospital where Eryn worked. As I looked at her, a stirring in my soul arose from her beauty alone; something in my soul cried out for her. I wanted to reach out and hold her close. That might make the situation worse so my hands stayed away.

I stood there not quite sure what to say. The events were still a blur. I knew what had happened. How the situation ended up where it did was the confusion. Sure, I was strong and fast but where the burst of speed came from that launched me over a bench and a carriage was still the mystery. The image played in my mind. No words came. She folded her arms and looked at me squarely. The smile was more of a smirk, but none the less lethal, as the previous one was. She was not happy.

"I'm waiting? Well?" Her weight shifted suddenly and she moved in and gave me a big hug. My eyes closed and focused on that feeling of the warmth her embrace gave. Her face pressed against me, revealing she was smiling. I did not know why she was irritated to start with. Before I could even form a sentence, she sighed.

"I had a whole host of reporters waiting for me after work. They followed me to my car. I was unable to get in for several minutes. They wanted to know where you were. Apparently, someone leaked it that you are staying here. I told them I did not know where you were. They seemed rather interested in the large man that jumped a car." She raised her eyebrows. I noticed the last part of that was a question.

I stepped back. To look her in the eye without my heart racing was impossible. This time was different. She was very serious through her faint smile. How could it be explained what was not understood myself? She went to her bag behind me. My hand found my chin and mouth and a dozen ways to try to begin this story came to mind.

I heard her rummaging, then silence. I was about to turn to face her when her hand touched my back and something felt strange.

"Wait," she said.

My shirt was far too small to cover me to my waistline and the shorts were so baggy two smaller belts strung together held them up. They hung rather low but still covered me. I could feel her other hand was now touching the beltline right above my right cheek like it was tracing something. It rather tickled and I laughed.

"When did you get this?"

"Get what? A bruise or something?

"No, this tattoo."

"What tattoo? I do not have any."

There was silence for a moment. "The one I am touching. It feels really weird."

All I could feel was the warmth of her fingers tracing and following the same pattern repeatedly to the point it started to form an image in my head. I could see a vertical line that went up then turned back on itself snaking back and forth across the original straight line. Each sequence or pass got bigger. It looked a little like a pyramid, but the passes were not straight lines but curved like the infinity symbol I remembered from school. I felt something inside me stir at the recognition of it.

Eryn stopped tracing it. Her hand went to the other side to check. Her fingers touching something on the other side and the image that had just started to fade reappeared in my mind stronger. I started to shake a little.

"Let me look. Hold still." She pulled harder on the belt strap and I felt my shorts ride a little lower. It was not as if she had not seen me before being my nurse in the hospital. I felt self-conscious. No one had ever really seen me naked besides the staff. My head tingled at the touch of her hand. I could smell her scent as if it were on a cloth in front of my nose.

"Okay, this is really weird. You have matching, mirrored tattoos on you. Now you jumped a car to save a woman. What are you going to do next? Fly?" she said.

Her big beautiful brown eyes greeted me with a smile as I turned. My hand went out and caressed her cheek. Her soul reached up to me through her smile. Something tingled under my skin and ran to my finger tops. It felt charged like feeling a battery touched to your tongue as a child. Was this her chi? Jason spoke of in the past. Was it what the Kung Fu movies referred to when they spoke of tapping into their own energy? It had to be along those lines. I would focus on this feeling when meditating next.

"If I can, one day, you will be my first passenger," I said as I let my hand fall to my side. She leaned up and kissed me. That is all I needed to see to make this day better already.

My size was already a problem. Now weird looking marks like tattoos adorned my waistline. Could this make my feeling of being a freak any less? A monster that looked like a Greek statue had come alive to eat the children of the world now roamed the street. I might as well be a zombie. I could see the headlines now. Me, some god awful picture showing me baring my teeth or something...in hand cuffs or chains getting hauled away into some full service freak show so the world scientist could study me some more. The best and the brightest had their chance to study me and failed.

Now my actions force me to hide like a child.

Something told me the world was not ready for what I was to offer or become from one bad experience. Even with my upbringing, negativity was not my outlook. I was not negative. It was fear of the future. Fate had extended its hand to me and slapped me religiously upside the head. Why? I was not sure I cared either.

I looked back at Eryn as she moved to the kitchen and began to pull out food in preparation for dinner. My stomach panged for a moment. Food was a good idea.

Walking over to the small wall that separated the kitchen from the dining area, I did not have to try hard to peer at what she was pulling out of the fridge. A couple of steaks sounded good. She tossed them into the sink after unwrapping them and turned on the water. As the blood began to flow in spirals down the drain, I found myself drawn to its pattern. Slowly the room began to spin. My nose caught the scent of blood.

It was not originating from the beef. It smelled acidic and foul. My heart began to race, and I felt my breath quicken as if running. The desire to cut into something overwhelmed me. Something appeared in my hands. The coldness of steel sent comforting chills up my arms. I needed to find an enemy and destroy it. My eyes went blurry.

Last thing I heard was Eryn calling to me. Then silence.

XXX

Confusion

It felt good. Saving a life made me feel like I had something to offer; I no longer feared being a drain on society. After lying in bed for so many years, with others tending and caring for me, it was time to give back. I thought about looking for a job in security, perhaps bouncing at a local club or working as a bodyguard would be my meal ticket.

I decided to visit a few local establishments at night. I had no decent clothing that fit. Canvas shorts would have to do. I did manage to find one 5XL shirt, but even that was a bit tight. I was bald, so hair was no issue.

The sun was setting and cast a brilliant yellow glow on the neighborhood where Eryn lived. Her house was on a hill overlooking the Puget Sound, right outside of Everett. Seeing the light dancing on the water always made me wish I could travel and visit mystical lands overseas. I imagined what it would be like to be a sailor in ancient times, braving the unknown. I would lose myself for hours in such times, deep in thought.

I knelt and let the sunlight hit my face; taking in its glorious rays and feeling my skin come alive. Tranquility washed over me for a moment, elevating the stress from the events passed over the last few months. It felt as if a slight weight lifted from me, chasing some of the shadows away that had been hiding my soul from the light in the universe. A smile crept across my face and a deep breath followed. It was unimaginable to imagine the horrors that had befallen me in those months. Peace calmed the stormy seas inside.

444

As light found its way back into my now open eyes, a silhouette stood in front of me. A funny, macho pose greeted my eyes as they focused on the same bad suit as last seen on the Sergeant. He had his hand on his hip, pulling his jacket back to reveal his badge and nine millimeter holstered on his cheap leather belt. It had the same scent to it which told me he had not cleaned it in the time frame which I had last seen him. He did not smoke but the company he kept obviously did. I could smell the stale stench with a hint of scotch.

"Sergeant Rick."

"Tathlyn, good evening," he said as he turned stepping to the side, seeing he was standing in my light. "Going out for a stroll?"

"Of sorts. Was there something that you needed or is this actually a visit?" I asked.

He paused, muttering something about my size under his breath, so I stood up.

I might as well have the upper hand, especially if it unnerves him. Taking a deep breath letting and it out as though it was a growl, my eyes locked on his. It kind of pleased me that I could sense discomfort on him when he was near me. It was probably not a very Zen thing to feel, but a number of issues he caused me became problematic even though it was all under the guise of helping. Perhaps the irritation that he punched me in the nose, even if he did break his wrist in doing so, was still lingering. There was a slight bulge on his right arm underneath his sleeve where his cast was still prominent. I decided to be cordial.

"How is the wrist?" I asked, trying to sound genuinely concerned.

There was no reason for me to care, because of the way he treated me. But being the better man...

"It is healing thank you. You know I learned a lesson that day," he said.

"Oh do tell!" I tried to not sound too curious.

"I should have just shot you. There would have been less paper-work, less follow up, and way fewer unanswered questions."

"I can only imagine your frustration," I said, unsympathetically.

"Not to mention the Ire of a certain nurse." I smiled at that knowing she gave him grief.

There was a long pause as he stood there looking out over the water. I am sure the same tranquility that calmed me stirred him on some level, even if he dressed badly. Rather than wait for him to speak, I decided to fill that gap. "I can only imagine the questions you must have that I am both unable and incapable of providing you answers to."

"You have no idea how hard it is to know there is something wrong going on right under my nose and I have nothing to tie it to. Not you, not anyone," he said.

"Why do you think I am responsible? My file is open to you. I was in a coma, remember?" My response came before his last word trailed off in his throat.

"You did not have to go through any physical therapy. You grew over two feet in nearly two months, and you were found in an area where you did not belong and is where the corpse of the priest that tried to kill you was found this morning in a refrigerator." He was very heated now, and after hearing what he just said, I could not blame him.

He had dropped a bomb on me, and I sat down on the steps and pulled my knees up near my chest. I did not think they would ever find him alive, with all the resources and shadow games that the church uses. To hear he was dead was a relief, but he was right. It raised more questions. His prosecuting gaze kept trying to reach inside my head.

"His neck was crushed, much like what would happen if you got your hands around his throat. That's my theory."

"Well Sergeant, your theory is wrong. I never touched that priest." His gaze did not waiver. In his hand was on a file of some sort. He handed it to me. There was a photo of a dead man lying on ta slid out slab. It was indeed the priest. I took a long look. Even in a post mortem condition, the features of his face stuck in my mind. The memory of his assault on me was not hard to recall and left me with slight anger rising up inside. Signs of asphyxiation were obvious, not just a broken or crushed neck, and his eyes were bloodshot to the point where there was no white left. Someone must have hated that priest.

He wore priest robes but they seemed really old and dark brown...almost black. The material was more like a canvas, not cloth, and the crucifix seemed larger than remembered. Barely visible there seemed to be small symbols carved into it that were so small, it amazed me that they could be seen in a photo. I felt something in my mind seized slightly that must have stirred an expression because the Sergeant commented rather quickly.

"You recognize something don't you? You have seen something before, possibly because you were involved. Don't lie to me, Tathlyn."

"Of course I recognize some things. He was in my face trying to kill me." I turned, looked at him, and laughed. "And you are a Sergeant?"

"Watch it boy, or I'll..."

"You'll what? Hit me? You are not an authority figure Sergeant. You serve the public. I do not answer to you in any..."

"I can have you arrested for murder."

"Fine, do you really want to know what I was looking at?" His stare told me yes so I divulged. "The material and color of the robes is not what he wore that day. It looks old. Secondly, his cross has symbols on it that do not look church related. In fact, I would wager they are from the occult." *How did I know that?* "Granted his actions support the church's concern about my existence, but why would he be dead now unless they are trying to leave no loose ends?"

Being on a roll, I continued, "What was the time of death? How long ago did they find the body? Your department knows exactly when released me from the hospital so you know full well with the time of death that it could not have been me. Unless someone timed the event to occur after the hospital cleared me, which would mean someone is keeping tabs on me."

"You are smarter than I thought. He was clearly on ice for several weeks. All this, points back to you, especially since you have a motive."

That statement made me laugh.

"Yes, he assaulted me. I technically would have a reason for revenge. If that was my desire, do you really think I would be that stupid now?"

He yanked the file out of my hands and looked at the cross through some sort of monocle that he retrieved from his pocket. He grunted when he saw the markings. Several minutes passed as he stared and made some notes in his little book. I sat and absorbed in the sun as it was now starting to dip even further. Waiting for his conclusion, my own thoughts began to wonder why the priest would have such strange scrawling symbols on his crucifix unless there was truly some sort of tie to an occult of sorts. Perhaps it was a secret order within the church...a big surprise that would be if it ended up being true. I felt eyes on me so I opened mine and looked at him.

"Let's say for a second I believe you. The guy belonged to a cult. If you were tied to them and meant for something sinister, then why try to kill you?" Silence gathered for a moment while I could see the thoughts churning around in his head. Something must have fallen into place in his logic for his eyes went wide. "What if he wasn't a priest?"

I had to admit, the logic did make sense because I am the one who put it out there. If he was a priest, then he was more than a priest. If he was masquerading as a priest, then that would explain a lot more. "But why try to kill me?"

He held up the last photo and I saw a familiar room – the morgue where I had woken up after being missing for weeks. The only thing missing was the room of my second awakening. Something inside me told me to tell him. For several moments, there was a wrestling match in my head over what to say, and logic kept telling me he would be a better ally then allowing this witch hunt to continue. I did not know where to begin so testing the waters a bit before telling him too much was my approach.

"Do you believe in the unexplainable, Sergeant?" A slow nod of the head told me he did not think it too crazy of an idea. Maybe my sanity was not in question still.

"Yes, I would have to say I believe there are dark forces in the world that are working against the good people."

"And you feel you are one of the good guys?" He gave me a sour look.

"I'm a cop."

"You have a point. You punched an unarmed, cuffed man who had surrendered, in the face."

"Look at you! You are lucky that's all I did."

"There's the cop I know."

"Just stop….for one second. Yes, I am one of the good guys. I just lost my temper with all my troopers down. Can you blame me?" he said.

"Actually Sergeant, yes. I had been awake for about 10 minutes." *Here goes.* I focused on that day. "What I left out of your report was this: There was some sort of magic at work…Now before you interject, just give me a moment to explain. I was in a room, strapped to a bed. A mortician was there and he ran when he saw me. After tearing free of my restraints and walking out of the room, I hit my head on the exposed light bulb." I paused long enough to look at him more closely. To my surprise, he was listening.

"Another man was there, other than the mortician. He simply vanished in that hallway you came through to the morgue." He nodded. "There would be no place to hide and we passed no one. That hallway runs under the road so they do not have to bring corpses through the lobby or across the main road. Then I turned around and the wall the door was in, the one you face when you enter was closing up as if it did not exist and Eryn's arm later got stuck inside that same wall. It was like the very fabric of the material itself melted together and sticky. It had hold of her arm. She was so scared. I had to be careful when pulling her free so it did not dislocate her shoulder. The opening closed right after she was clear as if it had never existed."

I turned to look at him. "Do you get it now, Sergeant? Somehow someone took me when I was asleep, had signed off with the hospital that I was released on my own accord, before the start of the morning shift. Who knows, they may have even manipulated time somehow. None of this evidence exists because the room closed up to somehow to hide the truth. It had to be some sort of magic!"

He processed my story. Any sane person capable of logic would see there was a pattern to the events, and I was hoping his rank was not honorary. The look on his face told me that he was getting it.

"So when you awoke, did they have you drugged? Like an intravenous bag in your arm? And this had you all disorientated?" he asked.

"Yes. Right after I cut my head, it healed. Next thing I know cops are lighting me up with taser guns."

"Healed? You mean it healed over time?"

"No, healed, on the spot. It closed on its own."

"Now you are messing with me. That's not possible."

"Do you have a knife?"

"You are crazy if you think I am going to hand you a blade so you can cut yourself with my prints on it."

"I don't hate you that much, Sergeant. Step inside."

I got up, unlocked the door, and stepped in. He stood on the porch for a moment shaking his head and mumbled something about him not believing what he was about to let me do, then stepped inside. I hunched down a bit and moved into the kitchen where I could stand at height. Grabbing a knife, I went to the sink and held it to my hand while looking at him.

He still had disbelief in his eyes as if he felt I was bluffing. Sure, I did not like the idea of hurting myself but it could not hurt as much as anything else already endured. He approached and stood on the other side of the island part of the kitchen where the sink was. With my right hand open, palm upwards, the knife in my left hand, I began to drag the blade slowly across my hand. The blood gushed out. After about two inches I stopped. His eyes were on the appearing wound the entire time, rather wide.

A moment passed.

"I don't see any change. Feel stupid? Let's clean you up," he said.

I held it closer to him and opened the skin allowing the blood to run freely. I felt a twinge looking at the crimson, but turned my focus back to him. I felt my inside get really warm like a switch was flipped.

"So you agree I am cut, yes?

"God yes, you are cut, a level one wound. You are crazy." His face grimaced.

I rinsed my hand off so we could see the wound better. The thought ran through my mind of the skin knitting back together. The itching sensation started along the cut and I felt the very ends start to pull in tighter and heat began to coarse from my chest down to that hand. Seconds passed and it increased in speed. The cut was closing faster. Blood stopped flowing out all together now and a light pink color formed in the areas that were mending. A moment later, it finished. I looked at the Sergeant.

His jaw was on the floor.

"I know how you feel. I could not believe it either." He just stared at my hand with his head slowing shaking back on forth in disbelief. "The reports in the hospital said this was happening while I was in my coma. I would not have believed it was real had I not seen it myself. I was unable to find the footage documented by the church. Surprisingly, it is not available to us, even when threatened with a subpoena."

He looked at me. "You do realize the danger here, Tathlyn. If the wrong people get wind of this, you are going to be dissected so scientists can find ways to reproduce this effect."

"I had not thought of that yet." I sat down on the floor right in the kitchen. It was easier than trying to avoid hitting my head on everything. The church thoroughly documented everything, so they know how my body reacts to injury. The scientific community had my case spread all over, but none of them had known anything past the original story. With the help of the police, the hospital had kept that quiet since the kidnapping and the attempt on my life. *Perhaps I needed to stage my own death somehow.*

The Sergeant had a look on his face that told me he had just come to the same conclusion. "You stay put. We need to keep you hidden for now. I have not told anyone on the force where you are staying."

"Neither has Eryn."

"Good," he said. "She should consider taking some time off."

"I guess I cannot get a job. This will not bode well with Eryn."

"Let me worry about that. Tell me, where did you really learn how to fight?"

"I honestly do not know. It is almost like instinct. I just acted."

"You acted?" he said, looking perplexed.

"Come on, Sergeant. I was sixteen the accident happened. You read my records; they documented all of it. Can you not accept there is no reasonable or logical answer?"

"Point taken."

"So I was going to go get a bouncing job at a local club. That's out, huh?" I said.

"I would recommend you keeping a low profile. If your name comes across the wrong person's desk, I won't be able to protect you."

"I think I can handle myself but will heed your advice to only go out at night if I need to get some air. Perhaps until this blows over, but I will not hide."

"Fair enough."

"I am confused about something, Sergeant."

"What is that, Tathlyn?"

"Why are you helping me or even caring if you hate me so much for going through your officers so easily?"

"I don't hate you. I believe you do not know what happened to you, and something tells me whatever this is, is beyond both of us."

His answer took me by surprise. I have never felt he was a man of his word or could even be trusted till now. My gut told me to not be so quick to trust. Something told me I may have just won an ally. I extended my hand. "Welcome to the weirdness of my life."

"I am not so sure I want to be on board, but I want to know what is going on," he said, shaking my hand.

I simply nodded my head and smiled as he headed for the door. He stepped out and turned back towards me. The look on his face looked genuine enough, but first impressions left lasting marks. I had to admit, I was confused.

XXXI

Memories

Rain fell hard outside, forming pools at low points in the back yard. Some were deeper than others were, and several turned into large puddles. Time drifted by while I sat in my bedroom on the floor observing nature for hours and passed in silence.

The variety of birds in the back yard exploited this moment to the fullest. Drowning worms that surfaced to escape the watery grave found themselves snatched out of the earthen embrace by the beak of robins waiting patiently above. I had to laugh at the irony of the situation to think you are saving yourself only to find death itself. This opera of savagery entertained me for quite a while. Tactics that I had never paid attention to caught my attention. You can learn a lot from animals.

Birds snuck up on their food as if they were predators in the real wilds somewhere. I had never thought of birds as true predators, but bearing witness to these events changed my impression. They would use everything from stealth to spring attacks where they exploded into action and pounced on the unsuspecting worm. I even saw a few swoop in from a low glide. I was amazed at the timing involved in that maneuver. I could not imagine how much it would hurt if they missed. I actually felt sorry for the worms. They did not have a chance.

Suddenly an image popped in my mind of being in a cold stream unable to move. My body was injured. Something had chewed me up pretty bad. I had a foreboding memory of waking up injured hours after the attack and being vulnerable. My only fear was the return of a large monster that I knew was waiting for me in the deeper waters near the middle. I suddenly felt I would be mad at surviving the odds then denied life because something bigger was hungry and had the advantage. The detailed images played out as if I was really lying there with failing strength. Every moment counted.

I knew that I was still sitting in my room, but something made me start coughing and sputtering, keeping me submerged in this half drowned state. Reality shifted and time began to fast forward. Darkness approached. My situation was dire. I could not call for help. There was no one to call. The image faded for a moment and the yard returned to focus.

I paused at my comparison for a moment. Something about that situation that just came to mind seemed awfully familiar. The cold embrace of the water around me crept painfully in. The pain caused nausea and weakness. Rain fell from the sky in sheets and made me feel like a drowned rat. Yet, I had never been in such a situation. It seemed so real even as a fleeting thought that grew into a reality. I actually had a feeling of dread and fear wash over me. It was very intriguing to have an emotion suddenly come forward. It had just been an image, but my brain was somehow feeling a real reaction to the situation; I felt fear. My breath quickened and panic set in.

This happened once before.

I closed my eyes and began working on some breathing exercises from therapy sessions with Doctor Price. I was trying to imagine a black dot on a white wall that was slowly getting bigger until the wall was black; then a white dot appeared and repeated the process until the wall was white. I repeated this process and focused on slow breaths in through the nose and out through the mouth. The feelings of dread started to slip away, replaced by peace. I repeated the cycle several times.

I finally opened my eyes and still felt moving water in a stream rocking my wounded body. Cascading water flowed down over rocks in front of me. The sting of the water in my open wounds spiked the pain. It was hard to see or focus on anything. Wind increased, making the rain go sideways. The only way to focus my eyes was to squint. As I looked through the torrential down poor over the river, I realized the window pane and the back yard came back into view. Images were blending...there was no rain in this dream. Reality and dream functioned as one.

I tried to ponder what was happening, where these new sensations came from as the images began to fade. Part of me was happy to see them go, yet another part was very curious why the experience seemed like a memory. I knew for a fact that I had never been in any raging river during a storm.

Sweat poured off my brow like water from the stream. I was shaking a bit and felt very cold. My muscles were fatigued. Heavy breathing lasted for a few minutes while I tried to clear my head. I felt unraveled for a moment; as the very fabric of reality had just split for a second and offered me a glimpse of what it felt like to be insane. In an attempt to refocus my breathing, my heart rate lowered back down after about seven breaths. My chest no longer felt like it was going to explode.

I played the recent events over and over. The freak changes that

458

were my life weighed heavily on my mind. The metamorphoses I had undergone were becoming more prevalent each day, yet it left me with more questions than answers. Two more tattoos had appeared – one on the small of my back in the center that looked like a compass with all eight directional points on it. The second on my neck, at the base, was something that looked like a rune. Eryn was helping me research it to see if we could find out what they all were and meant but came up with nothing. No records of such markings existed in any book Eryn found while looking at the library. That left one option... private book collections and possible occult materials.

I shuddered at the thought of looking through tomes that contained nasty rituals. I had never been a big horror fan growing up. Sure I had seen Dracula but I hardly called that horror. I heard stories from my parents and churches that I had attended that devil worship and the occult were synonymous. It terrified me, that one of the very things that from my childhood fears was now the very place I would have to tread. Now, Eryn was trying to make contact with some of the local Wiccan chapters to see if anyone there might be willing or able to help. So far none of them responded to her inquiries. I cannot imagine that you could just leave a message for one of these groups out of the blue and expect them to be willing to open up freely to a stranger. I do not care who you are.

The world's ignorance astounded me at times.

The irony of my current dilemma was not lost on Eryn or me. She knew how I felt about the church and my disdain for letting them be involved in my life. One of the priests that had watched over me when I was in the coma came to visit me a couple of times. I did not know of his exist-

459

ence until last week when I got an official apology from the church about the previous priest's actions. Apparently there was some mystery around where he had come from. I had to refrain from saying, "Ya think?"

Father Gerone was a young man about twenty eight or so, only a few years older than I was. He was very short and looked like he never ate due to the size of his frame. It made me laugh see him walking up because he had a jet black goatee and a serious look on his face as if he was on some mission from God that was beyond secret. His walk was confident, but he was not very coordinated; he always tripped coming up the walkway to the house due to the uneven sidewalk sections settling over time. His lack of hair made him look older than he was. He was, however, a nice man and showed genuine concern for people so our talks were not too painful, although his accusations of my affiliations did prove annoying. Just like being in a mass, he always opened our talks with a very lengthy prayer that had me almost asleep by the time he finished.

The hardest part was the questions. He asked me questions that I had no answer to, or any possible way of knowing. It was always the same theme. How long had I been interested in the occult? When did the devil approach me and promise me great changes in my life for power? Was I ready to repent? Yet he always asked me in such a way that made me feel guilt for the things happening to me. How could I be responsible for things beyond my control? Not getting labelled as a freak was now a life ambition. I simply wanted to figure my life out and did not dare tell him that we were actually going to ask for help on that level since the church could not provide any answers.

Movement out the window caught my eye again. The rain had stopped for the most part; it was a light mist now. I liked the rain. It washed things away and renewed life. I wished that I could step outside into the rain, and emerge out the other side back in my old shape or form and go exploring with Jason. Those days seemed so long ago and in part they were; I could never go back. That part of my life was over. My parents were dead. Dieter Gutermuth was dead. The new "me" was undiscovered. There was no clue to what my purpose was now. Science failed and medicine was not even at the same table as science was. Religion was an absolute travesty to me. I had spent a lot of time in prayer no avail. God was not speaking to me or was not home. Maybe I had angered him somehow or maybe the answer was what was actually happening was supposed to happen.

I did not have a clue who to turn to aside from Eryn's idea. My life continued to be full of strange dreams of slaying daemons. It made me shudder to think there was actual enjoyment in that. I felt in control being this close to insanity. One particular dream that I had involved a small village of people that apparently knew who I was; they were friends. In my dream, I walk in and countless people greeted me and called me all by my new name. Based on the look of the buildings, it seemed to be akin to the Roman era. There were tile roofs like the ones seen on villas from old pictures. The clothing and local garb seemed to be Roman like. I saw a few soldiers around wearing armor that looked to be from that era also. The houses were stucco and not more than a few stories tall at best.

They number in the thousands but small enough to know quite a few people there especially if you are a shop owner or market place urchin.

Legacy of the Defender

There is some sort of market filled with people looking at the wares for sale. Basic weapons, food, and clothing displayed on tables. The clothing is very basic but looks durable, made from wool or cotton, or some other materials. People moved about with purpose, something was wrong. Then screaming came from the other end of the market. One or two voices cry out then five, then seven, then a whole chorus of cries and screams. I rush to the other of the market place towards the noise only to find some sort of daemon is attacking the townsfolk and the guards are already dead. The people are calling to me by name for help in the panic and chaos. Next thing...there are weapons in my hands and I am moving with a purpose to engage.

I began to hack and these monsters with fury and vengeance. They see me coming and begin leaping on me from roof tops and other small structures. It took me many times of seeing this dream to realize that my size matches my reality. So the daemons try to topple me by getting up high, and using their weight to knock me down. One leapt from the left I duck and swing a blade up like a back hand and felt the steel bite flesh hard. A shower of ichor sprayed all over the ground; I rose up and swung at two more that tried to sweep my legs. The leg of is severed by my sword...the other is taken in the stomach lengthwise. It falls in two with bowels spilling on the ground.

Creatures with grayish green skin surround me, anywhere from four to eight legs, and lots and lots of teeth and claws. Quick count it is at least two dozen and one gigantic one.

"You."

With my sword leveled at it after speaking, it talks to me in some language somehow understood. It says something like "not yet" then dozens more swarm me. I am cleaving and swinging like a chef in a restaurant preparing a meal. Parts of daemon are flying all around and the ichor is flowing and spraying...getting on everything, including me. I am leaping and dodging, parrying, and striking with such ferocity that my motions are a complete blur through most of it. Daemon anatomy litters the ground and they just keep on coming. I take down the first dozen or so without breaking a sweat or getting hit.

Then the damage starts to accumulate. A bite on my thigh is moderately deep. These things have poison in their mouths, but I strangely am not worried about it. A claw on my abdomen leaves six marks horizontally; more of a light scratch but six of them will start to bleed a bit. The warmth of my own blood flows mixing with the ichor droplets on my skin, which are cold to the touch strangely enough. Several more wounds in various locations are all minor, but still add to the pain. The daemon blood, however, does burn when it hits an open wound, and a sick feeling that accompanies the pain, as it is very toxic.

I seem to know this in my dream because upon command my swords ignite and I touch them to each of the wounds to sterilize them and stop the bleeding. It hurts like hell, but I grunt through the pain in between swings that I am taking respectively at targets as they present themselves to me. They hesitate. The large one moves away and is casually eating some sort of beast of burden that I do not recognize but am not surprised to see. It cries in pain as the daemon has started on the backside of the creature slowly taking bites and chewing like it has not eaten in a while...like it is savoring what would be a good steak. I feel sorry for the beast but cannot get there to end its suffering.

Another horde has just arrived from the woods. They have charged into the fray right about the time I get down to only about six of the original total. I glance again and the big one that smiles at me with a mouthful of intestine that is bleeding and falling out of its mouth as it chews. I just shake my head and holler, "You can't hide behind your meal forever." Then I say a name as if I know this one...Something that sound like "Discus."

More daemons come. I continue to slay them left, right, and center. Six point counter attack, three point parry, and defensive parry-block combination into a whirling attack that manages to lure in about seven of them in and removed heads in one swing of both blades. I can smell and hear the searing flesh continue to cook as the heads hit the ground. They smell of burnt offerings to God in the Old Testament. It fills my nostrils with a smell that I long for...dead daemons. It allures me and entices me to engage further and further into the ranks without mercy or fear. I feel a threat from above me but far out of reach of my blades. The flyers have joined the attack now. I was waiting for that. Right when I have the battle figured out, it shifts again.

This is expected. I am now swarmed on all sides and getting attacked from multiple targets that are swooping in from the heavens. Something triggers within me, and warmth surges from somewhere inside me. The burning sensation took its toll on my limbs. This subsides and the flesh begins to knit itself back together. The blood flow ceases and my skin hardens like its liquid metal but flows and flexes with each movement. At this point in the dream, I realize that I am not even wearing armor. I have dual baldrics crossed on my back and a tunic that is silver. A cloak blows in the wind and moves with me.

The fight continues for several moments. The bodies of daemons litter the market place by now. It is well over a hundred that have been hacked into pieces. The garish nature of the fight has me even surprised at the violence level of which I am engaging. It is ruthless, I am slaughtering these monsters in such numbers that it makes me wonder how they can replenish their ranks so quickly, and keep coming at me with such ferocity and self-abandon. Something drives these creatures with hatred beyond what I am even capable of seeing. Even with my momentary lapse of drive to keep slaying them, which only lasts for a second or two because the dream gets good after I finish off the small ones, there is a panoramic view of the battle field. I cannot even count the carnage at this point. The fight is graphic, but nothing can prepare me for what I see as I turn and look.

Just like some sort of movie you see where the hero never runs out of bullets and the body count is insane, the pieces of daemon laying everywhere, broken bodies of townsfolk mixed in is sobering. Yet as I play back the dream I can actually still remember and see each of the daemons, what was cut off if anything or how they simply fell onto my blade in such a fashion it was not just skill but a manor of they almost wanted to die. The bigger one looks right at me as he jumps off whatever he was sitting on to watch the fray and laughs as he throws himself at me and I wake up. This is all very weird. Why does it stop there? I have seen a few seconds more where I start to swing but never what comes next. It is like having your video player eat the tape right at the final scene of a movie, so you never get to see it.

This almost traumatizes me more than the dream itself. All the gore and daemon blood, townsfolk slaughtered by the dozens, and I do not get to kill the bad guy whose name some of the people know. It is rather disturbing to me that I am more upset about that than the people that died. Just like fishing and the one that got away. I always feel unfulfilled when that dream occurs and I awaken, denying me the conclusion. It is always more graphic when I am asleep, or in the stupor I now call sleep.

I have told Eryn about this and that I seem to be having more and more dreams that all have the same theme. Violence and death on a scale that makes stories I hear about world wars pale in comparison. They have started to tie into each other also. Like chapters in a book. She seems to think I should find a hypnotist and see if they can dig around in my brain somehow to see if there is any sort of relation or if my mind is just tapping into a highly creative portion of my brain. I am not so sure about doing that because I am afraid of what they may find.

Shock factor aside I like the dreams because I feel like I am doing something rather than sitting around and being a freak. Something tells me Eryn would freak out if she knew this.

Why does blood affect me so?

The sight of it makes me go into a trance-like state almost every time with no memory of it. The last time it happened was at the sink when Eryn was making dinner. She said I was non responsive for about twenty minutes and it was almost like a panic attack. She was able to get me to sit. At least I did not collapse. That would be embarrassing to be this big strong man that collapses at the sight of blood. None of it made sense because when I see it in my dreams it excites me and draws me into combat. Yet in real life it shuts me down and perplexes me.

The sun started to peak through the remaining clouds like light showing through holes in a vapor canvas and painted the countryside golden yellow. The back yard was slightly still dark and dismal, lending to a melancholy mood that I was now feeling. A few squirrels foraged in the grass, hopping from raised spot to raised spot and trying to avoid an accidental bath. Birds were still in their hunt patterns and trying to capitalize on the earthen crawlers' plight. It always interested to me how rain always seemed to change the mood of the day. Yet it reset things and allowed for new beginnings. Just like taking a bath refreshes and revitalizes the human body, rain always seems to preserve life and keep the wheels of nature turning.

I rose from my spot on the carpet and noticed that I must have been sweating profusely by the dampness of the carpet. When I went to remove my shirt and put on a fresh change the clothes, I realized the clothing was not damp at all. Yet the carpet was close to being soaked. I went to the closet to grab some towels to place down. Yet again it did not make any sense how the carpet could be soaked while the clothes were totally dry.

Normally I would try to come up with something humorous to tell Eryn about this, but I found my thoughts were not in a funny mood. My humor fell short. I felt serious, almost like reality was crashing in on me in such a way that I did not find things funny anymore.

"Great!" I thought I am becoming as jaded as Jason and his crazy quest. I had nothing come to mind of how to tell Eryn of the freak water incident with a humorous twist. Perhaps it was best not to tell her at all. The last thing she needed to do was stress about leaks in the roof or freakish sweating. *Next thing I know she will be asking me twenty questions about how it happened.*

There arose in me a longing for her to return from work. I knew I loved her. What if she did not feel the same? It was not a hard decision to stay silent.

After all, silence was golden.

XXXII

Clues

Several days passed since my trance-like visions on the carpet. I felt like my mind was not just lost...but evaded me locating it. The hallucinations did not feel like visions or dreams. They felt like memories.

This was not possible!

Each day my journey into my mind took me to the surreal. The effects of the environment in each scene immersed to the point that my tactile senses came alive, whether it be a brisk, cold wind or the gentle dance of the breeze in the sun. The daemons had a foul smell to them. Many smells assaulted me. The rancidness of their breath found its way into my mouth. It tasted sulfuric. Saliva burned slightly when they bit me, and when their venom hit my bloodstream, I felt my body on fire.

These moments turned into hours. They came a few at a time or continuously, increasing my desire to experience these fights – to feel the life being choked out of the monsters of legend felt right to me. Holy vengeance channeled through me, wanting me to slaughter my foes and to relish doing so. This emotion became so strong it was hard to contain. The smell of their blood on the battlefield afterward was intoxicating, driving me to the next set of images that played out in my head.

It was like watching television, only better, and I found myself sitting there daily, stupefied. They came on suddenly, grabbing me like a paralysis, yet I did not want them to stop once they started. This existence consumed me, and I did not even know why yet.

An image had just shown large walls that were so tall they stretched into the clouds. I could not see what was behind it, only that the wall itself was covered in daemons the size of a large dog. They had wings and flitted about speedily. I had been slaying them with swords as fast I could swing. They fell by the dozens before me. Bodies decorated the walls like a façade. Blood covered me like a glaze and I felt permeated by it. My blades added to the disarray from the daemonic body count in my wake.

The vision shifted. My view flew backward and faded out completely, bringing me back to this reality. In previous days, the intensity was nothing compared to now. It felt hollow and false now as if I was looking through a lens at what my real existence should be. Yet I was still getting used to this new body. Its size, weight, strength, dexterity, and endurance had all increased beyond most of the athletes I had ever heard of. In fact, I was sure that defeating the warriors of modern sports would be easy.

I caught myself at the thought. Being cocky was never a luxury. The few things in my life that defined me never made me feel better than anyone else. A mental note to purge that way of thinking came to mind. This had to be a gift from God, life, or karma, best used to better the world somehow. Learning who I would transform into, was vastly becoming my soul purpose and these memories played a part. Even though my body was not visible in them...my shadow was. These events were things that never happened. Perhaps it was a vision of the future. One question remained beyond the obvious.

Why?

What could I have done to cause my life to derail so bad that my reward was a coma? Each wound left more than an echo that the incident had happened. Pints of my blood decorated the walls on dozens of occasions Eryn told me. They documented each event, but the records were now sealed. Something told me the church had footage somewhere, or perhaps photos to study. I knew the police did have some, but they were only of the blood on the walls and the stained or soaked bedding. The amount of blood that I lost was also not possible, further confusing the medical community as to how my existence continued. The body of a small man does not hold the volume I lost.

My curiosity was beyond obsessed.

I had never *seen* a daemon in my life, but did not doubt they existed on some level...so fighting hundreds upon hundreds was not logical. However, it was impossible to overlook the final facts. I was a giant with fighting skills that matched a seasoned warrior with muscles that normally took years to build.

Perhaps the hospital had allowed the government to experiment on me. Maybe they had some sort of crazy minion tucked away and they were taking me there to experiment? I ruled this out quickly because my growth happened after I awoke, and I imagined that they would have wanted to see their work in progress.

Wait.

Maybe that was what was happening now. Maybe they took me at night while I slept.

Again I ruled it out because Eryn was here when she was not at work, and we talked into the night several times a week and, in fact, did not sleep that often as a whole. She had become my lover, my confidant and my best friend since Jason was busy chasing down his own demon. I craved time with her. Being in her arms, even though they could not wrap themselves around me, seemed to be the only sanity. *My vision-like dreams are amazing,* but at the end of the day I just wanted to be with her. Nothing seemed to hold my attention as she did. Here I am, a monster, and one kiss from her tames the beast inside.

My thoughts turned to Jason for a moment. He came by once to talk, but all he did was speak of Bigfoot. There was suspicion he was getting closer and he started to think there was more their existence. We both saw the same specials, but he had the field experience. He was a ranger of sorts in his thinking. He shared stories of sitting and watching for days at a time and finding what could have been foot prints. Heavy rain had destroyed the real evidence, as they were not intact enough to tell by the photos he showed me.

He saw me after I came to live with Eryn. The look in his eyes and his demeanor told me that he was starting to lose it. He smelled of fear as his eyes tracked me from the ground all the way up to my forehead before stopping at my eyes. The fight or flight feeling building inside him was obvious to me even as I shook his hand. It took him hours to finally talk to me like before; as if I was Dietz again. Little did he know Dietz was dead now, only Tathlyn remained, and he was starting to fracture himself on the reality of what was real and what was fantasy?

As my thoughts drifted from that day, I found my memory had not only increased but also literally recorded everything like it was a movie. My mind could play it from any angle. Thoughts drifted to when I saved the woman. I could feel her in my arms and I jumped over a car. The image was as clear to me as when it happened. It was not a blur by any means.

Again, how was this possible?

Before Eryn had left for work, she left me a message that she had contacted a local Wiccan Coven. She did not necessarily believe in the old ways, let alone in any sort of magic, but after nearly being caught or pulled into the wall down in the morgue, and especially after what had happened to me, she found herself starting to believe in the possibility that there was more out there. She had never put much stock in the possibility of God, or if he participated in human life. I could not blame her lack of faith in a higher power before since she had never had any experiences of that nature.

My sudden growth, the appearance of tattoos on my skin, and the manifestation of this fighting machine mentality wrapped up in the body and soul of a big lover just blew her mind. She started to believe in something but was reaching out to a place with the wrong answers, in my opinion. With no answers that could even come close to explaining the complexities of my life, I accepted her searching. I did not think for a moment that a response back from someone in that world would come so soon. A woman named Diane had called Eryn back. She wanted to meet us right away.

What could we do, if anything, to find some answers? Science had failed. Medicine had failed, and the church, even though they claim they did not have a hand in it, tried to murder me. My options were limited at this point indulging Eryn's research and meeting with this person made sense. I hoped it was not going to be a group; being on display again was not an option. The conversation, in hindsight, was a bit of a travesty. My lack of enthusiasm frustrated her. She felt I should be more involved in searching for help elsewhere. She had no idea yet that I was seeing the visions now and that they felt like memories somehow, maybe even from someone else.

I did not have the proof I needed to stake such a claim.

This thought kept spinning through my mind. My hands felt bare, empty now. Like something was missing or belonged there. Another series of images flashed and I could have sworn, for a second, the swords from my images felt like they were really in my hands. Cold steel with some type of material wrapped the pommels. I could feel the weight as if something added its mass to me.

I opened my eyes and held up my hands, gently squeezing them as if to make a fist, but I could not. Sitting there in disbelief, I wondered if this was part of the dream like state. I did not notice Eryn standing there watching me. However long she was there was unknown. She gasped, causing me to look. Her mouth was open and a look of surprise was on her face. My smile faded when I realized she was staring at me in disbelief and pointing at my hands. Not knowing what she was referring to, I must have looked very puzzled. My eyes returned forward when a reflection of light glinted from in front of me. I turned my head and slightly gasped.

In my hands were two swords.

The sun reflected off the surfaces in the house catching every aspect. Two weapons made of a radiant material caught the light beams in the room. The elegance of the long blades had to be at least four feet in length made from some material I could not recognize. They had curved singular edges, slightly oriental, but somewhat different in the width at the end where it came to a wicked point. This metal had hues to it that were pearl like...that caught the light differently as I turned them in my hands. There was writing on the cross section right above the grip. Even pulling the weapon closer, I could not identify it.

Movement off to my left made me look. Eryn approached and knelt down next to me, a look of curiosity and surprise still upon her face. Her hands shook as she reached forward and touched the metal with one finger and retracted it quickly, then slowly touched it again. She was transfixed. The question of why I was holding two swords in my hands had not yet left her lips. I knew only one thought to be present. They felt at home. Something within me was not even surprised to find them there for a few moments until it hit me that I was holding two swords.

My expression must have changed because Eryn went into nurse mode. "It's going to be okay Dietz, just put them down. No one is going to hurt you." I must have been nodding my head or something in agreement. Her hand reached over and tried take one of them out of my hand when my grips suddenly loosened and she had one of the swords. Slight anxiety arose. My breathing increased and a word started form on my lips when I saw a flash of light and felt the sword back in my hand.

"Oh my God, how did you do that?" She was on all fours backwards like a crab, walking away from me. "How did you do that?" She actually raised her voice.

"Sweetie, I don't know what you mean. This just happened."

"Bullshit, you went out and bought swords today. Why? Where the hell did you get money to be able to afford those...and now you are doing magic tricks?"

"Eryn, I swear," I began. She jumped to her feet and walked to over to my jacket and fished her hand in my pocket looking for the wallet she had bought me. I was just as surprised as she was when the sword jumped back to me. My mind was wrapping itself around this and her reaction together.

"I can barely afford the food bill having you here. I can't have you spending that kind of money."

I sat there shocked. I had no idea things were tight for her, or for us, since we were essentially a couple. She had bought me clothes to wear, and we got a new bed a few days ago. Realization hit home. All my clothes fit, and the bed was huge. Bigger than anything seen growing up in a store or on television, let alone any catalogue. I was about to say something when she sobbed. I let go of the swords and was on my feet, ducking over to where she stood, wrapping my arms around her. She trembled...shaking a few times before she relaxed and fell into my embrace. I knelt down.

Her beautiful eyes welled up with tears. Streaks of moistened cheek glistened in the light as tears fell one by one to the floor or on her blouse. My hand went instinctively to her face, enveloping it as it may and she nuzzled her cheek and the whole side of her face into my huge hand. I felt emotion well up inside of me and before I knew it, the words came out.

"I love you, Eryn." I felt energy course through my hands and towards my chest. It hit my head and my mind reeled. Her hands held both of mine on the side of her face. She smiled. The tears flowing freely now,

"I know you do, and I love you too." My heart jumped and I soared over the planet for a second. "But where did you get the swords? How did you do that trick?" She pointed her right hand over to where I had let them go as she continued.

"We really can't afford anything, especially toys. I just don't..."

"I'll get a job then doing anything to help." She smiled and looked over to the weapons and a look of shock appeared. I turned my head to see what had caught her attention. There was no noise from their fall, even from falling on the carpet, not even a thump from my letting them go. We heard nothing. They were gone as fast as they had arrived. I moved to where they should be and stared at the ground...not sure what I was or was not looking at. I was suddenly saddened.

"Okay Dietz, where did you hide them?" she asked.

Burning.

The backs of my hands right were on fire as she said that. I winced. My flesh burned as a strange symbol outlined itself on my hands. The symbols were very small by comparison to my hand, but still large to a normal hand. The script looked very similar to the ones I already had. Burning flesh wafted up as my hands started to shake from the pain. Eryn was at my side with her first aid kit that she retrieved from the bathroom. When did she even leave the room?

My mind blurred from pain. This set of marks hurt...whereas the last ones did not. This was different, very different; it felt like something from within me surfaced. I felt energy move from inside. It flowed down to my hands and burst through my skin. There was no light or heat radiating off it but the pain was burning and my skin felt like it was melting. Eryn tried to look at my hands, but I kept pulling them back from her several times until the pain began to subside. She finally won the pulling contest to allow her to look. I felt her hands holding mine and to my surprise...she traced her fingers on the backside of my hand with some sort of pattern.

She had a curious look on her face and shook her head in disbelief. A troubling feeling, as if she was about to walk out the door away from me rolled off her. I did not know what to do. If she walked out, my heart would break into a million pieces and vanish. The feeling from her increased as if a monster came out of the woods. She could feel it getting closer, and I could feel her concern growing. Her eyes met mine.

"We need to talk," her voice trembled.

"I know. I just don't know where to begin."

"Something here is happening that neither of us can fully under-stand. We need to get some help," she said.

"From who? The Church? The ones that tried to kill me? How can we..." Her voice cut me off

"We have a meeting tonight with Diane. I think we should go. But not before you tell me how you did that trick with the swords."

"Eryn, it's not a trick. That is the first time the swords from my dreams materialized in my hands. Don't you think I would have told you about something like this?" I paused as she looked at me and nodded her head. "I have shared everything with you, but I do need to tell you that something else is happening even more so than before."

She got a look on her face that signified and "Oh God" moment. My head shook trying to reassure her that it was not as bad as what had just happened. She could handle probably about anything at this point, but I decided to tone it down for now.

"My dreams are increasing in intensity...to the point that I don't think they are dreams. They feel like they are visions of what I am supposed to do. Think about it. The church is watching me like they are expecting something to happen," I said.

"I know, Baby. I have felt that for a while, too, which is why I don't trust them. They already sent one priest and if they knew you were creating images to fool others they might think you some sort of heretic....well more than that, they probably already think you are," she said.

"Eryn, that really happened. I had them in my hand. Don't you believe you saw and even took one?" I asked.

"I don't know what I believe," she said.

I started to respond, but she cut me off.

"I want someone who has more of an open mind to take a look at you. Whatever you are dreaming, your mind is making you think it's real, and now it's affecting me too."

"Explain the tattoos." I held up my hands. "You saw it happen. Explain why I grew so much and so fast."

"Your body is trying to defend yourself to these spiritual attacks. I can believe that."

"What about the wall." I could tell by looking at her she was ready for that one. Neither of us could deductively reason that one out.

"Or the man that disappeared." My words unsettled her, I could tell, for she looked away from me and shook her head. Her hand came out of mine and she walked over to the table.

"Look, Dietz," she started and then sighed, "I want us to be able to enjoy life without bizarre things happening all the time."

"I know, so do I. My life has changed so much and with my changing my name, I had hoped it would have started something new for me, not a continuation of this freak show." I looked at her gently, "Can you call me Tathlyn though?"

"That's so weird to me, but I promise I'll try."

"Well my dear, it is my true name," I said.

"True?" she asked.

"Yes, I not only chose it, but it chose me."

"Okay, I will try to remember, Tathlyn." With that, she leaned up and game me a kiss. I felt the warm of her breath as she exhaled falling into the moment. The energy we shared danced upon my lips, and she tenderly kissed me...the passion grew. "I think you should take me in the bedroom," she said.

"Yes, my lady," the replay came without hesitation, and I picked her up without missing a lip lock. *After all,* I thought, *it is only four and we had till seven to get ready.* As I crawled on my knees with her in my hands, the thought of what happened to the blades crept in. My curiosity raced for a split second, and I forgot about all that as I set her down on the bed and smiled.

God, I love this woman.

XXXIII

The Coven

Traffic was heavy. The rain beat the road like an unforgiving army, pounding its enemy into oblivion. Visibility was almost nonexistent. I peered hard through the torrential sheets. There was no sign of the rain letting up. I would have thought that those that chose to live in this state, or were from here, heaven forbid, would know how to maintain a safe speed. The stupidity taxed my new Zen outlook severely. People drove way too fast for conditions and slammed on their brakes causing them to risk losing control.

French gestures flew from a number of vehicles. My dreamlike visions that put me into a bloodlust were nothing compared to the stress I witnessed on the face of the other drivers. This was life's gift: over-crowding and lack of intelligence make for a bad experience on the roads of Washington's urban sprawl.

Eryn drove. I had to crawl into her back seat and fold myself into a box like before. The suspension in the car protested. Things sounded a little more strained, which made me laugh.

The pheromone count must have still been enveloping the two of us because of being with her in the small confines of the vehicle. Her scent was so strong, bringing flashback of our intimacy all over again. I had my hand on her shoulder as she drove, gently massaging her. The time together before we left played deeply on my mind. Why did this meeting have to be

481

now? Love making was so new to me; it was indescribable in my mind to drink in the scent of her very skin. It had a drunken effect on me making me feel giddy. I understood what the phrase "drunk on love" meant. The uncontrolled passion for her was a caged animal. Many aspects of my life had changed forever.

I also did not dare think about those swords and tried with all the mental conditioning learned to keep them away from my thoughts. I was still mystified. Eryn saw it also. Something had to be real. Could be a ghost or spirit was messing with us. As unlikely as that was, because of how real it felt, it would certainly explain the Houdini effect.

We reached Redmond and turned up a hill that took us out into the woods. Light started to fade, and Eryn slowed down a bit as we started looking for the address. Mail boxes were poorly marked. Even with decreasing speed, we could not see the numbers very well with the down poor still in full swing. Diane's directions said to look for a plain mail box that would be obvious. I had to laugh at the description, with its vagueness. Trying to find *"fourteen eight seven four"* did not make sense until it stared us in the face. Right on this plain white mail box, mounted sideways and back from the road, the numbers were spaced just as such, but meant *"one four eight seven four."* The play on numbers felt overstated, but it was exactly as she said it would be.

A haunting driveway appeared. The darkness made it look like what a portal might look like, if they actually existed. Street lights down the road did not penetrate this darkness. The ominous warded off unwanted guests. There was a speaker box mounted next to the mail box as we pulled in. I heard Eryn gasp. The headlights on the car acted as though they were not even on as we pulled into the driveway.

"That's odd. Are you seeing this?" she spoke almost at a whisper. I looked ahead as well but was not sure if she saw something more. The power window lowering broke the silence further as I responded to her.

"They do not seem like they want guests, do they?" I chimed in and suddenly felt a twinge behind me outside. Chills covered me. Something unexplainable watched us from the woods. Unable to crane my head further, I whispered, "Roll up the window now." The feeling of chill turned to a definite sense that something was behind the car.

The speaker box crackled to life.

"Welcome, Travelers. The feeling you are experiencing is normal. Just relax, it will pass. Stay in the car and do not get out yet."

"She is not for real," I said. "Something is behind us not in front of us." I felt nothing from the darkened drive way, but a presence behind me told me something was indeed there. I twisted my torso for a better look. The light from the street lamps was nonexistent. Normally one would be able to see the street lamps from the shadows.

Darkness behind was impenetrable.

The speaker box remained silent for several more minutes. I could hear Eryn muttering something under hear breath that sounded like the "Lord's Prayer." She was worried now. The energy in the car changed. I patted her shoulder and returned to front facing in the car, the vehicle rocked in protest in my doing so. Her hand took mine and she hummed a few bars of something to reclaim what the silence had stolen. Moments passed. The squawk of the box began again, much more distinct and lower in volume.

"Pull forward now."

The air fluxed with energy making my skin tingle.

Movement on the white mail box right by the speaker caught my eye. The numbers written in the odd spacing moved closer together and did not have the same pattern anymore. "one four eight seven four" became one, then four hundred and eighty seven, then four." I blinked my eyes, thinking I was seeing things and heard a gasp from the front to signify otherwise. The numbers moved and regrouped themselves into a different arrangement. Could someone from the road see that amidst the strange darkness?

A sound came from beyond the gate. The area slowly began to illuminate.

The presence behind us came back, but the feeling was one of dread, like earlier. Some event took place. I could not glance behind anymore, but something told me we had just passed through some sort of protections set in place by this. The thought made me smile slightly. Not knowing what we were rolling into did have me on edge. Protecting Eryn was all that mattered to me, above all else. If she got hurt here, I would take this place apart. This thought kept coming to mind as my senses reached out. All seemed to be okay.

Eryn opened the car door. With the keys in the ignition and the lights still on, the dinging jingled out into the night. She left them on and stepped out to open my door. Out I crawled slowly like a snake shedding its skin. My ability to fit in the back seat probably compared to a clown car. I kept waiting for a game show host to jump out and hand us money for the feat.

My feet touched down. Something raced up my legs like chi, right to about my chest before a popping sound snapped in my head. As I stood up to my full height, I felt it again, this time it didn't make it past my abdominal area before it felt like something inside me pushed back whatever just travelled up me.

Then it hit me. There was no rain falling. The clear skies showed stars twinkling above. A feeling of longing followed by peace calmed my mind. The truth was there was a feeling as if I did not belong here on earth and had no idea why. The oddities of my life were in the back of my mind, and I was always analyzing my surroundings. My hands went up to show the universal sign for rain and shrugged my shoulders when I made eye contact with Eryn. This place had me curious.

Eryn was uneasy and took my hand. "I don't like this, Tathlyn. This was a bad idea. We should go." Before I could answer, from the shadows came a plain voice, female and soothing.

"Please don't. It is an honor to meet such a being," it said.

Eryn started to laugh. I was sure she had told them something to get a meeting. It had to be good enough to pique the interest of such a group...especially one so secluded from the public. A middle aged woman stepped from the shadow as the area lit up like daylight rather suddenly. Instinctively, my hand covered my eyes as they adjusted moments later. Eryn's hands went up to deflect the sudden brilliance as well.

Her breathing quickened. That bothered me. Because she was afraid, that put me on the defensive. I stepped forward to impose myself between the light this woman had brought forth and Eryn.

"Noble. Even now you protect her from nothing," she replied as she lowered a scarf from her face to reveal her gaunt features as if someone had stretched skin over a skeleton. Her eyes glowed as if something back lit them, giving her a mystical appearance, which made her look powerful. As she blinked, it became obvious there was light emitting. Her clothes seemed plain enough. A green dress flowed to the ground with a shawl over her shoulders colored an earthen tone. She held her hands out to her side and nodded her head with slight bow. "Blessings to you Eryn...and Tathlyn...is it? My, you *are* big indeed," she said with a toothy smile.

Her tone felt creepy. The kid of creeping feeling you get when something is not right. My view had to change, though. This was *her* house. This woman chose a way of life that was a bit off from the world. She probably dealt with things that would baffle me. I extended my hand to her.

"Come with me both of you, we have much to discuss. You may lower your hand there Tathlyn." She turned and walked away.

My hand returned to my side and I looked at Eryn, a puzzled look on my face. She smacked my rear to get me moving and tried to fake a smile. I could see through it. She was scared. Something was definitely off about this place. My senses were all over the place. My hand grabbed Eryn's and we followed gingerly behind our host.

It is funny how the mind misses certain things in new situations. I did not see a house when we pulled up, only a light that came on later. As we walked forward, I realized I did not know where or what we walked towards in this darkness. Diane's shape stayed ahead as an outline even in this strange light. We followed in her stead as she moved. Eryn's foot falls came behind mine and I made sure to keep pace with her. The air around us seemed thick like it hung heavier here on the ground. There were noises ahead...a murmur grew.

Light ahead appeared and grew, taking any peripheral vision away...not even the figure of our host. The murmur was now consistent with the droning of many voices that caught my ears. Crackles came from a fire appeared as we cleared the walkway. That had been diluting the many voices we heard on the way in. Diane walked into what looked like a clearing. She was about twenty feet ahead and moved towards a few shadows that within a few steps melded into the form of two people on either side of her now. All three faced our direction as we entered whatever this was.

A quick glance revealed a clearing about a hundred yards across. I could see several structures of odd design made with branched woven together, sort of like wicker. Hut like roofs on all of them hid a lot of the features with hanging debris and decorations of one sort or another. It appeared to be a village, almost medieval in design and décor. My unease turned to comfort and that troubled me. I did my best to hide it and stayed alert. The trio ahead now walked the ten or so feet forward, and all bowed.

"Welcome Honored guests to Shan Garran, may you find solace and tranquility while you are here."

She had a look in her eye that I could not explain. The bumps, where the hairs on my neck would have been, stood upright even though there was

487

no threat. I pushed the urge down and she was still talking, missing a few words. "...make your time here more of an experience. Do not hesitate to ask."

She gestured to her left. "This is Tolman. The other is Syreena, our leader." Her gesture went to the right. Both bowed again, and I locked eyes with the second woman. They felt vacuous and cold to me. There was still nothing obvious to detect. There was no response from her, simply a hand extended in a friendly gesture. I stepped forward and nodded my head. Her hand hung in the air so I gently took it.

Images hit me harder than any of my memories. I felt slammed with psychic wrecking balls. They hammered my defenses. The skin on my face felt like it was burning. I blinked my eyes a few times and suddenly Tolman was next to me with my other hand in his. Diane was watching from behind.

"This will take but a moment. We apologize for any discomfort you may be feeling. It will be over soon," Tolman said. I heard Eryn gasp behind me and tried to look, finding out my head would not move. It was stuck forward looking into Syreena's eyes. The pounding attempts to get in my mind and the burning sensation continued to grow. An object fell to the ground behind me. A third presence joined in the on the mental bombardment. Something inside me weakened.

"You got here just in time to help us finish the ritual, Tathlyn. Let us find out what you are. The power I sense inside of you is stronger than anything I have ever heard of. It is like a drug. We want it all."

A wave of energy rolled over me and turned the intensity up even more. My mind was on fire. I could not move and I struggled to breathe.

No sound came from Eryn. She was behind me, where my eyes could not see. Anger raged inside of me and threatened to overcome me if they continued. I had to calm myself down to continue to fight whatever these people were attempting. My mind tried to find my Zen place where meditation was possible.

Memories of watching the birds in their element hunting worms came forward. The rage reached a crescendo as the memory anchored my peace at that moment. Their assault continued to build, but my anger over it receded slowly. The words spoken by these three became blurry. It sounded like Latin at times but more guttural. My muscles went limp, yet I was still upright, unable to move. The fraction of time that exists between tranquility and acceptance held me in its sway. Energy rolled over me creating weakness that crept into my core. A fine red mist came from my skin, sapping my strength. My blood floated toward the fire.

A flash of heat came...then a voice, this time in English, "Diane, the portal is opening, his blood worked, its working, oh my ancestors, it is working. Fate has given us the divine energy source we needed to reach back to the past and avenge our fallen!"

Divine energy. What the hell is this weirdo saying?

My eyes opened and the entire area was bright. Energy was visibly swirly and building in intensity, above the bonfire in the middle of the clearing. For the first time, I could see hundreds of people in robes chanting and tracing symbols in the air. Strange symbols hung in the air for a moment before a swirling vortex in the middle of the fire sucked them in. The vortex grew with each symbol it swallowed.

The excitement in those around was evident. Their glee shone as this vortex collapsed into what appeared to be an opening torn into the very air itself. A loud whistling sound mixed with a buzzing sound and grew in my mind...along with a building sense of dread. I was about to witness something horrible before Eryn and I died. The peace that filled my heart gave way to a righteous fury, sudden and impacting. This simply was not acceptable.

Not if I could help it.

I felt a surge. My biceps flexed so hard they almost tore the tendons connecting to my forearm. A yell, much like a roar escaped my lips, and I felt eyes on me by the trio again. The mental weight of all three of them slammed me right in the forehead. This piecing sensation felt like the two hemispheres of my brain were about to be split in half. The pain was unbearable. My mind slid towards blackness. Like holes in Swiss cheese, the spots formed over my consciousness. Suddenly there was screaming. The pressure weakened a little. I could not see yet, but those screams were real.

"Something is coming through...."

"Everyone let ...."

"Stand your ground and contain it, we can't allo...."

Something came close to me that did not feel like a human. Another scream and a gurgle came from right next to me.

"Oh my gods, Tolman!" The sound of tearing flesh and snapping tendon filled my ears. Psychic energy lessened its grasp on me, and I could finally open my eyes to the horrors that filled my vision. A floating curtain like opening stood in the middle of the area that looked like it revealed

490

something on the other side. I could see creatures that resembled beasts from my dreams clawing their way out of it, leaping clear, and running on the ground at terrifying speeds. They took down a member of the coven and gored them with claws and teeth. Fine sprays of blood misted the air.

Next to me the two "witches" from the trio, Diane, and Syreena, were attempting to cast some sort of enchantment on the creature that I knew had to be a daemon. It was busy goring at the third witch and paid no heed to their feeble attempts. They did not see the two other monsters approach them from the side. They were gone in an instant.

Were we next? Suddenly I could move and turned my head quickly towards Eryn. She lay on the ground. The mass of moving monsters was eating the coven fast. I had to protect her. Time was running out. My feet found her side and crouched down.

A voice inside of me yelled that walking away from this situation would be a mistake. What could I do? I might be able to kill a few of them. My heart tore between saving my love and duty to kill what I somehow knew to be my mortal enemy. I felt the burning sensation in my mind growing stronger as the opening from God knows where got bigger. *"Perhaps those visions were about this precise moment. Maybe this is why I became so big to deal with this situation. Was it my destiny?"*

Daemons killed and fed upon coven members.

So many thoughts rolled through my head, tearing me asunder between protecting Eryn and killing these foul beasts. My hands started to itch terribly. I reached out to grab a hold of Eryn's clothing to drag her farther away from the horde that had completely overrun the area. It was time to be cautious while pulling her back. My eyes watched the horde of monsters the first fifteen feet or so without even looking down once. Then something happened. I suddenly felt incomplete, like something was forgotten or missing came over me. My mind started to long for something that I obviously did not have. The feeling crept down into my hands and an image appeared in my mind of those beautiful swords.

I did not even flinch when I felt them appear. Something cold and solid filled my grasp now and the feeling of something missing went away instantly. A surge of energy rolled from the ground up to my head. I felt complete.

Suddenly that presence from the road was behind me, and I spun ready to deal it due. To my surprise a man in plain clothes, very tall crouched down behind me, a look of surprise on his face. His brown hair was slightly hanging in his eyes, but I could see a glow similar to Diane's there. He was looking at the carnage. His eyes snapped to, focusing on me being right in front of him brandishing my swords. Powerful eyes looked to my hands and his surprise turned to a smile.

"I do not know what you are, my large friend, but you appear to be better equipped to deal with this situation," he whispered barely above the roar of the Wiccan feast going on behind me. His eyes moved to Eryn's body. "You cannot protect her and fight them at the same time. Go. I will care for her," he promised.

He understood my distrustful look by nodding and smiling. I looked at her then back to the horde in its blood frenzy. I glanced back to him. Again he spoke. "If you don't do something now that rift may turn into a portal, and if that happens, this may get really bad."

"It isn't bad already?" I asked, partly grinning.

"I imagine this is nothing compared to what happens next. I have her. Go!" he yelled. He closed his eyes, uttered a word, a visible bubble popped up around him and Eryn, and he pulled her close right as a few strays from the pile of monsters leapt our direction. "You have to kill them all somehow!" he screamed. "All of them! Now go!"

The roar of the feast behind made it hard to hear anything else he said to me. I could, however, hear the protesting of the daemons that slammed into the newcomer's shield. They began to circle him as if I was not even there. *Funny* I thought and stood up. They continued to claw and bite at the barrier. The cries brought the attention of two more of them to join in trying to break the enchantment around this new friend.

I got a good look at them. Some of them had multiple sets of limbs. It was hard to tell how many because they moved so fast. Claws flashed out and energy crackled over the sphere, showering sparks of various colors. Limbs retracted fast, shaking. Smoke poured off of a few of them. The man smiled my direction while pointing at them and drew a line across his own throat in the universal "kill them" signal.

My eyes dropped to the majestic blades. They vibrated in my hands. A voice in my head said three words.

"Kill them all."

I hesitated for but a second before swinging at one of the beasts. My sword caught its center length wise on the torso. It dropped down. The blade passed through like it was cutting butter. A shower of ichorous blood

493

sprayed the area. The creature fell dead. The remaining three turned and looked at me, with teeth bearing. Their human like faces had tongues and mouths, something I would have expected on a creature that was dog-like, mixed with lizard over tones. Speech came from them in chorus.

"Uut heeem. Keall heeeem," the creature hissed through bloody teeth and cherry red gums. Molten saliva sprayed outward as it spoke.

Time's mortal sway over my life came to a stop at that moment. I watched the muscles in their haunches tense up and ripple with the energy of the movement telegraphing what they were about to do. It was simple. They all readied for a leaping attack. As I watched the muscles slowly start to move, I could see the pressure of their movement ripple their skin as they sprang forward. Viscous spit dripping from their mouths caught the wind from their forward motion. The hanging saliva strings bent away from me as if the beasts had already reached full speed. I was still standing there watching this unfold.

I blinked.

Up came the left hand with the sword, taking the first one in the head, cleanly splitting its skull in two halves, still attached. The second caught the thrust of my right hand as it came behind my left with a stab that went right through the skull of the third with ease. I slid both of my blades free effortlessly and spun to my right taking the third with both strikes. I removed the head and the abdomen at the same time. I finished the spin, dropping to a knee before the pieces hit the ground in a sickening, squishing thud.

My positioning had me facing away from the main host. A feeling pulled me towards the rupture. Somehow the very fabric of the universe cried as it hemorrhaged its energy out into the world. I locked eyes with the stranger. He grinned at me and nodded again.

Turning towards the mass of monsters, a primal yell erupted from me that caught the attention of every one of them. It was almost comical to see them looking up with half-filled mouths, like children eating spaghetti and getting caught not exercising good table manners. A pause that seemed to last for seconds ensued as they looked at me. Then slowly teeth began to show, as the baseline growling became a blast of frenzy.

They charged.

A single moment of silence fell upon me. I felt like my brain had a seizure. My eyelids fluttered so fast as something hit my mind from deep within like a bolt of divine energy charged up from the ages passed down to me to deal with this moment. The picturesque image of several hundred of these monsters all coming at me like a tidal wave of teeth and claws froze in my mind. At that moment, I happened to see the scar on my forearm come to life. Teeth seemed to tear right through the flesh and a gaping maw formed right on my arm just like before. As my eyes fell to this open wound that did not even hurt, its eyes bore right into mine.

"Remember!"

I looked at the horde frozen and various elevations of their leaps. I could see the sharpness of their teeth and the razor like talons on their hands and feet. My eyes glanced back at the maw on my forearm to discover that nothing but the scar was there. It felt like someone drove a spike into my brain. My body doubled over for a split second as it felt like the sky split above me and rained lightning down upon me. My balance faltered for a fraction of a moment as a veil lifted in my mind.

I leapt at death.

XXXIV

Remember

The wind in my face invoked peace with its cool touch.

I leapt at my enemy. My mind reached back fondly of how it used to feel to ride my bike. It felt free, with no cares. It also made me feel refreshed and energized in some small way. It carried with it new meaning, scents of what was to come, and could keep you alive in the heat. So in many ways wind was a force for life, not just the power of nature that could destroy your home. It was a form of freedom now that represented so much more.

Steps quickened on my approach. My first set of targets flew towards me. Dropping lower on the move, my legs tensed, breaking me free of gravity and launching me into the air in a mighty leap. I flew towards a host of daemons that had come through a tear in the fabric of the universe.

What felt and actually looked like a bolt of lightning had just hit my mind portraying fuzzy images that started to come forward just like one of those creatures on a track in a haunted house. You can hear it coming; you know it is coming but from what direction it is coming is still unclear. Something inside my mind tried to work its way to the front. It was trying to tell me something and after seeing that maw of teeth on my arm again, there was some universal truth waiting to erupt into my frontal lobe. I imagined seeing myself yelling from within a glass prison, but I could not hear myself, no matter how loud or how hard the other me yelled. I simply knew something was there.

The first few denizens to fall to my blade came in fast with my ascent still increasing. I caught three of them in one swing of the left hand and five with the other hand. Their bodies literally erupted into bits of flesh as the blade passed through. They almost seemed like they disintegrated...if that was even possible. I heard myself laugh at that last thought. *What was possible?* I was living proof of the impossible. Those visions had prepped me for this day. Where the swords came from and why they felt so familiar were other questions I would ponder.

My feet found the ground again. The blades bit deep into the flesh of several more of them with terrific precision and speed. I caught phrases coming from them as they tried to coordinate their attack, and it was curious to me that what I heard was not English. I could understand this gutter speech. After all only so many of them could surround me but none of them was brave enough to come at me solo. There was always a wave of at least six to ten or more coming in with teeth and claws. They tried to bite or rend some part of me. In combat, a warrior does not always go right for the kill; you have to whittle your opponent down by letting the damage accumulate over time if you are smart so you do not endanger yourself. They clearly did not get this.

How did I know this?

The flip side of that theory is to all-out attack, throwing everything at them in hopes that one major blow will land, and then you can finish them off quickly when they are stunned. This tactic is for when you have multiple opponents that are all trying to kill you. Immobilize or kill each one you touch and move to the next. This is how you engage the different concepts when it comes to war. The Germans used the Blitzkrieg. It was very effective in taking every one of their opponents down that had many hardened facilities at the same time.

Where are these thoughts coming from? How did I know about combat strategies?

That option was not my idea to claim. By my count, there were over four hundred of them with more slipping through every second. Every second, several at a time died. The opening was no longer just a tear. It was a rift. Each stroke had to kill more than the number arriving for me to staunch the flow and figure out how to close the rift before it became a portal. As my swords rose and fell, I noticed a small part of them broke away from the host and moved over to the rift. Dozens more fell to my blades before I could afford another glance; what I saw brought confusion after the initial joy had passed.

For a split second, I was excited. Several dozen of them had begun to kill each other. They willingly exposed a vulnerable part of their anatomy to one another. Half of them took a razor sharp claw and opened that section up, spilling entrails to the ground with a gouting wound that bled them out in seconds. They spilled each other's blood and left carcasses behind. I did not fully understand their reasoning.

Daemons going after each other must just be part of the culture. Then I saw that the blood spilling out gave off energy. It moved like mist that flowed very rapidly toward the tear in the very fabric. It began to solidify and grow, and the realization hit me that the slaughtering of the coven had made the opening bigger, allowing more daemons to enter the glade. As

I watched in horror, seeing how much it expanded from a half dozen of them dying, the situation became dire.

How was I putting this together so fast?

Three crawled through the rift as I glanced over. Each second about seven of them died now. As my blades flashed through body after body of them, the numbers tallied in my head finished. There was about a minute before this would become unmanageable. A flash of light erupted from the ground again and looked just like electricity or lightning with its fingers reaching for the tear. A pressure in the area made the air feel heavy. The rift grew yet again. Natural forces that I knew to be standard physics changed before my eyes. The ground pulsated with a charge that kept leaping up and feeding the ribbon like dance of this enlarged opening.

Caution rose within; there was no doubt they had to die faster. Four more blows struck through many of them, leaving about thirty in my wake. Those three daemons joined the host while another group broke away and began to slaughter themselves. A curse came from my lips. More of them joined this time and made an accurate count impossible. It was more than a dozen. They just killed themselves or each other. As the dark magic saturated the positive energy in the air around me, my lungs took in this foul air with each breath.

A crawling sensation cascaded through my body with each tainted breath taken but carried with it a scent that gave me a slight rush and a stronger desire to eliminate them. Hunger-like desire fueled a growing need. My need to rid them from this place turned into a controlled fury. Instincts took over. Energy spread slowly out to the tips of my fingers as if something was holding it back, like water behind a damn or the rubber in a balloon. My insides were stretching to a point that could not contain the rushing effect.

Then something gave way to a flood. A surge hit me so hard I wanted to yell as it released with perfect harmony. My movement became an explosion and my swords spun so fast they began to hum. To my surprise flames ignited along the blades' edges. I still had no idea what these swords could do but accepted what had just occurred with a smile. The flames stretched out their warmth up to the tip of the mighty weapons. As they danced almost on their own accord, seemingly unaffected by the wind cutting across them, the flames extended out several feet from the tips killing several more daemons per swipe. Like an arc of energy, traces of light lingered but a moment, detailing the wake of my blade like a brush on a canvas.

The upper hand was now mine, for numbers mattered not. Elation filled me at seeing the daemons falling beyond my arms reach. The flames stretched out, consuming targets feet away. Dozens died in such a way that the flames burnt them from existence. Even the particles left behind by the disintegrating effect had disrupted and disappeared before they hit the ground, erasing all proof anything had even occupied that space moments before. In seconds passed, a hundred of them were gone with ease. The blades felt lighter.

Slight over confidence was certainly not the issue when something slammed me from behind hard, knocking me forward. I spun, taking it apart with ease as it was beating its wings trying to create distance. It was almost comical, the look on the things face as it was surprised it was already dead before it melted away.

Several dozen of them came around to my left as if they used the one just killed as a distraction. I postured to engage this next group when the pain hit me. Something burned through my veins. Multiple cuts on my body overrode the adrenaline. I did not realize what was going on until a knee dropped, causing me to pitch a sword. Spidering up my veins, a black pattern started to show through a slice in the cloth on my thigh.

Several hits came hard when my guard dropped, filling me with dread. Whatever this was now inside of me was debilitating. My blade dipped toward the dirt. Daemons began to tighten the circle. They knew exactly what was happening and pulled back to allow it to work. A sick feeling rolled through me as the effect expanded through me. Deep breathes came hard. My remaining blade clattered to the ground.

I wish I could say that was the only problem. Glancing at the portal again, two large hands reached through and grabbed a hold of the incorporeal sides. It took a moment for this to register as my attention snapped back to the circle of laughter now around me. Sweat poured from my brow. I tried to regain my feet but felt dizziness wash over me like when experiencing a newly formed tattoo. The burning all over was familiar, but I attributed that to the damage they had caused me.

The flyers broke away and banked low, following the ground. I had seconds. Glancing around me revealed the gargantuan hands continuing to claw and tear at the rift. Nausea hit and my hand tried to cover my mouth as if it could stop the inevitable.

502

That is when it became apparent.

The black lines on the back of my hand ran up my arm in a geometric pattern, but with a natural weave to it. Vision blurred. My senses reached out, trying to feel where the flyers would hit me next. The closest blade lay inches away. Retrieving it, my hand readied it the best I could. I did not know what all tattoos meant. What good was it if it could not help me out right now and heal me? Death stalked me. In the process, Eryn would die, falling to this darkness.

This was not acceptable! Almost right on cue, warmth spread through my body, starting at my core. Pain faded as this sensation flowed steadily to my hands and feet making my fingers pulsate. Nausea began to subside. My sight returned. The blackened veins in my leg returned to normal color as the color retreated to the wound on my thigh. Strength settled in my heart with this turn of events, giving me renewed hope to try to change the tide.

Something healed me.

My eyes fell to the rift. Whatever tried to gain access was huge. The giant clawing hand struggled to get a solid grip.

That is when the flyers hit me hard, bowling me over onto my back. One of them landed on me while the others continued and circled around. Claws dug into my flesh in several places. Rage hit me as a roar came from my depths, and I grabbed the beast by the tongue and thrust my blade into its eye. The flame ignited something in there because his brain boiled and popped, showering me with ichor.

Rolling to my shoulder blades, I picked up to my feet in a squat and looked for my other blade. It appeared in my hand with perfect timing as the "air cover" had tried to blind side me. Power from the swords now surged from me.

The flames reignited. Charging the rift to try end this and trap them was my only hope. I was no more than three feet away when sickness washed over me. The large hands had found their grip. A large foot appeared and forced the rift down, opening it farther while the mighty hands pushed up to the height of about ten feet from the four or so diameter it had been. A giant head appeared and trust through, adorned with a crown of sharp, blackened horns. Great big eyes, with blackened pupils, as if small black holes, sat inside the huge yellow orbs. Even its brow above the eyes was twisted and full of boney protrusions that blinked and made a disgusting sound of scraping bone. Its eyes locked on me and went wide. It made a sound as if overexertion was a word and a roar like sound filled my ears.

I stepped back on instinct.

Out stepped a monster that was straight up huge. His wingspan was at least twice his height as they unfolded. Great leathery gnarled wings, graying red in color, filled my sight. I could see some sort of material like dirt or dust falling from the folds, lazily coating the ground. As the grass died, it created an acrid smell and blackened the soil. Twisted and overdeveloped muscles flexed when the creature raised its powerful hands and roared while its huge tail whipped about from behind it and knocked me back several yards. It glared at me with intense hatred that turned into a wicked grin.

Out of thin air, a weapon as big as me appeared in its hand. Great blackened metal with twisted carving and horrific images adorned the blade.

Even where one would expect to see highly sharpened edges, a foul blackness existed. Running the length of the blade, a sickly glowing light pulsed down to curved tip, causing a green emanation to ooze from it. This fell to the ground like it had some sort of sludge inside of it. Upon contact with the ground, it spread like vapor for a second before disappearing, leaving a sick green glow on whatever it touched. The monstrous beast rose to its full height well over my own by almost three times. A pressure in my head grew suddenly and felt like it was going to burst.

Then it did.

The edges of my mind felt like they blew apart then collapsed in on themselves with a clap of thunder exploding inside my head. I felt pain turn from a furious storm to a placid ocean. Thoughts and images came flooding forward, bringing with them a whole other life that existed to me. Realization struck hard causing me to back pedal. The creature swung the massive sword at me, and even though both blades responded without even thinking about it, it launched me backwards.

Like a water fall of information filling my mind, it flowed into every corner all at once. Remembrance hit me with clarity and resolution as if I had been looking at a movie that suddenly jumped off of the silver screen and came to life.

I remembered everything.

I remember training with Malnuras on another plane of existence...where the city of Heaven was not a myth. My father was alive. He was an Archangel. He was also the General of Heaven's Army. Hundreds of battles great and small, all exploded into my memory at the same time. The memories flooded over the places of my mind, creating wrinkles in the brain to lock in a moment like a memory board in a computer. Millions of compartments for storing information filled up in an instant.

My balance almost failed. Thankfully, the space that I gave myself had been smart. Gasping for air, I looked from the ground up to the monstrous daemon in front of me and locked my gaze on his huge eyes. He looked back with a burning hatred.

This creature in front of me had been responsible for killing my teacher...and that teacher was actually a shard of God himself. How that was possible did not matter now. I simply knew it happened and that allowed the horde to access Heaven, killing hundreds of thousands of angelic guardians. Recognition must have washed over my face for it pointed to its chest with a huge arm that I could see had permanent scars on it from when it last met my blades.

"Amduscias," the daemon prince's voice gurgled. "You escaped us once. *Not twice.*"

I laughed strangely enough for one of my memories of this monstrosity was how much I angered it by denying it something. What it was I could now remember.

Something that it had obviously replaced.

A gigantic blade! It was not the exact sword from before. I had tossed that one down the well. My success there angered it beyond measure. That seemed like ages ago when in all reality it, had only been months. Hell had plenty of time to craft another one in one of its hellish foundries. This daemon blade was actually bigger and I did not remember the green flowing ooze or energy this one held. It was a nasty addition to an already horrible weapon.

He made a fancy gesture as if he was a gentleman swordsman beckoning me to a friendly duel.

I did not hesitate.

XXXV

Sacrifices

Holy hell he is big!

A moment of clarity hit me harder than ever. All the possibilities ever imagined came to a sudden epiphany in that very moment when I launched myself at this daemon lord. As a child, I believed daemons only existed in myth. On Sunday when you dressed up and put on your false piety to enter what you thought was God's house, one might hear these stories. This monster was neither myth nor legend; nor was it fake or a dream. It was big, horrific and, most importantly, determined to kill me.

With its flesh and blood, sinew and muscle, evil, and fear...all rolled into one very real nightmare, this dream became a reality in that moment. The true definition of childhood nightmares became a sick irony. Only there was no real fear in my heart.

I could see the very leathery skin ripple as time slowed for me. The bulging of muscles, as it flexed for a strike like a wound up spring, showed me that the tension building was tremendous. Its strikes, if landed, could decimate me. I had to be elusive. The pain from blocking such a blow would be unbearable. I would likely not survive a direct hit. For that fraction of a second I did not want to engage him, but only for a fraction. I was no fool. A strategy had already formed in my mind. This was what they trained me to deal with. I had to redirect the hits.

Energy flowed from everywhere around me and into me. A reservoir existed inside of me where my energy lived. It was my core, my chi, my life force. I could draw it from around me and build it up when needed, but it was finite. Every action took a small piece. Some took way too much. My defenses flared to life forming a protective barrier around me.

A vibration came from my blades as if in approval.

My eyes panned from the ground up one more time, studying his poise, muscle mass, movement, and weight distribution. Those wings and tail gave him an edge to keep me at bay and lend him balance. They also gave him additional strikes and other opportunities to throw a wrench into my plans. I needed to strike enough blows to create enough damage to weaken him. For I knew it would indeed anger such an ego to be touched by an opponent. Perhaps that was my ultimate tactic: to let him make mistakes and stay alive long enough to capitalize.

Heat flashed from him, which was interesting since there were no flames. This caused more of the decaying debris to fall from his wings, and his motion towards me started again. The particles fell to the ground behind him smoldering where they landed. It blackened the soil...before erupting into small flames. These brackish flames had patterns unto themselves. I could not smell the feted stench of it yet, but knew once engaged, those mighty winged would mixed it well into the air. That would become an is-sue. The myth involving daemons finally had some hidden truth. They did not actually have flames around them or live in them from my observation, but some sort of chemical reaction with something did create the illusion that they emanated flames.

I started with my swords high and to the right as to meet his blade in the over handed strike that came. Very predictable it was, but not anticipated. The very air would split as his strike fell towards me, emitting a faint sizzling sound as if the atoms themselves paid with their existence from the contact. The smell of ozone pushed ahead of his blade. At the last second, I dropped the angle of my swords over my left shoulder where his blade was to meet mine and dove into a roll under his left arm. Feeling the moment the swords connected, I let my wrist break just enough to create resistance and dove tucking my knees, and allowed my blades to drag along his. At the last moment, my head turned to the left. My body twisted and followed.

The swords snapped free of his blade, causing the maneuver to accelerate me forward into a roll over my right should while in the air. The extra force added to mine and brought my swords faster into his exposed ribs below his left pectoral muscle. I felt them bite flesh and an elongated, demonic roar told me how badly.

My feet followed my body around bringing me flat to the ground. Almost as instinct I imagine, his left wing pulled in tightly, like a rubber band snapping back, it came in fast to guard the damaged area. Ducking low I had to roll under it, unfortunately right through the trail of death it fanned out behind it. The burning ground ignited my shirt in places as I found my feet again behind the daemon.

A familiar voice in my head made me smile. A duet...long missed, spoke in harmony. "Watch the wing," they sang. A growl was my answer. Better late than never, to confirm what I already guessed.

"So glad you could join me, my friends. It has been too long," I said with the speed of thought. *"Why did you wait until now to speak?"*

"It was your journey alone to walk. We are not your guide this time. Nathanael told us to remain quiet and respond in kind when you were ready," they replied.

I am ready! I said mentally while ducking another swing of the huge blade.

He was fast. I could not believe how quickly he spun to face me while I was doing the same to posture for another strike. His wing muscles did not tense this time; it was his legs. I did not miss this fact. I saw the turn start from my peripheral to my right while moving the same direction. A small cloud of the powdery death came off the trailing edge of the great leathering wing just like the wind spilling off the wing of a plane. The cloud fell in spiral circles behind it for a moment...then my view of the particles became blocked as the wing itself closed in.

A sound, much like a sword coming out of a sheath, rang in my ears as I vaulted sideways in a barrel roll...my knees in tight and swords close to gain a faster rotation. It was not fast enough. Something cut me mid-air. The impact was just enough to throw my rotation off so I did not stick my landing. Unsure footing became a factor. My eyes moved from the ground to the wing as he spun, displaying a wicked, many fanged grin. His tongue fell out of his mouth with black ooze flowing from the puncture wounds he had inflicted with his own fangs.

A cackle ensued.

My eyes caught a sparkle coming off the blackened claw protruding from the tips of his wings. I could see a trace of red blood on the tip of one claw, running down a now fully extended razor of blackened bone. Another substance gathered near the tip, like a large droplet of fluid, and ran down as well. I could only guess what that was. The burning in my shoulder confirmed for me. He had poison glands on the tips of his wings that flowed from razor sharp protrusions.

We postured facing each other. My hands felt an exchange of energy flowing to and from my blades now. It was searing hot, so pure, rolling from me up the swords. Light traced its way off the edge towards the tip. Flowing back in to me was an awareness not noticed before. It was as though the swords themselves had nerves that fed information back to me on positioning from the ground and the proximity to the danger. I could sense *him* through my blades. The air he drew in cried out for help without the will power to resist.

Inside of my head, I could feel my eyes closed as I gently circled to the right. He sized me up. My mind could feel his muscles tense and relax with each step. They were very powerful, and the energy felt each time one muscle group flexed and relaxed was immense and caught me off guard from the expenditure. Then it hit me he was not breathing; his very existence was destroying life here as if he was consuming the ground where he stood.

A flurry of motion commenced. There was no competing with him. My parrying was redirecting. When possible...I dodged. My actions were but a fraction of a second ahead of him every time. That edge was fading fast. Steel rang off steel as I fought to position or reposition his blades away from me while avoiding his wings. Each blow he attempted to land took a little more out of me. He paused and began to pace to try to lull me into thinking I had a break.

He was getting stronger.

My inner eye snapped open as he exploded into action again. Spinning with great force, his motion built in his legs, generating momentum. His wings snapped out as if to slingshot the energy of his motion faster. I attempted to duck this time, for my shirt was still smoldering on my back. The fabric began to disintegrate after the initial burst of it caught fire. Dark flames still danced on my arm as the last of the doomed fabric disappeared, leaving me standing there in my breaches and shoes.

I was on my toes, knees collapsed to where my rear was on my heels spinning. The blade came in faster than anticipated. Had my stance not been low enough the blade would have taken my head off clean since my crossed blades were near my hips. There would have been no preventing it. Several swings gauged his distance from me just like pulling out a measuring tape. He was just outside my reach, but I was well inside of his.

As we circled, behind the daemon, the rift still grew. A few smaller fliers continued to slaughter each other to give that extra energy needed to fortify the portal. It must have been slowing down, but I could still feel its progress. A sense came over me that I had felt the minute it opened. Not sure what it was, my senses reached out yet again. My senses registered pain everywhere as if something siphoned the air around me of its life. I already knew the daemon lord was draining life from around him, but this was different. His power grew. My skin, even though still burning from the initial exchange, felt a sickening disturbance forming in the coven's dimensional pocket. It felt smaller than it was, almost claustrophobic.

My swords felt like if they were compensating for something, beyond my own energy and theirs. It flowed in a synchronous harmony. Like there would be harmony in ending a daemon's life. This was my first language in the physical sense.

The pain in my shoulder grew. It would be best to turn my healing on now, a mistake made early on in so many fights. I had waited too long to engage it. The sickness flowed through me, expunged out my pores like sweat forming on my brow and various other places. I felt better instantly knowing it would be several more moments before enough of the poison neutralized for the effect to weaken.

As the daemon spun his weapon back in an amusing display of swordsmanship, I caught a view of the portal for a few seconds around him.

The light around us bent towards the rift like a giant vacuum drew it in. Around its edges, tiny flashes of lights appeared when the air and streaks of light made contact with it. Just like a spark with gas or even pure oxygen it hit. The very positive energy of this place was fueling the growth now.

The smaller daemons had done their job. I caught a glimpse through the light display and could barely make out shadows getting closer as something prepared to come through. The opening was about sixty percent the size of the daemon prince now. How he had folded himself enough to fit through was certainly a feat, but now he could probably just duck and step through. Reality hit me. I was out of time.

It was a fully functioning portal.

He was still smiling and breathing heavily as he fed off the energy his presence consumed. Again it hit me that the longer he was here, the stronger he would become; unless it could only maintain what he had because he was not from this plain of existence. This was a curious thought cut short by sudden movement.

His wings snapped out again at me. Ducking, I dragged my blades along them, scoring deep cuts. Pressure gave way as they cut clean through to my target, the gland, and razor talon itself. As they hit, I snapped my wrists hard as it cut free. He howled. The ground shook. Tiny little pebbles jumped. Dust began to rise and drift.

Ichor showered the ground in a fan-like pattern, blackening the ground as it mixed with the already descending particles falling from the wings' folds. I watched in horror where it hit. Dirt decayed, creating large holes that continued to fall in on them, getting a foot in diameter. The smell hit my nostrils with a buffet of the wings, and I could feel and sense the muscles in his body tense in a spasm and he roared again like a child throwing a fit in a candy store.

I did not even see it coming. There was just a flash, a glint and movement before I realized his sword was clean through my chest in such a fashion that it just missed my spine but was sticking out my back. My left lung was punctured top to bottom. White spots filled my vision as the oxygen escaped. My diaphragm froze as my knees found the ground suddenly.

He had thrown his blade, scoring a direct hit.

How did his weapon get through my defenses so easily?

My first real thought of death lingered. Failure whispered its name in my ears. It seemed impossible. I stood skewered by the might sword. My breath heaved in and out, my eyes danced around sporadically. Slowly, the truth settled over my rigid body, standing arched and at attention, blood pouring from my torso and pooling around me.

Nothing daemonic should be able to get through unhindered. Disbelief, failure, and irony overwhelmed my mind. A soldier never throws his weapon unless he expects to die or does not care about the outcome. You cannot control the outcome without all your tools, Father used to tell me. He had done the unexpected and succeeded. If you are going to fail, it is better to die with your weapons in hand. Did' this creature not know that? Malnuras beat that into me every day until the day he gave me weapons that I could summon. Then he beat it into me again when I used it, for it was a last result only. I did not even feel any pain, which told me that my body and mind knew it was over, so the pain receptors simply disengaged. I had learned and seen first-hand that many warriors died a glorious death and felt no pain.

This was no soldier for he had no honor. My death would not serve God or mankind. Delirium began to set in. I could see him laughing at me...not just laughter but hysterics as if he knew the secrets of the universe and nothing mattered. I started to shake with laughter at the last part. No sound came out, however. I wheezed in exhausted sobs. His goals were to enslave or destroy mankind and this world. The idea of him caring about anything other than not angering his father was most likely the farthest from his mind. After all he was a daemon lord and our souls were like eating a truffle when plucked from a mortal coil. I felt the sword start to cauterize the wound.

What would my soul taste like? This thought did not even run its course when a twinge inside of me told me it was bad. Light began to fade;

he grew blurry and I repeatedly blinked as if something in my eyes told me to pay attention. Tears formed. My vision cleared slightly.

Gloating. He was actually gloating. About twenty feet in front of me he sat down hard. The oozing ichor ran from its wing still, creating a small crater behind and to the right side of it. I felt at peace in that moment and not defeated as I had from several seconds before. In the solitude of that moment, I realized my hands had found the blade sticking through my chest cavity. It hurt to actually lay hands on the blade as if it completed the circuit like a ground for electricity. My hands heated up as if I was holding a hot iron. I was a little confused, as if watching myself do something from very far away.

He spoke.

"It hurts? Blade not of the horde, but from the life," he motioned around us, "and feed faster as you weaken." He pointed at me and leaned in, breathing deeply. "Learned your tricks. Too simple. Your flesh burns, soon I shall feast." A long gurgling laugh escaped his lips; a slight trace of ichor was still present on them.

"Father... pleased...I finally assault... frail God's attention ...will weaken Heaven and make this place... ripe for consumption... eternity to feed. Many souls." Ichor sprayed the ground in front of him. At that moment, I began to push the hilt of the sword away from me. The resistance of the sealed wound made it difficult. For several minutes now, I had no air and did not know where my strength came from. I did not doubt but began to pray. My inner voice reached up to God, not in a begging approach but thanking him for giving this opportunity to serve man and for the tools he had granted me through my teacher and my master. I thanked him for Eryn and Jason, as misguided as he was, and said I hoped I could save them somehow. Intense pain started as the flesh gave up its bond to the weapon. At least I knew why it passed right through my defenses.

"You must focus to persevere," the chorus sang in my mind. With tiny movements and my one lung expired of air, the impossible happened.

An inch of the blade slid out.

"Father in Heaven, give me the strength to rid this world of my mortal enemy." The words exploded from my lips as I felt a small amount of trapped air free itself and flow out of me. "Your humble servant shall prevail this day, as the hordes of Hell do come my way."

Another inch.

I gasped for air, sucking it in like a glass of water to a person dying of thirst. Strength trickled back, but pain now erupted on my insides along anywhere the blade touched the grievous wound. I knew its vast energy, which it was pulling from the very air around me, lent life to this blade.

"I shall not fall before this evil this day," I yelled as a few more inches gave way and pain erupted tenfold inside of me.

He was laughing and almost rolling on his back. I found that to be very odd unless it was looking forward to another go at me somehow, even though another go felt impossible. I refused to die with this icon of destruction through my chest. The cackling slowed to a giggle. A glint in his eye told me that suffering had to be his prize right now, and he was eating well. The feeling in my charred hands was gone, to the point that all that was possible was to palm the blade and draw it forth. With each attempt to release it, more of the flesh stayed behind on the metal, slowly continuing to sizzle. The smell was disgusting; especially knowing it was my own.

Halfway out and he was still laughing and gloating. I expected at any moment that he would do something. My focus now was on healing. I did not know how I could do anything but maintain my balance and continue to withdraw this blade from me. Energy started to flow around inside and repair the damage. Thankfully none of the healing showed externally yet, as to not give away my attempt to act. With no idea of when that might happen, misdirection was buying me time.

A flash of light came from behind him right as the remainder of the blade came free. His head turned. Before he could speak something hit him square in the face, knocking him flat to the ground from a sitting position. He hit the ground with a tremendous force. Smoke rolled up from beneath his half buried face, driven into the ground; the skin was charred and boiling from the intense heat and damage. A foul smell filled my nostrils as the concussive force rolled towards me.

I did not even get a chance to let go of the blade as it slide from my hands. The rest of my flesh went with it, the entire hand of skin. I looked down at the burned muscle. Blood flowed from the back where the uncooked skin had torn free only moments before. There was not even time to be concerned. My healing focus turned fully outward. Not being anywhere close to fully recovered, the skin started to heal slowly and painfully. It was quite an amazing image to watch the flesh mend itself and come back from nothing. The energy within me flowed with such power. I could feel it as it tapped into my core, pulling all my strength left in reserve.

519

"Take this moment to heal...you are not the target of his ire," my blades declared mentally.

My attention diverted for too long. I looked up as a gust of wind buffeted me. The daemon was not prone before me but was now airborne and leaping or flying towards Eryn and the man putting the barrier over the two of them; only the man was now not standing in the protection of his bubble, but had moved forward. I was not sure why he would do this. Perhaps he could not maintain the protection and attack the daemon at the same time. Regardless, he did not remain in place but was now several feet in front of it.

This proved to be his mistake. Energy gathered around him that flowed to his hands as a focus point. Its brilliant light flowed over him like lightning. The color was light blue for a moment. There was a crackling sound heard from my position, even at my distance. Patterns both geometrical and arcane were appearing in the air as he spoke. His words were not audible to me. He had a daemon leaping towards him and his gaze was certainly in the air with a concerned but concentrated look.

I had to act. Seconds remained before the creature would land and kill this man for sure. Looking to the heavens, I felt the remaining energy within me surge through my limbs as if I had been shocked suddenly. With my feet beneath me, in a crouched position, healing energy erupted from deep inside as it rolled with blinding speed to my fingertips. I felt my swords strong in my healed hands. The cold metal was a comfort to my soul, driving back the feeling of incompletion I was experiencing in the moments before when I was nearly dead.

Time slowed. The need to act came into play. My legs flexed and gravity let me go. Whistling past my head, the wind picked up speed. Inside me, the energy waned enough that I knew landing was going to hurt, as I would probably not have it within me to do it gracefully. My eyes looked to my target. From high above, the daemon descended upon the man, and for a moment I was sad for not knowing his name. He bought me the time needed to take action, and I could not protect Eryn at the same time. As I watched helplessly, his valiant effort made the difference. Bards would sing of it.

He was about to die.

XXXVI

Answers

My ascent reached its zenith when the Warlock's spell erupted from his fingers a moment too late. I did not study any sort of arcane arts but had heard enough from my teacher and my master to know that the longer it takes to cast, the stronger the spell is. The air around me was devoid of energy at the last second before he finished his incantation, but I did not see it make its short journey towards its target. The monstrous body of my nemesis blocked my view of him a second later.

Another barrier appeared shimmering like a force field, but it appeared a moment too late. My angle put me high above so I got an elevated view of a hero's last stand, but I still could not see all of it. As the barrier exploded from the sheer force of the daemon smashing into it, the sound of shattering glass followed by the flash from the magic being released filled the area.

Energy rippled over the massive body of the daemon prince inducing a raging roar. As soon as the barrier broke, its skin boiled like it fell into a flash cooker. The putrid smell of this floated right up with the steam and smoke that rolled off the creature's body. I had smelled dead animals rotten for weeks in the woods that smelled better than what had just assaulted my nostrils. In a matter of seconds, a gurgling scream came from below.

Its massive body blocked my view of the event. One could only imagine the horrific death the stranger had just experienced. I cannot guess what it would be like to face such a menace without an edge of some sort. The warlock certainly had an edge, but it proved to not be enough or the effectiveness of his choices had simply failed. He paid with his life to buy me time, or perhaps he thought I was dead or dying. After all, it is not every day someone can recover from a sword through the chest. The wound still hurt, but the ability to disconnect from pain was rather helping.

After seeing me fall and bearing witness to what had just crawled out of the depths of whatever dimension that this portal connected to, he must have thought he was the only hope left. I felt bad for him and would certainly tell his story somehow. He died saving Eryn, also. That sacrificed meant we could live. That thought brought his importance to an even greater level. A heavy price was paid.

Whatever he had just done made a mess of the prince and had his attention just long enough. I must have created a shadow. Suddenly the prince spun and threw his right wing up to try to defend. The downward force added to the swing of both blades. Sparks flew as my left blade passed right through the protruding portion of the poison gland. It broke free, spiraling off to the side.

A surprised look crossed his face as my blade cleaved the gland continuing toward his now exposed head. My right blade caught him full in his left eye and sliced clean though to his huge cheek bone. The fluid burst forward like the inside of egg breaking and spilling out. The left blade caught and bit deep in to his forehead, right between his spine ridged eyebrows. His brow split to the bone, which shattered as the top third of the sword passed right through his frontal lobe. More foul fluids erupted.

My blades resonated with glee.

As I dropped further, the right sword sliced the cheek open to the bone, gouging it deeply and possibly through cleanly in some places. The initial impact knocked him back. Giant tracks ran down his face all the way to the bottom, emerging out from the grotesque, bony jaw. Ichor flew everywhere. He staggered backwards even farther. The hope that he was going to actually drop dead from one lucky shot disappeared as he caught himself and regained his balance.

The ground met me hard. My knees slowed the impact as much as they could, but due to fatigue, my balance was off. Rolling over my right shoulder with a left twisting dive to the creatures' right side, I found my feet and went immediately to a defensive stance. Ichor hit the ground near me and the soil smoked immediately. Momentum did its job getting me clear of the black rain

My protections reengaged, hoping for a different outcome. Not a moment too soon, his tremendous sword flashed out in a back handed swing. I barely had time to get both blades up. Even in a wounded state, the momentum hit me hard; both of my own swords struck back against me, allowing him to score a hit in my shoulder. Had my defenses not been on, I had no doubts it would have been worse, or over. Still the bite dug in and without hesitation drained some of my shield away.

I focused hard on restoring it, but the energy was not there. My healing still tried to finish repairing the grievous and mortal wound he had inflicted previously; it would not slow down with a second wound. There was no way the shield could take the brunt of his assaults and allow my body to heal in time. I cursed under my breath and hated making a choice of which one was more important. It was as though Father's voice was in the back of my mind. "Taking resources from one front to reinforce another battle front could cost you the one you take from, but win you the other."

In my mind, I weighed it out. I wounded his face, weakening him. He was crazed; making his threat level was far superior then before. As I dodged a swing of his sword, trying to find an opening with no avail, the reminder of the lethality came back to me.

I was not in good shape at all.

Several swings felt wasted batting and redirecting his blade away from me when the answer revealed itself. A swinging object is most dangerous at the tip because the speed of the weapon is fastest at the end. If I got in close, he could not swing very effectively, but being close to his claws would be less effective for me, too. His wings, if I stayed in front, would have a harder time hitting me.

Off came the shield; my healing boost kicked in again, giving me speed and strength right away. *Still far from full,* I thought while diving around the back of him appearing to be reckless. The tail connected once, but only a slap that knocked me off balance, causing a scraped knee. It started to heal right away, but the impact tore the rest of the fabric from the leg. I laughed. It may have not been much protection, but it was something.

It then dawned on me.

Where were my armored clothes?

How comfortable they were, too! That would have been helpful for this battle. The last time I had seen them was when they created a portal to try to kill me in the hospital. The irony of that moment was not lost on me. Thankfully, my swords had appeared to me when I needed them most.

The huge daemon turned to face me the exact way I had hoped. His blind eye could not track me as I came from his left. As predicted, the left hand led trying to catch me with a back fist to knock me back. He did not know I had hoped he would do this for I was ready. My left blade stuck hard on the side of his wrist and sunk to the hilt. I turned on the energy right as it sunk. The flames burned into the core of the bone, igniting the marrow to a boil.

The right blade came down with precision and severed the hand. He howled. Then he roared so loud…the ground shook, costing me my footing. Around me, the earth acted as though a meteor had struck. Rings of exploding earth shot up around me and out. Dirt, rocks, and other debris hit me everywhere. It got in my mouth but thankfully not my eyes. I coughed and spit while looking for a new angle to attack him. The taste made me sick. The blackened soil was diseased. Filth and vile excretion fell from his body; it destroyed everything it touched. It was not friendly to anything it touched. Now he had me choking on it.

It is hard to explain what I bore witness to just then. His movements became erratic and he staggered like a mechanical object that started and repeatedly stopped, only there were no gears or clockworks visible. Just a spasm-like twitching motion where he would move, then stop for a second, and move again rolled through his body. He was not looking around, nor paying any attention to my tactical position in relation to him.

"We do not trust this!" my blades spoke in but a whisper.

"Nor do I, he is hurt…but not done."

Logic told me that he was done. With each step, his movement became less coordinated. I caught a glimpse of the one good eye, fully dilated. He was not focusing at all…only shaking. The temptation to move in for the kill was overbearing. Yet instinctually, patience told me to hold off and watch. One does not attack an animal when it is in a death throw. A few moments passed while circling. I watched to confirm that he was done. His balance was starting to become an issue; the motions of his feet became labored. Tipping started to become a factor and I was convinced he was going to drop soon. His body twisted like it was going to fall towards me when I caught his eye again.

It gazed right at me.

Only my speed saved me. I brought my shield up in the blink of an eye, and he lunged in, ending his ruse. The attack was brutally fast. A side long dive was my reaction, but not very graceful one for my strength was not itself. I landed several feet away and rolled to my feet, regaining balance. Immediately something caught my eye.

A large book had toppled from some sort of stand. Rune like patterns adorned the front of it, with several geometric symbols. Metal bindings and clasps were present but not fastened. The material covering it looked very unique and made of some sort of hide like leather. A language I recognized but could not read was on the front. The enormity of this tome was not lost on me for it had to be at least two feet tall, eighteen inches or so across and nearly ten inches thick.

Maybe I should throw it at the daemon I chuckled. *I bet that would hurt.*

Legacy of the Defender

The wind to my left alerted me to duck and in doing so the blade I had been trying to avoid missed, but was dangerously close. It slammed the ground making a small crater that showered me with earth; it sparked and arced with blue energy akin to eldridge fire running the length of its blade. It left wisp-like tendrils of itself in the thin air to dance and slowly dissipate for several moments after the blade passed. This energy was also rolling around on the ground where the blade hit. Bugs and worms deep in the soil died crawling out into the small maelstrom, their lives stolen. Energy ran back up the wicked blade. It even jumped up from the ground to meet the sword's tip on several occasions before finally dying out.

I could see eldridge fire wrapping itself around the daemon's arm and making its way to his mighty bicep and shoulder. His skin rejuvenated wherever it touched. The boiled flesh from the magic barrier began to mend and his cheek began to close. I glanced to where the tome was and marked its location. It was time to end this and see to Eryn's safety.

Both hands tingled in anticipation of the vibrational impact from striking a solid object. The memory of hitting rocks with an aluminum bat came to mind. It hurt my hands each time the bat connected with a rock. Many years of training had taught me how to hold a blade just so I maintained a firm grip, but loosely enough so every strike did not resonate through my hands to cause fatigue and damage. The tingles had died down as I moved to reengage, knowing full well to parry would bring more of the same.

The daemon's large destroyed eye was not healing yet, so again I engaged on the side with a bad eye and a missing hand was my best strategy. The small stump was starting to protrude and regrow. Ducking the sword, but not the stump, my movement carried me to that same side. He connected hard, buckling my knees. I was face-down in the soil by the time I realized he had connected with my shield but not my actual flesh. It still hurt but prevented him from contacting my body, making me thankful for my gifts.

I rolled to my left towards him and then to my feet. Inside his guard was where I wanted to be. His sword could not get me there. With everything I had, I knelt and leapt straight up under his chin. Both tips of my blades extended at the last moment before impacting the underside of his jaw...meeting his misshaped, gnarled throat. There was only slight resistance in this less protected area as the blades punctured. They passed through the daemonic skin and flesh to find their mark.

They sank to the hilt.

A spasm rocked his huge form as the hilts stopped as far as they could go. The impact drove his chin up in the air as he staggered backwards, releasing his own blade that clambered to the ground a moment later. Several more steps, more off balance, it began to look like a drunken waltz. I held on tightly to my blades and looked over his shoulder in a rush, barely seeing past his now drooping wings. The daemon prince was stumbling towards the portal, still dozens of feet away. Talons tried to grab ahold of me, but could only enclose around the active barrier that had just saved me moments before.

He tried to squeeze and drive his claws into me. I could feel them pressing against the shield in such a way that it began to collapse. The only way that could happen would be if it was overloaded trying to protect me. His footing failed and over we went. I turned my blades with all I had and opened my arms to drag them across and through the inner parts of his throat. The disgusting gout of ichor flung to each side when we hit the ground, and his hand enclosed on me. Several huge claws found their way into my chest. I screamed. The degree of damage did not register yet, but he punctured my torso, taking my air. My own crimson life slowly flowed down his claws.

Light headed, cracked ribs, and bleeding, I managed to push up from his chest enough to kneel. In doing so, I inadvertently drove one of the claws in deeper into my back, causing pain which made me black out. I awoke on my side, fallen from his grasp and lying on one of the nasty leathering wings. My skin was on fire from that acrid powder residing there. It covered a large portion of my body and stuck to me with my own blood, sweat, and other daemonic fluids acquired in the last several minutes.

It burned.

Finding my feet was no small effort, but I managed to roll off the giant bat-like wing. Sickness washed over me and vomit followed. My protection was off, so my focus turned to healing, but there was no response. Everything inside was depleted and a horrible realization hit me. The portal was not only open but large hands reached through, bigger than the one lying on the ground at my feet. Panic washed over me. They tried to grab ahold of the special fabric around the portal but could not secure a hand hold. My head shook in disbelief, having witnessed this today. Uncertainty of whether another battle was possible in my condition flooded over me and despair took hold. It was not a matter of training at this point, but sheer will power. My knees gave out and I was down again before any decisions on the matter formed.

Air escaped from my chest. Flowing blood mixed with small air bubbles made it frothy and thick. I saw this kind of wound in the campfire runes so long ago. For a second, I remembered my teacher, bringing a faint smile amidst the chaos of combat. Glancing at the flow running down my skin, the pace was showing signs of slowing, which meant coagulation, but that did not solve drowning in my own blood.

My eyelids felt heavy, so heavy, and I just wanted to sleep. Breathing was laborious. Each draw caused shooting pains. They were the only thing keeping me conscious. Those large clawed hands continued reaching though and trying to gain access to my world. I was the only one that could stand toe to toe with whatever wanted through. My mind could not fathom the irony that getting this far only to fail was the plan, and I definitely believed in plans.

My imagination raced. How many sons of Lucifer could there possible be? I prayed only one. *Wait...* prayer. I looked up and offered a blessing to God, and although speech was not possible at the time, the words ever present in my mind were simply, "Thank you." Slight warmth encapsulated me for a moment...perhaps it was a blessing of healing, but it left a moment later. I felt cold due to fatigue and blood loss. Laughter wracked me with more pain. My clothes were gone...naked as my birthday.

Talk about being humble.

A few moments passed. The hands did not find a grip on the portal and a displeasured voice come from beyond, which chilled me to the bones. The language was guttural and very much like that of those before. It said one phrase.

"You will pay."

A roar ensued. The hands found a way to grab on and the portal started to throb as if being torn open. I could actually see fractures forming. Small pieces of material fell to the ground while some dissipated. Tendons, bigger than those of the monster I had fought, flexed in exertion. More of it collapsed but it fell inward this time. Only one thing ran through my mind: "Not again!"

Failure was not an option. A single memory, like a Minotaur in a ceramic shop, pushed its way to the front of my mind, crushing everything else that had been a concern up to that point. Large panes of glass formed in my mind that held a memory or feelings of affinity or affections that were in my foremost thoughts.

My eyes fell to Eryn where she lay on the ground behind me. She looked helpless now but had a strength that astonished me. I wondered if she would be okay but could not move to look. She had such tenderness about her that I loved and needed so much to have her love in return. The thought of never being able to hold her again drove me to look over that cliff of instant insanity for just a moment. I felt the desire to leap off of it, especially considering I might have failed my love.

Memories of my teacher lingered, how he died saving me. In reality, his death is what made me the man I was. I thought of him lying on the make shift alter where they had killed him to open the portal. He was part of

God...*the* God...who gave his life for me to survive by throwing me over a hill while he called down fires from Heaven. I thought of how they removed his finger and stuck it in an amulet which empowered the foe I had just slain. This weakened Heaven so the horde could breach its sacred walls. Right as I looked at this memory, a thought came crashing to the front, smashing all of the others. That moment destroyed everything I loved up to that point. I was on my feet without even realizing it. My fists clenched and an empowerment of rage coursed through me. I wanted to slay every one of these daemons and send them back to Lucifer in a container for him to choke on.

"Close the portal!" my swords yelled silently in my thoughts.

A voice, my voice rang out to the now destroyed glade.

"Close the portal!" they said aloud. Their voice did not sound soft and supportive, but commanding.

Again, I heard it.

Clarity came over me. My eyes focused on the now gaping hole that had one foot stepping on the bottom portion trying to force down while lifting with its hands. Time was up. Inside my mind, those precious shards of my memories came back together like a large puzzle, pieced together by some inner form of me. I almost laughed when a dejected image that I looked like as a teenager sat there, putting each broken piece back in place...but the picture was reforming. The dawning of a new age in my life was upon me.

Like one of my many projects and things I used to build, this one meant something more to me than anything. It was all happening in rapid pace; the last piece went into place. There was an image of Eryn. She was smiling at me. It was the day in the park when I gave her a flower and she was absolutely glowing. I felt like the luckiest man in the world that day. It hit me as the last piece affixed to the rest. She was my heart. My skills may be able to kill monsters and slay daemons for God and to save the world, but in the end, my heart needed her. She needed me now more than ever.

From my depleted depths, tendrils of energy shot from all parts of my body. A burst of energy left me and shot towards the portal. Latching on the areas that flapped in the breeze, this mental image of them stretched and reattached to the other side formed, just like wrapping a present. This filled my thoughts. My energy grabbed a hold of the portal and began to fold its sides down. The giant hands tore and clawed to no avail. A verbal outburst told me there was success. I smiled and continued to crush this portal down, and each fold gave confirmation because the icky sensation faded gradually. The portal was about a third of the way closed when the body of the prince rose from the ground. It floated toward the opening as if something was levitating it. I did a double take, for its head was that of a large unicorn. I almost could not believe what it looked like. The myth was true. Somehow he masked his true self. I guess we all have things we hide. As the body got closer, things got worse.

The ichor expunged from every possible wound on it as the body collapsed into a dried husk. Suspended right in the air its blood transformed into energy. The particles broke down and faded to a neutral color. The color went translucent save for the small jumps of energy that occasionally occurred before fading all together. Suddenly eldridge fire engulfed the clear mass as it floated towards the collapsing portal; it was as though this blood energy had tendrils of its own and began to grab the edges of the torn fabric.

Then it started to pull it apart.

Fighting with all my might I tried to counter it. My inner core of energy reserve collapsed inside me, and my own connection to the portal fractured and broke free. Trying to reestablish it was not working as my mind kept reaching out to grab it again and it felt as if it slapped my hand away. Maniacal laughter echoed through the glade. The air started to move towards the opening and began to interact with the portal like before when it was opening.

Then it happened. The silence before the storm simply vanished. Starting right at the portal, dirt vibrated on the ground breaking free then slowly moved towards it. Bodies of coven members began to slide before the suction took them and pulled them towards the portal. The bodies, like the big one before, flattened with a sickening, suction sound, as the red blood extracted. It had coalesced in a huge cloud of crimson before it flew apart, shedding its color and becoming raw energy. With each coven member's floating corpse, this process repeated, the blood coalesced from each. This energy shot toward the portal.

Everything here began to move.

A vacuum...It was time to go.

This area had a barrier around it that had kept prying eyes out and unwanted guests from entering. I had to rely on that barrier keeping whatever was here contained while I got Eryn clear. It had to hold. My thoughts turned towards getting that tome then on to my love. Turning back towards

Eryn, I ran. The air tore at my flesh, trying to take me with it towards this maelstrom of death about to consume everything here.

The vacuum reached where the large tome was. The stand it fell from lay near it and started to roll towards me. I leapt over it, feeling the suction grab a hold of me for a moment before my feet touched down again. Steps became difficult. All around me bodies rose up and moved towards the rift. One caught my eyes in particular and made me stumble for a moment. The face of the priests that tried to kill me months ago had just floated by wearing the robes of one of the Coven. I heard the coven leader mention names of all three, but I never a good look at him. My focused stayed on her at the time.

Anger rose.

It made no sense. One question hit me as I reached for the book. *Why would this group want me dead if they needed me here now?* I promised myself better answers to this quandary later and perhaps this book had some. It was a lot heavier than it looked and felt icky in my hands. Not having any clothes, I put it under my right arm...using the three of my appendages to claw my way forward. The ground shook harder. More topsoil came free in large sections. I could see the path behind Erin's form lost all its leaves. Even the light was bending towards the rift... just like a black hole.

Oh God! No!

A surge propelled me forward as if by an unseen hand. On the ground in front of me was the mangled body of the wizard that offered his assistance. He was a mess. Most of his torso was torn open but his heart and lungs, although exposed, were functioning. A look of shock must have betrayed my thoughts for he said to me without even moving his lips.

"I got this. Remember me...Sigvard is my name."

Pain stabbed me in the heart over his majestic sacrifice as my momentum carried me passed him. Scooping up Eryn, I clutched her using her using the tome to hold her in place. The winds tore at me filled with the dirt and debris. It was like being sand blasted. Particles embedded themselves into my skin pealing it away. I knew I could take it, but she could not. The book shielded her from some of it when thoughts of protection from the elements came to mind. Debris sliced at both of us. To my surprise a small version of my shield appeared. It began to drain my life to maintain it. My thoughts did not even think to question where this came from, but a thank you was a secondary thought.

Each step was harder than the last. It was difficult to find the way out. Strong winds still made it hard to keep my eyes open. The location of the path leading out was a mystery. My senses through my blades required me to be holding them, but my surroundings channeled through them when they chose to share. Occasionally I had to open them to peek. Faint light ahead aided me in finding the path now strangely lit, filled with bending light heading towards the portal. I passed the car we came in. The glass was already missing and the seats were starting to rip apart. Tires blew out right as we went by and it began to slide forward. Metal groaned in protest. The maelstrom of intensity finally forced my eyes closed, for even though the particles could not get through, the air dried them out. Blindly moving forward, my feet managed toward the direction we came in. I did not even know if we could get out. Air came through so there had to be a way.

A bright light appeared before me. Around the entrance, images cast from this source illuminated a fabric like illusion disguised like woods. It contained this area were the coven practiced their ways in secret. With them gone, the magic weakened. Trees threatened to uproot, creaking in protest as smaller limbs snapped and disappeared behind. Ripples rolled across the opaque protective barrier like waves as the stresses on this side taxed the magic that it contained inside here. It looked like what my mind imagined being inside a hot air balloon at night with spotlights out the outside. It flexed just like a container does when you suck the air out of it and it starts to collapse inwards. The tension made it quiver. It was clear, the covens dimensional haven was about to collapse.

I stumbled forward.

Blinding light hit me in the eye and pouring rain thundered. Internal reserves finally depleted and my strength gave out as my foot found pavement before I could even see it. The driving rain felt good as it washed the grime off me from untold places. As my body pitched forward, I managed to hold onto Eryn. We fell and rolled. The tome landed hard on the ground and skidded off somewhere. Ahead a car door opened and closed. Footsteps ran towards us. Not knowing what was about to happen I tried to get up but could not. We made it outside. I glanced again towards the barrier and saw the light upon it blinked out for a second as a figure moved into the light, blocking it for a moment. A shadow of a man cast upon that surface and then I felt hands on me pulling me up.

"Happy to see me?" the voice said. I recognized it instantly.

"We need to go now!" I yelled over the rain. "I need to find that...."

"You mean this?" A sly grin scrawled across the Sergeant's face as he raised the large home up. "Can you carry her?"

"Yes, forever." The words came and I knew at that moment, it was a lie. Tremendous fatigue had already won and I struggled to catch myself. "You better grab her." The world spun faster.

"How could a mighty warrior be so vulnerable?" I thought.

I had all my memories. My training and knowledge would dwarf most army generals. Yet my body was still subject to damage...just like a human, even one with an angel for a father. As I looked back towards the barrier while handing Eryn into his arms, a slight twinge of pain ran across my heart. The ripples in the surface flexed and I could see the integrity of it was about to fail. I turned to yell to the Sergeant to get her in the car when I felt my ear drums pop.

No one was safe until this was over.

XXXVII

Unity

The containment burst like a star going super nova.

A brilliant flash of light moved so fast that the human eye could probably not detect it except in hindsight or perhaps as a revelation in a dream. The rainbow spectrum of colors formed patters and runes for only a fraction of a second. That was the only warning I had and no time to react. For in that moment an object of scientific horror came into existence in the dimensional pocket we had just left, and it died within the same time span.

My face impacted the hood of the car with perfect accuracy to leave a facial imprint. Gravity shifted to behind me instead of below, but instead of flaying backward, it swept my feet towards it first. It was more of an insult to injury in my eyes because the daemon hit a lot harder. The winds shifted as if a hole suddenly opened into a vacuum chamber, sucking everything into a void. This is probably what it would feel like to be in a ship decompressing in the darkness of space.

An image flashed of a bubble popping and showering the area for micro seconds with the rainbow effects visible in the soapy opaqueness. Weightlessness took me up and away. I had nothing. No strength nor energy could help when I was not in control of my motions since all my abilities helped me defy the physics set in place to govern a planet or realm. Gravity had me in its claws just like where I had been when killing the daemon; only this time, the foe could not be defeated with steel or tactical maneuvering.

Mercy would play no role here.

The items before me began to peel away only to fly with me. Pavement, grass, and the earth itself erupted from its place for centuries taking trees out by the roots. Nothing was safe form my vantage point. The wizard Sigvard had bought us time... perhaps his actions slowed the inevitability of what just happened. I felt sorry for him dying the way he did. First he got his entrails introduced to the light of day by a large clawed foot. That was no way to die. Yet he survived long enough for gravity to rip him apart.

Suddenly it hit me. The wizard had all the time he needed because he was in the middle of it; he just had to survive long enough to do whatever he was about to do. Hours if not days could have already passed out here and with him inside based on my little knowledge of black holes, he has not had time to finish his incantation. I based my theory on the idea that he was still alive. I had to trust that he would finish what he started. That bore to mind one thought, however. What would happen out here if he was still finishing his spell and it took a day?

Changing my thoughts to survival, I looked behind me. Not enough debris was in the air to block vision. Light started to dim slowly. My vision was bending and blurring in slow motion. Yet my mind functioned normally, and my awareness of time still stayed the same. Only its flow around me changed. Like everything else I had no idea how much time had passed.

A thought hit me when closing my eyes to combat the effects of nausea starting to form in my core. I decided to use this time to relax and stop fighting the storm. My mind centered on myself, and pulled the conglomeration of the events of the day into one cohesive thought and began to file it away. Inside my mind was the answer I needed save myself. If the Sergeant managed to get Eryn to safety, then all was not lost.

Guilt filled my thoughts, not over concern for me but for being more worried about Eryn than humanity. Mankind was my responsibility. The issues at hand were larger than the sum of my and Eryn's life together. From this point forward, my thoughts included everyone's safety. Perhaps this was why angels had to prove themselves before they could take a mate...it was not because they were denied love, but because their duty was just as important. This journey was about keeping my oath as well as my family on equal footing.

Somber reflection took its hold as I focused on my breathing. My energies slowly crept out from my core to the tips of my fingers. The flow was so slow that I wondered how many years of my life fell away. How much of the depletion would be permanent? All this hinged on surviving this event, of course. My thoughts turned towards trying to turn on my healing and to my surprise, it came on. The warmth spread through me, pulsating as it flowed. My tired bones felt leeched of the core essence that empowered me. Only when I stopped fighting did it re-emerge to assess and reverse the damage done by overtaxing myself. I knew it would take time. Right now time around me slowed, but to my amazement, my conscious thought was unaffected, as if anything that went on beneath my skin remained unaffected by the effects of time.

My thoughts kept me company. With the ability to mull them over, it felt like this time was not a total waste. Hope that Sigvard, with his arcane abilities could deliver was starting to weigh heavily on me. If he did not, imagination ran amuck with the level of the devastation that would occur before the dimensional pocket collapsed and severed its connection to this world...to my world, which I was responsible for now. Focus on such things would only add to the stress of the situation. Eryn was with the Sergeant and trust, as minimal as it was, did fall to believing in the badge he wore, not in the appearance of his bad suits.

He did give off a "protect-and-serve" vibe. Perhaps my mistrust stemmed from his punching me in the face many weeks ago.

Why was S.W.A.T. at a hospital when I awoke? The randomness of this thought hit me but did not follow the thought process to its extent before I came back to the now.

To a have a total memory influx of gargantuan proportions in the middle of an epic fight that happened to be the catalyst of those returned memories has its own complications. I do not know the exact amount of time that passed in the other realm, but Father told me it was significantly longer than the time I spent in my coma. Six years to the day seems trivial. I know I had a physical body there and that it really was not just a spirit realm. There were all the same things to worry about there as there were here. Eating and sleeping were such a small part of the dynamic because surviving was a combination of everything.

In my wildest imagination, I could never imagine my dreams were memories.

I had all these skills and none of them fully prepared me because my mind was not in unity. Had my mind, body, and spirit been one, the outcome of today would have been different. I paused. The life I knew now was a series of tests...one leading to the next and each progressively getting harder. Perhaps that is the never-ending challenge. Maybe the steady progression is why life flows the way it does. A constant challenge to defeat or resolve greater problems; this keeps the mind moving forward and always sharp.

Clarity stuck.

A true warrior is always making his own way and seeking his own path so subconsciously, I have been taking the harder road all this time, not because I have to, but because it made me a better fighter. Lack of learning makes one stagnant, and stagnation is the killer. The feeling that rolled through my mind was applause like I heard it from the firm hands of my master. Trials do not have to be exponentially tougher, but if you have no reflection from the last engagement to seek out better results through better decision making, then you cannot streamline and improve the process. The trick is you have to keep the mind challenged, not simply seek a tougher opponent. Eventually, your path will take you to the pinnacle of your career as a warrior. You either live or die.

My job was to stay ahead of the attempts the horde made to gain access to Earth and this was certainly one of them. Right now more daemons could be coming through and I was not in a position to act. Physical movement was just not possible. Calling my swords would not help. My options seemed to be limited when it hit me. If I could have slapped myself, I would have.

I could teleport.

Laughter ensued inside.

The acceptance that this was who I was finally hit home with no more questions, other than knowing how continue my studies every day to be the best Defender possible. My thoughts relished in the Zen moment of it all. Doubtful that my enemy could overcome physics, the very laws set in place from the beginning of time were constant. The energy and skill it would take for the horde to get at me while gravity held me would be monumental. The exception being...I could get out.

Healing finished its job.

More laughter. "Yes Tathlyn...you can teleport," they chimed. "There is no point in slapping yourself now."

It was time to open my mind the rest of the way to the possibilities because all that I had seen should not exist according to man's calculations. They always fall short of realizing that life has no limits, and God did not limit man. My skills came from his training. The runes were simply a reminder that my abilities developed by my teacher were part of me. They had to start the process by building the runic network inside of me. I was not invincible or unstoppable by any stretch of the imagination. I was formidable. Did Malnuras and Father know the outcome of my decisions? Is my path preordained? Not that it mattered if I was predictable to my father. Making him proud did rank high in my priorities.

It was time to get out of here.

The energy inside of me reached its crescendo. I visualized the road behind the car in my head even though only part of it was even visible, hoping that this dilation field did not reach the car yet or expand too far so I would not appear back inside of it. A wave of nausea rolled through me as perception began to warp...dizziness ensued. The hold that space and time distortion had on me did not want to let go at first. I did not move for several moments internally. A strained sensation inside my mind made the blood in my head pound with each beat of my heart, and I realized that my shield was up fully the entire time. Knowing full well that I could not teleport with it off, the risk would be great. Prayer for guidance came to mind, but the answer was inside of me. The stresses about to tear at me would try to tear me apart so I would have to overtax myself to start the process with my shield up and drop it at the last minute. Without a choice, I started to build up further.

At first the vision was minimal, like holding back a dog when it was trying to run away. As the pressure built, it became like trying to pin a man in a wrestling match. It took some skill, but it was possible. You might not get away without a few scrapes, but you were not always worse for the wear. I felt like my eyes were leaking tears but realized it was blood, for my vision turned red.

The vision turned into trying to wrestle a bull without a rope and one hand tied behind my back. I was having difficulty grabbing a hold of it at the beginning. My hand kept losing grip as it was trying to toss me aside. Determination finally won out when I grabbed a hold of its head and threw my legs around the great neck. Death would be the only thing prying me from this. It bucked and slammed me into everything possible, trying to break me free, but I prevailed and hung on. It felt like blood was running down my throat now.

Something inside my mind snapped.

Suddenly I was in front of a car with my hands on the hood. Its tires spun on the pavement and great clouds of black smoke rolled off the rear of the car. The noise sounded like it was ripping the black top up, and the road was protesting the grievous wound and crying out. Bucking wildly back and forth, the rear end of the car was practically bouncing, and as it came down the pressure against me increased. My hands began to crush into the car. The hood crumpled around them. I pushed with tremendous force to break the car free and before I knew it the nose of the car caved in. My hands and arms went into the fan which promptly shredded them...breaking the fan in the process. The pressure in my head burst. Pain exploded in my eyes. They felt on fire.

Something changed. The pressure subsided.

"It is done," a voice in my head declared all distorted. It was not my swords speaking to me, but based off the phrasing it was the wizard finishing his task.

As I fell into blackness, hands caught me.

I recognized the feeling. Soft and gentle the sensation was as they cradled my head. Voices unclear called to me in muffle tones. A second set of hands grabbed a hold of me firmly, surprising me at how strong they were. They guided me into a back seat of a vehicle. I crawled in. The car did not lower any.

More muffled voices.

I focused on turning my healing on and was thankful it responded so quickly. Within minutes I watched the red retreat from my eyes – a welcome sight greeted me. Eryn sat in the front seat holding onto my now healed hand. Her lips moved and slowly noises turned into words. She was crying and smiling as she spoke.

"Time...you better...that...sense...."

I smiled at her and tried not to look like a dog with water in its ears. The road flew by as the car traveled at a high rate of speed. I looked behind me still not hearing everything she said. A cataclysmic sight unfolded behind me as trees uprooted and flew the direction from which we came. Cars, houses, and fences all broke apart and got sucked towards the place we had just been. People hid in their homes as they broke apart around them and flew helplessly toward the vortex. The winds outside howled as the car cut through it. I looked back at Eryn. She was screaming and hitting my arm.

"What...in…were...make...alive...they...it...natu...."

The wind increased. Its force buffeted the car heavily. The Sergeant evaded flying debris as best he could. Much of it hit the car and some of it even cracked the windows. It occasionally felt like the tires lost grip on the road when the car maneuvered around something toppling towards us. Several impacts happened that I swore were going to flip us. Eryn was terrified. I was sick over the loss of human life all around me.

"How...you...we...it...taken...survived...you...truly...touched by...must like...very much...hear...now? You...this? we...to...die." The sentences were not making sense so I reached out and touched my chest and then touched her on the forehead. She nestled her face in my hand and closed her eyes, her face shrouded in fear. Finally, the missing pieces filled in. I could hear again.

"Tathlyn are you...you had us really worried...happened in there?

Things moved as if in a dream, slowly, yet horrifically. I stared, still dazed.

"You're going to have to wait a few more minutes," I did my best to say; very sure it sounded like some degenerative disease had taken root in my brain. The wind lessened a little but objects toppled towards the gravity well behind us. I remembered hearing that term in a science fiction movie but could not remember which one.

As if by magic, the forces pulling on the car subsided like it broke free of a magnet. Glancing behind I could see everything sucking into a giant cloud that rippled with energy. Several moments passed as I watched. Eryn stopped crying and looked behind. Only the occasional sniffle found my ears over the roar of the engine. Winds diminished. Debris fell to the ground just like watching a tornado dissipate; the only difference was there was not much of a debris pile. The ground past a certain point was a crater.

"What happened in there Tathlyn?" The inquisitive tone came from the Sergeant. Silence held my tongue, not sure where to start. The truth was too unimaginative to speak of, yet something told me not to lie to him. I decided to go a different route. I did not know I could fully trust him with it all so I summoned a sword to my hand as I spoke.

"Hold your hand up."

"Why?"

"Do you trust me since I am letting you into aspects of my life that may satisfy some of your questions?" I asked.

"Tathlyn what are you doing?" Eryn protested...her eyes curious, as she did not know where I was going with this. She looked at the sword tip dipped just below the seat and barely out of sight.

"Hold up your left hand and do not turn around," I said to the Sergeant and waited. He sighed and did so but more so out of not wanting to press the issue. Eryn watched as the sword drew a line in the meat of his palm. He yelped slightly and did not pull his hand back. A small crimson line ran its way down and dropped off his hand.

"Do you swear to me that your intentions to me are genuine and that you will never betray me, on your life, for you know full well I can kill you at any time?" His chuckle caught me off guard, but his head nodded with a sigh.

"Yes, Tathlyn, I will not betray you. Now, what in the heavens happened in there? Did an anti-gravity bomb go off or what?" His sentence ended and silence hung in the car as if it was a phone commercial for long distance.

"Then I have a story to tell you." Eryn looked over at him. She had a curious look on her face and her brow furrowed slightly. She shook her head and looked at me. At first I did not catch that she was trying to get my attention. The car stopped around back of a house and she was acting very weird with her expression as if she was trying to say something. After another few seconds, she finally spoke.

"Tathlyn, he is hiding something." The Sergeant stepped out of the car and opened my door. In doing so, he poked his head through the window. Eryn looked at me as I was backing out of the car in a crawling fashion. She was worried.

"It is okay. We will be safe," he said.

She hesitated but removed her seat belt and opened the door. Joining me around the drivers' side on the side walk, she glanced behind us. Trees cut part of the view out but also hid the back yard from a lot of prying eyes even in a slightly urban environment. Several miles away a large cloud of dust rose up. I took her head in my hands and kissed her gently. She trembled for a moment then relaxed.

"Let us go inside where we can talk." A sudden ease settled over me as I stepped towards the door of the house and crossed from chaos to calm. I glanced at him waiting a few feet up. "We need to get you inside because you *really* are naked." The stress on the last word "really" made me look down in confusion.

I was still without clothes.

XXXVIII

Catalyst

This day keeps getting better.

I walked in the house not sure what to expect. It was the first time there were any good vibes between Sergeant Rick and me. A short time ago, we stood in Eryn's house and he saw my ability to heal. Trust was a hard word to use. He passed a test that day and told me to keep my head down. His appearance was not just odd, but peculiar.

His house was rather sparse and was void of any real furniture. Some strange pillows adorned the floor with a low table, and I would have felt funny sitting there naked. I stood just inside the door and waited until he checked outside one last time. Caution was fine by me.

Eryn made a wash room request and was already half way down a short hall by the time I made any observations. I looked down at my body for the first time, watched the runes slowly rotate, and pulse. It was like watching a painter change his mind in the middle of a painting; each rune would form then shift to another one. The raised scar tissue was gone where the runes moved. I deduced my mind knew where they belonged and re-sponded with some sort of mark. The hypnotic patterns drew me in easily. All those memories tried hard to remind me of who I was. It is amazing it took seeing Amduscias.

I needed to take it easy right now for a few minutes. A glance up at the wall caught my eyes.

There were paintings on the walls. The theme surprised me, for there were lots of pictures of mystical creatures and some of the angels watching over mankind. I looked closer and, to my surprise, the armor on the angels was highly accurate, right down to the cloak I had seen in Heaven. Closer examination brought my weapons to my hands for the angels were standing on a solid gold wall. In the background, there was a portal...with a very large man in front of it. Daemons flowed through the opening and the man and the angels cut them down.

Something in the room changed.

"Do not be alarmed," a soothing voice came from behind me. I spun around quickly to find no one. My eyes panned the room. The voice had a distinctive sound. One heard before but in another place. I suddenly felt less threatened and lowered my blades. An angel materialized before me in all of her splendor, fully armored and just as beautiful as I remembered them to be. She offered me a nod. "My lord, please forgive the secrecy over the last few months. I feel bad for misleading you this entire time." My jaw dropped. Not from the recognition of her face but at the words she spoke. I looked around the room then back to her.

"Where is the Sergeant, and why does he have these paintings? Did you tell him of this event?" She smiled. I heard Eryn coming down from the hall.

"Hey Sergeant, whoever your lady friend is could you tell her I had to borrow some...." She froze as she walked into the room. Her eyes beheld the majestic beauty of an angel. White and blue wings were in full view tucked neatly on her back. The beautiful craftsmanship of the armor radiated light. The golden hair fell to her shoulders as if there had never been a hair out of place. Her gaze fell to me, and she just stared. Eryn stood transfixed.

"Would you like to tell me how you got that picture and where the Sergeant is?" Again the smile.

"Tathlyn...she *is* the Sergeant," Eryn whispered, barely audible and full of awe. She could not take her eyes off the angel and she walked slowly forward to gaze up at the majestic being towering over her close to my height. Eryn did not speak a word... she simply hugged her. Laughter rolled from my mouth at the sight of this. I was sure it looked even funnier to them for me to be standing there naked.

"As I was saying, please forgive the web of deceit I had to weave to help guide you on your journey. I imagine you have hundreds of questions, but first let us get some food. I am famished. Allow me to change back to something less shocking."

There was no flash or dazzling; she shifted back to the form of the Sergeant and motioned us into the kitchen. Her hand waived and the table filled with food. A bundled item wrapped in burlap sat on the table chair closest to the door. She walked over and picked it up.

"But first, here are your clothes," she said.

"My clothes...you mean? How did you get those?"

She raised an eye brow as if she was saying, "Are you really going to doubt me now?" I walked over thinking that she would be handing me a set of my big clothes from Eryn's house. As I undid the brown twine, a feeling of familiarity came over me and the desire to get into the wrapping was just like a present. With two fingers the twine snapped. The burlap fell away to reveal something I had just been thinking about a short time ago. My armor was a gift from my teacher. It looked brand new. My loin cloth worn for all those years that I washed by hand several times a week was even there. I held up the shirt admiring it as if it was new to me.

Eryn was at my side looking. Her eyes were still wide with amazement while she munched on some carrots. She was looking at the material and got lost in the pattern. She reached out and touched it, not saying anything. I stood there and let her look for a few minutes while she touched the foreign material, a mesmerized look on her face as she processed.

After a few moments, I leaned over, "Let me go put my clothes on so we can talk. I'll be just a moment." I left, finding the bathroom. It was apparent how the bathroom gave away that a woman lived here. It was full of fluffy things that gave definite proof of a lady's presence. The towels were all matching and fresh. There were little soaps on the counter in a bowel. It was obvious she did not need to wear real clothes because she seemed to be able to change her appearance, and the armor seemed to come and go on command, like my swords.

While dressing, the conversation was easy enough to follow.

"Are you really an angel or is it some sort of illusion?" Eryn's voice said audible through the door.

"I am an angel."

"Why pose as a man. I mean…why not just be you without wings?" There was a pause. I re-entered the room right at the end of the silence when the "Sergeant" began to reply.

""My real name is Celuine. I have been here for about five earth years." She turned towards me. "My job was to help trigger your memories, Tathlyn. Establishing myself as a police officer, I watched over you. It made sense to join the police and eventually S.W.A.T. to prepare some men in the event we needed help. An information leak allowed the church to send someone to be there to watch you when it was not possible for me to be there. In time, I learned that someone within the church had taken a personal interest in you, and I traced the story back to a priest with a twin brother who was part of the Wiccan Coven. He began to siphon information from his brother."

"I spent years putting out that fire and burying your unique problem under a mound of paperwork when I learned they were planning something. They wanted to use the energy to create a psychic battery for their project. I thought that they were trying to tap into higher levels of magic at first...then whispers in the covens suggested they wanted to create a gateway back to Salem. The time right before the witch trials...to change the tide and if that was successful then the Spanish Inquisition was the next target. They were so dedicated they did not care how it affected time. Essentially time travel seemed to be silly as an attempt but they were supposedly going to try. The priest that tried to kill you was the Wiccan brother. He had already killed his own brother to take his place at the hospital when you were to wake from your coma. They knew the day of your return. His intent was not to kill you but to trigger the change that would increase your power. They were going grab you after the funeral."

"Somehow they knew that cyanide would not kill you, but it technically did. So they could not take you from the graveyard. My direct involvement started with being there waiting for you to awaken in the morgue where I put you while your body grew. I had to keep you sedated with substances that you would not be able to find nor understand here on this planet. I kept S.W.A.T close on maneuvers in case the coven made a move to try to grab you. I did not plan on you taking out trained officers that easily, so I had to make it look believable when you were apprehended."

"I thought you might actually hide away at Eryn's, but instead you started going for runs in the park and saving young mothers from certain death. It did not occur to me that you would confide in me if I started leaning on you about what was going on, and I had hoped that the Coven would lose track of you. A tracking device put on Eryn's car reported to me her whereabouts but was set to notify me if you came near this address. By the time I got here it was too late. I was unable to enter, but I ran into that wizard outside. They kicked him out of the coven, but he still kept tabs on them. Apparently he disagreed with their goals."

"They made contact with daemons that tricked them into opening a portal so they could mount a full invasion force. Daemons told them to lure you here and use your power to open a portal. You walked right in the front door and handed yourself to them before you were ready. They knew when and where you would be there so they started the ritual knowing the exact moment of your arrival. It is all in that tome. I glanced while waiting for you to free yourself."

It was my turn to raise an eyebrow. This all fit together way too nice, for it not to be true. Had I known, I would have not gone there. This event is what triggered my memory and brought me to unity. Had Celuine not helped me change, things would have been much worse. I looked over at her standing there stoic but in her Sergeant form. There was no expression on her face as she spoke. It was all factual. Emotions did not burden angels, but a struggle was apparent.

"It appears I owe you my life in spite of all the underhanded efforts."

She shook her head and a hint of the emotion came through. I looked at Eryn. Her eyes fixed on me. She was unconscious inside the glade before the attack happened, and I could feel the questions inside her growing, but she remained silent. She was a sponge right now. After a moment of silence or two, I looked at Celuine. This affected her. I did not know why.

Eryn Finally broke her Silence. She looked right at me and had a very quizzical look on her face. I had no idea what she was thinking when she finally spoke. I did not even think to discuss what what happened in the glade, but realized that the unanswered question was in the room now.

"So what happened in there Tathlyn?" she probed, a very stern look in her eye, like I had dragged her into something.

"Well, the ceremony was in full swing when we walked in. They did something to us which knocked you out but held me in place. They drained my life force through my blood, to power their spell to open a portal on this side while I could not move. That explained why I was so weak and had difficulties recovering. I was low on blood. I did not even know that is what they were doing."

"When the portal came into existence, they had a coven member ready to leave," Celuine interjected. "That's in the book, too."

"When the portal opened, a swarm of daemons poured through. I could not move until the daemons killed the three creatures subduing me, so I could defend you. That is when the ex-Wiccan member Sigvard came in and shielded you while I started killing daemons."

"With the swords you can summon?" Eryn asked.

"Yes. I did not have this armor, though, which would have helped in that last fight."

Eryn nodded. She was following quite well.

"I was killing the daemons as they poured through but not fast enough. My memory still held me back for it did not return yet, so I had no idea I could close that portal. I just knew it needed to be done somehow."

"You can do that?"

"Yes, it is part of my skill set. I fought and killed Amduscias when entered the area, but he gravely wounded me. He almost won." Celuine's eyes widened. She lost all composure and shifted back to her angelic form.

"Wait...you killed Amduscias?" she added with clear emotion in her voice now. Her head shook in disbelief.

"Who is that?" Eryn asked.

"Lucifer's son," I responded looking her in the eyes.

"Not just Lucifer's son. He was a high level daemon," said Celuine.

"*Thee* Lucifer?" she said.

"Yes. He was about twenty feet tall with a wingspan about twice as wide. He was very formidable. I have faced him twice. Each time he has technically killed me." Eryn's face went white. The mental and emotional impact of hearing this had to be hard. She started to shake and I placed my arm around her until she stopped, trying to soothe her. "When he died, his head changed to its original form...A unicorn head. It was rather disturbing."

"That is disturbing indeed," commented Celuine. My comment about the daemon prince's head went right over Eryn's head.

"So you have died three times then?" she finally asked with a sad look on her face. I did not respond right away and she looked right at me. "How many?"

"Four that I can remember." Her head shook in disbelief. I stopped and just held her. Celuine looked at me patiently and waited for me to continue. It took a moment for the words to sink in before she sighed.

"I fought the daemon prince to a standstill on the first exchange. The second part of that fight, he pulled a move that impaled me and gloated as I was dying. The Wiccan outcast got the daemon's attention long enough for me to heal. I reengaged the daemon prince but not before he took the outcast down. We then fought for several more minutes. He managed to poison me at some point, and I cut off one of his poison glands."

"After a ruse that he was done, he almost beat me, but my skill and tactics won out. I felled him. Then something even bigger tried to come through. I was unable to close the portal, but it could not get through either. Whatever it was told me I would pay and then the portal changed into a black hole."

"Here on earth? How is that possible?" asked Eryn.

"It did not happen here because that place was a dimensional pocket.

The Wiccan's removed their holy place from the Earth for the ritual, but the daemons did not know this so when they sprung the trap and the portal opened, it was not Earth. The portal would not function properly and essentially got stuck," Celuine said.

"How do you know that?" I asked.

"I studied portals centuries ago. They do not work properly in dimensional pockets. They are not stable," she replied. "You also would not be able to close one in a dimensional pocket because you have not learned that yet."

I laughed. I believed I was prepared. Suddenly my confidence turned to amazement because my training shortened by the attack on our camp, but also my first attempt had failed in training long ago. It was lucky that we averted disaster.

"At that point it was about getting out with you. The gravity pull was immense and we barely made it out. The Wizard was not dead. I found him eviscerated on the ground on the way out, holding his insides together by magic. He said he had it. Funny he kept using that phrase. You know the rest."

Moments passed and Eryn and Celuine sat there looking at each other, eating silently. One more important question came to mind but not wanting to overload the situation, I waited.

"Celuine, how do you know about the fight in Heaven since you were here?" She looked at me, with slight surprise I asked in front of Eryn. I wanted her to know everything. She had to realize that as much as I loved her, the planet needed defending. Celuine sat there. Her hesitation was unclear. So we waited.

"I was called back. The ability to move back and forth is part of being an angel. Your teleportation works only in the realm in which you are standing. With training, you can bridge worlds. My father can speak to me telepathically, so he called me home to help defend."

"You mean God?"

"No. Mathias, your Master." That admittedly caught me by surprise. I smiled.

"You mean our father?" Her Jaw dropped. Slowly her head started to nod and a smile began to spread. This added to my confusion. First my father is an Archangel, but not just any angel. He was the in charge of the defense of the City of Heaven. He is a General.

Now this! A sister. My sister...Unknown to me. Someone that shared my blood on my father's side. OUR father's side. I looked at her in her male human form and laughed. "You are going to have to be in your female form for a while until I get used to this. This is a lot to process...again!"

She shifted back. Eryn sat there as mystified as I was. My upside down life finally righted again.

"So you are the one. Father refused to speak of it because he felt ashamed that he could not be a part of your life. It pained him. He never told me your name or location. I could not come visit you. He felt it would easier that way.

"That would have changed my life drastically if you had."

"This explains why Father sent me ahead while you slept. It was not our time yet."

"Was it fate for me to be chosen for this? To replace the Defender?"

"No. We took a chance. You showed compassion to a monster that your society has feared because though the years, he had to pull back to the shadows. The Defender could no longer teach mankind because they had advanced beyond his ability to reason in matters of Heaven. So from the shadows he watched and waited; answering the pull to find the portal when they opened, dealing with the incursion, and closing the portals. Then along came a boy, with a heritage hidden from the world. A boy who was not scared of the creature. Sasquatch reported that to our father while you were dying that day."

"Several came before me, I was told. They died. The knowledge of dealing with one's own death was too much for most human minds."

"It had to be a hybrid. You just so happened to be one."

"Wait...So if God is Father's father...That makes God my grandfather."

Celuine nodded.

"Holy shit!" Celuine frowned at, me most likely because of my language.

Eryn sat in silence, overloaded by everything. She had a smile on her face as she looked at me...at *WHAT* I was...and who I was. A man whose father was an angel and his grandfather was God. *THEE* GOD. Her mind was processing fast.

Celuine continued to speak. I tuned her out as I watched my love absorb all she could. Several more minutes passed before she finally burst out.

"So this means you were there and she was there on Heaven's walls. Was this an invasion? That must have been just as weird knowing that you were in a hospital bed in a coma. Did you paint those?" she asked, pointing back to the living room.

"Yes. A few weeks ago." Celuine looked at me. "Your bravery to go after your teacher to save Heaven is legendary now. Even the souls in Heaven speak of it. Yet you play it off as if it was nothing. I saw you from a distance while you recovered. You had a few conversations with "Our" father before he sent you on your last quest to return home. Had you not figured it out, you would not have woken up when you did, of course. Possibly worse."

"Yes, there was hundreds of thousands of the horde coming at me. Diving through the portal seemed like the only option. To stay would have meant death. I can face hundreds to several thousand...not hundreds of thousands...not yet anyway. I hated running, but when I saw their target was me in my hospital bed, I had to act."

"It is good you acted, Brother."

Eryn got up and moved into the other room to look at the painting. Silence overflowed the room and pressed itself into the kitchen like a hurricane making land. With everything in the open, the moments filled with contemplation. To say, "I felt lied to," was a gross understatement, yet the understanding of why everything had to be the way it was became clear. My mind took longer to open and allow the memories to flood in than those that helped draft me anticipated it would take. I gathered this by Celuine's own account of being the backup catalyst for me. Had she not done this, there is a good chance nothing would have happened. It took both her prodding and my seeing the daemon prince to trigger the influx of those astral memories.

Eryn came back in from the other room. I rose to my feet. She cried silently. Tears rolled freely and more so than any other time before when emotion came to bear. She walked toward me and reached up, touching my cheek. More silence followed, simply a tender hand upon my cheek melting the wasteland of ice inside of me even further. I felt something inside of me fall into place. Completion. One can only relish the feeling for what it is.

"You saved Heaven from being overrun somehow, didn't you?" A heavy sigh came from her as she gazed into my eyes. She always knew the truth when she saw it and was always the first to declare when she knew the answer. Her honesty was a beacon of morality. This right here was worth fighting for to me. A woman's tender touch could turn the tide of wrath back on itself like two waves on the ocean canceling each other out.

I simply nodded. Words could not come forth at that moment. Silence deafened the room. Celuine stood in the doorway, silent and stoic. I could not look at her the same way. She was not just an angel in the form of a man, one I had and wanted to hit so many times while dealing with *him*. She was my sister. It was her job to push me till I remembered. I could not express my thanks properly, so I simply nodded when she hugged Eryn. A squawk of a radio broke the silence.

"Sergeant?" Celuine walked to a shelf and picked up a hand held radio. It had not gone off once while we were there. It kind of surprised me, but then again, nothing really did anymore. I was sure there must be a good reason for the call.

"Talk to me," she replied, her voice now back to that of the man I knew.

"You know that guy you had us keeping tabs on?"

"Yes, what is the update?"

"Well sir, the locals up in the hills out by Flowing Lake said someone is firing a gun in the woods and chasing something. A neighborhood watch caught a glimpse of the target you were concerned about running evasively. The car you had us track is there."

"Well that's good, keep an eye on him. Run interference if you can till the target gets away."

"We can't sir, the target is hit and there are other players"

Celuine looked at me and I already knew what it meant. Jason had found the Sasquatch and was trying to kill it. She looked at me and nodded. Both of us could get there on our own. I was about to turn to Eryn when the house shook gently. My first instinct was to cover her in a doorway, so I pulled her towards the kitchen.

"That is not good," Celuine shouted as the shaking turned more violent and the entire house protested. I knew exactly what it was. A portal was opening close by, which meant some sort of natural disaster of the earth shaking variety would accompany. Thankfully the closest one was dormant. I grabbed Eryn's face and with intent, kissed her.

"We have to go now. Stay here." I looked to Celuine, who was nodding.

"If Sasquatch is down, that means he will not be able to deal with the portal opening. You are going to have to do it and stop Jason."

"I know." I thought hard about Jason and an image came to mind of where he was. The lake was about twenty five miles from here. I knew the area well because we met the girls there the day I died. The room began to spin and flux. Energy flowed through me from my core to my hands and feet, and I felt her lips touch mine before everything went black.

My sight came to focus on a forest floor. Pine needles covered the ground like a soft and prickly blanket. If one was to lay down with a sleeping bag on it, as I had many times in my younger years, it served as a good soft bed. Sunlight tried to reach down through the canopy to the floor. Tranquility shattered with the crack of a rifle off to my left. The ground shook violently. I took a knee.

I surveyed the area. Jason was close. His scent was on the breeze. He was an accomplished hunter and knew his skill, for the scent was subtle. A glance quickly in front of me told me it was clear. Suddenly, a feeling came from behind.

I turned around on my knees and my eyes saw a familiar hairy face, a face that was not doing the traditional peeking from behind a tree. He stood perfectly still. Dark fur was matted and saturated with blood in several spots. His breathing was labored and hard to control. Using only his eyes and chin, he pointed behind me. I was about to spin when the head of the Sasquatch exploded followed by a sharp crack of a rifle. The body did not even fall lifeless. It turned to opaque dust and fell to the ground on a gentle breeze.

Shock took hold of me and I just stared, feeling tremendous loss.

The tree had one huge hole and one smaller hole in it. While lost on this, I did not catch the movement to the side from the ground shaking all around still. Celuine was behind and to my right, trying to stay even on her one bent knee and braced with a tree.

"The rifle did not kill him. That shot missed."

"I know, but what di..." I did not have time to finish my sentence as the area exploded into action. Several daemons sprung from the forest revealing their position. Through the trees, there was another familiar sight. The energy weapons the horde used to assault Heaven were here, only a smaller mobile version. It walked towards us, firing as it came. Smaller daemons trailed behind it to feed the creature. It had just consumed one and was preparing to fire again. Hands pushed me down. I hit the dirt hard and rolled in an attempt to gain my feet.

Celuine had knocked me down and took a blast meant for me. She saved me from serious damage. A look of intense pain crossed her face and she fell hard not moving. The ground around me erupted from more bolts of energy. Rolling to the side behind a large tree, I jumped up trying to assess the situation. Several of the mobile energy creatures had me pinned. My shield came on, but I did not know if it could stop that type of weapon.

To my right, I sensed movement and turned to face it. Swords were in my hands and powered on as strong as I could make them charge. Fire ran the length of the blades. My eyes locked onto one of the creatures flanking me. It had just finished consuming a daemon. I had no time to react. It was about to fire when the part of it that would release the energy when suddenly destroyed and the familiar crack of a shot gun went off. The energy released, adding to the blast. Thirty feet of forest around it ignited like napalm. Running around the area, I caught movement and turned to face the assailant.

A friendly bearded face stood before me. Covered head to toe in ichor, Jason appeared sporting a shot gun, a rifle, and a machete hanging off his belt, also coated in ichor. He ran to my tree as the one he just passed exploded into a burst of embers showing the area directly around us again. The area started to burn.

"You're a sight for sore eyes," he laughed. "Is this what you do for whomever?"

"More or less," I responded, surprised at how accepting of the idea he was.

"Good, there of them coming from some type of rift or portal. I assume you can deal with that as well?" he added with a touch or seriousness, a side of him never seen before. "Several of them carried large stones...strangely enough. Any ideas?"

"I have no clue about that, but I cannot be good." I smiled remembering how many times we pretended. "Just like when we were kids, huh? Only this time the monsters are real," I replied

"Yeah, no kidding, my imagination was pretty vivid, I just never thought you could see the daemons, too."

I looked at him with my jaw down.

"Why do you think I became a hunter to begin with? They hide and look like trees that have multiple root systems. I have never seen them walk before, only grab, and consume animals. Whatever these smaller things are, they consume them before firing."

"Daemons. The smallest type. Leapers."

I tried to assess how many there were, but the earth shaking made it hard. I knew what these things could do, especially the larger models. While I was thinking, Jason jaw dropped for a moment before he continued.

"It is like they were waiting for something here all these years. Now I know how they get here."

"They are the ammo," he said, looking at me. I nodded. "Seriously?"

"As I ever can be. You have my back?" He nodded.

XXXIX

Reality

The forest erupted in flames.

Around us, the first salvo of energy blasts hit close. For several minutes, one or two at a time came spaced apart. Now it was constant, unrelenting bombardment. I did not know if Celuine was dead, but I owed her my life. She knew the risk most certainly, but it was not my style to leave someone down. I had to get to her. Exploding trees, dirt, and debris turned the once quiet forest in to a war zone.

They had us pinned down.

Celuine's body lay fifteen feet away. The exact location of her wound was not apparent. I was unable to determine if getting to her was worth a suicide run. My honor dictated that no matter what, I had to try.

The barrage cleared a lot of branches, taking cover away quickly. My enemy was not just trying to finish her. We needed to keep moving. It was a simple matter of tactics, but then again, so was keeping your head down. I was no good to anyone while stuck in a fox hole. My blades were thirsty for battle, or perhaps my desire to cut daemons to bits tried to override getting to my angelic sister. Both plans drove me toward action. Even after I scoop Celuine up we would need an egress point.

"Cover me when you see me disappear!" I hollered over the sounds of destruction. Jason nodded in reply. I quickly peeked around the cluster of stumps and tried to time it to avoid getting a face full of energy. Three tar-

571

gets in a one hundred and twenty or so degree arc at various ranges availed themselves. They took no care in hiding and kept firing repeatedly. I pulled my head back and pointed the direction I was looking a moment before.

"You can do that?" Jason questioned with excitement, barely able to contain himself.

"You would be amazed at what I can do. We can discuss it later. Give me three shots when you see me fade." Several energy blasts hit the tree above us, showering wood chips all over. Smoke thickened as more foliage and trees caught fire. That did not make me happy. I thought of the first lightning storm I watched destroyed a whole forest. That was a decimation level event. It still made me sick at the thought, but I chose to focus on my target. One of the daemons fired from behind some large bushes, affording a bit more cover than the other two. This offered me more cover from bullets fired that general direction where my teleport would carry me.

I focused on my target. More blasts came in hard and fast, signifying more creatures joining the fray. Trees began to fall and offered a little more to hide behind as they piled atop of one another creating a small barricade. It did not offer any protection from the opposite side.

Jason hollered, "GO...GO...GO," right before I finished activating. Why did my vision have to go so blurry every time? I closed my eyes when things shifted.

I reappeared behind my target and heard Jason fire his salvo. Several screams ensued from the smaller feeder daemons telling me he had a hit his marks. The idea to turn them invisible was moot. Jason needed to see them, so that would be counterproductive here.

Several of the smaller ones failed to notice I was there until they died. Others around them stood like before in Heaven's assault. My swords swiped several times and bodies burst into nothingness. They did not know I was there until I was slicing them apart. The makeshift line ran behind each of the living weapons. It still intrigued me how they gave themselves up to die. A good start if you ask me.

I cut through the last one in this group and saw the tendril reach back to grab for another volley, but its strange gnarled hand found only air. My blades scythed out, removing its appendage and causing it to howl and turn. It called out in some strange tongue. It did not have a visible mouth from which it cried out. Instinctively both blades connected, severing its head. Greenish ichor sprayed the area as a choking sound started and ended when it fell over dead. The body turned into an explosion of ash as it hit the ground and faded away.

Looking to the left, I saw another creature about ninety feet away fire on Jason's location. It was an easy stride through some light cover making it easier for me to stay hidden. I charged, killing the firing daemon before it could grab another energy source. Taking their head was easier on these smaller versions because I could reach them without having to leap. The creature toppled over and landed right on several of the smaller ones in the line behind it. Several got pinned beneath its body, making them even easier targets to dispatch. It was a matter of cleaning up the before they could call for help or attacked me themselves.

Things did not go easily for long as the third creature saw me coming and turned to fire. Another blast flew at me and glanced off my shield. I moved evasively till I was right on it. A straight shot to my shield could be bad. It was not a theory I felt like testing. It let out a high pitched shrill, cut short when I removed its head. Soon they would know I moved within their ranks, compromising their tactics.

"You must move faster. A portal must be close by," Sabathiel said in a singular voice.

"He must deal with the ones he finds. If he gets surrounded it will remove his advantage of position," Radueriel added to the dialogue.

"You are the Defender now Tathlyn. You must take care of yourself and deal with the task. No un-needed risked should ever be considered except as a last resort," they said in unison.

"Agreed my friends. The threat level here is growing. Caution will be exercised."

Explosions echoed through the trees. Hope that Jason and my sister were okay hung heavy on my mind. It killed me to leave her on the ground with no proof she yet lived. This was the second time I found myself in a mess and had to worry about the life of another within the same day. I refocused on Jason and reappeared next to him a few moments later. He just about jumped out of his skin. The look on his face told me that he was relieved. The horde decimated the forest. Taking cover low to the ground was the only thing I could do here. With my size, low crawling still made me a little vulnerable. My armor made the feeling of being a duck on a pond a bit more bearable. Such odds were not the problem; it was the location and I was about to change that. I could teleport one other person but the farther the range, the longer it took and we still had a portal to find.

I grabbed Celuine and looked to Jason in one swift motion. She was remarkably heavy even with her daintiness in her angelic form. Perhaps it just came as a surprise to me that she weighed as much as she did. Mathias told me that sometimes a magically created weapon had a property called weighted...for when it struck that extra weight made the wound more severe. He had also explained how some beings had more mass to them, even though they looked the same. That was probably the case here. I smiled at how things in my new world were exactly as they should be even if appearances misled.

"Follow me and try to keep up," I said quietly, making a beeline for the place cleared moments before. Crashing through the fallen timbers was not as easy as I had hoped. Celuine was over my shoulder as we ran, but moving through the smoke filled forest slowed me down. Jason stayed right behind me, matching my pace. Something told me he would move faster on his own even with my stride. His ability to choose a path then was second to mine growing up for I had lived out here longer. His ability superseded my skill, for he was a ranger of sorts when not working.

Nearly a quarter mile passed. The daemons ceased pounding that location for a moment, so we stopped to assess Celuine's wound. She was barely alive, and it would take a lot out of me to fully heal her. I trusted she could heal herself if I brought her back to consciousness. Her wound was through the back plate, right at the base of the neck. The armor took the brunt of it, but something had gotten through, hurting her badly.

"Keep watch. This is will take a little bit."

Jason nodded. He went to a tree and began setting up quick hunters blind to conceal himself. My focus shifted to Celuine. I removed the plates as gently as possible. The front came off easily enough, but in the back plate, jagged metal bent inward, digging into her spine. The pressure on the spine must have pinched several nerves causing her body into a coma. This would take its toll on me.

Energy charged in my core for a moment before I turned my focus to her. I needed to reduce the swelling in the soft tissue. My fingers tried lifting the plate slowly. Several moments had passed before anything budged. The blast embedded it in the bone. When it finally released, the blood flow increased rapidly.

My focus sharpened. The memory of the day I healed Malnuras flooded back. Emotions surged. It clouded my thoughts for a moment, taxing my concentration. That day, using this ability had knocked me out and allowed the horde to capture him, and Heaven fell because of it. The weight of what was at stake here was not as great. Failure would mean the life of an angel, my sister, not a walking avatar dying again. It was not an option either way. Earth needs its Defenders, and Heaven needs its angels.

The tissue repaired slowly and the damage to her vertebrae even slower. She breathed a little easier now but was still unconscious. I focused on knitting fibers together and increasing blood flow to the area. Her pulse strengthened and slowly her breaths became deeper and deeper until her eyes finally opened. Slight panic washed over her and she started to fight until her eyes locked on mine and she relaxed. My senses tingled as she closed her eyes and her own healing kicked in. Celuine smiled for the first time since I had seen her in this form.

576

"Thank you," she whispered as she sat up, shaking some cobwebs out of her head. Damage like that tended to leave one paralyzed so it made sense that her abilities failed for a moment, rendering her helpless. I handed her the breast plate. Holding up the rear piece, my thumb pressed hard on the twisted metal and it groaned in protest before bending flat. Several jagged edges later it was flat again. She stood feeling much better than she had been, for sure. I helped her refasten the armor.

"I need to go for the portal. Can you handle these things now that you know what we are dealing with?" I asked.

"They will not gain tactical favor a second time. We fell into an ambush set for the old Defender. They are not expecting an angel and a hybrid Defender. Take your friend with you. I will handle this. Meet me back at my domicile. I will not be long," she assured me.

Jason had made his way back to the camp. He took one more look at Celuine and smiled. She looked back at him as she walked by shaking her head. I could tell what he thought before he did and why would he not? She was beautiful and a warrior but the key component was she was an angel. If she ever got permission to marry, it would most likely be someone important. His grin did not fade after she left camp, and it made it hard to look at him without knowing how he felt for I was that way with Eryn.

"We need to go to where the portal is. Can you take me?" He nodded yes and pointed towards south east.

"There is something bigger there that is not like these smaller things. It stands on two feet. The creature knew the direction of my approach before I got anywhere near it. It was focusing on some strange circle of light floating in the air. Is that a portal?

"Yes, that sounds like what I need to find. We need to move fast before reinforcements come."

"The creature is smart and doesn't stand still," Jason added. "I can kill it if I can get line of sight. I tried to get a bead on it once but had to run away. That's when I saw Bigfoot running from me."

We moved through the forest. Jason led expertly. He did not disappoint me with his speed. We paused for a moment to listen to the forest. Our enemies were not close by at the present.

"I have a question," I whispered "As kids when we ran around in the woods; you could really see these things I just fought? How did you know they were daemons?"

"It was a guess. I knew something was up where I could see them and you could not. They tried to blend in. Occasionally, I caught them moving. A few years ago I saw one kill something. So whenever I see them, they die. It is all I've done since you were hurt, but looking for Sasquatch was my focus."

He paused and stared at me. "So why did you come out here? To stop me or to help me?"

"There is a lot I can't explain right now. Just know something: My title is Defender. The Sasquatch was the one that chose me to replace him because of what happened that day when I told him to look out. I will tell you more as soon as we have time, but we have to get to that portal. If you know where it is, take me to it. Otherwise, I will have to spend a lot of time and effort finding it."

"Let's continue then." He took off at a rapid pace. "I hope you can still keep up." It was obvious he knew where he was going.

Sounds of battle rang out to my left. I heard the distinctive chimes of a sword hitting something hard, causing it to vibrate. Many times it was the after affect from a successful kill...A smile crossed my face knowing Celuine was close. Perhaps it was time for mankind to get more involved in protecting their planet.

I wondered if Jason would be up to the task. He was tough. But could he handle the changes to his reality? His outlook, when he visited me in the hospital, showed that he was a fighter... his cause was noble as it pertained to me, and a misguided sense of honor. But what I saw today made me think that was a ruse. His heart was indeed in the right place.

We ran at a fast pace for about ten minutes then slowed. Motioning me to get sneaky, Jason pointed at something off in the distance about eighty yards away. I crept forward into cover. Sure enough, there was a portal open. It angled toward us, so it looked oval and close to eight feet tall. Jason was right. There was also a large pile of stones, carved or cut in irregular shapes on the ground. Next to the rock pile stood an arch way. Strange they built and arch as if marking the spot to build a structure or mark the area as a marshaling point for future invasions. The horde was getting confident that it would be able to return to this exact spot and construct a building. Motion caught my eye.

Some sort of creature moved about. One I had anticipated. A hybrid was there with a daemon. Hybrids not only commanded, but also added a serious threat. We had no way of knowing what else was here.

Talk about ugly.

This thing towered over the medium sized daemon that stood guard. The hybrid looked like it had some sort of scales all over it. By all appearances, it was male. He seemed to be looking around often and focusing in certain directions at times. Suddenly he would trace symbols in the air, and an energy wave rolled out into the woods. I got a distinct impression he was giving commands based on where his attention focused and how he moved his hand, but I could not be certain. Occasionally he would look at a scroll.

"Can you take him?" I whispered.

"Yes, but he always seems to know when he is being targeted. I had him in my sights earlier and he moved almost as if he knew there was danger. It was creepy."

"Then I will distract him. Give me about a minute, and then take aim." I was able to focus my energy on the area. I could see the clearing and that made memorizing it easy enough. My energy gathered faster than usual. That should have triggered a warning. Something was strange, but I dismissed the thought not wanting to over analyze.

Perception shifted.

I stood inside a ring of protective barriers not viewable from a distance. Runes hung in the air suspended by the arcane. He spun to face me and hissed in a guttural voice something almost like English. His face disjointed and I could see he had mandibles and four eyes. His hands only had two fingers and no opposing thumb. Without hesitation, he charged me.

He was fast...faster than any creature I had ever faced. His attacks came furiously. My posture went defensive as he engaged. Just being in close proximity to me, dark energy grabbed a hold of my core. The closer he got the worse it was. Swipe after swipe he made, trying to hit me. My swords deflected each one then scored great cuts on his arms with each attempt he made. He did not relent.

My shield triggered on its own with his proximity. I jumped back, creating much needed distance. Not wasting a moment, he charged again. He never closed the distance. Part of his head exploded followed by a crack of the rifle. On the perimeter, small flyers took to the air in typical flight patterns and set up angles for a pass at me.

Behind him, the runes flashed and the portal vibrated. From the hybrid's body, several of the plates opened and tiny flyers appeared and started to feed on his flesh. They started to grow right before my eyes. This was familiar. He was a Hybrid Summoner Daemon. I charged at him with both swords engulfed in flame. Energy flashed from the tips of the swords, obliterating the body and many of the small creatures eating it. When they died, they were four times bigger than when they emerged from the hybrid.

The runes flashed again. Now images of an angel in the woods appeared. I smiled. Celuine cut down the daemonic weapons and decimated the trailing energy sources, as they stood there stupefied. About a dozen of them remained. Some moved and fired, other stayed stationary. This hybrid directed and coordinated everything. With him gone, the coordinated attack would cease, I hoped.

Over my shoulder, a group of about thirty flyers came in low. They had no idea what they were facing. My position in the open for an enemy would be too hard to resist. The small ones all had the ego of an ant taking on something much bigger. They always thought they could take me in a one-to-one fight...even though they watched me destroy a whole flight of them seconds earlier. Shots rang out from Jason's direction. He was doing plenty of damage. I lined up my targets and as predicted they came in fast and low to try to sweep my stance. Shifting at the last second out of the way, both my blades passed into the path of the small fliers creating death by cutting clean through all of them. Remnants of them dematerialized as they hit the ground and simply disappeared.

Jason ran down from his elevated area. He had his shot gun out and advanced like a S.W.A.T. member would. His stature was determined and alert. I was rather convinced he was very efficient until he tripped over a root. I laughed for a moment before waiving at him.

"That was impressive. You really took care of them."

I laughed.

"That, my friend, was nothing. There are daemons the size of dragons, the big kind fly with four sets of wings and walk on six legs. Those are hard to take down. Nowhere near as hard as Lucifer's son. He was formidable." Jason looked at me as if I was crazy.

"You do realize what you just said, right?"

"Yes, I do. There is a lot about me you probably will not understand right now, but in time I will try to explain. Right now I need to close this portal. Keep watch."

I centered myself. A deep breath flowed into my lungs with a slow exhale, and I turned my focus to the portal. Slowly, energy flowed. Tendrils of energy moved toward it and grabbed hold of the edges just like before. The edges began to fold in on itself, slow at first, and then another flow of energy came from me to grab another side of it and began the same process. Within moments, several tendrils had the portal down to almost nothing.

A small popping sound occurred and it went away. I looked at Jason. His eyes were wide. He just stood there in shock for several minutes before shaking his head slowly. I could tell by the look in his eye that disbelief was starting to fade and wonder was setting in.

"What have you been doing all this time that you were in a coma?" he said, finally finding the words.

"I was learning to fight daemons and to do that," I pointed towards the portal's last place.

"You were right. We do have a lot to talk about." There was movement to his right. He spun, leveling his shotgun. Out stepped Celuine from the trees and she stopped for a moment until he lowered his weapon. She had a smile on her face expressing she enjoyed herself for the first time in a long time. Jason stared at her seven foot frame while she approached.

"I might as well get this over with," she said. A motion behind her blurred and majestic wings unfolded and extended. The perfect white on them caught light from the canopy and began to glow with searing brightness. My hand shielded the intensity. Jason stood there nodding his head in excitement. I had seen this splendor but on a grand scale amidst a war muting the magnificence. Even after the siege broke and I moved around the city a bit, I did not see many of the angels. Among all of that gold, a white pair of radiant wings was not such a sight.

583

"Can you do that?" he asked.

"No, I am only half angel, a nephilim," I said.

"Seriously?" he questioned with a look of utter disbelief. "Wait, it is your father right?"

"My father too," replied Celuine.

"Unbelievable!" Jason remarked, unsure of what to ask next.

I laughed.

"Let us depart. I have some explaining to do and I am hungry." I felt a slight tingle in my shoulder and was not sure why.

He laughed hard. That made me smile.

XL

Duty and Honor

Synchronous Dance

A synchronous dance of steel and air

Step forward they purrs are you brave do you dare.

In one sweeping motion, they glide to and fro

Blurry is the timing and lethal is the flow

The firelight glistens and reflects off my blades

Stepping through motions, feet mimic my wade

Legendary foes springing up all around

Through them I slice but none hit the ground

My mind is in focus, deadly is the dance

The link that I have with my hands, they've no chance

The intimacy lies with each or my blows

Knowing they rain down death on my foes

Tomorrow my test I take in my head

Knowing if I fail that I will be dead

The trial tonight is to play out this dance

I will give no mercy or allow any chance

Legacy of the Defender

My motions draw near to the end of the night

Sweat of my brow catches rays of first light

The sun rises slowly to reveal it all

The fields of battle summon me with its call

I will not go weary from this night to the day

This battle is won with each step I portray

I see the horde rushing to fall on my steel

They will soon know that with me there's no deal

Fore fathers above guide my blades strong and true

Know that my goal is to fight and honor you

This legacy will balance by the strength of my blade

Today I fulfill sacred oaths I have made

Alone I will stand on this field I've prepared

A line in the earth shows a boundary declared

Horizons do darken and blot out the sun

I smile at the tactic for I've already won.

A treasure was gone – one the world never knew existed.

The weight of it all landed on my shoulders. I felt the Sasquatches passing for several days.

He might even be the last one. I did not need recognition for my efforts, but my state of mind found contentment. Was the world ready to know the truth?

My defeat of Amduscias was a bitter sweet memory. He claimed to be a son of Lucifer. There were not any records or history to back his claim up, only several references describing him. He did have the fabled unicorn head. That was more terrifying to be honest. He was *damn scary* as he was. His defeat at my hand was not an open contestation of his true rank. Why else would such a nasty creature be granted not just one but two incredibly powerful swords?

We could not dispute Lucifer's reaction.

One had to wonder if he could just walk into a hellish forge and order up another instrument of death so easily. Was there a surplus of them around? What kind of arsenal was at their disposal? I cannot imagine every denizen of the daemon horde would have the kind of resources needed to get another one so easily. As funny as these questions were, I had to know my enemy, and that meant knowing their weapons.

Yet this one did.

My blades were unusually quiet.

I asked them several times if they were okay. They said they were excellent. But I know that during that fight with Amduscias, they went above and beyond with their contributions. My fear was that my actions overtaxed them, and it could be weeks before they recovered fully. I spent time meditating with them. Several times they spoke of sensing daemon presences, but none revealed themselves to us.

Yesterday it took many hours to explain the situation to Jason. His boyish charm was gone. Not much was funny to him anymore. Reality found its mark. He knew the world as it really was now. It was a day to silently mark in his mind that he was not a mundane any longer. He confirmed his own sanity. His mind was awake. There was no going back to sleep.

All was quiet.

We staying at Celuine's house and enjoyed getting to know her. We talked into the night and got very little sleep. The idea of what I was settled in a bit more with Eryn and Jason. They were still in awe that the world was not only much bigger than they had imagined, but it also more vulnerable. Both had a different way of looking at me now. I would feel the same way had things been reversed.

It was dinner. Celuine shared her experience when Heaven called her back.

"A feeling came from Heaven for me to return. I had no idea what was happening. As an angel, we all share a connection to the city. Something felt wrong. So when evil creatures overran Heaven, the energy felt tainted. Part of me expected it was a call to retrieve the souls outside the walls of the city. As Tathlyn knows it is a choice when a believer dies. Heaven may be a city, but it is also what you want the experience to be. People choose to exist outside the walls living in the smaller cities or towns. When hell invaded Heaven, those people chose to stay and did not desire to live in a cloister. Even in death, it appears some people want a simple existence. So when the call came, I figured it was to recover those outside, and never expected to find Heaven's walls breached."

"That must have been a surprise...and not a welcome one," Jason said, feeling the seriousness in her voice.

"It was horrific," Celuine added with distant look crossing her face.

"I agree. It was beyond description," I interjected. "That must have been shocking."

She continued her tale.

"Denizens reap more from a live kill on Earth. Their only real drive is to kill while the soul was still in the body. This was the whole reason to siege Heaven. To distract God and keep him busy. Grandfather is too busy protecting Heaven to answer prayers or involve Himself with humans."

Eryn's jaw dropped.

"So God really is not listening? He does not care about us anymore?" she asked.

"It is actually the opposite, Eryn. The task falls to angels because of the copious amount of energy needed to power the shield. With several hundred billion daemons in Heaven's realm, it has Grandfather taxed. It is like a virus in his body. He cannot get out of bed to do anything. He can only hold on." Celuine gazed at Eryn and something took place between them. Eryn nodded and smiled back.

Celuine looked at all of us.

"God loves every one of the Children here on Earth and throughout the galaxy. Earth is not the only place where his angels protect. We have the ability to answer some prayers if the person praying has very strong faith. This keeps what few of us there are very busy. The Defender exists for this reason. It is now Tathlyn's responsibility to deal with invading daemons."

She turned to look at me.

"Brother, seeing you close the portal moved me. I did not know it was the Father's apprentice until much later. But it moved me because it has been mankind's destiny to defend Earth against the horde. It is long overdue. Every candidate failed for hundreds of years. We thought the concept was impossible until the Sasquatch found you...an angel and human hybrid. That was the key all along. We needed mankind's determination to succeed and the human fortitude mixed with an angelic bloodline."

I blushed a little bit at her praise. It was strange to have a sister...let alone one that was an angel. I was still adjusting to knowing my father really existed...in Heaven. It was no pun to say this. The joke would be lost on anyone not in the room. Celuine stood up and gave me a hug. Eryn began to weep. Jason bowed his head to hide his response.

"I painted that scene right after returning to Earth and right before you awoke," she said.

I looked at her paintings. The detail made me realize how much you can miss when you are right in the eye of the storm.

"So what was your funniest moment training?" Jason asked

"That would be getting swallowed by the large flying daemon. This dragon-like creature was one of the hardest tests of my training. I cut two of the wings off making it very mad. The daemon rolled over on me then managed to swallow me. When I carved up his insides, he spit me out. I felt like a giant spit wad flying through the air."

Jason laughed. Celuine had a confused look of amusement on her face. Eryn looked mortified by my story. Then piped up

"That explains some of the wounds I saw on you during your co-ma!" she said. "I met your earthly parents. They knew something was wrong when the church convinced them to stay away and let them handle it." Celuine's eyes widened and she added to what Eryn said.

"I remember now. The scientists involved were paranormal investi-gators working with the church behind closed doors. They wanted to dissect you. I had them shut down and threatened to have them investigated for fraud since they were not actually who they claimed to be. We destroyed the data. Any news of your situation became uninteresting. I told the church it was damaging to the family. Funny thing about the church is their devotion to family. The church kept a priest there...not like he could do anything. They have no power and their faith is challenging at best."

"What about this twin who killed his brother?" Eryn asked. "That was damaging enough with an imposter roaming around a hospital mas-querading as a man of the cloth." I had to admit. That part still bothered me that they had access to me when I was not able to protect my body.

Celuine looked at all of us. It was clear that her strength ran deep. But even the water in the deepest pool still circulates. There was tension in her voice during this recanting. She held poise and composure the entire time like it was an interrogation. Something about her changed at that mo-ment. She was somber...almost sad. She finished her thought.

"I was there unseen often, but occasionally they allowed me to task another angel to stay in your room. We kept an eye on you. I started to question that decision but remembered that the Sasquatch had still been doing his duty so resources, as thin as they were, had to make due.

We processed all the information from the night before and the previous day's conclusion. *The reasons behind the decisions may not always be clear. They just are.*

I was out in the yard working out with Jason. He asked me for instruction almost as soon as we returned. Celuine retrieved an extra blade and let him borrow it. It was a decent sword. The angelic make was obvious to me. His eyes lit up when he held it and swung it around for several minutes without even looking at me. It was strange being the teacher now.

His fighting skills were still apparent.

Since the day of the accident, his skills had improved. I wanted to ask him where he honed his skills, but something told me the answer was one that I did not want to know. We exchanged blows on an eight to twenty ratio in the first few minutes. He fought well. I remembered stories he told me where he faced several at once in his early years and walked away. Holding back was not hard. My actions and reactions masked my intentions. I did not want to give the slightest appearance of what I could actually do.

I allowed Jason to continue his repetitive attacks for a time. It was easy to keep it simple and start with the basics without letting him know this was the basics. He fought well considering that his training in weapons was self-taught. I smacked him with the flat of the blade several times to show him his openings. All hits served a purpose...to humble the student and toughen them up.

After all, was it not Malnuras and Father that daily beat the daylight into and out of me? This is what toughened me up and gave me the edge to manage pain. The key was to recognize it was there and measure your response to it.

The topic of the day was Bigfoot. Jason wanted to know everything that I knew about this creature. It had not only eluded him for six years but also remained a clouded mystery to mankind for the better part of known history. A great sadness was set over both of us. It was a great loss. Jason recognized that a mighty warrior fell doing his duty and had died with honor. He also recognized that Bigfoot saved his life many times. The series of questions that came at me were not ones I would have expected so soon. My friend's anger and hate melted away to compassion.

"So you're telling me that you have met him before? I can't imagine having a conversation with it, or him." The look on his face was a betrayal of his fascination and admiration that developed since the battle. Jason's bullet hurt the creature, but the daemons finished the job. My guess was the Sasquatch could heal the bullet wound over time.

"Well, I saw him once. The siege of Heaven was over. Malnuras's body was back in the city. I was recovering in the city for several weeks. My father brought him when he came to visit me."

Jason's eyes locked intently on me. Mine used to fixate on him when he told me stories. This role reversal was an adjustment for him. He felt as if I did not see him as a warrior. That had to be emasculating. My opinion mattered more. He fought gang members twice his size and won. So size did not intimidate him.

The flurry of my strikes did.

"So that was a bit of hero worship by that point, I imagine," Jason added. "After all, you got to watch so many battles of him defending the Earth and now you got to meet him. I feel so stupid for going after him thinking I could kill him. I wish I had known."

"You did not kill him, Jason. The daemons did. That was an ambush set for him and their planning paid out. You or I involved just added variables that a very formidable enemy needed to compensate for. The fact that you saw them so many years ago, hiding in the forest, tells me this has been in preparation for a while. Since they needed to get the smaller daemon here to sacrifice, that took some planning. They built up a force here so slowly that the Sasquatch did not detect anything. That worries me. It also means when portals did open, those things slipped through. I doubt they are indigenous to Earth."

"I shot him. Had I not messed things up, he might still be alive," said Jason.

"How do you know you did not tip the balance of that engagement? Maybe your presence put him on greater alert. Maybe he would not have lasted that long and more would have come through the portal had you not started shooting. Did you not chase him for miles?" I asked.

"Yes, I did...through several properties, in fact, along the lake." He had that guilty look in his eyes so I went defensive and let him keep swinging for a few moments until he slowed and stopped. Several quick breaths followed while he stared at me.

"Everything happens for a reason, Jason. It may not be as it should, but there is a purpose for everything. Sadly, not all of them are good. He found peace after several thousand years of fighting. He has earned his rest."

"He is dead. How is that peaceful?" Jason asked.

"Celuine told me last night when I asked what had happened to his spirit. Heaven is his reward; to live in peace and tranquility."

"What was Heaven like?" he asked.

I smiled at the question, for my presence in the afterlife was a dichotomy of truths. My faith in God was there all my life, but my belief was not hardcore. As a sinner, I have walked the streets of Heaven. But sin is not in Heaven; those existing there have free will and no desire to be sinful. I searched for a way to describe it but decided to simplify it.

"It was like everyone was happy. I do not want to use a term like a *higher level of consciousness* but when the city fell under attack, there was no fear. The souls did not show fear. There were no negative emotions. They enjoyed their life and did not worry about what was going on. I heard them ask questions and they showed concern, but faith was absolute. They knew God would protect them."

Jason smiled. "It would be nice to have that kind of guarantee that everything will be all right."

I nodded and resumed the workout.

A series of different combinations was on my starting lesson plan today. He already knew the eight angles of attack. Since he favored one weapon, he used strikes with offhand grappling techniques. His style worked for him. I quickly executed a series of strikes so he could see what it looked like at full speed then slowed it down. He followed the mechanics, including the foot work.

It was rather warm. My shirt was on the porch. Several times he stared at the runes moving on my skin. They could be a little hypnotic. When I first got them, I spent many days staring at them...it was easy to get lost. I tapped him upside the head to bring him back to reality. It smarted a little and he rubbed his ear furiously.

"Hey, what was that for?" he griped

"You asked for this, so pay attention."

"I am, it's just, and I don't know...something on your skin looks funny."

"What? Where are you looking?" I responded with curiosity. He pointed to the runic pathways that allow me to use my whole body for gathering energy when I teleport. One of them looked damaged. That area bore so many wounds from previous battles; it was hard to remember which one did the most damage. The daemon prince had an arsenal of weapons he brought to bear on me. He hit me multiple times with most of them. My shield took the hardest beating ever that day.

That had me thinking, especially since when I healed, the runes were floating magic on or under my skin. It was hard to imagine anything could damage one of them. Perhaps a magical assault targeting the rune could cause an issue. I did notice that the muscle was tender in that spot. I did feel things catch a little at times, which certainly had never happened before. For some reason, the area felt a little weird when he mentioned it. Eryn would look at it when she returned from work.

We continued to train. Hours flew by. Jason impressed me. In mere hours, he excelled from where he was.

A car approached. I dismissed my swords and waited behind where the gate would open. The fence was tall enough to hide me from the outside. No neighbors were close, but the fence was a good privacy screen. Moving toward the side of the house where the shade was, I waited in the darker area until I heard a familiar voice. The gate opened and Eryn stepped in. The smile on her face was a wonderful sight to me even though she had only been gone for five or so hours.

"I thought you were at work," I greeted her with a surprise hug.

"I called in. There were more important things to for us to do." Celuine came through the gate in her Sergeant form, carrying shopping bags. I looked rather puzzled.

"Are you shopping for Eryn?"

Her smile told me it was for herself. I tried to figure out why she wore such bad suits as cover for her role. She laughed and walked inside. I kissed Eryn and was about to inquire when she silenced me with a finger and mouthed the words "thirty minutes" before she entered the house. I nodded and turned back to face Jason again.

"So what's going on?" he said as curious as I was. I knew that he had a fixation with her, but he was just as in awe of her as I still was. In the last few days, Celuine spoke several times about her roll and she looked forward to acting as a liaison to Heaven. I could not speak directly to Father yet, but she could. She reported to him on my behalf. His responses were not very long. But she advised me he was looking forward to seeing us soon when his duty allowed.

"I do not think this has anything to do with work."

"That is too bad. I am itching to deprive more of these things of their lives."

"In time you will, I imagine. Resume," I said, calling my swords and waded in.

We returned to sparring. My shoulder suddenly hurt. This was strange to feel pain when there was nothing wrong with me. Jason withdrew still swinging his blade.

"What's wrong? Is your shoulder still bothering you?"

"It is. I need to gather my thoughts."

The shade called to me. My thoughts raced more than usual. Even with my memories back, my mind still wrestled, compartmentalizing all the new memories into my original body. Meditation helped. I sat in the shade and tried to place myself into a trance. Time passed. Something felt wrong though and all my attempts to self-diagnose my condition seemed to fail. My healing helped a little, but it felt like something tore into me every time I moved. The energy pulsed over me and stopped at the damaged rune before moving farther along.

I stirred out of my mediation when Jason sat himself down next to me and took a drink from his water bottle. He wiped his brow.

"I can't get over how big you are. It's as if you are not even the same person. If only your mom could see you now. She would be shocked. I do not think even the truth would matter and there is no way she could handle this," he trailed off for a second, and if I did not know better, I could have sworn he choked on his words. Silence crept in. Moments passed.

I continued to rub my shoulder and let the healing flow.

"You know I looked into your parents' death. It was very odd the way the car crashed. I have a fee..." I held up my hand. He looked at me, wondering why I cut him off. The truth was I already knew that they had to die for me to be ready. It was probably some sort of no attachment policy, or it was merely supposed to happen. Maybe the Coven did it. Perhaps it was God's will. I never bought the idea that it was his will cause pain. A final reason came to mind. It might have been someone's desire to trigger the change in order to help my body catch up with my mind.

He tried to speak again. "Dieter, I'm sorry... I didn't mea..."

"Do not," I said and looked at him. He stared at me like at the hospital when he saw my rage first hand. I could still smell fear rolling off him, but it was healthy fear. There was no panic. I got a similar feeling from daemon blood. I did not get off on blood but just liked obliterating daemons and the threat they posed. That much was just part of who I was and yes, I did love to fight my enemies.

"Okay Deitz, it was just a thought that we had not had a chance to discuss. I won't bring it up again. I did not mean to upset you."

"Call me Tathlyn," I whispered. "You did not up..." I never finished my sentence.

He slapped me right on the shoulder and pain exploded. It flowed over all my meridian lines and I felt it travel the same pathway along the runes that connected on the outside. "Something is wrong," I said and fell over convulsing so hard it looked like I was trying to snap my own back.

"HELP! Celuine...Tathlyn needs you!" Jason shouted.

His voice sounded like he walked away. The volume diminished.

Everything went blurry. Inside I felt like fire. Just like the poison. My hearing faded. I turned my healing on full as a last act of defiance. Inside of me, it felt like something ripped my soul out piece by piece. Rage collapsed the walls of serenity and in one motion ran its claws down the exposed emotional nerves, causing an overload of every meridian and chakras at once.

In that moment of pain and anguish, time stood still. I could not move nor react. Logic was impossible. The alarms inside of me that used the runes as both detection and healing fired impulses all at the same time. Something foreign was wrong. How long this went on I do not know. Blackness never came, but a living nightmare commenced.

Suddenly Eryn was over me. My eyes tracked Jason and Celuine as well. The pain resided. I was on my back on the hard wood floor of the living room. Hearing slowly returned... My energy pathways burned. The flow was running on high as if I was building up enough energy to launch a ship. I was cleansing.

"Lay still," the duo in my head said. "Relax." So I did.

A tinging sound, like a small piece of metal falling in a glass bowl echoed in the room. Repeatedly the sound came, with no pattern or rhythm to it. My energy returned to normal like an engine whose rounds per minutes dropped to idle. Hands helped me sit up when they saw me try. The burning sensation was gone, but I still felt the effects of something indescribable.

"That was really bad!" declared my blades. I could feel them on the floor next to me. They appeared on their own. My hands were resting on the hilts.

"Okay, what in the hell was that?" I declared with my voice rising.

"We don't know, but it was buried in your rune and must have been shooting some sort of synaptic signal down your runic lines. Eryn pulled this out." Celuine held out a bowl and a small razor sharp pin sized needle that looked like it was for taking blood. It bounced around in the bowl. It was over an inch. It looked like it partially dissolved...

"This is ridiculous. How come with all my training and conditioning a needle can do this to me? How am I supposed to protect the world or you when I cannot protect myself? I cannot believe that something that small could..." My voice trailed to a whisper. It hit me. There was no surprise when I realized it. The answer was obvious.

"I know what it is."

They all stared at me.

"What? Did you fight a giant porcupine and lose?" Jason interjected in his usual smart ass tone. Eryn looked worried, and Celuine was puzzled as well.

"No, it is from the poison gland from Amduscias' wing. It broke off inside me when I fought him. He hit me so hard, he broke his own injector."

"Daemons are created to be lethal to man. Amduscias was no different. Except that his essence is also poison to humans...and angels. This should have killed you."

Eryn's face went pale.

"How could this stay inside you when you healed yourself?" Eryn asked, as the nurse in her wanted answers. I think she had about enough of the bad for one day. I cannot say I blamed her. Sadly, I was used to it when

I was in daemon-ville, but I had grown lazy since returning home. My guard was down once I had my friends around to care for me.

"When I was healing myself to stop the bleeding, I closed the outside first without thinking. It was only minutes after my memory returned did I go back and heal some more, but it was obviously not enough to prevent this. I sealed the thing inside of me." I stood up and put on my armored shirt. It was obvious now that I needed to keep this on most of the time. I retrieved my cloak from the second bedroom and put it on too.

Celuine stood. I noticed that she was smaller and in female form wearing a nice dress. She looked amazing. *Spectacular* and *stunning* came to mind. Regardless of how much I loved Eryn, this woman, this angel, defined the word *beauty*. The shopping bags must have been for her and she brought home a dress.

"You look great. I love the new ... lo..."

Celuine suddenly released her angelic presence into the room. She tensed and began to look around...

"Shhh!" she fired back, looking around. The needle in the bowl vibrated louder. It moved so fast there was a buzzing noise, and it grew louder. Like a little jack hammer, it cracked the bowl it was in. Pressure in the room increased; accompanied by that gut feeling this task would never end. The house started to vibrate.

"Wow is that little thing doing this?" Jason inquired, looking at the bowl.

It was not conceivable the enemy would attempt an attack so soon. My gut was never so wrong. I donned my cloak and tied it while looking at

Eryn. She walked over. I lowered my head and put my forehead to hers.

"I have to go chase this down. They are not going to give it any rest." I looked to Jason and Celuine. "Take care of her. Do not let her out of yo..."

The room exploded with energy.

A pressure wave knocked me back. I lost grip of Eryn. It launched Celuine right through the front window. As my body impacted the wall hard, timbers and drywall did not break through; however they cracked hard. Eryn landed near the kitchen and hit her head solidly on the wall. Blood flowed into her eyes. I fell on all fours and scrambled over to her. Placing my hands on her, I dumped my life force into her while a maelstrom of energy vortexes swirled around us. The drain took over and I did not even twitch a muscle. It worked.

Her eyes opened.

"Get in the kitchen!" I yelled over the noise. She scrambled to move across the debris littered floor. I turned to face where the blast came from. The light was bright. A shadow danced a bit in front of me while I fought to focus to see what it was. All I could do was shield my eyes.

"Where are the others?" I heard Eryn yell behind me.

"Celuine is out the window. Jason was..." I found I did not know and I looked again at the light.

Jason was gone.

This was a portal. Heat radiated from the other side like a fire...like a searing white hot fire.

"Oh God, no!" I screamed.

The light dimmed and a shadow moved in the opening. I could see the outline of the rip in the fabric. It was not a normal portal but simply a slice through it. The light was blocked then unblocked, creating a sort of blinking effect like waving a hand in front of a dimming light. Something moved on this side. I stepped to the side of the room towards the wall nearest the portal. It was not in the center nor was it aligned with any walls. To get a better idea of was going on, I side-stepped the light. When my eyes adjusted, I could see a large clawed hand holding onto something. It tried to pull its hand back through the opening...just like a monkey grabbing a banana through a hole then trying to pull it back, The hand was too big for the opening; only this was no banana, it was Jason, crushed in his grasp. Blood ran from his mouth on the hand's first attempt to retract.

I could not tell if he was still alive.

The vortex in the room roared with energy.

My swords came into my hands as all my defenses and abilities came online. I raised my blades to strike; the little metal piece leapt out of the remnants of the glass bowl and disappeared into the torn fabric of space. Down swung my arms to sever the wrist and save my friend.

In a quick motion, almost blurry, the giant clawed hand thrust forward then pulled back enlarging the portal with Jason's blood and twisted Jason's body even more in the process. He screamed as he disappeared into the void. My strike missed entirely and slammed the floor breaking it. I was about to thrust a blade into the maw when I realized I could not risk hitting Jason.

Celuine crawled in the front door right as I stepped back about to dive through the opening...with her dress torn to bits by glass. She bled everywhere. I felt a hand on my right arm, gentle yet firm. I turned my head to see Eryn standing there without a fear in the world, her face still bloody from hitting her head. She shook her head.

She knew what I was planning.

"Don't you dare! I just got you back, and I am not going to lose you a second time."

"He is my best and only friend. I cannot leave him," I said.

A voice came from beyond that was laughter. "Father, I have him, father.... I will bring him to you..." The rift started to close slowly. I had moments to act.

"Eryn I love you. I cannot leave him to die this way and now that that piece is out of me, I am better than good. I have to..."

"NO...NO...NO, you don't, don't leave me alone here. I can't bear the thought of you leaving. If this can happen to you it can happen to anyone," she sobbed. I glanced at Celuine. She propped herself in the doorway. She raised her hand waiving me to go.

"I will protect her with my life. I am sorry I had to take your parents, but you were too important not to fulfill your role. I was wrong." She breathed heavy and coughed up some blood. "I'll be fine, and I will protect her. Go Tathlyn. *Dammit, go!*"

Eryn's hands were on my face. I turned towards the sliced opening still sealing up.

"You can't be serious. How can you do this? What about your duty to Earth? We need you! What about your pledge to protect me?" I was having a hard time seeing now due to tears forming. She was right. How could I leave, he was but one man and my duty was here.

"I'm pregnant."

I stared at her then back at Celuine, who nodded her head.

A daemonic scream filled the room and a giant mouth pressed itself against the torn fabric of air. Its feted breath and rotten teeth actually reached into the room. The invisible flowing fabric formed the face and when its mouth moved, so did the fabric giving me a face to see.

"Whoever this whelp is, he will suffer like no other. I can come for you now, no matter where you are. Run little manling. I will catch you another day." The portal was smaller; the giant shot two fingers in and tried to tear it open. A roar ensued and suddenly there was a big eye looking at me. "I will come for your whore and eat your child."

A look of rage crossed Eryn's face and she pointed.

"I don't want that thing near our child."

"Then I will take the fight to them, my love. Keep a candle in the window for me." I kissed her more passionately than ever before. Looking to Celuine I smiled.

"My wife is your charge now, Sister. Do not fail me."

"I love you Eryn, queen of my heart. From the moment I saw you, I wanted to make you mine." Crying, she smiled at me and touched my face one last time.

"Go kill it."

The words rang in my ears as I turned toward the portal and, with a mighty leap, dove headlong into the rift. Forces tore at me from everywhere.

Heat cooked my skin and started to boil my blood, but I felt my protection compensate to keep me alive. A burning sensation ran head to toe just like when my first rune appeared. My only thought was to save Jason and keep Eryn safe by diverting my enemies away from her.

Behind me, the portal closed.

Tumbling on every axis, I fell forward into nothingness.